Under the Spreading Chestnut Tree

Val Scully

www.underthespreadingchestnuttree.co.uk

Under the Spreading Chestnut Tree
Second Edition
ISBN: 978-1-291-70718-2
Copyright Val Scully 2014

For Jane Nicholson
1956 - 2013

Chapter One

September 1919, Adlington', Lancashire

They said the gypsies stole my brother, but I was not so sure. It wasn't until later that I found out what my sister was capable of.

From the moment I heard the faint cry in the distance, my heart froze. It was almost a premonition. I was crossing the yard, carrying a pail of milk from the cowshed to the kitchen. The golden September sun was slanting low, casting half the yard in shadow: I had just moved from chilled shade into surprising warmth and stopped for a moment to enjoy the sun on the back of my neck. Quartz in the yellow sandstone walls glittered and I was filled with one of those tingles of happiness that surprise us sometimes in the course of everyday life. I put down the heavy pail, closed my eyes and turned my face to the sun. At that very moment I heard it, and our world changed forever.

My sister's voice. I knew it instantly. The high-pitched sound came again and I ran to the gate, grasping its rough timbers with my fingernails. There again, louder this time and clearer. She was shouting Dad. I turned and echoed her call across the yard. He wouldn't hear: he was in the forge. Torn, I turned back just in time to see her emerge from the woods, running across the field towards the farm, her pigtails flying out behind her, her long skirt held up to one side, right arm raised in a frantic wave. 'Get Dad! It's Bertie!'

I dashed to the forge, my feet sliding on the cobbles, and reaching the great doorway, I called to him. He had his back to me, and his head bent over his work. He didn't hear me: my call had coincided with a blow on the anvil. 'Dad!' This time he heard, for he paused with his hammer held high, the powerful arm lifted above his huge shoulders. He straightened and turned to the door, where I must have stood in darkness. Dazzled by the bright light of the furnace, he would not have been able to see my expression, but he'd caught the urgency in my voice.

'It's Izzy, Dad, she's just run out of the woods shouting for you. I ... I think it's something to do with Bertie.' At that, the hammer hit the stone floor with a crack that hurt my eardrums, and he moved past me like a giant tree falling. By the time I caught up,

5

he was beyond the gate and half way across the field, almost level with the horse-chestnut tree. He reached Izabel and I saw him grasp her by the upper arms and bellow into her face. 'What do you mean gone? How can he have gone? Gone where?'

I touched his arm: 'Dad, let her speak,' for she was crying and gasping and couldn't catch her breath.

He shook her again. 'Speak child!'

'By the river. We stopped for a rest and a drink, and I took our shoes off so we could have a paddle. We lay on the grass to dry off, and I must have fallen asleep, but it can't have been for more than a few minutes, and he was gone! But Dad, his shoes have gone too! He can't put them on by himself! I think someone's taken him!'

'Show me!' He held her by one arm in an iron grip and half-dragged her back across the field so fast that she couldn't find her feet and if he hadn't had hold of her she'd have fallen to the ground.

'Dad!' I called unheeded, 'I'll go and get Alf and Bess. We'll find him,' I finished lamely, though in my heart I knew we would not.

It's strange. Now, at the distance of all those years, I can think of that day, of the search that went on into the night, of the questions and recriminations, the crying and the shouting, and it's almost like the dream of something that happened to someone else. There are moments of clarity: I remember how I stood for hours at the five-barred gate watching the lights of torches flicker amongst the trees, hearing the men call to each other. The night was cloudless and cold and my breath faded ghostly into the air. I remember how numb my toes and fingers were: I must have stood so still, afraid of moving in case I missed the cry that would tell us they'd found him. But I knew in my heart that they would never find him. I can't tell you how I knew: there was just a deadness inside of me. I thought of his little sturdy body and tried to reach out my mind to feel where he might be, but I couldn't bear the thought that wherever he was, he was gone from us.

It had been such a dry summer: the river was low, and the place where we paddled was a calm shallow pool with a soft beach. There were no footsteps in the sandy soil other than those Izzy and he had made when she walked him into the water. She said she'd

6

carried him back to the beach, so though there were two sets of footprints going in, there were only Izzy's coming out. The grass where they'd sat was flattened, and the basket of fruits she'd bought at the market was still where she'd left it when she awoke and saw he was gone. The shoes were the thing: Bertie hated wearing shoes, and if he'd toddled off by himself, none of us could imagine him picking them up to carry. I'd had a moment of inspiration: he was a mischievous little monkey, what if he'd picked them up to throw in the river, then overbalanced and fallen in? But the grassy bank was soft and the water-level so low that we could see there was no disturbance to the soil or the reeds.

After the first frantic searches, calling and calling, we combed the area, fanning out from the spot, some of us on our hands and knees. Alfred gave Bess one of Bertie's vests to sniff, and we watched in hope while the collie ran in circles around us, whimpering. I remember that as we watched the frantic dog, Izzy reached out to touch my hand, but I could not bring myself to hold it, nor to look at her.

Dad and Alfred strode into the river with elder sticks, and soon other men appeared and joined them. Someone came in a rowing boat and brought nets and poles to comb the shallow river-bottom.

The twins were only nine years old, but they searched the roots of trees and amongst the ferns in silence, their little faces wet with unheeded tears, until I was instructed to take them home. I'll never forget Mum's face when she came to the door at the sound of the gate: the lift and flare of hope, and the collapse of hope into despair. She turned from us without a word and we followed her into the kitchen, where our aunties wordlessly gathered the twins to them and pressed their faces down into their dark curls.

I returned to the search, and by now the neighbours had gathered and people were muttering about strangers in the area. On market days, Adlington bustled with traders and travellers, salesmen and seasonal workers, so there was no shortage of suspects. It was soon accepted as fact that Izzy and Bertie had been followed as they left the market square and set off down the lane towards the woods.

And now it was night-time and the search went on. Above the woods, the stars shone like smithereens of glass on a black

7

shroud. A dog barked once, and a shooting star traced a short silver line above the horse-chestnut tree: the briefest of lives, leaving not a trace.

Eventually the torches gathered and the lights grew larger as the men assembled and began to move towards the farm, but so slowly and silently that I knew they had no hope.

When finally Izzy and I were sent to bed, we lay sleepless and speechless, side by side like carvings on a tomb. The distance between us had never been greater. My thoughts were my own. What she was thinking I find it hard to contemplate, even now.

I know my mind turned back to the night he was born, just two years before. The memory of that moonlit night is as fresh-minted now, over twenty years later, as it was then.

I'd retreated to the workshop, unable to bear the noise any longer. The moon was full and bright and the candles on the horse-chestnut tree were glowing: it was spring but momentarily it felt like Christmas. The still air smelt sweet and warm. The latch was freshly oiled and I closed the door softly behind me, resting my back against its familiar ridges and breathing in the warm air, moist with resin. Moonlight lent a silvery sheen to the vice and the woodworking tools in their neat rows above the workbench. My feet made soft crunches as I moved forward through the coiled wood-shavings to Granddad's oak chair in the darkness of the furthest corner.

Gradually my chest relaxed and my heartbeat calmed itself. From the other side of the wall came the gentle clinking of halter chains and snuffled exhalations of horses.

Mum's cries were calmer now, deeper and more regular. The baby was coming. My aunts were brisk and competent, bustling about the kitchen and bedroom with confidence and barely-suppressed excitement, placing soothing hands on the heads of my little sisters as they passed. Dad was sitting to attention at the table, sometimes bowing his head in silent communion with Mum's suffering a few feet above his head.

My job had been to keep them supplied with water for heating on the range, but now they had enough, I could do nothing but wait with the rest of them.

Drawing my knees to my chest, I remember I curled in on myself, letting my hair cover my downturned face, and inhaled

8

deeply, forcing my breathing to slow and steadily soothing the banging of my heart. From the barn behind me came snuffles from soft muzzles, and chains chinked gently as the horses moved in their sleep.

The moment the child's first cry pierced the air, I might have been asleep, so warm was I in the nest of my own breath. I lifted my head and listened intently, straining to discern the tenor of the hubbub of voices drifting in its wake. Soon one sound repeated in many voices separated itself from the rest, unmistakable now: boy.

At last...at last...I was glad for them.

Moments passed in the silvery stillness while my thoughts drifted.

Finally, gathering myself, I uncoiled and stretched to my full height, smoothed my clothes and ran my fingers through tangled hair, gathering the waves over my shoulders to tumble down my back.

When I stepped into the kitchen, a perfect tableau presented itself: my sisters gathered around their father, the twins stretching up to see the tightly-swaddled bundle he held across his chest.

'Esther love! You have a brother! Come see!' His blue eyes were alight with a joy I didn't think I'd ever seen before, and I remember the briefest prick of resentment in my throat. But I could be nothing but happy for him: the uncharitable thought that rose in me was instantly suppressed as I felt his free arm encircle my shoulders, bringing me close to the tiny scrunched face like a closed fist. My own face must have softened and I reached to lift the sheet from his crumpled brow to reveal a shock of damp red hair.

I was aware that Izabel was trying to catch my eye, but I resolutely refused to engage, focusing instead on looking up at my father. 'Congratulations, Dad, he's...well, I'm sure he's going to be lovely!'

Dad's loud laugh broke the spell, and he dropped his voice to a whisper. 'Well, he does have a face like a cat's bum at the moment, but he'll no doubt turn into a handsome bugger like his old dad!' And with that, he kissed each of his daughters once on the top of the head, and went back upstairs to see whether his wife was presentable yet. He would sit with her: the little chap could have his first feed, and we'd all have to endure the clucking of the proud aunties.

Izabel waited until she heard the latch of the door above our heads, and then said in a low sing-song voice, 'Hallelujah. The saviour is born unto us.'

'Izzy!'

'Well, for God's sake, we all know where this puts us, especially you, dear sister, no longer number one for darling daddy. How will you bear it?'

Little Rosie and Lily looked from one to the other with incomprehension. Turning my back on Izabel's sneer, I took the twins' shoulders and guided them to the table. 'Come on girls, we'll have a celebration! Cake anyone?'

'Can we really have cake? It's nearly midnight!'

'So? Mum baked it specially, and it's not her fault the little fellow chose to arrive this late, is it?'

Watching me lavishing the little'uns with loving attention, Izabel's nostrils will have flared in that way she had. 'I'm going to bed,' she announced.

'Night then.' I didn't turn round, let alone try to dissuade her, so she stomped off to our bedroom and no doubt lay seething in the darkness.

When I finally got to bed, Izabel was still awake, and I could tell by her breathing that her thoughts were teeming. She must have willed herself to keep still and silent until I slipped in beside her. When I lay down on my back and pulled the blankets over me, I heaved a great sigh, for I was so tired, but she misread it and spoke: 'You know what this means, don't you?'

'Not now, Izzy. Go to sleep: I'm exhausted.'

'We'll be out on our ears. He'll get the farm. Us girls can go whistle.'

There was no answer. Frustrated, Izzy turned away, dragging the blankets with her, muttering into her pillow.

I stirred and asked her what it was she'd said.

I remember there was silence for a moment, and then her voice came low out of the darkness: 'I said: we'll see about that.'

10

Chapter Two

*' what will you do now
with the gift of your left life?
Snow, by Carol Ann Duffy*

The idea came to me when I was sitting on the front step in the sun. I'd collected the keys from the letting agent without really knowing what my intentions were. I just knew I had to get away.

It had been an unbelievable twenty-four years since I'd been in the house, and the procession of tenants and maintenance tasks had been dealt with entirely by the obliging agent: 'No need for you to come up, Mrs Keaton, we can deal with it.' So it had come as a surprise to both of us when I'd rung and instructed them to let me know when the latest tenants had moved out.

It had been so long that when I rounded the corner and drove along the terrace, it had taken me a minute to work out exactly which house it was. I drove to the end and did a u-turn, before slowly pulling up in front of 144. The ones on either side had a distinctly more vibrant look, with bright curtains and flowers in the garden, whereas 144 had faded nets and utilitarian paving slabs. I'd forgotten how narrow the frontage was: my MX5 was the same length as the low stone wall, and the missing gate was like a lost tooth.

The front door was still green, as it had been when I was a child, and the familiar bulge of the stone step was slightly worn by the years of footfall. In grandma's time, that step was chalked every day, and I smiled when I ruefully remembered how often I'd had the backs of my legs slapped for getting chalk on my skirt. After she died, a piece of highly-polished brass had been fixed to the front step as part of the orange-and-brown seventies overhaul that mum had done to prepare the house for renting. Nobody had polished it though, and after a year it had disappeared.

An impulse had come on me then, and so there I was, sitting on the stone step with my back against the faded green door, legs stretched out and my face turned to the sun. The street was quiet: it was the middle of the morning in early September, the time of year when parents breathe out and teachers breathe in.

11

I sat there a long time, just savouring the sunshine and letting my thoughts drift. I was conscious of the warmth from the wood seeping into my back, and felt muscles relax that I hadn't known were tight. The ebb and flow of a conversation between two women in the distance was growing louder, and I was aware of them falling silent as they approached, but I felt under no obligation to open my eyes and pass the time of day. They started talking again after they'd passed, but I couldn't even be bothered tuning into it. It didn't matter. It was strangely liberating to be in a place I knew, or felt I knew, where nobody knew me. What a delicious feeling. It was a bit like when I'd gone to university, changed my name and dared to be different.

That had been fantastic: what a kick I had got out of shedding my old skin and deliberately presenting myself at Nottingham as someone new. No longer shy bookish Annelise but trendy, confident Annie, up for a laugh, confident, outgoing, gregarious, soon part of a big group of mates who had an absolute ball.

It was so vivid it could have been last week: incredible to think it was twenty-seven years ago.

It had all come flooding back when we'd taken Mark to Leeds, and then two years later when Rosie started at Lancaster, both times being driven away in floods of tears which I knew were partly jealousy. They had it all to come, and what now for their devoted parents? Eskimo day, that's what.

"You locked out?" A man's voice. I hadn't heard him. I kept my eyes shut and hoped he'd go away. "Ah say," local accent, louder this time, "are you locked out?"

Not going away then. Languidly, I opened my eyes. Old man, cloth cap, shopping basket, back to the sun. "Sorry?"

"I said," he knew full well I'd heard him, but he was evidently a persistent bugger, "are you locked out?"

"No, just enjoying the sun."

"Only we like to keep our eyes open round here, tha never knows..."

"No, it's ok, I've got the key, thanks."

"You the new tenant then?"

"No, I'm the owner."

12

"Never!"

"Pardon?"

"Tha's never Maggie's girl!"

I opened my eyes properly now, taken aback, and remembering my manners, I got to my feet and went to the wall to shake hands. "Yes, hello. Did you know my mum?"

"Ah did that. Walked to school together, me and Maggie." There was no mistaking his wistful tone, and he bent to put down his basket and take a better look at me. "Ee, love, you're the image..." he stopped, shook his head slightly and then looked up at the house.

"The image of who?" I knew I didn't look like mum, and was immediately intrigued. My turn now: it served me right. "The image of who?"

He completely ignored me, peering from under the peak of his cap at the guttering. "Tha wants to get someone to look at that gutter."

"I will, but please tell me who I remind you of."

Slowly, he lowered his eyes and looked into mine, then said quietly, "Just someone I used to know." And with that, he bent to pick up his basket and left without another word.

I watched him walk away towards the far end of the terrace, cross the narrow side street, and unlock the first door of the next stretch of houses. As the door closed behind him, I had a sudden memory of a curtain of plastic strips in primary colours that used to hang there all summer long, and billow out into the road when a draught blew through. An old man had lived there in my childhood, but it couldn't possibly be the same one, though his height and bearing were similar. I'd never seen any sign of a family. That old man would have to be, what, over a hundred now. He used to sit outside on a folding chair on sunny days, smoking his pipe, and he always said, "Owdo?" when you went past, though he never seemed interested in receiving an answer.

I'd never given that old man a single thought in the intervening years, and yet I could conjure him up now as clear as day. Shaking my head slightly to dislodge the memory and the vertiginous sensation of looking down the well of forty years, I turned back to the house.

A woman was leaning in the doorway of number 146, only a couple of metres away, smoking and watching me. Startled, I said, "Oh, hello!"

"Did I make you jump?"

"Yes, you did a bit."

"You own it then?" No pretending she hadn't been listening. I liked that.

"Yep, my grandma left it to me years ago. She died while I was at university. It's been rented out since. I'm Annie." I stepped forward and held out my hand. She took a last puff on her cigarette, reached out and dropped the dimp with a theatrical flourish, then delicately stepped on it, swivelling on the ball of her foot. I knew the scene, and she knew I knew. In as near an imitation as I could manage to John Travolta's incredulous shriek, I yelped, "Sandy?"

Turning, she looked back over her shoulder and drawled, "Tell me about it ... stud." It was so perfectly done that I burst out laughing and when she'd finished her flounce, she did too. By the time we'd both subsided into giggles, she extended a hand. "Beth. Nice to meet you. Want a coffee?"

Still smiling, I stepped over the low wall between the two yards and followed her down a narrow corridor into a bright kitchen.

'So, what's the plan then?' She really didn't mess about, this one. 'Instant alright? Only you look like a filter kinda gal.'

I sat down at the kitchen table and considered my answer. 'I don't know really. I'm at a kind of crossroads.'

'Mid-life crisis, is it? Luxury. Empty nest syndrome? Lucky bugger.'

'Well yes, got it in one.' Bemused by her directness, I went on, 'Both, actually. Cliches abound.'

'Just because it's a cliche doesn't mean it's not real.'

'No, no it certainly doesn't. You got kids?'

'Yep, one girl, two lads, no dads.'

'Ages?'

'Ellie's twenty-one and the lads are teenagers. Jason's left school and specialises in hanging around street corners terrorising the old folk. Adam's fifteen and aspires to do the same.'

I must have looked horrified, because she smiled as she set the mugs on the table and sat down. 'They're not bad lads, just bored and shiftless.'

'There's a lot of it about. What about you? Do you work?'

'I do a few hours cleaning at the juniors and a bit of home care for a couple of old folks. This and that, you know. We manage. So anyway, back to you and your crisis. What's the plan?'

'Well, I'm not sure.' I suddenly felt self-conscious: my problems seemed too self-indulgent to spread before this brisk, capable woman.

'Come on, I've clocked the car and the handbag, I can see we've got different lives, but we're all sisters under the skin and all that. Come on, cough. Take me out of myself for a bit. Tell me a story.'

I studied her face to see whether she was laughing at me, but her smile was kind and her eyes candid. It would be a luxury to articulate all the feelings that had been swirling around my head, but I decided to confine myself to practical matters, for now, anyway.

'Married nearly thirty years. Husband away a lot on business, attended by his pulchritudinous PA.'

'Pulky what?'

'Pulchritudinous. Beautiful. Sorry, I love a bit of alliteration.'

'Teacher, are you?'

'Not any more, no,' I smiled. 'Anyway, two kids, both through university and in work. They're ten years older than yours and got launched before the bottom fell out of the employment market. Rosie got married in August, and all of that kept me occupied, but now ...'

'What? Go on.'

'Well,' I took a breath. 'I don't know what to do with the rest of my life.'

'What do you want to do?'

'That's just it, I don't know. I...' I almost blurted it all out, but stopped myself. 'I don't know whether I want to stay with Paul. I just feel ... dead inside. Well maybe not dead, half asleep, sleepwalking.'

'Anything else?'

I looked up. 'How do you mean?'

'Is that it? No worries? No deaths? Nobody drownded?'

'Drownded?'

'Albert and the Lion. "No deaths, and nobody drownded, fact nothing to laugh at, at all." '

'Ha! I've not heard that for ages! My granddad used to recite that!' Suddenly I welled up.

'Don't get upset.' She missed nothing. 'Nah, get upset if you want to. Have a good cry. I'm just going to the loo.'

Alone at the table, the tears brimmed but did not fall. I got up to distract myself from having a complete meltdown in this stranger's kitchen. I had a look at the pictures and notes stuck to the fridge, the cheery red gingham curtains, the shiny white tiles with red grout, the glass on the windowsill with a clump of parsley rooting in the water. The back yard was paved: plant-pots, buckets and even an old stone sink were arranged about, all stuffed with late summer bedding plants. Three giant sunflowers were trained up the end wall, their faces basking in the sun. I didn't try and look over at the garden of 144. I wasn't ready.

By the time she came back, I'd got a grip. Or so I thought.

'So, who's died?'

'My mum. We were never particularly close, but you know, towards the end... And last year, my closest friend. At 49. She didn't even make 50. It makes you think.'

'Of course it does. Sometimes we need something like that to shake us up a bit.'

'How do you mean?'

'My mum died when I was four. You don't get over it really.'

Shocked, I waited for her to go on, but she seemed unwilling to elucidate and fell silent.

'How do you think it affected you?'

'Lots of things really. I'm not very girly. I had two brothers, and my dad was a bit of a ... rough diamond. But the thing is when you learn that death can come any time and take beautiful young mothers with loving families, you know it can come any time and take anyone, so you'd better get on with it.'

16

'Get on with?'

"Enjoying life. You never know. That's all I'm saying.'

There was silence for a while. 'Another coffee?'

'If you're sure I'm not holding you up or anything?'

'Sure. We've not got to the bottom of your dilemma yet. I'm hoping for some juicies.'

"Juicies?'

'Passionate groping at the golf club. Quickies with the gardener. Old boyfriends contacting you on Facebook.' She adopted a simpering voice and clutched her heart. 'I couldn't help it. He re-ignited my libido, put me in touch with my younger self, all that malarky.'

I gaped, unable to believe it. How could she know? Or was I really such a cliché?

She caught my expression and laughed out loud. 'Ha! Juicies! I knew it! Come on, spill the beans.'

Abruptly, I got up. 'It's ok, thanks for the coffee. I'll have to be going now.'

'Oh come on, don't be like that. I'm sorry. I've obviously touched a raw nerve. Let's go back to the serious stuff. Come on, sit back down and have another coffee.' In a wheedling, sing-song voice, she added, 'I've got Kit Kats!'

Mollified, I sat down. 'Oh go on then, as long as you've kept them in the fridge.'

'Yes indeed. No other way to keep them. So tell me about your mum. We can leave the juicies till a wine night.'

I looked up at her sharply, but saw that she was teasing, so I told her about Mum's death six weeks before the wedding. 'It's strange, even though you've been expecting it, you're still not ready. So anyway, as you say, it made me think.'

'So what are you going to do?'

"Well, I've been thinking about taking a kind of gap year.'

'How do you mean? Digging wells in the Congo?'

'No, from my marriage. A kind of gap year from my life. While I think. And try on a different skin.'

'Sounds like a plan. What would his nibs say?'

'I don't know really. I need to think it through. How I'm going to put it to him and everything.'

17

'Where would you go?'

'Well, I was thinking I might live here. Next door, I mean. That's why I've come. To have a look, try it on for size. Only I got a bit overwhelmed when I saw it. I've hardly given it a thought for all these years, but you know, it was my grandparents' house and I spent all my summer holidays when I was a kid. Mum worked, you see, so they used to bring me up here for the six weeks.'

'Flipping heck! That's a bit ... From being how old?'

'A baby really. She was in the police. They both were. It was unusual in the sixties I suppose. It wasn't until later I learnt to be proud of her. At the time, it was ... well it was hard. But Granddad was fantastic. What a lovely man. Grandma was a bit of a tartar though.'

'Yes, I've heard.'

'Oh, of course! Have you always lived here? We might have played together when we were little!'

'If you don't mind me saying, I think you're a bit older than me, but yes, I might have seen you around, and your gran was, erm, a bit of a legend around here.'

'Yes, it's funny how you see things differently as you get older. I'm interested to find out a bit more about them both. Grandma was brought up on a farm that used to be not far from here, but she never took me there or even talked about it. My mum was born there but she got out of Adlington as soon as she could, and she'd never talk about her family. In fact, come to think of it, I don't think she ever told me anything about her childhood, certainly not the farm.'

'Chestnut Farm. Yes, it's still there.' She gave me a curious look.

'What?'

'Oh nothing. Another time.'

Chapter Three

Nothing was ever the same again. That autumn and winter we went about our business in virtual silence, our heads down, frightened of looking into each other's faces for fear of what we would see. Dad seemed to have become smaller overnight: his massive shoulders drooped, and I often saw him standing alone, staring into the distance. When he came out of his painful reverie, he would consciously straighten his back and rub the back of his neck, sigh deeply and then turn back to the life of the farm.

He once caught me watching him. I had been leaning against the trunk of the horse chestnut, alone with my thoughts, and he hadn't noticed me as he led one of the Shires through the field. The canopy hung low, though most of the leaves had fallen and the branches were almost bare. The coppery leaves were crisp underfoot. I saw him pause and pick up a conker, distractedly polishing it with his thumb, then stand staring at it with his head bowed. After a few moments I realised that he was crying, helplessly and soundlessly. I hesitated for a long while, struggling with my own grief and the distress of seeing this powerful man, the centre of my world, so overcome and shaken by emotion like a great tree in a storm.

Eventually, the horse grew restless and whinneyed, breaking the spell. I moved forward, hesitant, wanting to comfort but also to be comforted. No words would suffice. I thought of Cordelia saying: 'I cannot heave my heart into my mouth.' As I came out from under the skirts of the tree, he heard my footsteps, and looked up. All I could say was, 'Oh Dad'. He lifted his arms and I walked into them, helplessly sobbing into his chest. He held me, stroking the back of my head gently and rumbling, 'There there. There there.'

I don't cry prettily, never have. By the time I'd calmed down, the front of his waistcoat was sodden, and I started dabbing at it ineffectually with my hanky, which was already wet through. 'Never mind, love, you'll feel better for that.' In a brighter tone: 'Look, I found a beautiful conker: we haven't played at all this year. I've still got that twelver from last year. We'll have to....' His voice suddenly cracked and broke, 'Thing is, what got me ... it's the colour of his hair, yours and Bertie's.'

19

It was the first time anyone had said his name in weeks. I looked into my father's eyes then, and I saw such pain that I had to look away.

We all coped differently. The twins were subdued but capable of bursts of energy and hysteria. They were a welcome distraction: even telling them off felt like a relief, and the more disproportionate the reactions to their frequent misdemeanours became, the more watchful they grew.

But the real worry was our mother. By the time winter closed in, she had given up pretending she could carry on. Her grief was agony, her focus inward, and nothing served to distract her. I saw her knock Dad's arm away when he tried to comfort her. I tried to persuade her to take on some of the outdoor jobs, just to get her away from the house: the very fabric of the place seemed to vibrate with pain. Things that Bertie had used or liked or even touched would draw her and hold her, and we seemed to be watching her life drain away in the power of her grief, which was a kind of anger: it burned with an intensity which scorched us all, and in time we turned away, defeated. The only time we saw a softening, a slump, was each night as she drew the curtains on another day when he had not come home.

And as for Izzy, we hardly saw her. Less than a month after Bertie's disappearance she had come home flushed and purposeful and announced that she was moving out.

We were just sitting down to eat another silent, desultory meal that no-one wanted. A place had been set for her, although no-one knew where she was: she hadn't been seen all day. It was dark outside, late October: the lamps and candles were lit and the curtains drawn, but it seemed no-one apart from Dad could muster any curiosity about where she might be. She had become something of a pariah, not just in the neighbourhood, but even amongst us. Terrible things had been said that could never be taken back. When I thought of how she might be feeling, I found that I simply didn't care.

I knew she had had another restless night, because of course that meant I had too. I had even considered dragging some blankets onto the floor and sleeping there, but it was so cold and I was so very tired. When I woke up in the weak autumnal dawn, she had gone. I thought nothing of it until mid-morning when I noticed that the hens

20

were still shut in their coop. I put my pail down on the cobbles and went to let them out and scatter some seed in the yard. The chickens were Izzy's responsibility and she was usually reliable, in fact I had always resented the theatrical way in which she'd present the eggs each morning, as if she had laboured in some way and deserved praise. More than once I had offered to swap the hens for the milking, which was my job. I wouldn't really have gone through with it, as I was fond of my cows and the way they patiently stood and endured the indignity of me pulling on their teats. There was a companionship in cows that you never felt with silly hens. The warmth of a cow's flank against my forehead on a morning, and their gentle lowing of need and relief was a pleasure I wouldn't forgo easily.

Even Mum reacted. 'Where on earth to?'

Triumphant and glowing in the lamplight, she cast off her shawl with a nervous flourish and lifted her chin. 'The big house. I'm to be a ladies' maid.'

Dad stood up. 'What do you mean? You're needed here.'

Instantly defiant, she turned on him. 'No I'm not. You've got plenty of help here. I'm going to live where there's light at the flick of a switch, and hot water, and fine things. You can't stop me. I'm sixteen and I can do what I like.'

Normally, Dad would have put her straight about her insolent tone, what she could and couldn't do, the right way of doing things, but he simply sat back down and went on with his meal, his expression indecipherable. The twins were wide-eyed at this turn of events, and all eyes were on Dad, but he just quietly cut a slice of the loaf and reached for the butter. Izzy remained standing in the same position, her hands on her hips, ready for battle, but it never came, and after a while, we all went on eating apart from Mum.

'Right then, if that's the way you all feel, I'll go and pack my bag.'

I couldn't stop myself. 'You haven't got a bag, and don't think about taking Gran's valise: she left that to me.' They were the first words I'd spoken directly to her since that terrible day. She glared at me with real venom and then swiftly went upstairs, where we listened to her banging about in our room, her clogs resounding on the bare boards. A muffled footfall told me she was standing on

21

the rug by the bed, and I knew she'd be taking the embroidered pillowcase from her side. Our maternal grandmother had made a pair of beautiful white linen pillowcases for each of us, 'for our trousseaux' and until she died they had been carefully stored in tissue paper in the bottom drawer of the dresser in our room. We'd loved them so much and been so in awe of such finery that after the funeral we had gone to our room to gather together all the things she had made for us: the dressing-gowns, the nighties and the stuffed toys. When Izzy had opened the bottom drawer by which Gran had set so much store - 'Such beautiful girls deserve beautiful things' - we sat and wept at the sight of them. The crisp starched white cotton, the ribbon and lace, and best of all, our initials embroidered in ornate copperplate script with delicate flourishes which seemed to promise bright futures. Izzy had decided then that she was going to sleep on hers to feel closer to Gran, though I secretly thought it was because she really believed she would one day sleep in a bed befitting such finery. To be fair to her, she had continued to meticulously rotate her pair each washday so that they would wear at the same rate. At the thought of this, my heart softened, but I still could not bring myself to go upstairs and talk to her.

Eventually, we heard the latch and she came back downstairs more slowly. She was carrying Gran's valise. She looked directly at me and said, 'Don't start. I'll bring it back.'

Mum hadn't moved since Izzy's announcement, and her dinner remained untouched. She rose now and stood looking at her defiant daughter. Eventually she whispered, 'Must you go tonight?' and her voice seemed to creak with lack of use.

Izzy was unmoved, in fact she seemed to bristle with sudden haste. She looked away, found her discarded shawl and wrapped it tightly around her shoulders. 'Yes, they're expecting me. I've a room ready.' She faltered, then: 'I'll come round in a few days to tell you about it. And bring the case back.' She was almost at the door now, and when she turned back to say goodbye, I saw that that her knuckles were clenched white. Then the door banged and she was gone.

That winter was so hard: frost hung from the eaves and never melted from dawn to dusk. The house was dark and quiet, and we moved slowly, our hands, faces and voices muffled against the cold and the pain.

To her credit, Izzy visited us often, and never empty-handed. In her basket, she always had something from the big house: a game pie, a stone bottle of whiskey, a pair of thick woollen socks, a couple of venison steaks. At Christmas, her presents were lavish and frivolous: a delicate perfume bottle for Mum, glass necklaces for the girls, a book of poetry for me, a kite for Dad. She never stayed long, rarely made eye-contact with any of us, and her smiles were full of secrets.

Mum stayed in bed, attended anxiously by her sisters and by me. After Christmas, she stopped eating altogether apart from soup, and she seemed to shrink into the mattress until she barely disturbed the blankets. The doctor was baffled: he said he could find no evidence of any physical illness. He shook his head and left us to our despair.

When he'd gone, I went slowly upstairs and sat with her awhile. Her face was the colour of the pillowcase, and there were hollows under her eyes and in her cheeks. The threads of grey had overwhelmed the copper in her hair. Without speaking, I sat down beside her and reached for her hand, which lay in mine like a dead leaf. She turned her face away from me and held my hand weakly.

'Mum.' I spoke softly: everything about the room seemed muffled and airless. She didn't move at first, but then slowly turned her head to look at me, as though her eyes were focusing from a long way away. She didn't speak, but lifted her hand, reaching for my face. I bent towards her hand, took it in mine, and pressed it against my cheek.

When she spoke, her voice was like the rustling of dead leaves. 'So lovely, my Esther.'

I couldn't help it then: the tears came in earnest, brimmed and fell down my cheeks. Her thumb softly drew across my face and she cupped my cheek more firmly. 'Don't cry darling. You're a strong girl. Don't cry.'

She never saw the spring. She died on the last day of January.

23

We sat with her through the night before the funeral, Dad and I, and though I kept the fire going, the kitchen seemed cold to its heart. Outside, I knew the ground was frozen and I pitied the poor soul who had to dig into it. For days, the hoar frost each morning had been thick, coating the cobwebs on the eaves, which reverberated in my breath but did not melt. The breath of the horses blew ghostly on the air, and the chickens huddled together in the corner of the coop, unwilling to come out, even for food. The bare arms of the chestnut tree had a bloody cast in the light of a wolf moon. Bertie was out there somewhere, and not for the first time I found myself wishing he was safely dead and buried in our churchyard where we could tend to his grave. There would have been a kind of peace in having the grave opened so that his mother could be close to him once more.

At the funeral, no-one knew what to say to us. We were a family suddenly blighted by events so dreadful that others seemed to hesitate to come close for fear of contamination. Instead, they gathered their children to them, their little boys impatient of the unwelcome hugs and unexpected kisses, the wives leaning gratefully into the shoulders of husbands suddenly appreciative of their presence by their sides.

As we stood in the doorway of the porch to receive the congregation, I scanned every approaching figure for one that I would recognise as Izzy, but still she did not come.

My old teacher, Miss Ashworth, arrived alone. Her fine, erect figure, for so long my hero, was a welcome sight that spoke to me of worlds of possibility away from here. At the sight of her, my heart lifted: she always had words of comfort and words of inspiration, but this time, she could only say, 'My dear,' and press into my hands a small volume of poetry, which I saw was Tennyson's In Memoriam. In answer, I pressed it to my heart and leant forward to kiss her cheek.

The bearers, four of Dad's closest friends, were lined up ready to shoulder their burden, when we all turned to see a closed carriage pulled by two fine black horses coming swiftly up the lane. The coachman pulled on the reins just below the church, and the gleaming ebony flanks of the horses were clouded by heat rising. The door opened, and a gentleman in a long black coat stepped out, before turning to hand down three women, all in dark clothes with shawls over their heads against the cold.

The gentleman strode towards Dad and held out his hand. 'Mr Grenfell, I was so sorry to hear of your loss.' He shook his head. 'Terrible, terrible.' He indicated the three women. 'I hadn't been aware that your daughter was in my employment, I'm afraid. Since my wife died, my housekeeper has dealt with staffing. It was she who told me this morning. I've come to pay my respects. I do apologise for our tardy arrival: a problem in the stables.' He stepped back to allow the three women to pass into the church, took off his hat and followed them.

Dad managed a smile for me and his sisters-in-law, 'A real gentleman, Mr Farnworth.' Visibly strengthened, he nodded to his friends over by the bier, straightened his back, put his arm around my shoulders and stepped back to allow the bearers passage.

As we followed the coffin, I looked down at the worn stone floor, and only lifted my eyes once, as we passed the Farnworth family pew. Izzy's eyes met mine with an expression I found hard to read: dry and haunted, yes, but something else I couldn't catch.

Dad and I sat side by side against the wall in the front pew. He sat up very straight, and his bulk seemed massive and reassuring by my side. The girls had clung to their aunts' skirts since daybreak and would not be separated now, but huddled in the opposite pew between them, their sobs mingling and choking, their shoulders trembling.

Behind us sat Dad's sister with her husband and daughters: she reached over once to squeeze my shoulder, but I couldn't turn to acknowledge it for fear of crumbling.

The service passed in a blur and I took no comfort in the words. There seemed to me no justice, no plan, no reward. I could only think of the indifferent universe and the image of the rainwater washing away the flowers from poor Fanny Robin's grave.

Soon, it was over, and we were back outside in the frozen air, following the bearers around the back of the church and up beyond the yew-tree. When they came to a halt at the open grave, I saw that it had been dug when the earth was soft and crumbling and had since frozen. Hoarfrost clung to the soil walls, and I looked down with cold horror and a sudden sense of falling. I must have

25

made an unexpected movement, for my father grasped my elbow more tightly and I leant in against him, surrendering myself to grief for the first time.

The first time I saw snowdrops, their delicate heads bowed but their slender stems powered by the life-force, I resented my mother for leaving us, for giving up on life when she still had all of us to live for. And that resentment released me from my mourning.

In time, I grew to miss her properly, and pity for her replaced the pity for myself, for all of us in our loss and hardship. But at the time, my heart was so battered and bruised, my days so long and hard, that I felt nothing but a quiet determination that no more grief should come to my family.

Chapter Four

When I finally opened that green door, my shadow stretched the length of the hall and dust motes danced around it. The floorboards were bare and unvarnished, but the stairs were covered by a newish carpet held in place by the same black metal rods I'd known as a child. I was sharply assailed by a vision of my grandma sitting half-way up the staircase, as she had been the last time I'd opened this door unannounced, not long before she died. She had been annoyed to be seen in all her tiredness and vulnerability, and the visit had not been a happy one.

I stepped into the hall, closed the door and was instantly plunged into darkness. The leaded glass of the fanlight above the front door used to cast its jewel colours onto the floor, but I saw now that the window had been boarded up. The door to the front room was closed, and would remain so for now. My beloved granddad, the gentlest of men, had died in that room: not a peaceful death but a painful and a vocal one. On his last day, I was allowed to see him for the first time in several weeks. I remember it was a Sunday in late January. The wind was bitter, the roads from Manchester were icy, and the eleven-plus results were going to be revealed the following day. So much hung on whether I'd passed or failed that I could barely sleep, and I'd been told so many times how much the extra lessons had cost that I felt sick with dread.

When we finally pulled up outside the house, the curtains were drawn though it was only midday. A neighbour opened the door and went before us into the back parlour, where grandma was sitting in state, an imposing figure in black, her back to the window: watery grey light tried to filter through the thin curtains. She showed no recognition of our arrival but sat bolt upright, staring straight ahead, dry-eyed, her mouth a clamped down-turned line. Mum and the neighbour went into the kitchen to whisper whilst I stood, mutinous and terrified, in front of my grandma, and focused on the gleam of her hat-pin to stop myself from crying.

When I heard the door to the front room open and softly close, the doctor walked quickly through into the kitchen, briefly touching my head as he passed. More whispering, then my mum appeared in the doorway, a handkerchief clutched to her mouth.

Without a word, she turned me round by the shoulder and took me back into the passage, where she softly tapped on the door and then opened it. There would be no answer to her knock.

The air in the room was stale and wraith-grey and I couldn't breathe. I stood at the open door, clutching the knob for anchorage, and watched my mum bend over the pillow I couldn't see. She stayed still for a long time, then straightened up, and made a movement with her left hand that seemed to mean I should come forward. My hand wouldn't let go of the doorknob, and at first my feet refused to move; feeling sick and faint, I took a breath of the rancid air, and clutching the back of my mum's cardi, I moved round her bravely.

The bed seemed vast, a mustard counterpane I loathed. If it hadn't been for the lumps of his feet, I wouldn't have believed there was anyone in there. I saw a curled hand like a yellow talon lying lifeless, the frayed edge of a pale striped sleeve, then the pillow, on which there lay a yellow skull. Saliva filled my mouth and I had to swallow hard, twice, three times as I convulsively grasped my mother's cardigan. Skin like yellow parchment stretched tight, eyes staring lifelessly at nothing. Mum bent again to the pillow and whispered something, and slowly the sightless eyes closed, stayed closed, then opened and closed again. When they opened again, they seemed smaller, more awake, as though he had dragged his soul back from the ceiling, where it had been seeping through on its way to the frosty January air. Those faraway eyes drifted down the wall behind me and finally came to rest on my face.

My mother bent to whisper in my ear, 'Go to him, sweetheart, and sit with him while I talk to the doctor. Go on, he won't bite.'

So I sat by the bed on the hard spindle-back chair and stared, horrified, into the bottomless pit of his pupils and the yellow whites of his eyes. I thought for one terrible moment that he had died with his eyes on my face, but then the corners crinkled in their old familiar way. He closed his eyes for the longest moment, and a slow smile curved across his face. I looked down at his hand where it grasped the counterpane like a claw, and watched it relax and unfurl, then lie open, palm up. The pressure of grief in my chest welled up so that I could hardly breathe. I took a great gulp of air and

28

gathering his hand in both of mine like a bunch of twigs, I bent down and kissed it, sudden tears overflowing down my cheeks and trickling onto his fingers. I felt his hand stir, and slide to cup my damp cheek then move gently to rest in the tangle of my curls. He sighed, and it was like the rustle of a breeze through dead leaves, then he whispered something I didn't recognise, but now I know was 'Esther'.

I don't know how long we stayed like that. I sobbed softly and tried to concentrate on holding the moments, feeling as though if I stirred, the spell would be broken and he would leave me. I remember being thankful that the tangle of my freshly-washed hair masked the musty smell of the counterpane. His hand rested like a weightless leaf in the curls at the side of my face.

Eventually I remember other hands taking me gently by the shoulders and guiding me out of the room. I hung my head and took no last look. Later that night, I heard his voice for the last time, and it was raised and angry, not his voice at all. My mother told me he didn't know what he was saying. Some words sounded German to me, though none of us knew he had any other language than his soft Lancashire burr. I never told anyone that he had said the word Esther.

I paused a moment to let my eyes get used to the gloom, and soon found an instinctive sense of orientation in the space. As I walked slowly down the hallway, I trailed my fingertips along the wall for reassurance: when they found the door of what used to be called the parlour, my hand found the familiar knob straight away, and although its turn was looser, the whole action of opening it - 'Shut that door! There's a draught!' - catapulted me back to the nervous child I had been.

The fireplace was gone, but I could conjure it easily, and beside it my lovely granddad, sitting in his chair, smoking his pipe, bending to tap it on the grate, and lifting his head to turn his gentle blue eyes on me and smile with a warmth that lifted my heart.

It seemed to me at that moment that no-one in my life had loved me with such simplicity. For him, I had never fallen short. The thought gave me a confidence, a centredness that felt new. I don't know how long I stood there, but by the time I moved across to the window, something essential had taken root.

Through the window, I could see that the yard was paved like Beth's, but devoid of life and colour. I was surprised to see that the outside toilet was still there, though presumably boarded up: the door wasn't visible from where I was standing. Was it possible Granddad's woodshed was still standing too? Hastily, I got the keys out of my handbag and went into the kitchen, barely registering its transformation, to open the back door. I stepped out into the yard and rounded the kitchen extension, and there it was. Weather-beaten and bedraggled, with cracked windows and rotten wood, but still standing. I felt a surge of happiness and must have been smiling stupidly when Beth appeared in her own garden. 'What's tickling you then?'

'I was just feeling an affinity for this shed: both battered and weather-beaten, but still standing!'

'It's funny, that shed. People are always saying it should be knocked down, but there's something lovely about it, like one of those ramshackle places on allotments.'

'Yes, exactly that. It was my granddad's. I helped him build it. Well, I sat on a log and watched and handed him nails and brought him drinks. He did woodwork in it. He used to say it was his bolt-hole. I loved that shed. It smelt of wood and pipe smoke and mint imperials.'

'It still might: I don't think anyone's opened the door in thirty years. They wouldn't dare, it might collapse.'

'And the outside loo as well! I can't believe it's still there! He made me a swing in there.'

'Eh? You had a swing in the privy? Or do you mean he sat and whittled a swing seat while he did his business?'

'It was hung from the doorway and I used to bang my head on the cistern but I didn't have the heart to tell him.'

'Oh bless! That's brilliant! He sounds like a lovely man.'

'He was. He was.'

'Shame about his wife, though, eh? Old Izzy was well-known around here. No wonder he called it his bolt-hole!' She leant on the wall with her arms folded. 'So, how's it going in there? Bit grot, isn't it?'

'Yes, a bit bare and dark, but decent. Even the windows are clean.'

'I know: I did them when the last lot moved out.'

'You? Why?'

'I told you, I do a bit of this and that. Cash in hand, you know. It's a nice house, just a bit ... unloved.' She looked at me, a question in her eyes.

'Hm, I've been feeling a bit unloved myself.' A surge of unfamiliar determination straightened my back. 'Well, my friend, it has loved and lost; it has been used and abused, neglected and taken for granted, but it shall love and be loved again!'

Chapter Five

At last the days began to lengthen and the earth unfurled from its long winter sleep. The daffodils that year were glorious golden trumpets heralding the birth of new hope. I was proud of my bountiful crop, and in a spirit of reconciliation, I cut a huge bunch, wrapped them in muslin, tied a ribbon and set off one April morning to see Izabel at Farnworth Manor. I had never been through the gate before, never having had cause, but as I walked across the meadow and over the brow of the hill, I stopped to look down into the shallow valley in which it nestled. The low sandstone wall encircled the park of natural woodland, and the house lay at its centre, glowing golden in the spring sunshine.

The original house was beautifully symmetrical, in the classical Georgian style, but the eastern side had a more recent addition which I guessed to be an extension to the kitchens, as the neat lines of a freshly-planted kitchen garden were laid, south-facing, to the front of it. The stable blocks were behind the house, I knew, for Dad had been there often enough.

As I passed through the wrought-iron gate and started up the drive, a large pond which had been concealed by the trees came into sight: it was fringed by reeds, apart from a natural beach from which it was rumoured that the squire entered the water to swim. Moorhens pottered and pecked on the beach, and the still waters reflected the parapet and chimneys of the house against blue sky.

We still called Mr Farnworth the Squire, though it was a long time since his family had owned any land in the village. He was often away: he had other properties in London and abroad, and since his wife had died in a riding accident in the woods, he rarely stayed here, leaving the house to be run by a modest staff, all of whom were devoted to him. The central doorway was approached by a flight of four stone steps: the Squire was a friendly man, warm and well-regarded in the area, but I wasn't brave enough to presume to knock on the front door, so I went round to the right, and passed the kitchen garden, where a girl was on her hands and knees planting seedlings of lettuce. I gave her good morning, and was astonished to see when she turned to respond that it was Izzy.

Clearly startled to see me, she got to her feet and hastily dusted the soil from her skirts. With barely concealed resentment, she said, 'What are you doing here?'

'I ... just came to see you and bring you some daffs. Look, aren't they lovely?'

'I've got my own daffs, thanks. Just as good as that.'

'Well, that's charming. Can't you just pretend to be glad to see me and accept the gift with good grace,' I couldn't help it, 'as befits a ladies' maid?'

She looked up at me sharply and her chin jutted. 'I am to be a ladies' maid!' Mrs Cobham says she'll train me after my seventeenth birthday. There's no ladies in residence at the moment, so we don't need one, but when we do, it's going to be me.'

'Ah, I see.' Somewhat mollified, I cast an eye around the kitchen garden. 'So for now, this is your job?'

'We all have a few different jobs: it's only a small staff. I look after the vegetables with one of the gardeners, and I help with the cooking. But I also do the rooms with Molly, when visitors come and that. Not fires, that's for the skivvy. I only do the clean jobs, bedding and towels and airing the wardrobes. Mrs Cobham gave me gloves and told me to take care of my nails to keep them nice for when I do ladies' hair and things.'

I felt quite touched by her anxiety to impress me. 'Can you have a break and a chat? Maybe you could show me a bit of the house? Is Mr Farnworth in residence at the moment?'

'No, but his son is.' She flashed me a look.

'Oh yes?' I smiled. 'What's he like then?'

She turned her back on me and bent to lift the seed trays. 'Nice. Friendly, like his dad.' I knew this tactic. She didn't want me to see her face. I waited until she straightened up and turned round. Yes, she was blushing.

'How friendly?'

Predictably, she rose to it straight away and flashed, 'What do you mean, how friendly? Mind your own business.'

I persisted, trying to keep my tone light and teasing, but she wasn't having any of it, and for the first time, I felt alarmed. I modified my tone. 'How old is he?'

'Same age as me.'

I waited.

'He's nineteen.'

'You're sixteen.'

'I'm seventeen in a month, Miss Picky!'

'Was he in the army?'

'Yes,' her eyes softened unmistakably. 'He looked lovely in uniform.' She gathered her wits again, 'What's it to you, anyway?'

'Just interested. It's good to have lads about again, isn't it?'

She smiled at me properly for the first time, 'Oh yes, it certainly is,' and although I held my smile, I felt a chill in my chest.

She gathered her things together and led the way into the kitchen, where there was a jug of lemonade with a beaded lace cover, standing in a bowl of water on the draining board. I sat at the long kitchen table and looked around me. The room was light and airy with whitewashed walls and deep shelves holding every kind of pot and pan. Herbs hung from a drying rack over the fire, and a jug of daffodils stood in the middle of the table, illuminating the wood with their yellow glow.

'This is a lovely kitchen,' I said. 'It feels ... happy somehow.'

She sat down on the same side of the table as me, and again I thought how clear it was that she wanted to avoid eye contact.

'It is. I love it here.'

'Where's your room?'

'On the top floor. I share with Molly for now, but when I'm a ladies' maid, I'll have my own room.'

'What other staff are there?'

'Gardeners, stable boys, a valet and a chauffeur, but they're only here when Mr Farnworth's in residence.'

I waited. 'And women?' My tone must have been sarcastic, because she bit back: 'I've told you the women!'

'So there's just you and Molly and Mrs Cobham?'

'Yes, and a couple of others who come to help when they're needed, but they don't live here.'

'So do women ever come to stay? Has Mr Farnworth got a lady friend?'

35

'Not that we know of, though the chauffeur hinted that there might be a lady coming in the summer. I hope there is. Maybe Mr Farnworth'll marry again. He's only forty-five. They'd maybe settle here. There could be parties, and balls, and motor cars and footmen...'

'And what would his son think of that, do you think?'

'Oh, he'd like it. It's too quiet here for him. He gets lonely,' she stopped and looked at me, then got up and took the glasses to the sink. 'It's great having running water. And electricity. You can't imagine. You're living in the dark ages.'

Chapter Six

When I turned into our drive that evening and pulled up on the crunchy gravel, the movement-sensitive lights made my pupils contract painfully. I reached for the remote and while I waited for the garage door to open like a stage curtain, I sat floodlit, the house directing its interrogative gaze through my windscreen. The imperative beep of the garage alarm snapped me out of my reverie: I had driven home on automatic pilot, my thoughts elsewhere in time and place.

Paul was away, for which I was thankful. I couldn't have faced either curiosity or indifference: I wanted to be alone with my thoughts. He didn't ring or text, but that was nothing new. I would normally have called someone for a chat, watched a film or had a look at Facebook, but for ages I just sat at the kitchen table in the gathering darkness, letting my thoughts wander. The idea of moving out seemed suddenly daunting, and I couldn't settle to making plans: too many thoughts and memories had been stirred up like silt, muddying my mind. I had been doodling on the back of an envelope, indecipherable swirls and loopy flowers, then names in flowery copperplate: Stanley and Izabel. My granddad's name had suited him so well: soft-sounding but solid, dependable. And Izabel? Such a lovely name for such an embittered, bad-tempered old woman. What had my granddad ever seen in her? Had they ever been happy? Had there been a time, before I knew them, when they loved each other and she spoke gently to him? And who was Esther? As I gazed at the names, the faces of their owners swam into view and I began to try to visualize them as young people, when their names were their own, before they were parents or grandparents, as they might have looked when they met. I searched my memory for any anecdote my mum might have told me, but there was nothing but a blank. I had simply no idea how the family had come to lose the farm, if indeed they had.

It had been a long time since I'd written anything longer than an email or a shopping list, but after a while, I went up to get an A4 pad from the study, suddenly possessed by the need to put something down on paper. I got myself a glass of wine, sat down and spread three blank sheets on the table. I headed them Past, Present and

Future then stopped, intimidated by the enormity of the effort of channeling all my swirling thoughts down my arm and out into the world. Present and Future were the imponderables, the ones that needed objectivity and solid ideas. The past I decided was the place to start. If I could exorcise all the memories that today had stirred up, I would be able to see things more clearly.

The child I had been seemed like another person, and I felt protective of her. But she was me. She might not have been spared a thought for a long time, but she was still there, deep inside me, the kernel of what I am now. It came to me to write about her in the form of a story, as though it was something that had happened to someone else, and suddenly the words started to flow:

In deepest Lancashire for many a long summer, sixties city slicker Annelise became "ower Annie": possessive naming of the pale skinny child with the Salford pallor, the abhorrence of pigs and mud and gaslight.

Regarding her traitorous parents from the gloom of the front parlour, she'd watch them say their hasty goodbyes and dash off back to their busy lives. Her silence would last for days; bookish, immobile and alien in the corner of the room.

"Ye want to get out an get some fresh air - do ye good." But for days the child would refuse to leave the house.

Alternately belligerent and bewildered, her grandmother scolded or cajoled according to her mood, Grandma's moods being the dominant weather system in the small terraced house. Indeed, turbulence was often felt beyond its confines, and the child had noticed early on that the neighbours on either side never met her grandma's eyes when they acknowledged her presence.

"Morning Izabel."

"So it is."

"Looks like a good drying day today."

"No, it's going to rain this afternoon." Uttered in a tone that brooked no opposition: woe betide anyone who disagreed with Grandma, even mildly.

"Oh I think I'll get the shirts done though."

"Yer daft if you do."

Washdays were Mondays for Grandma. Rain or shine, out came the tub and the washboard, the wooden grabbers and the mangle: the tools of her martyrdom would not be denied their pivotal place in the week's rotation. When the weather dared to defy her, summer rains wantonly drenching the flags, she would simply force the washing back through the mangle and then drape sheets, shirts and bloomers from wooden racks suspended from the ceiling and propped round the fire. For days afterwards, condensation ran down the walls, and anyone foolhardy enough to want to look out would have to risk the strap for putting fingermarks on the windows.

Nobody called, but Granddad was often out, returning home to a tirade about what a fool he was to be mending that hen-coop for Mrs Alker, whose husband wasn't as poorly as he pretended.

Surreptitious surveillance from the upstairs window confirmed to the watchful child that the women knew what time Izabel chalked her front step and swept the path: their times coincided, but not with hers. Often they'd get up from their knees with unconscious symmetry, briefly survey their freshly whitened steps, nod at each other, fold their arms across their flowery pinnies and stroll to the pavement to put their heads together and murmur in subdued tones about what poor Stanley had to put up with. They felt for the poor man - such a lovely man, he'd do anything for you.

Granddad, meanwhile, went about his business, eyes habitually downcast, submissive, acquiescent, and apparently indifferent to the verbal batterings and the silent child. Every morning he boarded his bike, weskit buttoned, his butty box strapped to the back, and left.

Each evening he reappeared, his arrival announced by the creak of the back gate, and the ticking of his bicycle coming up the yard. Eventually, the back door would open on Grandma's kitchen domain.

"Ayup, ower mother."

"Ayup."

"Alreet?"

If he was lucky, he'd get an affirmative: "Alreet." If he wasn't lucky and a storm was brewing, Ower Annie would vacate her chair and vamoose.

39

Bare feet on the hot chalk of the front step, squinting into the evening sun's unaccustomed glare, ears buffeted by the maelstrom at her back, she'd survey the front field and sniff the air suspiciously for a whiff of pig. If the wind was in her favour, her nostrils would involuntarily flare with the draught of undeniable sweetness. Her hibernating poetic soul would stir and lift its head attentively.

Oh, the air! The gradual expulsion of soot-blackened sixties Salford sediment from small lungs, pushed out by the cleansing draughts of Pennine air drunk deep. Here it began. From walking to school in lint masks on smog days, to infusions of air that shimmered green in the heat haze and made you drunk on freedom. From fear of pigs to worshipful rummaging under warm hens.

The day she was there to meet him at the top of Sandy Lane, the summer could begin for Granddad. For days now, he'd squinted into the west as he'd slowly pedaled home, searching for her silhouette on the brow of the hill and at last there it was. Bambi legs akimbo, white arm waving, halo of chestnut curls glowing in the late afternoon sun. His back would straighten and his chest expand, and his eyes would crinkle unseen.

Drawing near, subduing his smile, his greeting as gruff as a billygoat. The cool cookie would pointedly respond with an urban hello, a shy glance upward from under her fringe. He knew that the 'ayup' would come, initially ironic but soon well-meant and as natural as breathing.

Allies, for the first few days they'd walk home in silence, until the day she greeted him with a feather, an egg, a hunk of sheep's wool, and once a bedraggled comic she'd found in a den. By then, their buoyant and chatty entrances subdued Izabel, bossily bustling about the kitchen in her wrapover pinny with her hat still on.

"Shut the door."

"It's a lovely evening, why don't we...."

"Shut. That. Door."

Instead of doing as he was told, she knew that if she looked round she would see him defiantly propping it open. The worm had turned. This grandchild who stayed all summer, and looked her in the eye while she was getting the strap, had let the air in.

They'd be full of plans, him and the child: walks, picnics, a coach trip to Blackpool. One time, she grudgingly agreed to climb Rivington Pike, scandalised by the child's suggestion she should leave off her rubber corset and stays, but then overcome with regret and envy when she had to admit defeat and let them stride on ahead to the top without her.

The day he announced he was going to make the child a swing in the outside toilet, she thought he'd taken leave of his senses. Undaunted, the two of them went out to the woodshed with a jug of lemon barley water, and the child sat on the wood-chopping stool, rapt, watching with avid eyes as he crafted a seat from a plank. Later, there was laughter from the end of the yard, and Izabel was drawn to go and see what they were up to. He was holding the child by the waist and swinging her up and backwards until her head touched the cistern, then dropping her swiftly and smoothly back towards the entrance, shouting. "Measure it! Measure it!" while she shrieked with laughter, helplessly waving a tape-measure above her head.

He put her down in the end, and sat on the low wall while he got his breath back. The child lay spread-eagled on the hot flags, panting and giggling exhaustedly. The warmth of their laughter included her, so she sat down beside him and pressed her arm against his shirt-sleeve, letting his heat suffuse her skin.

Summer on summer, the child grew taller, until one day she observed that the hatpin was level with her eye. "Eee, grandma, am bigger than you!"

Sharp as a tack, the woman flashed back, "Aye, 'n yer 'ead's bigger an all."

But there was no more belt after that. No more, "Hold yer 'and out." The belt he used to sharpen his razor hung on its hook, left to its original purpose, and there even came a day when the child, now a teenager, could pause in the doorway, lift the belt and stroke its soft brown leather, thinking only of her Granddad and the fascinating skill of the cut-throat razor rasping over his neck-hairs, the way he whipped up soap in the white lather-mug, then tilted his head and bent the soft cartilage of his nose-end to one side to get those last few gray sprouting bristles. When she was small, he used to tickle her tummy with his chinny-chin-chin, and as she grew, his

41

goodnight kiss would scratch her face in a way she loved, always ending with 'butterfly kisses', fluttering his eyelashes against her sleepy eyelids.

I wrote it in a kind of trance, the words flowing easily from my pen. The sensuous pleasure of ink on paper came back to me: as well as a feeling of deep peace, I had forgotten how much satisfaction there was in the act of creativity. All the meals I'd created with loving care vanished in minutes and the satisfaction was transient, lately feeling as though it was hardly worth the effort. I used to make clothes when we were first married, curtains and even bedding, but it more through necessity than any creative impulse. I enjoyed decorating the house for Christmas, occasionally making wreaths or candle-holders with pine cones and bits of greenery, but really it was such a long time since I'd made anything that would last.

This would last: this was truth, my truth. In the act of writing it, I had understood: it was insight, preservation, continuity. My mother had deliberately removed herself from this story, from her unhappy parents, from this town where her roots lay buried deep. And although she left her daughter here for long stretches of time, she had done so through necessity: at least, it had seemed necessary to her, devoted as she was to her job, to earning money so that we could have more things, bigger and better houses.

I had hoped, while mum went about the business of dying, that we could become closer, share intimacies, confide secrets. I had hoped to get to know her before she took her leave, but as always, self-sufficiency and independence were her priorities: she seemed to believe that showing affection, revealing her interior life or stories from the past would entail some loss of face, some show of vulnerability, so whatever secrets she might have had went with her to the grave. She got her way in the end: she usually did.

No matter what happened in the future, I was determined to reconnect my own daughter to our family's roots. Without roots, how can we grow? Rosie, I knew, would love this little story. Only connect.

Chapter Seven

That night I slept eight solid hours, and woke in the centre of the bed, spread out like a starfish. I lay still, watching the light grow stronger and savouring the feeling of peace. I felt happier and more peaceful than I had for years.

I took my time getting up, showering in thoughtful silence and wrapping myself in a long, soft towelling dressing-gown. As I padded down the stairs, the silent house seemed to hold its breath. The marble kitchen surfaces gleamed in the soft autumn light. Pouring myself a glass of apple juice, I opened the patio doors and stepped out into the garden. It had rained in the night and everything had a drenched freshness: the air was sweet and moist with resin. Beyond the trees, the sky was pale blue and gin-clear. In the distance, a pair of pot-bellied golfers studied a green. I stepped out of my slippers onto the damp grass, savouring the unfamiliar sensation on the soles of my feet.

The decision was made already, and I didn't even feel the need to justify it to myself. How he would take it I couldn't imagine, but would soon find out. I only hoped that things wouldn't get nasty. He had so much power over me, and I'd let it happen. Financially, things could get very tricky. My only power lay in the importance he placed on his image: he would hate his colleagues and his friends at the golf club to know all of it, let alone Rosie and Mark. There might come a time when I would have to tell him everything I knew.

By the time I was dressed, I had the wording, and sat down at the kitchen table to compose a note, which I folded into an envelope and placed on the top of his pile of mail.

I got some steak out of the freezer, checked the salad drawer and even decanted a bottle of Cabernet Sauvignon to air: he couldn't accuse me of neglecting him, and I wouldn't want him to feel completely abandoned: it would be enough of a shock for him to come home this evening and find the house silent and dark. I couldn't think of a time when that had ever been his experience.

It's surprising how having such a small boot focuses the mind: if I'd had a car the size of his, I might have been tempted to take more, but I got all my basic clothing needs into the one suitcase which would fit, then stuffed the corners of the boot with towels, shoes and toiletries. The bedding I rolled into a bale and wrapped with my dressing-gown cord so that it wouldn't spread over the gearstick. Finally, I packed my rucksack with laptop and some other bits and pieces, and stuffed a good bottle of red wine into the webbing pocket that was meant for water. I'd do a shop when I got to Adlington, but I didn't yet know how well-stocked the shop in the petrol- station was, and reasoned that there was no point in suffering unnecessarily.

When I was ready, I just went. There was to be no farewell tour: I reassured myself I'd be back to visit, anyway. I was fairly confident I could keep our relationship on an even keel, at least at first. I pressed the remote, and the garage door slowly raised like a theatre curtain. I took a deep breath and pulled out onto the drive, looking down the leafy avenue to left and right. It was mid-morning, and the street was deserted. A small red car appeared at the far end, and I recognised the Robinsons' cleaner as she drove past without a glance.

A sleek Siamese regarded me from the wall opposite, its almond eyes narrowed and its face impassive. That said it all, really. I was off.

The ring-road was clear, and as I drove round Manchester I reflected on the geography of my life. Leafy Cheshire had never really felt like home: I'd felt a fraud ever since my parents had uprooted us when I was seventeen. My brother, at eleven, had settled into his new school with barely a backward glance, but I'd stubbornly refused to move schools, and doggedly travelled across the city to finish my A-levels in Salford. In one of the many rows about it, my mother had once actually let slip that they wanted me to make what she called 'a good marriage', meet a nice boy 'from a good family'. The air had changed in an instant. I had stopped my random raging and stared at her with open-mouthed horror. There, it was said. And it was indefensible. We both knew that. I had experienced then a sudden certainty, and my mind was made up. I had actually been wavering: always a bed-lover, the thought of three hours on trains and buses every single day had been appalling to me, but from the moment she said those words, she and I both knew I would do it, and never miss a single day.

So when I brought Paul home from university, they were gleeful at his middle-class credentials, his 'good family', his interest (feigned at the time) in golf, and his avowed intention to get a job in Manchester and live in Cheshire. These were all things that I held against him, even then, but love and lust are strong imperatives. If they'd been aware of his need for control, his amorality, his capacity for deceit, his sexual proclivities, his cannabis habit, his musical taste or his real opinion of them, they would certainly have felt differently about their prospective son-in-law, but he was a schmoozer good and proper, and they never suspected a thing.

So here I was, skirting Manchester in a clock-wise direction, heading north, winding the clock back, past even Salford, into Lancashire, to the very village Mum had fled half a century ago. Why? What had driven her?

When I pulled up outside the house, there was no-one about and I was hungry, so I dumped all the stuff in the hall and drove back to the chippy on the main road, then wandered along to the canal bridge to sit and eat my fish and mushy peas. The steps down to the canal-side were still there, but the path had been tarmaced and there were bright barges tied up along the banks. If I thought hard enough, I could conjure up a picture of my granddad and his skinny little red-headed granddaughter dangling their fishing nets into the murky water. I don't think anyone had ever taken a picture of us there, but the sepia scene seemed real enough. In contrast, the canal water was now a glittery bluey-black instead of muddy sludge brown, and laughter rang out from the beer-garden.

The shop was surprisingly well-stocked for one so small, but very pricy: Beth had told me that everyone did their weekly shop at the giant Asda on the edge of Chorley. The small parade opposite had once been a hubbub of butchers, bakers, greengrocers and gossip, but now three shops were boarded up and the other was a dismal-looking charity shop. A group of teenagers were lounging round the war memorial, smoking and texting, the stone soldier above them gazing out across to Rivington Pike, as oblivious of them as they were of him.

I'd just got back to the car when my phone rang: Rosie.

'Hello love, how did it go?'

'I think I might get it, Mum, I did really well. You know when you just feel right? I felt dead good, clicked with the panel, had lots to say but kept an eye on them so I knew when to shut up? Anyway, hope so. I should hear before the end of the week.'

'So you really want it? '

'Yes, I do. The people are lovely and the offices are great. You know when the architecture's been really well thought-out? It's just two storeys high and kind of semi-circular, with a glass wall: everyone looks out onto greenery. You'd have loved the toilets.'

I laughed, 'Oh yes, you know me and my toilet fetish!'

'No, you know what I mean: natural light, lovely soaps, proper towels. Where I am now, they're horrible. You don't feel like anyone cares about you as long as you're doing your job. Anyway, how's you? What are you up to?'

I drew a breath. 'I'm having a few days away.'

'Away where?'

'I'm just up in Adlington.'

'Adlington?'

'You know, where the house is, the rental house, my gran's.'

'Oh, yeah, right. How do you mean, a few days? Is Dad with you?"

'No, he's flying back from Geneva this afternoon.'

'Then going to Adlington?'

This really wasn't computing. 'No, he'll be going home. But I won't be there, I'll be here.'

'In Adlington?'

'Yes.'

'Is there a hotel?'

'No, I'm staying in the house ... for a bit. Look, if you speak to him, I'd rather you didn't tell him where I was. Just for now.'

'What do you mean? Have you left him? What's he done now?'

I didn't really want to do this over the phone, and I wasn't sure I really knew what to say, so I didn't answer, which Rosie interpreted wrongly. 'Mum? Are you ok? Are you crying? Shall I come?'

46

'No, no love, I'm fine, in fact...' I almost said that I felt better than I had for quite a long time, but decided she didn't need to hear that. 'I just need some time on my own. Would you mind if I rang you back in a few days?'

'A few days?' There was silence while she thought about it, and then, in a low, slightly sulky voice: 'What if I hear about the job?'

I relented. 'Oh, of course ring me! Ring me anytime, just as normal. Like I say, I'll be ready to talk to you about it in a few days.'

'Does Dad know?'

'No, no he doesn't. I've left him a note. He'll be ok. Don't worry about your dad. He won't be ...' If I'd said it too quickly, it would have come out bitter. 'He won't be lonely.'

'Oh, I get it. Again, huh? After all that. Is there anything I ... Well, if you're sure you're ok?'

'Yes, yes I am love, I promise. Ring me when you hear, hey?'

'Yes, ok, will do. And you ring me or text me if you want me to come. I can be there in an hour, you know.'

'Yes, love, I know. And thanks. Love you.'

'Love you too. Bye then.'

'Bye love, and good luck.'

'Thanks. Bye. Mwah.'

'Mwah.'

Less than five minutes later, my phone rang again while I was driving. When I saw that it had been Mark, and that he hadn't left a message, I decided not to ring back and go through what I knew would be a rather more shrill and indignant version of the conversation I'd had with his sister, so I texted him to tell him I'd be in touch and not to worry.

When I opened the front door, I had to climb over my pile of stuff to get to the kitchen and put the kettle on, gasping for that cup of tea that always tastes so delicious after fish and chips. While it was boiling, I made myself a passageway and brought the bags of shopping in.

Beth had left the cupboards immaculate, and I had all the time in the world, so I opened the back door and took my tea out into the garden. Yard. Quite a contrast with the garden where I'd drunk my apple juice this morning: this was all cracked flags, crumbling bricks and rotten wood instead of manicured greenery, but I surveyed it fondly and with a real sense of anticipation.

In the early days, when I was teaching and used to do my own cleaning, I could never be bothered with a routine. I'd just wait until the detritus piled up and you could draw a picture in the dust, or we'd run out of mugs, then blitz the place. It meant you got a real sense of achievement: I subscribe to the view that dust is just matter in the wrong place and life's too short to stuff a mushroom. I'd had to up my game when Paul got promoted though: all those bloody cream carpets and canapes. I could measure the last fifteen years of my life in flipping canapes.

'Enjoy your chips then?'

A teenage boy was leaning over the wall, his earphones in and phone in hand.

I mouthed an answer but made no sound.

'Eh?'

I did it again.

'I haven't got any music on. I just keep them in so I don't have to talk to anyone.'

'I'm honoured.'

Instant sulk. 'Just thought I'd be friendly. Forget it.' His head disappeared below the wall.

After a bit, I got up and leaned over to look at him, sitting on the floor with his back against the wall. A tinny cacophony was issuing from his ears. Knowing better than to let him know he was being watched, I left him to it, but later, when I saw him through the kitchen window sitting on a bench in the sun, I poured myself a glass of water and strolled outside.

The earphones were still in, so I trod on an empty can that was lying in my yard and saw him register the noise, though he tried to pretend he hadn't heard. I sat on the opposite wall, where we could clearly see each other, and spoke in a normal voice: 'Got the afternoon off, then?'

48

'Yeah, study leave.'

'In September?'

'Well doh.'

'When are your mocks?'

He straightened up a bit and jutted his chin. 'Soon'.

'That's unusual.'

He gave me a long look. "What's it to you?'

'Nothing. Just wondered.' I drank my water and went back into the house. When I looked out again, he had disappeared.

I was enjoying stocking the cupboards, but the house was suddenly too quiet, so I got my laptop out and looked for a wi-fi so that I could have the radio on. Finding a strong signal from one called Travolta4me, I followed my hunch and went round to knock on Beth's front door.

After a few minutes, the window above me slid open. 'What?'

'Hello,' I said brightly, as though we'd never met, 'I'm your new neighbour, Annie. I wondered if you'd mind me using your wi-fi until I get mine installed?'

'DannyZuko,' and the window slammed shut. I should have guessed.

The afternoon passed in a contented flurry of nesting, and soon I was able to stroll from room to room and know exactly what objects were in each one. It was wonderfully soothing: I was so used to the static in my head when I moved around my marital home: all the voices of all the objects the four of us had accumulated in twenty years of affluence. Socrates was right: It's surprising how many things in this life you can manage without.

More than once, I glanced at my watch and calculated how long it would be before I'd have to face the music, and finally, just after six - I knew he'd have watched the headlines while he mixed his gin and tonic - my phone rang.

'Hello Paul.'

There was silence, then the chink of ice against glass. After a moment, he still didn't speak, so I said, as casually as I could muster, 'How was your trip?'

'Fine, flight was chocker though.'

49

'Did you get a meal?' This was ridiculous. Why was I even pandering?

'No, I was looking forward to a home-cooked steak.'

'I've left it between two plates in the fridge.'

'Yes, I saw that. I won't say thank-you as you should be here to cook it.'

I bit my lip but kept my tone light, teasing. 'You can do it just the way you like it. There's plenty of salad, I checked.'

'Thank-you, I appreciate that. Nice homecoming.'

Ok, he was going for heavy irony. I didn't respond. I didn't want it to escalate: it had all become so predictable, and this was exactly what I wanted to escape from. I wondered how I'd have felt if he'd been upset, concerned, even hurt. This way made it easier.

There was silence punctuated by chinking ice. Finally, he said, 'Oh well, suit yourself,' and the line went dead.

In the silent room, the enormity of what I was doing threatened to overwhelm me, and for a moment I thought I was going to start crying, but right on cue, a cheery 'Coo-eee!' rang from the back yard.

I took a deep breath and called, 'Coming!' in a breezy voice.

She was leaning on the wall having a cigarette, so I said, 'You should give that up, you know.'

'I know, the kids say the same, so at least it does some good.'

'How do you mean?'

'Well they're so disgusted by my bad habit, it puts them off doing it themselves.'

'That's not the point.'

She took a last puff and ground out the dimp in a bowl of sand she evidently kept for the purpose. 'I know, but hey…Anyway, do you fancy coming round for tea? It's just me and Adam tonight. Any attempt at conversation with him is like dropping stones down a deep well and never hearing the plop.'

'How can I resist such a delightful invitation? I'll bring my Wildean wit. Can I bring anything else? Grapes? I have grapes. Yoghurt? I have plenty of yoghurt. I took great delight in stocking the fridge with only myself in mind. White wine, too. I have white wine.'

50

'Oo, I think we could have a little drinkie-poo, don't you? I've got a bottle of vodka and some tonic.'

'What time shall I come round?'

'Any time you like. I'm doing a spag bol and the pasta's not on yet.'

'Oo, well if it's spag bol, I'll bring a cheeky bottle of red I happen to have about my person. Great, I'll just nip and have a shower and I'll be round by seven. That suit you?'

'Yep, just hop over the back wall when you're ready.'

'Lovely, thanks Beth.'

Under the shower, I reflected on how long it had been since I'd had that kind of casual invitation. Some of my neighbours in Knutsford were quite friendly, but generally it was couples, and our social calendars were planned well in advance. Even the book group had developed a distinctly competitive air when it came to catering.

By the time I locked the back door, the light was going and there was a distinct chill in the air. Beth's door was open: Coldplay and the delicious smell of bolognese wafted out on the evening air.

'Knock knock.'

'Come in! Adam, get Annie's vodka and tonic out of the fridge, love, would you? Ice? Put her some ice in, sweetheart.'

Adam grunted and laboriously heaved himself out of the chair. 'Please?'

While Adam did as he was told, I sat down at the kitchen table and put a small vase of flowers in the middle.

'Ah, lovely! Thanks Annie. I can't remember when anybody last bought me flowers!'

'I gave you some on Mother's Day,' he rumbled resentfully.

'Yes, you did love. Sorry, I'd forgotten.' As he turned a mollified face to me, I clearly heard Beth mutter, 'I think we'll draw a veil over where you got them from though.'

'What?'

'Nothing. Have you got yourself a drink, love? How's your vodka and tonic, Annie? Thank God it's Friday, eh?' She took a sip from her glass, then reached out to chink mine. 'Cheers. Welcome to Adlington.'

'Cheers, and thanks again for inviting me.'

'I didn't know whether you'd be looking forward to your first night of solitude.'

'Oh, I get plenty of solitude. My husband's away a lot and of course the kids have got their own places now.'

Adam muttered, 'Wish I had my own place.'

Ladle in hand, Beth bent to kiss his head. 'Oh now, don't! How could I carry on without you, my baby boy?'

Squirming away from her embrace, he retorted, 'At least I could get away from flippin' Coldplay.'

'Put your earphones in if you don't like it.'

'I thought I wasn't allowed to have my earphones in at the table?' He was already reaching into his pocket, but Beth tapped him on the shoulder with a plastic sieve. 'You're not.'

He turned to me. 'Did you see that? She wants reporting.'

I was laughing at them both, evidently so alike and gruffly affectionate. They kept up the banter throughout the meal, but as soon as he'd finished eating, Adam leapt up. 'I'm off out.'

In a tone that brooked no opposition, Beth said, 'Sit down please. Third degree time.'

Rolling his eyes, Adam sat back down and recited as if by rote: 'Matt's. Computer games. 11 o'clock. Yes, I've got my phone.'

'Promise?'

'Promise.'

'No, look at me and promise. I'm having a drink and relaxing tonight with Annie. I don't want to be out scouring the streets for you. And if I ring you, answer it. Now promise and you can go, but put your plate in the water.'

When he'd gone, she poured us both another glass of wine and said, 'He's a good lad mostly, but we've had our moments.'

'It must be hard with no man around.'

'Who said there was no man around?' She winked and took a sip. 'Shall we go and sit in the front room?'

'No, I'm alright here if it's ok with you. So go on, tell me about the man.'

'Nothing to tell, just someone I see a bit of when it suits. How did your husband take it?'

I'd been hoping for a bit of distraction, but Beth was like a terrier with a scent, and she soon ferreted out a summary of the state of my marriage. Despite the wine, I managed to withhold all the details. 'Thing is, I'm never lonely when he's away, but when he's home, I feel as though I don't exist. It's been like that for ages. His indifference just drains the life out me. It's like he's like one of those Dementors in Harry Potter. I've just been getting more and more depressed. It's pathetic really, in comparison to some people's problems, so I don't really like talking about it. Thanks for asking though.'

'So what triggered this then?'

I gave her a furtive look, which she caught and interpreted correctly, or almost: 'An affair?'

'Not exactly, although emotionally, yes, I suppose it was an affair.'

'Facebook? Old boyfriend?'

'Got it in one.'

'Are you still in touch?'

'No, by mutual agreement, well at least after he accepted that I meant it about I refusing to sleep with him. Thing is, I felt so alive while it lasted. And I thought, I can feel like this again. I am attractive, at least to someone. I can be funny and interesting and have things to say. Paul noticed a difference: he said once, 'Oh, the worm's turned, has it?' I'm not at all sure how he's going to react.

'How do you mean? What might he do?'

'Well, he could cut off my allowance. He could start divorce proceedings. He could lie. He's a very very convincing liar. He could...' I paused and looked at her open face. 'He could get very nasty. But anyway, so far so good: he's just a bit disgruntled that he's got to cook his own steak tonight.'

'Ha! He'll cope. But I'm interested in the nasty bit. How nasty? He doesn't hit you, does he?' When I didn't answer straight away, she burst out, 'Bastard! Even in the leafy suburbs, eh? ' She reached over and squeezed my arm. 'Don't worry, you're safe here. I can handle myself and I've got two big lads.'

'He wouldn't make a scene, not in a million years. Anything he does, he'll make sure we're alone.'

'Well, if he finds out where you are, we'll make sure you're never alone, don't you worry. So anyway, what are you going to do with yourself while he gets used to the idea?'

'I think the first thing I've got to do is find out about the farm. It belonged to my family and if there's the faintest chance I could claim it, or even have some relatives I don't know about... I know it's a long shot, but the more I think about it, the more I think my Mum and Izabel were hiding something. They hated each other's guts, could barely be civil to each other. They only kept it going for Granddad's sake. Meanwhile, this house is all I've got. I'll occupy myself by renovating it: I used to enjoy decorating. In the long term, if I settle here, I might try to get involved with the community, do a bit of voluntary work maybe?'

'Hm, not much in the way of a community around here I'm afraid. You'll have to do better than that.'

'Well, I'm just going to concentrate on getting the house how I want it for now. Might do a bit of family research, play the music I like, eat what and when I like.'

'Avoid Marmite.'

'Eh?'

'It's a killer, Marmite.' She went on in a sepulchral voice: 'A woman alone, a jar of Marmite', and shuddered, shaking her head and turning her face away.

Thoroughly tickled now, I felt laughter rising in my chest like champagne bubbles, and giggled, "No! What? Tell me what to be afraid of! There's a jar in my cupboard right now!' I clasped her hands across the table, 'Don't leave me alone with it!' I felt drunk, not only on the vodka and wine, but also on the heady liberation of being profoundly silly.

When we subsided, I said, 'What on earth was that all about? Marmite? It's like a Monty Python sketch! What put that into your head?'

She laughed as she got up and put our plates in the sink, then sat back down and looked suddenly serious. 'It sounds daft, but it was one of the scariest things that's ever happened to me. I nearly died in a freak Marmite accident. I'd walked the kids to school, and you know what it's like, you don't get a chance to make your own breakfast for rounding up stuff and herding them out the door. I got

54

back and thanked God I'd got the house to myself. I did some toast and slapped the butter on nice and thick while it was still hot, and then a slick of Marmite, only there was too much on the knife, so I licked the knife, and just as I licked it I did this kind of hiccup and the Marmite flew to the back of my throat and slicked across the top of my windpipe and suddenly I just couldn't breathe! I was trying to get breath out and coughing and inhaling Marmite and gulping for air and trying to drink water or gargle or something and all the time my eyes were bulging and I thought this is it, I'm going to die of Marmite inhalation! How bloody embarrassing! And then suddenly something shifted in the back of my throat and my nose and I could breathe, and oh boy did I breathe! I've never got over it!'

'You're not suggesting I shouldn't live alone because I might get killed by Marmite?'

She smiled, 'Nooo, I'm not suggesting anything. I'm just telling you to beware the unseen dangers of independent life.'

Suddenly the smile died on my lips and a well of morose regret rose up in its place. 'Because you know, I've thought that. Maybe it's my fault that things have fallen apart for us. It takes two to tango. Maybe I should just accept ... well, there's something I can't accept, but maybe I should just appreciate what I've got, preserve the status quo. And who's going to look after me when I'm old?'

But Beth wasn't having any of it. 'Oh, for God's sake. You might not get old. Plenty don't.' She looked bitter for a moment, and I thought of her mother. She got up, briskly, 'You only get one life, missis, so think on. Let's go and watch Bridesmaids.'

Chapter Eight

The following morning, I awoke with a sore head and cursed the second bottle of wine, but reflected that I'd had such a good night, such a laugh, that it was well worth the hangover. I didn't actually remember going to bed, so it was amazing that I'd managed to find my way to the bathroom during the night to drink a pint of water, which had been miraculously absorbed into my body, and without which I no doubt have felt worse. I reached for my mobile and saw that there'd been a missed call from Paul at eleven o'clock: I was glad I hadn't taken my phone round to Beth's as we'd both have had our tongues liberated by alcohol: he'd no doubt finished the bottle of wine and gone onto whisky. It occurred to me that if we were to keep our relationship on an even keel, I mustn't talk to him when either of us had 'a drop taken', as my mum used to say.

I lay still, loath to move my head again. As I lay there exploring the ache like a tongue probing a sore tooth, I remembered the description in Bonfire of the Vanities: for the first time in my life, my head did in fact feel like an egg with the shell peeled off. When I'd moved it to pick my phone up, my brain actually did seem to roll like a yolk made of mercury. My gums ached. My mouth was like the bottom of a bird-cage. The curtains were tissue-thin, and the daylight hardly glaring, but my eyes ached to look at it.

Eventually, I summoned enough determination to get myself to the bathroom and take a couple of painkillers. I made myself drink another pint of water and staggered back to bed. Before I went back to sleep, I made sure my phone was on mute.

By the time I surfaced again, the drugs had worked and the sun was staring in through the curtains more insistently. I turned over tentatively, and finding that I could stand up without any ill-effects, I slipped into my dressing gown and shuffled downstairs to make myself a coffee. I could hear music through the walls, and instead of feeling it an intrusion, I welcomed the novel feeling of companionship. I wondered whether she felt as bad as I did.

I'd ring him when I felt more human. Let him wait.

An hour later, having fortified myself with a big bowl of muesli and another coffee, having showered and dressed in my comfiest jeans and floppiest shirt, I curled into an armchair, took a deep breath and called him.

Just as I thought it was about to go to answerphone, he picked up. 'Well?'

I was determined not to rise to it, so I gave him a cheery, 'Good morning!'

After the briefest silence, he returned the greeting. 'What time are you coming home?'

My turn for silence. 'I'm not. I said. I'll be away for a bit.'

'Look, Annie, what's this about? Come on, get it off your chest, but make it snappy. I'm playing golf in twenty minutes.'

I let that linger on the air for a bit before I said in a gentle voice which I hoped had not one jot of sarcasm in it. 'I'm okay. I just need a bit of space.'

'Space? You've got a five-bedroomed house with an acre of ground and a double garage! How much fucking space do you need?'

I took another deep breath and when my voice came out, it sounded more placatory than I'd intended, but it was clearly not the right time to lay my cards on the table. 'Look, Paul. Just give me a few days, hey, and then we'll have a talk. Is that okay?'

'Well it'll have to be, won't it? It seems I don't get any say in the matter.'

There was so much I could have said, so much I wanted to say, but most of it had been said before and I knew he would just switch off, so I didn't answer.

It surprised me when his voice came again, so quietly that I almost missed what he said and it took a moment to process: 'I miss you.'

It had been so long since he had said anything remotely affectionate that I was startled, but I only had to remind myself how manipulative he could be, and suddenly I knew what to say to keep him calm: 'I miss you too.' I'd been missing him for fifteen years, but now was not the time to go into that. 'I'll phone you on Monday evening at six, okay?'

Hard again now: 'Right. Fine. Goodbye.' And the line went dead.

I wouldn't dwell. I got up more quickly than I should have done, and went out into the yard to top up on vitamin D.

There was no-one in Beth's garden, but the neighbour on her other side gave me a cheery wave, and a chap pushing a bike along the back lane nodded at me as he passed. The early autumn sun was warm and welcome, and my spirits lifted and swelled. I'd go for a walk, that's what I'd do. I'd go and find the farm.

My boots were in the hall, and as I straightened up from putting them on, I caught a glimpse of my reflection and realized that my hair was a mass of frizzy curls, but I couldn't be bothered sorting it out, let alone straightening it. I didn't have any make-up on either, but what the hell did it matter? I tied a jumper round my waist and set off without even taking my phone.

I knew vaguely where I was going, though I didn't know what I'd find when I got there. At the end of the terrace, there's a short row of slightly bigger houses from the same period, presumably built for mill supervisors; they have fine stone porches and sash windows. I struggled to remember the name of the little boy who lived in number 182 in the sixties. He was a big blond lad, always leading the games and seamlessly moving us on from Cowboys and Indians to Earthlings and Martians. It suddenly came to me that he'd had a Dalek costume and had been chillingly good at extermination. David Topping, that was it: I only knew that because my grandma had hated him and used to spit out his name and call him a 'dirty little Turk'. Which seems strange, come to think of it. Maybe she meant 'tyke'. There had been quite a gang to play with, and it never seemed to matter that I didn't know anyone's names. By the time I'd been coming here a few years, they just accepted me every summer and probably never noticed my absence for the rest of the year. I never liked to draw attention to my outsider status by asking who was who: I'd see them coming and just swim out to join the shoal as it swept past the house on its way to the Common.

Such freedom, unthinkable now. We were out all day, and nobody worried, not that we were aware of anyway. We'd either be driven home by hunger or called home like dogs with selective deafness. We'd laugh and whoop and lose balls and boomerangs, play endless games of hide and seek, climb trees and build dens and fires. We swam in the river in all weathers, even in a thunderstorm once. That had been exciting, the electricity crackling through the trees and the gods throwing thunderbolts. Some of us got belted for our stupidity when the grownups got wind of it. We caught taddies and sticklebacks, and I remember how excited I'd been when I got my own net, but one of the lads stole it and I never got it back. Oh the pain of childhood.

When did things change so much? How different the world seemed by the time I had my own kids. I'd done my best to give them freedom, but always there was that undercurrent of 'what if?' When did things change, and why? I remembered the shock of the Moors murders: I was the same age as one of the victims, and Manchester was dark with fear, but out here I don't remember it having any impact on our freedom.

When I reached the end of the houses, I was astonished to see that the Common looked entirely unchanged, at least from where I was standing. The road carried on in a straight line, tapering between high unruly hawthorn hedges to the width of a single vehicle, and in the distance it might well still be unsurfaced: I could still feel the crunch of the ash. There was still no footpath: overgrown ditches were just discernable at each side of the road. Still no fences, either: all was verdant and unruly, looking much as it must have done since the Enclosures. I knew there was a new estate off to the left, but it wasn't visible from here. The houses on the other side of the road were more modern, but they'd been here in the sixties, and little had changed, just pvc double-glazing, satellite dishes and more cars on their paths.

Beth had told me that the man who lived in the farmhouse was a nasty piece of work, so I doubted I'd be invited for a look round, but I was determined to find the farm, so I stepped off the end of the pavement and set off along the narrowing road, breathing the sweet air deeply and consciously lengthening my pace. I knew it was off to the left somewhere, and followed a kind of gut instinct along a lane which had suddenly appeared between the high hedges. I had no real memory of the farm, never having been taken there, and only being vaguely aware of Grandma's association through overheard remarks. Whoever lived there had delivered our milk in the fifties and early sixties, on a little horse-drawn cart with a tall churn on the back. I had no memory of their faces and it startled me now to think that they might well have been close relatives. I had often admired the skill of the man who could scoop a perfect gill and

60

pour it into my outstretched jug without spilling a drop. When they first started delivering it in glass bottles (such progress!) Grandma used to stand it in a bowl of cold water on the floor of the kitchen. Good grief, when did I become a witness to living history? I suddenly felt ancient, as though my childhood had happened in black and white, or even sepia.

I was abruptly wrenched out of my melancholy musings by a shout, but I couldn't see where it had come from or whether it was directed at me. The lane had become a muddy path bordered by ramshackle fencing, and a few small black and white horses of the kind often seen on urban waste ground grazed the long grass over to my right. There was a cluster of low stone buildings a few hundred yards away, but nobody visible. I looked back at the ponies and saw that a huge horse-chestnut tree dominated the centre of the field. I don't think I'd ever seen a bigger or more beautiful solitary tree, its outline tinged with the golds of early autumn. The air around me was still, but as I watched, a wave seemed to move through the leaves, rising and falling like breathing. I was drawn to climb over the fence for a closer look. The shout came again, louder now, and echoed by the deep bark of a big dog. As I jumped down from the fence, an imposingly tall lean man appeared over to my left, striding towards me behind a straining Alsatian. I stood still where I had landed.

He stopped a few metres away and yanking the dog's leash, commanded it in a voice that rattled my ribs, to sit. It sat.

His cap was pulled down low, but I could still see the glitter of hostile eyes. The collar of a well-worn Barbour was pulled up, and his mouth was set in a tight line. In the silence that followed, my voice sounded a little puny, even to my own ears.

'Hello. Sorry, is this your land?'

He didn't answer at first, and his stillness was unnerving, so I started talking, hoping to disarm him by friendly neighbourliness; but faced with continuing immobility, I soon descended into nervous gabbling and finally stumbled to a halt.

'Sorry, I'm new here, well not really new, I know the place from way back, well, not this place, but the road and the Common, well, a bit. From the sixties really, but nothing's changed much, so far as I can see. But anyway, I was just exploring my old haunts, where we used to play, and actually, I was looking for Chestnut Farm, and I saw that tree, and I thought maybe...'

Still nothing. I couldn't decide whether to simply turn and climb back over the fence or launch myself jauntily forward in the reckless hope that he wouldn't set the dog on me.

Suddenly, I felt my temper rise and grab my tongue. 'Well this isn't very friendly. I've just told you I'm new here. You're obviously trying to intimidate me, which is hardly fair seeing as you haven't even answered my question. And anyway, if this is private land, why are those horses tethered? I've a good mind to report you: they haven't got any water and that one's cropped all the grass it can reach so it's hungry. Why don't you just mend the fences then they can wander? And get shade. And things.'

The silence was deafening, and then: 'Things?' Was he smiling?

I jutted my chin and put my hands on my hips. 'Yes, things! Horses need things, you know.' I couldn't think of a single example.

'What kinds of things?'

'Well shoes, for one. And brushes, for another. They get ticks you know. And worming tablets, I bet.'

'Worming tablets?'

'Well, I don't know about worming tablets, but I do know they need care. And if you don't mind me saying so, these horses don't look very cared-for.'

'They're not mine.'

'Well what are you doing here then, shouting and intimidating me? I wasn't doing any harm. I was just going to see that tree. In fact,' I jutted my chin again, 'I am going to see that tree. Right now.' There was no discernible reaction, so I set off across the field, though my back prickled with apprehension.

Chapter Nine

It was the summer of 1920 and we were struggling to get the crops in before the rains came. The glass foretold heavy rain. We'd hired extra hands at the fair, but still the work wasn't going fast enough. All the talk was of tractors and combine harvesters, but we were still doing everything the old-fashioned way. Dad was working too hard, we all were.

Walking back from the fields alone one late afternoon, I ducked under the skirts of the horse chestnut to sit a while in shade. The boughs were weighed down, heavy with leaves the size of a Shire's hooves. My shirt was sticking to my back and I thought longingly of the river, but I still hadn't the heart to swim. I had an hour or so before Dad got back, and the girls were in charge of the tea tonight: I'd prepared a chicken that morning, and they were more than capable of doing the salad and potatoes. I had a stone bottle of water, and I had just sat down on the dry soil when Izzy appeared, ducking suddenly under the low-hanging boughs, clutching her skirts. She sank to her knees and then keeled forward in slow motion until her forehead touched the ground. Tired as I was, I sprang to my feet and rushed forward, bending to lift her shoulders. 'Izzy! Izzy, what's wrong?'

She groaned and slithered out of my grasp. I hastened back to the trunk to get my bottle of water and lift it to her lips. Believing her to be overcome by the heat, I rolled her onto her back and splashed her brow with water. She groaned and clutched her stomach, then rolled onto her side with her knees curled up. It was then that I saw the blood on the back of her petticoat. I got up, indignant. 'Oh, you're such a drama queen! Get away with you. Go to the house and sort yourself out. Honestly! You'd think no-one else had ever had a period!' I stamped back to the trunk and sat down again to swig from my bottle.

Her voice was hoarse and she caught her breath as she spoke, her cheek scraping against the soil. 'Esther, help me. You've got to help me.'

I stopped drinking, the bottle rested cool on my forearm, and looked at her in silence, a chill in my heart.

She continued to lie on her side, but as I watched she turned her face into the soil and coiling in on herself, emitted a long, deep groan then lay still. Rooted to the spot, I looked on in horror. It seemed an age but can only have been moments before she turned her face from the soil, and it had dissolved into an ugly thing of mud and tears.

Slowly, I got up and lifted her petticoat. She lay unresisting as I turned her onto her back and took her under the arms to pull her deeper into the shade away from prying eyes. Her drawers were soaked with blood. Gently, I eased them down and saw that some of the blood was solid with the texture of liver. My heart was beating hard, and my gorge rising, but I gently lifted her bottom and pulled her drawers away, wrapping their contents in the fabric as best I could. I couldn't look, but hastily rolled the sodden cotton into a ball and put it away from her.

I pulled her skirts down for decency: the risk of one of the workers passing was growing greater by the minute. Overwhelmed with the enormity and the horror of what had just happened, I slumped back beside her, and we lay stupefied, legs akimbo like a pair of discarded rag dolls.

Wordlessly, I passed her the water bottle and wordlessly she took it, though she sat holding it and staring straight ahead for some minutes while I gathered my scattered senses. 'Come on now, drink something. How does it feel? Do you think you're still bleeding?'

In answer, she dissolved into sobs again and the bottle rolled away, its contents melting into the parched earth.

I hitched myself closer to her, and reached an arm round her shoulders, wriggling for comfort against the scratchy bark. 'We need to get you into the house and cleaned up. I don't know what'll happen now: maybe you'll stop bleeding. I don't know who we can ask. Dad mustn't find out: it'd kill him.'

At last, she turned to me and her black eyes were softer than I'd ever seen them before. The thick lashes were stuck together in clumps, and mud and mucus streaked her face. I looked sadly into her eyes, then bent forward to try to rescue some of the water. There was a trickle left, so I searched the hem of my skirt for a clean bit, wet it and then wiped her face as best I could. She still hadn't spoken.

64

'Come on, let's see if you can stand up.'

Shakily, she pushed herself sideways onto her knees, then grasping the trunk, she pulled herself up and stood with her head resting against it, looking down at her skirts. Catching sight of the bloody bundle on the ground, the tears came again.

'Look, we need to make sure you're ok. If you can walk and you look presentable, you can get yourself to the house and clean up. Or,' I suddenly had an idea that possessed me with certainty: 'We can both walk together to the river. We'll just look like we're having a swim together and it'll get most of the blood out of your clothes.'

The look she gave me spoke volumes: and at last there was a kind of hope. 'But what about ... the baby?'

'It wasn't really a baby, Izzy, not really. How many periods had you missed?'

'Two, I think.'

I knelt down. 'Do you want to look?'

She shook her head and turned away. 'No.' She looked down at me then. 'But will you look? I need to know.'

I decided then. 'I'll come back later. I'll look and I'll tell you what I see. And I'll bury it. But for now ...'

She interrupted, 'Somewhere proper?'

'We'll talk about it. For now, I need to hide it.' I bent down and picked up the bloody bundle, wrapped it more tightly, then reached up to push it into a knot hole just above our heads.

She turned away and took a few unsteady steps. I saw that there was blood on the hem of her petticoats, so I bent to lift the cotton into a loose knot, then I took her arm and we slowly moved out from under the protective arms of the tree. Anxiously, I looked around, but there was no-one nearby, just a couple of farm-workers visible in the distance. Holding Izzy round the waist in what I hope looked like a sisterly embrace, we slowly walked across the meadow towards the trees.

I hadn't been to the beach since that day, and it was almost an affront to see it unchanged. The indifference of nature indeed. By the time we reached the water's edge, Izzy's gentle sobs had subsided into hiccups and she had a fixed, concentrated look, staring at the water in silence. I would have given anything to see what she could see in her mind's eye.

I couldn't mention Bertie, not with her in this state, so I sat her down on the bank and asked her how she was feeling. 'We need to check whether you're still bleeding, Izzy. There's no-one around. Will you look, or shall I?'

Weakly, she shook my hand away from her arm and turned away from me. 'I'm not. Not much anyway.'

'Are you ready to go in?'

Without answering, she undid her shoes, got to her feet, and walked into the water. I stepped out of my clogs and followed her, gasping as the cold plunged my legs into ache. It took a few moments to get used to it, but I waded forward until it was waist-deep and felt instantly more alive and invigorated. Izzy stood still with her back to me, staring into the water.

'Swish your skirts around a bit to get rid of the blood.'

Obediently, she agitated her skirts and then went still again. All spirit seemed to have left her.

'Does the father know?'

'No, and he mustn't. I don't want to spoil anything.'

Instantly, my anxiety rose. 'What do you mean? You're not going to risk it happening again? Who is he?'

She turned to me then, and there was no mistaking the pride in her expression. 'Who do you think?'

'Oh, Izzy, it's a story as old as time. Don't end up one of those girls.'

'What do you mean, 'one of those girls'? We're in love!'

'Yes, I'm sure you are, but is he?'

'Of course he is! He loves me. He's not like all the other boys. He talks so lovely and he's so kind and gentle. And he gives me presents. All the time! Where do you think I got your Christmas presents?'

'Don't involve us in this: you're not doing it for presents I hope!'

'Of course not. We love being together. He mustn't know about this. Nothing must spoil it.'

'But Izzy, he's gentry. You can't believe you have a future together?'

66

'We're going to get married as soon as I'm eighteen.'

'I'm sorry Izzy, but you mustn't depend on that. Men want to marry virgins. You've given him what he wanted. He'll tire of you and want a fresh bride. You must know that! How can you think you can keep him?'

She turned on me then, angry and sparking fire from those black eyes. 'What do you know? You've never even had a proper admirer! You scare them off with your miserable face. Besides,' her eyes glittered with malevolence, 'everyone can see that your heart belongs to Daddy.'

She saw that her words had hurt me, but closed in for more. 'You think you're so superior, so smug in your cosy little farm. When I'm mistress of Farnworth Manor, I shall ride through your farmyard in a coach and four, with footmen on the back! And you'll be an old maid, living alone or with your precious daddy, waiting on him hand and foot, and think yourself happy. I despise you. You don't know what happiness is! And until you've lain with a man, don't lecture me about how it all works!'

She pushed past me in the water and waded up the banks, lifting the heaviness of her skirts and wringing them out as best she could. Then she turned and kicked my clogs into the water in her temper, picked up her shoes and walked away.

Slowly, I lay back in the water and let my hair spread about me, my upper body floating while my heels rested on the soft mud of the bottom. I looked up at the bright blue sky and the canopy of emerald green leaves and thought about what she'd said. It was true: I did think too much of my father. Boys who'd shown interest in me had barely got a look in. Besides, there had always been so much to do on the farm, and Mum had relied on me to help looking after my younger siblings. I was only two when Izzy was born, and had often been told how I'd burst into tears when I'd seen her. They put it down to jealousy, but I remembered how frightening she had looked, with a mass of spiky black hair and an angry-looking red face, like a demon being laid next to me in my bed, with flailing fists and kicking feet. I had been horrified by the sight of her.

Suddenly, I was overwhelmed with self-pity. I hadn't deserved that. And after everything I'd done for her, including the horror of the last hour. From now on, she was on her own. I'd leave her to her fate: she'd be used and discarded, and if she came crawling back, I'd show her the door. I even considered telling Dad, but decided against it for fear of breaking his heart all over again.

When I eventually surfaced from my reverie and climbed the bank, I felt cooled and refreshed with a new resolve. I would start to take notice of the young men I knew. I needed to think about my future. Izzy was right: I couldn't stay with Dad forever. Miss Ashworth wanted me to train as a teacher, but that didn't appeal to me. I loved to be outdoors and couldn't imagine any other kind of life. I would find a husband who'd help to run the farm, and we would look after Dad and have a family of our own. We'd need electricity, mind, and running water.

Full of my own thoughts and a vision of a better future, I tripped over something on the path and almost fell. With horror, I saw that it was Izzy's bare foot and that she was lying face-down in the ferny undergrowth beside the path. For the second time in an hour, I found myself on my knees calling her name frantically.

She stirred in my arms and lifted a weak hand to her brow like a swooning lady in a play. Impatient now, I said, 'Come on, get up. Stop play-acting.'

She opened her eyes and gave me a weak but unmistakable glare. 'I'm not play-acting. Do you think I'd choose to be found face-down in the bracken? I must have fainted. You made me angry. It's your fault.'

I stood up and let her fall back, 'No it isn't. It's the heat and the cold and the blood-loss. Don't blame me for your temper tantrum. I'm going home. If you want any help, get up now. If you don't, you can lie there and rot for all I care.' As I stood glaring down at her, I saw her recognise my determination to leave her. She struggled to her feet with much groaning and no assistance from me. 'Don't forget your shoes,' I said pointedly, and set off back towards the farm. I listened for signs of her following me, and when I heard a twig snap, deliberately speeded up.

When we got to the gate, the two casual labourers were leaning against it. One said, 'Now then, that's a sight for sore eyes. Two pretty girls in wet skirts. You should have called us if you were going for a swim girls, we could have had some fun.' He winked lewdly.

'We managed to have fun without any help from you, thank-you gentlemen,' I replied. Remembering my resolution, I ducked my head and gave him what I hoped was a coquettish smile from under my tousled hair: 'Maybe next time.'

I caught the frankly astonished look on Izzy's face, and saw her bat the man's hand away from her skirt.

'Oo, the dark one's a tartar, but I fancy her freckly friend,' said the other one.

As we walked away, I smiled to myself and imagined Izzy's glowering demon-face behind me.

Dad was at the pump washing himself down, and I called out to him as we entered the farm-yard. 'We've just been for a swim, Dad. We had a play-fight and fell in. Just going to get changed before tea.' He looked up and waved in assent, and we passed into the kitchen where the twins were bickering over the chicken.

'Just let it rest on the table girls. Dad likes to carve, you know that.'

When we got up to my room, I saw Izzy look around and take in the changes, but I also saw that she was white. Brusque in my manner and my words, I told her to hang her wet clothes up, put one of my nighties on, get a towel and lie down on the bed. 'But be careful. I don't want any blood on my sheets.'

Obediently, which was a worry in itself, she did as she was told, while I towelled my hair dry and changed into a fresh dress. When I was ready, I saw that she was asleep. Her face was still very pale, and her jet black curls spread across the pillow like hot tar. Feeling nothing, I went downstairs for tea. Dad didn't ask where she was.

I took a plate of chicken and a glass of water up to her after I'd eaten. It was eight o'clock and beginning to go dark. The casement window was open, and the smell of cut hay drifted in from the fields. The air in the room was still and the heat oppressive. She didn't stir, and when I laid the back of my hand against her brow, it was no surprise that it came away damp with sweat.

Sighing, I left the plate on the bedside table and went back downstairs. I had no energy left for anything else that night. My bones ached with the day's labour and stress. I made my excuses early, and crept into bed beside her. I saw that she had drunk some water, and gently lifted the side of her nightie to check that she wasn't still bleeding.

I knew no more until the dawn chorus woke me: I'd lain in the same position all night and awoke stiff and sore. As I slipped out of bed, Izzy stirred but didn't waken. I had a moment of tenderness but dismissed it: saw her leather shoes by the bed and decided to take them instead of my clogs. I knew Dad wouldn't be awake yet, so I slipped into an old dress, carefully lifted the latch and tiptoed down the stairs. The kitchen door was trickier, having a creak that was hard to avoid. I opened it as much as I dared and pressed myself against the door-jamb to squeeze out through the gap.

The air was warm though the sun hadn't yet risen: a pinkish light bathed the roof of the workshop, like a colourwash of watery blood. There were always tools propped against the wall, and I bent to retrieve a trowel from amongst them. When I got to the fence, I looked out across the field: the whole scene was cast in that curious pink and the horse-chestnut looked unnatural, as though it was painted on a backdrop in a melodrama. I climbed the fence instead of opening the gate, and swiftly crossed the field, ducking beneath the skirts of the tree into cooler, moist air. I paused then, safely hidden, and considered what to do. I could look, as I had promised to do, but the sight would stay with me forever. Or I could not look and bury the thing as though it was a chicken that the foxes had had. I could do neither, but stood for a while and tried to think of it as a child, of our own flesh and blood.

The ropes of Bertie's swing creaked forlornly and the first light of a pink dawn crept under the boughs.

I decided there was another way. I reached up and felt in the knot hole. Thankfully it was now dry, which made the whole thing easier. I stood for a moment holding the bundle in both hands, with what I hoped was a kind of respect.

I chose my spot carefully, not wanting it to be a place where anyone would sit. I considered burying it beneath the sad little swing, but the thought was too poignant. Around the other side, part of the trunk juts out, so no-one would lean against it. I measured three lengths of my foot away from the point where the trunk rises out of the earth, and I knelt and began to scrape the soft soil. I soon came to a root the size of my thigh, and dug round and underneath it

70

until there was enough space for the bundle to be protected by the root.

It felt hypocritical to say any kind of prayer: I simply didn't believe there was anyone listening. But I did feel I should say something, so I whispered, 'There there little one. I'm so sorry you never had a chance. I hope you didn't suffer. I'm not going to hide you really. You'll be here, in my favourite spot in the world, for as long as this tree stands. You'll be part of it. Part of nature. And when I look at it from now on, or come and sit here, I'll always think of you.'

As I slipped back into the house, I heard a floorboard creak in the room above my head. Izzy. She had gone to the window, so when I opened the bedroom door she didn't hear me at first, but turned, startled. She saw that I was dressed. 'Where've you been?'

In my new, indifferent voice, I replied, 'Where d'you think?'

'What did you do with it?'

'I buried it under the chestnut tree.' I saw her think about raising an objection, but then she stopped herself and asked, 'Did you look?'

I lied. 'Yes,' I said, 'there was nothing to see. Only ... like liver.'

She lay back down on the bed with a sigh. 'I feel awful. Really weak and sick. I don't think I can go to work. Will you go and tell them? I don't want him to see me like this: I look like death.'

I just wanted her out of the house now, so I ignored her question whilst I washed and got dressed, ready for another day of hard physical work. Of course, in the end I went to the big house and told Mrs Cobham that Izzy was ill with a fever. She gave me a long look. Finally she said, 'Tell her to look after herself. We can manage here, especially now the young master has gone off to university.' Again that look. 'She'll not be paid, mind.'

I was disturbed by Mrs Cobham's manner, and wondered how much she knew, but on the walk home, decided it wasn't my worry. I relayed her message to Izzy, who dismissed it with wave of her hand and lay back on the pillow. 'I'll be better soon. Just a few days to get back on my feet, and I'll be good as new.' She went

71

quiet, and turned away from me. I waited a few moments, then I said, 'Which university is he going to?'

'Um, Oxford I think.'

'You did know, didn't you, Izzy?'

She didn't answer for a while, and I knew she was crying. I left her to it.

It turned out to be the best part of two weeks before she was up and about, and fatefully, she was there when Stanley arrived.

Chapter Ten

I didn't look back until I'd reached the outer branches, which softly swept the ground like a petticoat. I brushed the leaves apart and stepped through into a cool cave, my heart pounding. The sheltering dome of leaves and branches was so thick that I was immediately plunged into a kind of underwater half-light, and saw that nothing grew there save the sinuous roots which knotted the moist earth. The trunk was the width of a barn door, and its musculature reared up diagonally to disappear into the canopy overhead. I thought of the powerful beauty of the Sagrada Familia, where stone pillars became muscle and sinew, animal and leaf. I felt curiously as though I'd entered a church, the air cool and silent, the atmosphere expectant and elevated.

I had one of those moments of recognition that you sometimes get. A frisson, a special pulse in time, almost a sense of homecoming.

Rapt, I pressed my back against the rough bark and looked up into the depths of the darkness of the mighty branches, where leaves the size of dinner-plates layered away into the distance and shimmers of green light flickered as the outer layers shifted and whispered in an invisible breeze. As my eyes grew accustomed to the half-light, I saw that the dark green sky above me was dotted with the lighter green sputniks of conker pods.

My hand on the bark, I stepped carefully all the way round the tree, exploring its crevices with my fingertips and looking up, all the while conscious of flickers of movement just outside my field of vision. At eye level, there were several worn carvings which I couldn't decipher, and higher up, a deep knot-hole which I refrained from exploring with my fingertips. The lowest bough, just beyond my reach, was deeply scarred by two ridges about eighteen inches apart, their edges raised and puckered. In both, the thin and tattered remnants of old rope were embedded in the flesh of the tree. It was this that arrested me: children had played here. I searched my memory, hoping to uncover a flicker of recognition: it would be wonderful to locate a memory of swinging under this very tree, but the only swing I could remember was the single rope which we used to launch ourselves out over the river.

73

Softly, I sat down in the space between two roots, and leant back into a gentle hollow, cradled comfortably against the trunk. It's not often you come across a place so entirely untouched by modern life, so powerfully present, in and of itself. This tree must be hundreds of years old, I thought. People will have sat in this very spot in the nineteenth, eighteenth, maybe even seventeenth centuries. Men, women and children. In winter and summer, in peace and war, in public and in private, in poverty and prosperity. They'll have rested here in the cool shade, lovers will have met and embraced, children will have played, people will have sat alone just as I'm doing now.

When I reached the lane, I hesitated. It was tempting to go on towards what I took to be the farm, but I was suddenly ravenous and the thought of a bacon sandwich lured me towards home. By the time I reached the pavement in front of the bigger houses, my stomach was growling, so when I saw the old man coming towards me, I intended just saying hello and hastening home to my frying pan. But when he saw me, the thunderstruck look on his face made me stop: 'Are you ok?' A small grizzled dog at his side nuzzled my ankles blindly. I put my hand on his arm, but he continued staring at me with his mouth slack. At my touch, he jumped and seemed to gather his wits.

'Are you ok?' I repeated.

'Yes, sorry I thought for a moment there ...'

I waited, anxious to be gone now I knew there was nothing wrong. 'Shall I walk you home?'

He chuckled, his eyes crinkling, and scratched his brow beneath his cap. 'That's a relief. You'll never guess what I thought.'

'No, go on.'

'I thought I'd died.'

I couldn't think what to say, and looking back, my response sounds ridiculous: 'On your feet?'

He chuckled again, 'People do, you know. One minute they're walking along, the next everything stops. You might not know when it happens, that's the thing.'

74

'You mean like a chicken?'

He turned and smiled directly into my face and I saw that his eyes were as blue as sapphires embedded in a walnut. 'Yes, exactly like a chicken.'

He turned and slipped his arm through mine, 'You don't mind do you? Only I feel a bit shaky.'

I was seized with an idea. 'How do you fancy a bacon butty? Would that help?'

His face lit up. 'Oh yes, we'd love that, wouldn't we, Laddie?'

I was still concerned about his health, despite the smiles. 'Did you have a pain or anything?'

He looked at me significantly, and said sadly, 'No love, no pain. Just a bit of a shock.'

It came to me then. 'You thought I was her, didn't you?'

There was a moment's hesitation before he said, 'Yes, yes I did.'

'We're here, come on in Laddie. Is he blind?'

'I think he still sees shapes. He doesn't miss his bowl when I put it down.'

'Does he like bacon?'

'Oh yes, we like bacon, don't we Laddie? And a nice strong cup of tea.'

'For Laddie too?'

'Yes, only he has it without sugar. We don't want to rot his teeth, do we Laddie? Eee, I haven't been in here for years. I was a boy last time I was in here.'

'Where would you like to sit? Make yourself comfy: I'm just nipping up to the toilet.'

By the time I came down, he and Laddie were outside looking at the woodshed. 'Ee, I can just see Stanley in there. I used to come and talk to him over the back wall. I wasn't welcome in the house, no-one was. Your grandmother, you know, she was ...'

'A bit of a tartar?'

'Yes, she was. As you know.'

'I don't know you, do I? I mean, did I know you when I was little?'

'No, I don't think you'd remember me. My name's Leonard, by the way. I know yours. I remember you, with your lovely red hair. You were like a little pixie, always smiling. My dad used to look forward to you coming past, you lit the day up like a matchstick, he used to say.'

'Was that your dad who used to sit outside? He had a curtain of plastic strips in his front door?'

'Yes, that was him.'

'Owdo.'

He laughed. 'Yes, he was a man of few words. Owdo - that was one of them.'

'Would you like to sit outside? I'll bring a chair out.'

'I'm alright, I'll just potter about. You get the bacon on.'

'How do you like it?'

'Crispy please.'

'Would you like an egg on it?'

'Oo yes, with some pepper. Smashing, eh, Laddie?' The dog was lying on its side, basking in a patch of sunshine between the shadows of the chimneys.

He came in while I was doing the bacon, to supervise the thickness of the butter of his barm-cake and the strength of his tea. Laddie was awoken from his slumbers and drawn in by the smell of bacon. I poured the dog's tea into an old cereal bowl, cooled it with water and set it down on the hearth next to his slice of bacon. The three of us sat contently chomping and slurping, and finally Leonard wiped his mouth and fingers on a napkin and leant back in his chair to regard me with smiling eyes.

'So, Leonard, who did you think I was?' When he didn't answer, I said, 'I know I don't look like my mum. In fact, I don't look like anyone in our family. Never mind the hair, nobody else even had green eyes. I used to really believe I was adopted.'

'Oh, but you do.'

'I do? Who?'

'You're the image of Esther.'

'Who's Esther?' Though even as I said the words, the ghost of a whispered name came to me.

'Your grandma's sister.'

'But I met grandma's sisters: they were called Rosie and Lily. Twins.'

'Esther died long before you were born.' His voice had taken on a dreamy quality.

'I'm amazed. Why did no-one ever mention her?' I cast my mind back: surely mum would have told me about her, but I simply had no memory of her name ever being said out loud, apart from that once. Something made me keep that to myself for now. I felt profoundly sad, bereft by the absolute loss of someone I never even knew, someone who clearly meant something to my granddad.

'You seem very ... Did you love her?'

'Aye, love, I did in my way. I was just a boy when she died, and she was a grown woman. I'd be, what, thirteen.' He looked at me again. 'I saw it that first day I met you, sitting on the step. You had your hair tied back then, but when I saw you just now, with it all curly and wild, it was just like seeing her again.'

'I'm intrigued. Tell me about her, Leonard.'

'She was the Estate Manager at the big house, and I was one of the gardeners' lads, a pot-boy really. We all loved her. She was so beautiful and clever, so full of life, full of ideas, always moving. Everywhere she went, people straightened up and bucked up. She was so smiley, and always had a kind word. She was like a flame, going about, lighting other people. You felt warm just being near her.'

I smiled at his rapt expression and when he smiled back, he looked younger and his face was lit up by his memories.

'My granddad knew her, didn't he?'

The question hung on the air for a moment, then he went on as though I'd never asked it.

'It's when you smile you look most like her. It transforms you like it did her. When she was concentrating or having to tell someone off, she looked proper fierce, and that temper! But it was gone in a flash, and then she'd be all smiles again and you'd feel it was worth it.'

'Did you get told off much?'

'Oh yes. I was a lazy little bugger, forever skiving off to go fishing. I got the sack in the end.'

77

'Did she sack you?'

'No, she told one of the supervisors to do it, so I never saw her again. I was heartbroken, but it taught me a lesson. I couldn't believe it when I heard she'd died. I had no idea what her age was, but I reckon she'd not even be forty. It was just before war broke out.'

'How did she die?'

'I don't know, but it were quick. I didn't hear about it till she was gone. She'd only been ill a few weeks: it was a shock to everyone.'

'I can't believe no-one ever mentioned her. Can you think why?'

He looked away, suddenly furtive.

'Leonard?'

'I don't know, I was only a lad.' He was definitely avoiding my eyes.

'But you were friends with my granddad. Did he never mention her?'

He got up. 'I'll side these plates, eh, then we'd better be going. Laddie'll be wanting his nap.'

I got up and followed him into the kitchen. I'd try a different tack. 'So the big house? Where was that?'

'On the Common, past the farm, in a valley in the woods. Farnworth Manor. Beautiful, it was, sandstone. We grew all sorts.' He'd somehow side-stepped me and was heading for the front door. Laddie had hauled himself to his feet and was panting behind him. 'Thank-you for the butty, love, and the chat. We're off home now, aren't we Laddie? See you again love.' He was in the front yard now, and turned to me with a smile, evidently relieved to be out of the house.

'You're welcome. Any time. It's been nice talking to you. Just tell me one thing before you go, though.' I watched him carefully, and he was determinedly looking at the guttering. Defeated, I went for what I thought was an innocuous question:

'Why did they knock it down?'

He looked at me then, 'I don't know love. The family went to live in Switzerland during the war. The Squire's wife was German, you know.'

Frustrated now, I felt myself snap and my voice raised an involuntary octave, 'No, I don't know. Because you won't tell me anything!'

In answer, he smiled ruefully and walked away, muttering and shaking his head. 'Temper temper, just like Esther.'

When he'd gone, I felt suddenly sleepy, and lay down on the sofa for a nap. By the time I woke up, it was late afternoon and the clouds had closed in. I made myself a coffee and fired up the laptop, wandering outside with my drink while it booted up. I thought of Leonard leaning over the gate talking to Granddad. It dawned on me that there was quite a difference in their ages: Granddad was born in 1901, the year Queen Victoria died, as he was fond of telling me, so it was easy to work out that he'd have been thirty-eight when war broke out. If Leonard had been thirteen that year, he'd only have been forty when Granddad died in his sixties. So although they were friends, it perhaps wasn't surprising that they'd never talked about anything personal. I'd been a bit sharp with him but reassured myself he'd understand.

I cast about in my mind for ways to find out about her. Now that Mum, Uncle Aiden and their aunties Rosie and Lily were gone, there was no member of the older generation left. There was no chance there were any letters or family Bibles: Mum had never been one for keeping old things, in fact I still couldn't forgive her for not keeping Grandma's treadle sewing machine for me. It was the only thing I'd asked for, and I'd been incredulous when I got home for the long vacation and she'd casually mentioned that it had gone into the house clearance.

I'd meant just to check my emails, but found myself googling Esther Grenfell: nothing. She could have been married, of course. There was no point in going any further until I'd talked to Leonard again. When I tried Farnworth Manor, I didn't hold out much hope of finding anything, so I was surprised to see a reference to it having been used as a base for the Ministry of Food in World War II. There were no pictures, though, and no detail beyond that. It seemed reasonable to suppose that the family who'd lived in Farnworth Manor had had that name, at least originally, so I refined my search to Farnworth Lancashire, but kept coming up against references to the town of that name, which is just outside Manchester.

Before I gave up, I thought it might be an idea to write to Chorley Central Library's Local History department, so I found an address and sent an extremely waffly email. I doubted very much that any reply would be forthcoming.

I closed the browser, feeling a bit down in the dumps, and was immediately cheered up by a couple of funny emails: I forwarded them to Rosie and Mark with a short note. Then I wrote to my cousin Gordon in Australia, just telling him I was doing a bit of family history research and asking whether he knew anything about Esther.

I thought about writing to a few people to let them know where I was, but simply couldn't be bothered: I could hardly tell them what I was doing when I barely knew myself, and anyone who wanted to get in touch could get me on my mobile, so I shut the computer down and went out into the back-yard. I was staring at the shed, lost in a reverie, when I heard a window open and a low moan. I looked up, startled, and she was hanging out of the window like a rag doll. 'Beth?'

'Nyyrrr.'

'Beth? Are you ok?'

She looked up, laughing, and then clasped her brow as though laughter made her brain ache. 'Oww, I feel horrible!'

'Still? I felt awful when I woke up, but I'm ok now. Are you sickening for something?'

'Naw, I'm alright really, just had a bit of a relapse this afternoon. I saw you striding away this morning in your seven league boots,' she added, accusingly.

'The wonder of drugs. Between the hangover, the headache, the angry man and the mad dog, I'm relieved to have survived the day.'

'Angry man? Oh, you went to the farm did you? He's a nutter.'

'Who is he?'

'Nobody knows. He's been there nearly a year now, and no-one even knows his name. He just shouts and growls at anyone who goes near. And as for that dog! Bloody terrifying. It's like a hound of hell.'

'Does he farm, then? What does he do?'

'No idea. I've seen him go past in a blacked-out Range Rover. He must eat, but I've no idea where he gets his food from. And drink. He certainly drinks.'

'How do you know?'

'Empties. The bin-man told me. He's very law-abiding with his recycling, I'll say that for him.'

'Does he own all that land, where the big horse-chestnut is?'

'I don't know the one you mean. I never go past, no-one does. It's not on the way to anywhere. There's plenty of places to walk on the Common without going past there.'

'Where does that road go?'

'It's just a track really, I think it finishes at the farm gate, doesn't it?'

'There are ponies in the field.'

'They'll be gypsy ponies. They come and they go. They camp in the woods. Anyway, can't stand here chatting, I'm going out tonight and need to make myself feel human and look presentable. You doing anything?'

'No, I'm looking forward to a bubble-bath, a herbal tea and an early night. I'm hoping I'll be back on form tomorrow. Thanks for last night, though Beth. It was well worth the hangover.'

'You're most welcome, neighbour. Your turn next time. I like curry.' And then she was gone.

Later, in a bath lit by candles, my mind drifting over the day's events, I felt the stirrings of real curiosity. I was going to follow this up. I wanted to know about Esther, about why she was never spoken of and what had happened to her. I had a hunch it might be linked to all the things I didn't understand about my grandparents. After I'd made the decision, it gave my mind a focus, and as I blew patterns in the bubbles, I felt more relaxed and content than I'd been for years.

81

Chapter Eleven

Dad had just finished a shoe for the bay gelding when I took him his tea that morning, and as he stood up and patted the horse's haunch, I saw him notice the tall young man with downcast eyes who stood behind me in the doorway. As the father of four daughters, I know that before the war, Dad had been used to lurking lads, but he'll have seen straight away that this one was different. All the boys who used to come to call on us were bright-eyed and over-eager to ingratiate themselves with their 'Yes sir, no sir"; farm boys usually, strapping lads who knew the lie of the land.

When he stepped into the smithy, this one kept his eyes on the stone floor, and it wasn't until I whispered, 'Go on,' that he lifted his head and spoke, though his eyes remained downcast.

'Am ... am looking for work ... I've just got back ... I ...' he tailed off. 'Am good with me hands and I wondered if you could do with a 'prentice.'

I saw Dad's surprised expression: such a pale young man, tall and broad-shouldered but so thin, so hesitant - hardly a natural candidate to be apprenticed to a strapping blacksmith. Dad took a sip from his mug, then blew on it, rolling his eyes at the lad, who continued to look at the ground. 'She allus makes it too hot, don't you love?'

He fell silent again, and we all studied the ground, while the gelding shuffled and tossed his head, impatient to be off.

This wasn't going very well, and Dad clearly hadn't recognised who it was, so I decided to help things along a little. 'You remember Stanley, Dad: he went to school with me and Izzy.'

He had an expressive face, my dad. His tanned features erupted into a pantomine and I could read every thought as it crossed his face. Stanley? Stanley Aspinall? This was never Stanley! That daft little lad, always running and laughing? Always muddy, liked making the girls scream by putting frogs down their frocks and taddies in their drinks? Bright-eyed, talkative. Not like this... And then it dawned on him: the lad had surely seen a different kind of mud now, mud with blood in it, and worse: his face settled into an expression of tenderness and pity.

'Stanley?' He looked up then, blue eyes squinting in the shaft of sunlight that illuminated the older man's halo of curls. Their gaze held for only a moment, but a world of understanding passed between them. He dropped his gaze again. 'Aye.'

Dad turned away briefly to put down the tongs, and when he spoke his voice was gruff. 'Aye, well, 'prentice, eh? You want to be a blacksmith?'

'Yes, or a farrier. My dad was going to teach me carpentry when we got back, and I'm still keen on wood, but he's ... not right now ... he's not up to it. I thought I'd like learn to work with metal.'

Dad looked beyond Stanley then, to where I stood illuminated in the doorway. Though my face was cast in shadow, my stillness must have spoken to him.

'Well, I could certainly do with a hand in here today, so we'll see how you do. Esther, will you go and find the leather apron the last lad wore, and get him some gloves, while me and Stanley here talk terms.'

I couldn't help it: Dad teased me later that I'd raised on tiptoe before I turned, in a way I'd always done when I was excited, ever since I was a child. I was in the kitchen making a pie when he came in unexpectedly in the middle of the afternoon. He was wiping his hands and smiling broadly, in unusually high spirits. 'When I saw your pony tail bouncing away across the yard, I knew you had a soft spot for our Stanley.'

'Dad! Lower your voice! He'll hear you!' I realised too late that I'd not been quick enough to deny it.

'It makes me laugh when I think about you lot when you were kids: it was always him and Izzy running wild, getting into scrapes and coming home with butter-wouldn't melt faces.' He put his arm round my shoulders and kissed the top of my head. 'You were always so serious and easily hurt, always left behind, or the victim of their pranks: the one locked in the hen-coop or stuck up a tree. Those two running away like a little pair of raggle-taggle gypsies.' He squeezed me tight, crushing my shoulders together, thankfully briefly, and kissed my head again before he released me. 'Oh sweetheart, my tender-hearted Esther, always bringing home the injured bird, the rejected lamb, the orphaned puppy, the retired pit-pony. And now there's Stanley, eh?'

I turned away and hid my blushes in some business at the range, thankful that no-one else was hearing this, especially not Izzy.

Stanley had gone by the time she came in for tea. She'd taken cider to the field-workers to celebrate the end of the harvest, and the fresh air and exercise had brightened her eyes and flushed her skin. Her unruly curls had escaped from her ribbon and she had a tousled, over-excited look that gave me a chill.

'What's this I hear? We have a handsome young man in the forge?'

Too quickly, I snapped at her, 'Who told you?'

'Ooo, sister mine, do I detect a little blush on those freckly cheeks?' She came over to the range and ran her fingertips down the side of my face, then jumped back pretending she'd been burnt. 'Ouch! Good heavens, something's stoking your fires, my pretty!'

Dad's voice chopped her down abruptly: its tone brooked no challenge. 'Izabel, wash your hands and help your sister.'

Instantly deflated in a way she never would have been before that day, she took the kettle to the washstand and did as she was told. He was talking to Rosie when she brought it back, so he didn't hear her whisper in my ear, 'Let's just see who the apprentice prefers, shall we?' She didn't know who it was then, but she soon would.

Inevitably, during tea, Dad mentioned his name. 'I'll take Stanley over to the big house at weekend, introduce him to the stable lads and let him get to know the horses.'

I couldn't help looking straight at her, and her face was instantly transformed into unmistakably triumphant glee.

That night, she spent ages carefully taming her hair in strips of rag, and when she appeared at breakfast, there was an excited glow about her. It was obvious that she was keen to see the impact of her womanly charms on the childhood pal she hadn't seen for five long years.

As soon as the gate creaked, she sprang up from the table and was through the door into the yard. Taken by surprise, Dad looked across at me, genuinely puzzled. I could only roll my eyes at him with a rueful smile, before getting up to side the table and get the little ones off to school.

When I opened the door to walk Rosie and Lily to the gate, they were sitting side by side on edge of the stone water trough, and I

85

caught a barely-concealed note of resentment in Izzy's voice as she got to her feet and said, 'Well, I suppose I'll see you later then.' Always the actress, her face managed to convey bewilderment, frustration and scorn in the look she gave me as she flounced past.

When I re-entered the kitchen, she was standing with her hands on her hips. 'What's up with 'im, then?'

Just to be awkward, I said, 'Who?'

'Benjamin the flippin' bullock, who d'you think? Stanley flippin' Aspinall, that's who! What's up with him? He barely looked at me, barely spoke! He's not like the same lad!'

'Well, he's not the same lad, is he, Izzy? Think where he's been and what he's seen. He'll probably never be the same again.'

'Oh you and your bleeding heart! He doesn't want you mooning over him like a sick calf! How's that going to get him back on his feet? He wants some fun, that's what he wants. He wants bringing out of himself.' Her voice grew thoughtful. 'Yes, that's what he wants: a bit of fun.'

When I took the men their tea that morning, I stood watching for a few moments before I spoke. I saw that here was a slight tremor in Stanley's hands when he passed Dad a cloth. Later, when we were alone, I asked Dad how he was doing, and he mentioned the shaking. 'But when he grips a hammer or works the bellows or lifts the hoof of a giant Shire, he's strong and steady. Beyond the necessaries, we work in silence, but it's good to have the lad in the smithy with me. Mind you, I chide myself for thinking of him as a boy. When I think what he's been through ...' News of the suffering of the Lancashire Fusiliers had filtered home with the wounded. He shook his head, 'If he doesn't deserve to be thought of as a man, who does?'

Over the next few days, Stanley was assailed by the full arsenal of Izabel's feminine wiles, though I was relieved to see that he seemed immune to it all. The poor lad couldn't even cross the yard to the water closet without being invited to admire a piece of sewing, a chick, a picture in a book. She became unusually domesticated, which was a nuisance as she was too impatient to do anything properly and often wasted ingredients or left the kitchen in a mess. The two men were being kept supplied with fresh lemonade, inept cakes and malformed biscuits. I soon withdrew and occupied

86

myself elsewhere when she was in the kitchen, often watching from upstairs as she chattered and flirted. It seemed to me that the more indifferent Stanley was to her charms, the more Izzy redoubled her efforts.

One hot day, I was upstairs putting freshly-laundered sheets on our bed when I saw her leaning through the top of the stable door, wafting her face with a homemade fan fashioned from offcuts of wood and fabric, and declaring it to be too hot to work. 'Why don't we go for a swim, Stanley, eh? Like we used to.'

Was I alone in finding our swimming-place unbearable to think of? But no, she was persistent and, it seemed, immune to shame. 'Dad? Are you going to give Stanley the afternoon off?... Pleeeease?'

In truth, the heat in the smithy must have been unbearable, and the idea of a snooze after lunch will have been an appealing one to Dad. I saw him come out into the yard and stretch, pushing his hair back from his damp forehead with the back of his hand.

'Aye, go on lad. You've earned it. Get yourselves a bit of picnic. No...' I knew he'd been going to say no hanky-panky, mind, but stopped himself. No doubt he didn't think it needed saying. He knew that Izzy would be safe with this one. The question of whether Stanley would be safe with Izzy would never have crossed his mind.

'If you're sure, Mr Grenfell. That'd be grand.'

Jubilant, Izabel swung open the door and bowed low, teasingly indicating the route to the cool of the kitchen. 'This way, milord. Allow me show you the delights of our estate.'

Stanley smiled and wiped his face as he walked past her towards the kitchen, and my heart turned over. I sat down on the bed and stayed quiet, hoping they didn't know I was there; I knew I wouldn't be able to act naturally if I went down to the kitchen while they were making their picnic, and I couldn't bear to contemplate Izzy's gloating glances.

By then, I'd forgiven my mother for dying, and sometimes had little chats with her in my head. She spoke to me now: 'Go on, ask them to wait. Get your things and go with them.'

'I'm not going to do that.'

'I know love, I know. Our Izzy has set her sights on the lad, but I wouldn't give up just yet if I were you.'

87

I felt a blush creep up my cheeks: I often thought that there was something in the way Stanley looked at me, an intensity in his eyes, however briefly I saw them. But those moments were so fleeting, and we were never alone. I suddenly felt a wave of sadness and self-pity. The loss of Mum and little Bertie was still painful and raw. I could smell him in the fresh laundry: when we were making the beds, he'd loved to be tossed into the air from clean sheets stretched out between me and Mum. His little wooden cot had been in the corner of this room, and I remembered how I'd loved to pick him up and plant kisses on his bare belly. He would squirm with delight, waving his little fists in the air and gurgling giggles through toothless gums. His cot was in the workshop now, achingly empty and dusty with wood shavings and old mouse-droppings. Granddad made that cot when Mum was born, and now they were all dead and the cot seemed to be crumbling into sawdust. Tears wet my cheeks now, and I let them fall.

While I cried alone on the bed, stifling my sobs with the clean sheets, I heard Izzy's laughter in the kitchen and a brief occasional word or chuckle from Stanley. Her footsteps clattered up the staircase: she'd be going to get towels, and I thanked goodness that I'd closed the bedroom door. Soon she was descending the staircase at a run, the kitchen door banged and the sound of their clogs moved across the yard. I summoned myself to stand up and go to the side of the window to watch Stanley open the gate. As he turned his back to close it after her, she looked directly at the window where I was hiding and ostentatiously blew me a kiss, before laughing and turning away.

Mortified, I watched them walking across the meadow towards the river, each carrying a bundle wrapped in white cloth. When they got to the stile, Izzy seemed uncharacteristically unsteady, prompting Stanley to hold out his hand. I saw Izzy take it and keep hold of it, but I was heartened to notice Stanley's arm bend slightly as he attempted to pull away. Izabel held on tight and slid a sly smile back towards the house.

Chapter Twelve

The next morning, I was up bright and early: I had slept wonderfully well, and woke up full of ideas. I had no paper, so that was the first thing to go on the list I scribbled on an envelope whilst I ate my breakfast. I needed some more basics for the cupboards: balsamic vinegar, some herbs and spices, more milk, but I also wanted to get some new curtains, a coffee machine, some fairy lights. Paul had been acidic in his disparagement of the lights I'd once put round our bed-head, so I'd dutifully squashed any tendencies to 'twee' or 'fey' ever since. Now I could indulge my bohemian proclivities to my heart's content. I didn't want to drive anywhere today: I had other plans, so I decided to walk down to the newsagents on the end of the next row down, to get a paper and see what else they offered; I set off at a brisk pace down the rain-washed street.

It was a lovely surprise to find that the newsagent stocked all kinds of interesting spices, fruits and vegetables in a small fresh food section at the back. He was a friendly Asian man and wanted to know all about me, so by the time I left with my provisions, I felt I'd provided him with sufficient information to give him a bit of gossip to spread.

On impulse and full of bonhomie, I reached across to shake his hand: 'Annie.'

He gripped mine with a laugh, 'Anil. People will be getting us mixed up!'

Walking back up the hill, I passed Leonard's house just as he was opening his bedroom curtains. I gave him a wave and resolved to call round and see him later to apologise for biting his head off.

That's if I survived my morning visit.

When I turned into the lane an hour later, there were no people, dogs or ponies to be seen. The great horse-chestnut tree was back-lit by iron-grey storm-clouds and gathering swallows were swooping close to the ground, but I strode on, determined not to be distracted from my purpose. As the lane grew muddier and the farmhouse grew closer, my pace slowed. I saw that the farm-buildings were low and made of local sandstone, blackened with age and pollution: at this distance it was hard to separate the farmhouse from the outbuildings, but by the time I reached a five-barred gate, I could see that there was a cobbled yard with barns or stables on each side and that the farmhouse faced the lane.

It was a strange feeling looking at that house and thinking of my grandmother living there as a girl: I could barely imagine it. The roof was low and steeply-pitched, and at first I thought it was single-storey, but then discerned the casement windows tucked deep under the eaves like shy eyes peering out from under a fringe. The front door seemed to be dark old wood, and I wondered whether it could possibly be the same one that she'd used, she and her sisters, all three of them. There could well have been brothers, for all I knew. With family secrets and child mortality, I actually had no idea how many great-aunts and uncles I'd had. But I was going to find out.

There was no sign of the dog, and no sound coming from the buildings. At first I thought he might be out, but then I noticed the front bumper of a vehicle sticking out of one of the barns, and moments after that, I saw that there was a large mesh cage built onto the side of the house and in the bottom of it, a dark mass that could well be the dog. I'd soon know.

Bracing myself, I stood up straight and reached out my hand to lift the latch, but then decided against it, reasoning that if the dog moved and its cage was open, it would be faster to jump back over the gate than to struggle to close it to keep the dog in.

Maybe I'd just stay here and shout. The thought of trying out Beth's high-piched coo-eee to summon Mad Max made me giggle somewhat hysterically: emboldened, I put one foot on the gate and lifted myself onto the middle bar. It was getting darker, and as I looked up, a heavy drop of rain hit me on the forehead.

Oh sod it, I'm here now. Here goes. Slinging my other leg over, I jumped down into the mud and stood still, waiting for a reaction from the dog. Nothing. Deciding that it was better to get this over with while there was still a chance of jumping back pretty sharpish, I shouted in as deep a voice as I could manage, 'Hello? Is there anybody in?'

Instantly, the air exploded with deafening barks accompanied by rattling metal as the Hell Hound repeatedly flung itself at the bars. If he was in, I wasn't going to need to go any further to make my presence known. Sure enough, seconds later the front door opened and he looked straight at me. I couldn't see from this distance what his expression said, but I stood my ground and watched as he went round to the kennel and bellowed at the dog to shut up. It subsided into the back of the cage with a shocked whimper, and sat down, growling softly.

He stood with his back to me until he was sure the dog had settled, and I saw how very tall and lean he was, with wide, powerful shoulders, held straight and still: he moved with a fluid economy, like an athlete. He was wearing jeans and a dark top, and I saw now that he had a full head of light brown hair: from this distance, he certainly looked younger than I'd previously thought, maybe not much older than me.

When he finally turned round, he stayed where he was, and though he spoke in a normal voice, his words cut through the oppressive air and clearly carried to where I stood, my hand unconsciously gripping the top of the gate in readiness for a hasty retreat.

'What is it now?'

I wasn't going to raise my voice, so I answered as though he was standing in front of me, which, if he'd had any manners, he would have been. Moments of silence ensued, punctuated by ominously heavy raindrops penetrating my hair.

It worked. He cupped a hand to his ear and said in a terse voice, 'I can't hear what you're saying.'

I considered a flippant answer but instead, started to walk toward him as though it was the most natural thing in the world. Even from that distance, I saw his jaw clench. 'Stay where you are.'

I pretended not to hear, lifting my hand to my ear in a gesture that echoed his own, and carrying on walking. He watched me in silence, his hands held by his sides, elbows slightly bent, as if in readiness to pull a gun. In the same instant that I noticed his stance, I saw that he was wearing a formal collared shirt under a round-necked jumper, and it suddenly came to me that he was military. Call me psychic, but the intuition hit me like a thunderbolt, which is exactly what came a moment later. I stopped walking while I recalibrated my approach hastily. Living alone, hard-drinking. It pointed one way, and I was out of my depth. My courage left me in an instant, and as the rain began in earnest, we stood and looked at each other, mutually baffled.

There came a point when I realized that if I were to retain a shred of dignity, I would have to take my leave with good grace, because I certainly wasn't going to be asked in, and if we were taking bets on who had the most willpower, I'd have backed him at a million to one.

But he spoke, and when he did, his voice was lower and tinged with wonder.

'You're really not scared, are you?'

'No. Well, a bit.'

'But not really. Why not? I'm a nutter. Everyone knows. Why aren't you scared?'

'Because you recycle.'

His expression was incredulous. 'You're not scared of me because I recycle?'

'That's right. It shows that you are inherently a civilized and law-abiding human being.'

He laughed, a great explosive shout that set the dog barking. Without looking over his shoulder or changing his stance one iota, he commanded it to shut up and it did, mid-bark.

'So.'

'Annie.'

'I didn't ask you your name.'

'Well, there it is anyway. What's yours?'

His voice hardened. 'My name is no business of yours or anybody else's. I don't bother anyone and I ask them not to bother me. Now, Annie,' he gave my name an ironic inflection, 'I'd like you to leave.'

I considered how to reply without burning all my bridges. I'd got him to laugh. It gave me courage. I could over-step the mark by teasing or pushing my luck, so I played a straight bat. 'My grandma was born on this farm.'

'I haven't the remotest interest. Kindly leave.'

'But I have.' Silence, which was encouraging, so I went on. 'I've just moved into her house on Park Road.' I didn't know how to continue, so I waffled, which is something I've always done well. 'I might stay, I might not. I'm just deciding. At a bit of a crossroads, you might say. But while I'm here, in Adlington, I mean, I thought I'd like to find out more about them, my grandma and granddad. Like I say, she was born here, and I've just found out, amazingly, that she had a sister that she never told me about! Can you believe it? I used to stay with them every single summer when I was a kid. We lived in Manchester, you see, and my mum and dad were in the police, which was unusual in those days, Mum I mean, not Dad, and anyway, this sister, Esther, she was called, she was the Estate Manager at Farnworth Manor, which was over there somewhere.' I gestured vaguely towards the woods. 'And apparently, an old man tells me, I'm the spit of her, the sister, I mean. Well, you can imagine!' I'd really hit my stride now, and I averted my gaze from his face for fear of what I might see there. 'I'm fascinated and I want to know more, but I don't know how to find out, so I thought I'd come here and see who owns it now, and if there were any things left, from their time, I mean, I know it's a long shot, but, you know, boxes in the attic, family Bibles, that kind of thing.' I was running out of steam and the rain was trickling in rivulets down my face and neck.

I looked at him for the first time in my monologue. His hair was plastered to his scalp and the set of his jaw was rigid but I thought I saw something in his eyes: I chose to interpret it as a gleam of amusement and not the mad gleam of a man driven beyond endurance who was going to go inside and come out with a gun.

Inspiration struck. 'And my granddad, what a lovely man he was, so quiet and gentle, and my grandma, well she was a bit of a battle-axe, but the thing is, I don't think it ever dawned on me that he must have fought in the First World War, but he did, you know, and I've got his medals to prove it. I found them when my mum died and I wrote to the Lancashire Fusiliers Museum and they sent me his war records, and he was only fifteen when he joined up. Can you believe they'd let a fifteen-year-old lad go and fight in the trenches? The things he must have seen!' I threw a quick glance at him and saw immediately that I was right. Instead of feeling gratified, I stopped talking abruptly, feeling as though I'd found myself standing at the edge of a river about to dive in without knowing how deep it was or what I was going to hit my head on.

I took a step closer to the edge. 'Do you happen to have been in the army, by any chance?'

The look he gave me contained multitudes.

Chapter Thirteen

As the days grew shorter and the golden light of autumn came again, Izabel kept up her determined focus on Stanley, and I found it in my heart to be glad to see him blossom. I don't think it was purely her doing: the work suited him, and he was eating well. She had gone back to Farnworth Manor by then, but almost every day, she would find some reason to come home, though it was a good mile's walk across the fields. Stanley would often eat with us after his day's work, and if Izabel managed to get away, she too would share our evening meal.

Those were livelier meals than we'd had for some time, thanks almost entirely to Izzy's ceaseless chatter. She would always have some story to tell, though I often doubted how true they were, but it was good to see Dad laugh and Stanley smile his slow shy smile.

One evening, we had just sat down to tea: there being no sign of Izabel, I had not laid her a place, so Stanley was alone on one side of the table opposite the twins, whilst I had taken my seat at the opposite end to Dad. Without warning, the door banged open and there she was: it was clear to see she was bursting with news, but Dad told her to wash her hands and set herself a place before she started. He was used to her over-excited entrances, and had just started telling Rosie and Lily about an albino foal that had been born at a neighbouring farm.

I watched as Stanley moved his chair to one side to make room for Izzy, giving her a shy smile when she came to sit beside him. She looked wonderful: glowing with good health: her cheeks were rosy, her eyes bright, and her hair piled up in a new style I hadn't seen before. Wayward curls fell loose in ringlets on the tanned skin of her neck. I felt a sharp stab of envy and a wave of self-pity: I hadn't even run a brush through my hair today, and it was days since I'd looked in a mirror. Again, I resolved to make some effort with my appearance: I felt my youth was simply slipping away from me.

Finally she was allowed to speak, and all was revealed: 'Mrs Cobham says my training is to start immediately! It's so exciting! Mr Farnworth is bringing a party of his friends from London for a weekend in October, and there are to be three ladies in the group.' She looked around the table with shining eyes, and I think we all felt a stirring of excitement too. 'And,' she paused for effect and her eyes seemed to grow bigger: 'Guess what? The rumour is that one of the ladies is very special to Mr Farnworth: there are only two other gentlemen in the party!' Triumphant, she said, 'What do you think of that?' Not waiting for an answer, she rattled on: 'So I'm moving into my own room and shall have a uniform! Mrs Cobham will begin my training tomorrow, and next week I'm to be taken to Rivington Hall to spend three days with the ladies' maid there! I just can't wait!' She beamed around the room, and her beauty glowed in the mellow golden light from the window.

After she'd gone that night, walking part of the way with Stanley, I felt so sorry for myself that I was short with the girls and even, at one point, with Dad. He noticed immediately and looked up from the fireside where he was sitting with a newspaper. "Are you alright, sweetheart?'

I embarrassed myself by starting to cry. He got up and came to the foot of the stairs, where I was clutching the bannister and sobbing like a baby. He put his arm round my shoulders and led me to the sofa, pushing a soiled hanky into my hand and patting the seat beside him. "Come on love, tell Daddy.'

'No, it's nothing. I just sometimes ...' I tried to get up but he held me firm, patting my head with his other hand with a weight that made my brain rattle.

'Is it Izzy?'

'Partly. I just ... sometimes I feel so sorry for myself.'

He was quiet for a time, and I really think it hadn't dawned on him before that I was anything but content with my lot. Suddenly, I longed for my Mum, and the tears came thick and fast.

When he still didn't say anything, I finally gathered my wits and wriggled free to stand in front of him, sniffing and dabbing at my face with my pinny. He was staring into the fire and his face looked bereft. I felt terribly guilty and wished I'd got to my room before I'd let my self-pity overwhelm me. 'It's fine Dad, don't worry. Just the wrong time of the month. You know women.'

He snapped out of it then. 'Don't I just! Surrounded by them, I am.' Subsiding, he looked up at me wistfully. 'I'm sorry love, you don't get much fun, do you? I don't think. I just get on with it, like, but I forget what it's like for you. I don't know what I'll do when you leave to get married.'

'Pah! There's not much chance of that, is there?' Sorrowfully, I turned away and made for the stairs.

The next morning, he was in the kitchen when I came down in my dressing-gown. I hadn't slept well, and sat down wearily at the table, unable to summon any energy for the day ahead.

'Morning sweetheart, I've made us a pot of tea. We've got an hour before we have to get the girls up. I want to talk to you.' This was a tone I hadn't heard before: in the last year, whenever he wasn't working, Dad had either been silent and distracted or full of false cheer.

I felt a stirring of something like hope. He put the cosy on the teapot, fumbling with giant's hands to get it over the spout. Then he poured us both a mug and sat down opposite me.

'I've been thinking.'

'I hope you were sat down.'

He flicked a smile at me, 'Enough cheek,' but refusing to be diverted, he went on.

'There's things to talk about. Serious things. Things that affect all of us. I've not faced them, there's been too much going on with ... you know ... everything, but now things are settling down a bit.' He spread his hands out on the table, and I looked down at them, marvelling at their strength and size. It was so rare to see them still. I'd seen pictures of titanic figures carved by Michaelangelo whose every vein and sinew pulsed with life and power: these were similarly god-like hands, albeit scarred and calloused and dusted with fine black hairs.

With one forefinger raised, he counted out a list on the fingers of his other hand: 'One, you. Two, Izzy. Three, the twins. Four, Stanley. Five, the forge. And six,' here he held up the forefinger with a flourish, and I had the distinct impression that he'd practised this speech, 'the farm.'

I held still, hardly daring to disturb his thought processes. My heart was fluttering with excitement.

He reached for the teapot, something I'd never seen him do before: I saw him realise that only one finger could fit through the handle, and he used his other hand to steady it as he poured. The milk jug handle defeated him entirely, so he lifted the thing bodily, like a giant picking a flower. 'Have a drink of tea while I get my thoughts in order.' We both took a sip in silence.

'Right. I'm starting with the things that are sorted. Izzy's got a good job, she's happy and she's on her way. I'm not thinking about her love-life. She's young yet.' I kept my face still.

'The twins'll be eleven next year, old enough to start work in the mill. That's not the life I'd want for them, but it might be their only option.' I was startled by this: they were children still, and I had barely given a thought to their future: the idea of them working in a cotton mill was horrible. That would not happen if I could help it, but I wouldn't interrupt him just yet.

'Now, Stanley's a grand lad, and he's a stayer. He's a natural blacksmith and he loves the job. I can't tell you what that means to me, Esther. Well, you know. Thing is, the smithy is what I love, that and woodwork. Between us, he and I can make decent money. We can take on bigger jobs and build up more regular customers. I've heard smithies are closing in the cities, but there will always be plenty of work out here. Thing is,' he paused and sighed, 'I'm getting on a bit now, and I've been thinking about the farm.' He stopped, and I looked up at him with real surprise. It had never occurred to me that anything would ever change. The farm and the family went on, as they had for centuries, surely?

'Thing is, love, I'm running the farm down. We've only ever farmed half of what we own, I've only planted oats this year and I haven't bought any new stock for a few years. The horses will stay, of course. We love them and they work hard for their keep. Other fellers are buying machinery to do what horses do. That's not for me. We only need one field for growing fodder and another for pasture for the horses and the few cows. I'm thinking of selling most of the land.' My eyes wide, I opened my mouth to speak, but he held up a hand to stop me.

'Now then, back to you. You're my rock and you've got us all through this terrible time. But now it's time to think about you. You're, what, twenty now?'

I smiled gently, 'Nineteen.'

His face softened, 'Eee, nineteen eh? And look at you. Worn out, you are.'

I bristled and straightened my back indignantly. 'No-one looks good in the morning!'

'Hold your horses, that's not what I meant! You're an outdoor girl, Esther, and for a year now you've been stuck in the house, doing all the cooking and cleaning and laundry and childcare. It was only when I looked at you last night that I thought how hard you work. All the things your mum did too. I just took it for granted: everything just carried on like before. But it's not right. Your Aunty Nellie offered to help after Alice died, but I refused it. I said we'd cope, but I didn't think what that'd mean for you. And now look at you!'

I looked up sharply, but saw that he was laughing, and I smiled too. He reached out and swallowed my two hands in his.

'Now, Mistress Esther. You talk. Tell me what you want.'

Shy now, I shook my head and looked away, overwhelmed to be the focus of anyone's attention. 'I just don't know.'

'Come on sweetheart,' he tugged on my hands. 'Tell me what you'd like to do with your life.'

I was at a loss, until he said, 'If you could walk away from this farm, where would you go? What would you do?'

'Dad! I could never walk away from this farm!' Suddenly my eyes were full of tears. 'What are you saying? Do you want me to go?'

'No, no, of course not! That's not what I meant. You can live here as long as you want to, love. But you need to think about what you want to do with your life.'

'You're not going to sell the house, Dad, are you?'

'No, no, sorry love, I'm making a mess of this. What I'm saying is, I've decided to look into selling or letting the land. We can live well off the smithy: now I've got Stanley and the country's getting back on its feet, there's more work than we can take on. We'll keep the hens and the horses, put the cows out to pasture and we'll be able to get a housekeeper, and you'll be free. That's what I'm saying. Free to do what you want to do. So what do you want to do?'

Suddenly my mind was filled with ideas and visions, a mosaic of scenery, faces, books, buildings and impressions that I would struggle to put into words. 'I don't know. I thought hard, and began slowly: 'I love to be outside most of all. I do know that. And I think you're right: I've been inside too much and it gets me down.'

He nodded and kept quiet.

'I suppose one day I might like a family of my own, but the way I feel at the moment, I don't even want to think about it. Housework and looking after children: I've had enough of it this past year.'

He still didn't speak, so I carried on. Now I was just thinking aloud. 'I love reading, and ideas, but I don't want to be a teacher. I can't think what else I could do.'

'You want to be outside.'

'Yes, that's it. I do think I'd like to help people somehow, but I don't want to be a nurse.'

'I'll tell you what,' he sat up decisively. 'Why don't you go and talk to your old teacher, what's she called?'

'Miss Ashworth.'

'She'll know things that we don't. She'll have a different ... what's the word?'

'Perspective.'

'That's it, perspective. Talk it through with her. But I want you to know that whatever you want to do, I'll support it.'

I heard shuffling footsteps upstairs: it was time to get the girls up for school. I must have made a movement, because he put his hand on my arm to stop me getting up. 'Just a minute love, before we finish. I'm going to make some enquiries about selling the land. What would be your thoughts?'

'Well, like you said, we'd keep fields for pasture and fodder, and of course we'd keep the vegetable garden, in fact I'd like to have a bigger plot, extend the flower-beds and maybe have a greenhouse? Could I use the land against the old barn wall? Where the midden is at the moment, maybe knock down the old pig-sties. That wall's south-facing. What do you think?'

'Yes, that'd be grand. I've meant to get round to moving that midden for years: easterlies stink the house out! What about a potting shed? I'm sure Stanley would love to build you a shed. I keep seeing him looking in the workshop.'

'Oh Dad, that'd be wonderful! I could grow so much more if I had a greenhouse! I could grow more variety of flowers, too, and sell them, so it wouldn't just be for us. And herbs. And fruit: I've neglected the orchard: I could expand it. I could have my own market stall, or maybe my own shop here on the farm. I could make it into a real business!' I couldn't believe this might really come true. That I could be released from the drudgery and do what really made me happy. 'Do you mean it, Dad?'

'Of course I mean it love. It's a great idea! We'll leave it for now, but you go and talk to Miss Ashworth and have a think, and I'll ask around about the land.'

'One thing, though Dad, we'd keep the horse-chestnut field, wouldn't we?'

'Oh Lord yes, no question. We'd have to change the name of the farm if we lost that tree: it's over two hundred years old!'

'And another thing, Dad. Could you find out about getting pipes and running water?'

'I'd already though of that. Wilfred Hodge has it already and he says his wife's a different woman! We might even get electric. What about that?'

I couldn't speak. Life could change overnight. I'd learnt that a year ago in a terrible way. And now it could happen in a wonderful way. I sat at the table for a long time, lost in dreams, with tingles of excitement running up and down my shoulders. The girls were late for school that morning, but I simply didn't care.

Stanley noticed straight away. When I took them their tea that morning, he was sitting on the horse-trough, whittling a new handle for a hammer. As he stood up to take his mug from me, he said, 'You look well.'

It was the first direct remark he'd ever made to me, and I didn't know how to respond. I looked him straight in the eye and said, 'Thank-you,' expecting him to look away, but he didn't.

It's a strange thing: it had never occurred to me before that there's a certain length of time when it's fine to look at someone without speaking. When that moment had definitely passed, I broke the spell, instantly embarrassed. 'What is it?'

He still didn't look away, but instead answered, 'I was just looking at you. I'm sorry if I embarrassed you.'

'No, I ... well, I just wondered what you were thinking. I thought I must have a smut on my face or something.'

He turned away then, and looking out across the field, lifted his cup to his lips and drank deeply. For the first time, I noticed threads of red-gold in his hair, which curled onto his collar. Confused, I turned to go, but turned back when he said quietly, 'Would you like to know what I was thinking?'

My first impulse was to deny it, but I was in an exhuberant mood, 'Yes, actually I would.'

'I was thinking how beautiful you were.'

I must have been haunted by Dad's comments from last night. My voice was flat, accepting. 'Were.'

He turned back to me then, and smiled. His shoulders seemed to block out the sun.

'Are.'

My high spirits left me, and I turned my face away. Having no idea whether I was being teased or complimented, I decided to leave, but he touched my arm gently and an electric shock ran up my shoulder to my neck.

'I mean it. You're beautiful. And you're even more beautiful because you have no idea that you are.'

I should have left then, but I was suddenly so suffused with languid warmth that I doubted I'd have been able to walk away even if I'd wanted to.

I could only brush it off. 'Well, freckles and red hair aren't to everybody's taste.'

'I wouldn't say your hair was red,' he tilted his head to one side to consider it. 'At the moment it's goldy-red, like copper. Sometimes it's darker, like burnished bronze.'

In for a penny. 'And the freckles?'

'Ah, well they've faded a lot since you were a child.'

'You barely noticed me when I was a child!'

'Oh yes I did, Esther. You were so sweet and soft-hearted, and sadly, for daft little lads, that's red rag to a bull.'

'You were horrible to me.'

'Now now, don't be mard. We had fun.'

'You had fun.'

He smiled. 'Anyway, that was then.'

This had gone far enough. Izzy would be livid. I gave him the full beam of my new, confident smile, said, 'Yes, and this is now,' spun on my heel and stalked away across the yard, my hair bouncing down my back.

Chapter Fourteen

'So go on! What happened then?' Beth was all agog. Apparently I was the only person to have succeeded in getting through the gate in the past year, let alone to have any kind of conversation with him.

'Well, it's funny but I just suddenly thought, that's enough for now. I mean, it was a bit much, wasn't it, barging into his privacy and rattling on like I was on flipping Oprah. I'm lucky he didn't set the dog on me.'

'He likes you. He's bound to. Look at you. And him, a man all alone.' Warming to her theme, she went on: 'No company,' she winked theatrically, 'especially no female company, if you get my drift.'

'Oh, I get your drift alright. Forget it. Far too scary.'

'So go on, what did he say when you said were you in the army?'

Suddenly it seemed like a betrayal to describe the look on his face and the way he'd abruptly turned and gone inside. What would I say, anyway? Haunted? Hunted? Agonised? Angry? All I knew is that it had stayed with me.

'He just went.'

'Without saying anything else?'

'Yes.'

With a wave of her hand, he was dismissed. 'Ah well, you win some you lose some. There's probably nothing in the farmhouse anyway.'

'You're probably right. I do wonder who it belongs to, though. I'm going to sign up to Ancestry this afternoon and see what I can find out. It's a project. I'm looking forward to getting my teeth into it. It'll be like detective work. I hardly know anything. Mum just wasn't interested in talking about the past, and my grandparents were both dead by the time I had any interest. I do know my great-granddad was a blacksmith as well as a farmer. I didn't even get a chance to have a look at the buildings: I'll go back when I've got more information.'

'How do you know he was a blacksmith if no-one ever told you anything?'

'It's funny, like I say, mum had no time for the past or anything old, and I was always the opposite. I really wanted to see a ghost and I never did, but once this thing happened that convinced me. I knew Gran had grown up on a farm, and that mum had had to work there when she was in her teens, but she never ever talked about it and ran away to the city as soon as she was old enough. Anyway, one time when I was about eighteen, we went with her workmates to see a psychic in Bury. Well, I was young and cynical, though I secretly wanted to be impressed, and we all sat in this chintzy sitting room with big bay windows looking out onto a huge garden, and this woman started talking, and it all sounded like a load of trot to me and just random, and then all of a sudden my mum blushed beetroot and looked shocked and tearful, and I thought, what did the woman just say? I hadn't been listening, so I whispered to this girl sitting next to me, "What did she just say?" and she said, "Something about a man in a leather waistcoat sitting on a big grey horse in her garden." So I looked out of the window and there was no-one there, and I looked back at mum and she still had that startled look on her face: in fact she was looking like she might burst into tears, but no-one else seemed to have noticed.'

'Woo!'

'So I didn't say anything until we were on our own in the car on the way home, and then I was really cool and just said, "What did you think of that then?" and she didn't answer at first, and when I looked at her she had tears running down her face. So I said, "Mum? What's wrong?" and she carried on driving but then after a bit she said, "It was my grandpa." And I asked her what she meant, and she said, "My grandpa was a blacksmith on the farm, and when I ran away he was heartbroken, and he died a few years later, long before you were born."

'It was probably a set-up. Cruel, those things I think. One of her workmates will have given the psychic woman the info.'

'The point is, there's no way in the world she'd have told anyone at work that she'd been brought up on a farm: she had this big thing about it, and she said that she'd always had a guilt complex about her grandpa and she'd never told anyone about him because she was so ashamed of herself, but there was this woman who didn't know her from Adam describing him exactly. Apparently she'd also

106

mentioned his curly black hair and thick moustache and something about his boots: that girl hadn't told me that, but even the horse was right because the woman had said it was huge and grey. Mum said it was a shire called Dolly.

Beth was impressed, though I could see her struggling to explain it.

'Anyway, there you go.... After that, I got really keen on finding out about my roots, and when I got my first car, I came here with my boyfriend and became all besotted with the country and wanted to live here. I loved D.H. Lawrence at the time, and all that earthy man stuff, Lady Chatterley, the Virgin and the Gypsy, and mum was horrified when I brought a lad home with long black hair and a neckerchief. It didn't last long: he was uncouth and I had aspirations.'

Beth laughed, 'Oo yes, Lady Chatterley. We used to pass that round. Learnt a lot from that, we did. I still like a bit of outdoor rumpy-pumpy, don't you?' I know I smiled, but I must have looked away, and she saw through me. 'No rumpy-pumpy, eh?'

'Nope, none at all.' I felt alarmingly close to tears all of a sudden.

'How long's it been? You don't have to tell me, but it'd help.'

'Help what?'

'Well, it'd help to know where you're at with your marriage. If you want to talk about it, like, but if you don't, it's ok, honest. I don't like to pry.'

I gave her a rueful smile. 'Yes you do.'

It was a relief when she laughed. 'Yeah, go on then, I do.' Then she was serious, and leant across to hold my hand. 'But you can trust me, Annie. We're friends already aren't we? Just if you want someone to talk to, I'm here. '

I squeezed her hand. 'You're right. I appreciate it, Beth. I was thinking about that. All my other friends are couples and they all know us as a model marriage. You put a front on, you know, perpetuate the lie.'

'Has he got someone else then?'

'Yes, he thinks I don't know, but obviously I do. It's a long time since he was careful. This is the third one that I know about, and it's lasted the longest.'

'Who is she? His P.A.?'

'Yes, so they're away together a lot, most weeks in fact. If there's no sales trip, there's an overnight stay in London. Head Office.'

'And how is he with you?'

'Well, perfectly polite, just indifferent and disinterested. No eye-contact, conversation confined to the house and the kids. We used to row. I was mad as hell about the first one and he begged me to forgive him. It would never happen again, didn't know what had come over him, all that. But then of course it did happen again, and I just couldn't be bothered fighting it. And then, something...something happened that meant no going back. The kids don't know, and I...sorry, I just don't want to talk about it. Anyway, I kind of switched off. I had my mum to look after, and Rosie's wedding. We just lead separate lives. He plays golf a lot when he's home, spends a lot of time in his office, on the computer. I do my own thing. I think he likes the stability, keeping up appearances and all that. I don't think she's married. I've never asked. For all I know, she might be happy with the status quo too. I expect we'll find out soon enough.'

'Is that what this is really about then? Forcing his hand?'

'No, not really, nothing as purposeful as that. Or maybe unconsciously that's exactly what it is. I've lived in a state of inertia really, and coming here has kind of snapped me out of it. I don't want to go on like that. All my confidence has just ebbed away, and I've let it happen. So no, no sex. He used to make a half-hearted attempt occasionally, but I just pretended to be asleep and he soon gave up trying.'

'God, I don't know how you've stood it. The bastard.'

'It's funny, I don't see him as a bastard. He's basically a decent man, just a bit vain and self-satisfied. I've been kind of passive and philosophical about it. Like marriage is just society's way of helping a people to stay together long enough to bring their kids up. Well, we've done that. But, you know, being here, away from the comfortable stasis, I can feel myself coming back to life.

I've only been here a couple of days, but I've felt all sorts of emotions I thought I'd lost. Contentment, for one. Just standing in the sun with a cup of tea. Anticipation: I'm looking forward to decorating and nesting. Peacefulness, just getting into a smaller bed by myself and lying in the middle. The laughs with you. And curiosity. I'm really hungry to know about Esther and all that, find out about my family, it's like detective work. I'm looking forward to getting going.'

That afternoon, I made myself a study space in the front room. I had no desk, but had found a decorating table under the spare bed which would do for now. There was only a dim ceiling light with no shade, and the afternoon was dark with leaden skies, so I set the table up under the window, thankful for the grubby nets as I'd have felt rather exposed being only a couple of metres from passers-by. While the computer warmed up, I thought about how quickly I was getting used to living in close proximity to other people: I'd expected to find it claustrophobic and intrusive, but I felt curiously happy and safe. The nets would go.

Before I started on the family research, I thought I'd have a look at the farm on Google Earth. There was no Street View, but I got a real kick out of zooming down on the buildings I'd only really seen from a distance. The pictures had clearly been taken in winter as the chestnut tree was a dark skeleton in a bare field. It was difficult to discern anything about the farm from above, but I knew I'd be going back, preferably when I knew he was out. He'd have to drive past here to get to the main road, so I'd probably ask Beth what she knew of his routine, and maybe take her with me for security.

I was just about to close Google Earth and create an account on Ancestry, when I had an idea. It was without much hope of finding anything that I started to scroll away from the farm and over the woods. The dark stain of winter woodland was large and shapeless, so I zoomed out to get a sense of its size. It was difficult to estimate the area, but it was certainly big. Judging by the comparative distances that I knew, I estimated it could be about three miles across and roughly oval, bordered by the Common all along its nearer edge, the new housing estate to the west, what looked like a large mill to the north, and the river to the east, beyond which the road ran to Chorley through a patchwork of conurbations.

I zoomed in as far as I could and scrolled round the perimeter to look for any sign of roads or tracks, but could find nothing until I arrived back at the farm. Beth was wrong, the track didn't finish at the five-bar gate: the ghost of it could just about be traced down into the wooded valley, though it was clearly long-disused and overgrown. Following what I assumed would be its trajectory, I hovered over the centre of the woodland, where a pale area showed like skin through thinning hair. Assuming that was where the manor house must have stood, I zoomed in rather too quickly to see anything. The screen was filled with pale, pixelated shapelessness but there was something about the sandy shadows that caught my attention. I clicked out a few times, and began to discern a hazy shape that my eye didn't at first recognize. Whilst my brain whispered that could be a chimney, my finger kept up a cool and steady beat of clicks. The unmistakable shape of a very large quadruple chimney-stack materialized before my disbelieving eyes.

The house was still standing. At least, part of it was. If it had not been so dark and forbidding outside, I'd have pulled my walking boots on there and then, but I told myself to calm down. It would wait.

Chapter Fifteen

That Sunday, I went to see Miss Ashworth, who still lived in the tied cottage near the school. I'd heard that the new teacher lived nearby with her widowed mother. As I walked, I considered the job of school-teacher. I'd enjoyed school, but that was mostly down to Miss Ashworth, who always kept me provided with books to read when I'd finished my work ahead of the others. For a short while, she'd tried to make me into her assistant, and I had tried to help, but so often she would find me with my head in a Dickens novel or a poetry book when I should have been helping the little ones with their sums, that she soon gave up on me and recruited my friend Mary, who was much more keen and biddable.

I'd stayed on as long as I could, aware that if I stopped going to school, I'd have to help Mum with the twins, who were energetic toddlers by the time I was eleven. I was dimly aware that Miss Ashworth had ambitions for me, although at the time I could conceive of no other future than the farm.

When the door opened, I could tell by her eyes that she already knew who was standing on the doorstep. We'd often credited Miss Ashworth with psychic powers: those clear dark-blue eyes had a way of looking into your soul. Mary and I used to call her The Mistress of the Perfect Pause because she had a way of standing utterly still, her head cocked to one side like a listening blackbird. She never had to raise her voice: when she was disappointed, never angry: she only had to speak more softly and the culprit cowered from the simple fact of her disapproval.

'Come in, come in! What a delightful surprise! Come through, my dear.' She led the way down an oak-panelled hallway adorned with etchings, and I thought how like a tall, slender young woman she looked from the back: her clothes were discreetly modern and her salt-and-pepper hair cut into a neat bob. 'Would you like a cup of tea or coffee? I bought a slice of walnut cake in Chorley yesterday: we can share it.'

Miss Ashworth never baked, having declared in class one day that life was too short. I remembered how smitten I had been with this idea: I was ten years old, and helping Mum with the baking was one of my weekly chores. I often enjoyed it, but increasingly frequently I resented time away from my book: I'd contrived a book-stand out of wood off-cuts, so that I could continue to read while I peeled and beat. Miss Ashworth had never complained about the flour in between the pages until she once came to my desk and ostentatiously wafted her gilt-edged edition of Great Expectations over my copybook. A fine snow stuck to my freshly-written words and clumped in my inkwell. I learnt my lesson.

I followed her into sunny sitting room at the back of the house: French windows opened onto a small garden and a large oak roll-top desk dominated the room. She had clearly been working, and I apologised for arriving unannounced.

'I hope I haven't interrupted you.'

She called from the kitchen, 'You have, but it's a welcome interruption. I must confess I had a surreptitious peep from the front window before I decided whether to answer.'

I laughed, relieved and flattered by her honestly. It was eight years since first she'd invited me and Mary for afternoon tea. Both farmers' daughters, we had gazed with astonishment at the bookcases, prints and postcards that adorned the walls. Miss Ashworth had been to university, but even more impressively, she'd been to Egypt, and transfixed us with tales of embalming methods and tombs containing riches beyond our imaginings.

I stepped out into her garden, always fascinated by the uses people made of their plots of land. It had once been cultivated, with a neat lawn and flowery borders, but now the grass was like a meadow with a well-trodden path to a seat in the shade of a fine oak tree which bordered her property.

'Would you like to take tea outside?' She had appeared beside me carrying a tray.

'Yes, please, that would be lovely.'

'These autumn days are so precious: I sit outside whenever I can. How do you like my garden now it's au naturel?'

I followed her through the long grass, 'I love it like this. Did you decide life was too short for gardening too?'

'Ha! You remember that pronouncement, do you? Do you know your mother told me off about it one time when I met her in the market? She said you'd become a proper little radical, refusing to help with the housework on the grounds that "life's too short" and "dirt is just matter in the wrong place."

As she set the tray down on a low rough-hewn table, she laughed in that delightful tinkling way I remembered so well. 'Such a unique child. So serious and thoughtful. You used to sit in a shaft of sunlight, your hair all ablaze with ideas and indignations about the injustices of the world. You were the only child I've ever known who was moved to tears by the beginning of Oliver Twist.'

I remembered that: it broke my heart to find out that children could be born to mothers who died, and that a child could be so unloved, treated so unfairly, or allowed to walk all the way to London simply because nobody knew or cared. I had been chastened by that story, and I honestly think I saw the world differently because of it.

She patted my hand. 'So, my dear. How are things at home? Are you coping?'

'Coping. Yes, that's the word for it. We're coping. It's been a terrible year. I'd never have believed life could change so much from one year to the next.'

'Indeed, from one minute to the next.' She poured the tea and offered me a piece of cake, which I declined.

'I insist. It's a modest slice, Esther, and you look too thin, if you don't mind me saying so.'

'No, I don't mind. I know I'm not looking my best. I hadn't realised how tired I'd become. But first, tell me about you. Retirement suits you.' I looked at her properly for the first time. 'You look very well, and I like your short hair.' It struck me that she actually was much younger than I'd previously thought.

She read my thoughts. 'You are thinking that I look younger, I believe. I always found that the age of one's teachers was either astonishingly exaggerated or a matter of supreme indifference. Don't you agree? I am the same age as your mother would have been, forty-five. Now you are wondering why I left teaching. I am a positive Sherlock, am I not?'

I laughed outright and said the only thing I could think of: 'Elementary, my dear Miss Ashworth.'

'I was in receipt of a small inheritance when my father died, so I am now a woman of independent means and may spend my time as I wish. I read, I write, I travel: I am in heaven.'

'That sounds like a wonderful life.'

'It is. I awake every day and give thanks. Not that I believe anyone is there to be thanked. I give thanks to good fortune and good health. And now the war is over and I even have the vote. My cup runneth over.'

'Yes, it's a new start for everyone.'

'Indeed. A new world order must be forged. For one thing, we shall not rest until you too have the vote, my dear. You should not have to wait until you are thirty to be considered as intelligent, well-informed and capable of good judgement as a man. I'm sure you agree.'

I was ashamed to think that female emancipation had rarely crossed my horizons. The activities of the suffragettes had seemed remote, confined to the cities: they had seemed to have no bearing on my life.

I saw that she had intuited this too, but was too kind to say anything, and we ate our cake in companionable silence.

'I am still involved in education, however. Perhaps you have heard of St Peter's School, in Preston, sometimes called the Brook Street Club?'

'No, I haven't.'

'It was established a long time ago by a dear friend of mine, Edith Rigby. You might have heard her name in connection with an act of vandalism she committed in the vicinity before the war.'

It still meant nothing to me.

'She set fire to the wooden bungalow that the MP, Lord Lever had built in his grounds on Rivington Pike. It was a protest for which she paid dearly.'

'How?'

'Imprisonment. Restraint. Force-feeding. The usual ways in which the male establishment deals with women who have to much to say.' There was a bitterness in her tone that I had never heard before, and I was astonished to think that she knew a real suffragette, in fact that a woman from Preston had been treated like that.

114

I could only say, feebly, 'In Preston?'

'No, in London. She is a wonderful woman, eccentric, magnificent and utterly unique, the most caring person I have ever had the fortune to know. She has suffered for it, but remains unbowed. "To thine own self be true." She acts, whereas others only dream. The inequalities of life have preoccupied her all her life, though she was born into a comfortable family: an accident of birth merely, as it is for all of us. The school, or club, is for mill girls. I teach there once a week.'

'A school for mill girls?'

'Yes. Many of them have to leave school at eleven due to the financial imperatives which govern their lives. Edith decided that she could enable them to continue their education whilst simultaneously earning a living: the school is open in the afternoons and evenings for the purposes of education, recreation and conversation. I and other members of the Women's Social and Political Union support her endeavours in any way we can.'

'My father is talking of sending Rosie and Lily to the mill.'

'You astonish me. I had not thought it of your father.'

'It's not what he wants for them, and it might not happen. We had a talk on Thursday. He is thinking of selling the land.' I gave her the gist of the conversation, and, perceptive as ever, she homed in on the reason for my visit.

'And so, my dear. You will be freed from your duties!' Her eyes gleamed with vicarious excitement. 'What are your thoughts?' I told her what I'd told him, and she smiled and nodded as I outlined my plans.

When I'd finished painting a shining vision of a cosy, unambitious future, she seemed about to speak, but thought better of it and reached forward to hold both my hands in a gesture which echoed my father's. 'I am so pleased for you, Esther. You deserve every happiness, my dear.' She got to her feet and brushed crumbs from her skirt, then sat down beside me again. 'What are you reading at the moment?'

'I have hardly any time for reading, I'm afraid. I have a volume of poetry by the fireside, but as soon as I start to read, I fall asleep.'

115

'What a shame. There are so many new ideas in the air. But I do understand. I cared for my father for a short time before he died, so I briefly had a taste of what life must be like for people who are obliged look after others. I am too selfish, I fear.'

'Is that the reason you never married?' I had asked the question before I thought it through, and I held my breath for fear she would be offended.

But I need not have worried: she answered as though it was the most natural question in the world: 'Partly, yes, though if I had married, it would not have been to a man who required my full attention. In my opinion, I was never suited to being a mother. That requires a level of selflessness of which I fear I am incapable.'

'I must admit, the past year has put me off the idea of ever having a child of my own. I suppose that precludes marriage.'

'By no means, my dear. You must read Married Love by Marie Stopes. You are young yet, but as time goes on, if you still feel the same, it will simply be a matter of finding a man who shares your inclination. Edith has been particularly fortunate in that regard: her husband Charles is a doctor and supports her every endeavour to the hilt.'

I waited, expecting the usual questions about my non-existent love-life. My aunts asked me every time they saw me whether I was walking out with anyone. But the question never came. Instead she asked, 'So what about that prodigious brain of yours? What interests you, Esther?'

Again, I was nonplussed. For the past year, I had barely had time to think, let alone summon any intellectual curiosity. It struck me that, for all her wisdom, Miss Ashworth had a faulty understanding of my life. She had been honest with me, so I would respond in kind. 'Looking after a family without running water or electricity doesn't lend itself to cultivating interests, Miss Ashworth.'

She smiled gently: 'I appreciate that, Esther, and do please call me Maud. I can imagine the sheer tediousness and physical effort required, though I have never experienced it myself. I simply wondered whether you had any thoughts about your intellectual development and imaginative life, now that you are soon to be released from domestic servitude.'

116

'I imagine that the planning and cultivation of my market garden will occupy my mind nicely, and as the business grows, I anticipate that I will develop new skills. I will also have time to visit the library and read again. The first thing I shall buy with my earnings will be a reading lamp! I cannot wait for electricity to be installed!'

Miss Ashworth (I could not yet bring myself to call her Maud) had become thoughtful: she seemed to come to a decision about something, and abruptly stood up. 'Come and see me again soon. I'd like to hear how things are progressing for you and your family. And when you are at leisure to read something, tell me, for I have something I think you'd find most apposite to your needs and stimulating to your ideas.'

I took my leave of her with a kiss and a hug. Apart from a brief kiss at the funeral, we had never done more than shake hands before, and I felt it a great step forward in our friendship.

When I got home, Izzy was there, full of news about the imminent arrival of Mr Farnworth's party, particularly the ladies. 'Apparently one of them is the daughter of a mill-owner from Manchester, and she's a great society beauty, but that's not the one who's special to Mr Farnworth: that one is called Freya Hertig, and she is from London! But the best thing is: she wears trousers! Can you believe it? I can't wait to see! She is to have the bedroom adjoining Mr Farnworth's: we are scandalised!' She giggled and looked anything but.

Dad was more interested in the menfolk: 'So when do you say Mr Farnworth arrives?'

'He's coming on Wednesday, ahead of the rest of the party,' and then she turned back to me to speculate about the dresses and hairstyles she hoped to see. 'At Rivington Hall, I saw such gowns as you wouldn't believe, Esther! Finest silks, and such colours! We had to practise the fastenings, and I got to wear one of cornflower blue satin! I felt like a queen! And one of the ladies' maids did my hair in this wonderful style with tortoiseshell combs, and then I had to copy it on another girl. We had such a time of it! There was a emerald green gown that would have suited you so well, just the colour of your eyes.'

117

Behind her, Stanley appeared from the workshop, smiling at me over Izzy's head. Surprised to see him on a Sunday, I blurted out, 'Hello! What are you doing here?' which sounded most unwelcoming. She whirled round, exclaimed in delight and hooking her arm in his, said, 'Let's go for a walk and I'll tell you all about Rivington.'

Giving me and the girls a wry look, he smiled and walked away with Izzy. Dad shook his head, laughing, and put his arm round my shoulders. 'Poor lad never got a chance to answer. He's working on something in the wood-shed.'

Trying to keep my tone neutral, I asked what it was. Dad smiled down at me and kissed my hair. 'He's asked me not to look, says it's a surprise.'

'Who for?' I really had to get into the habit of thinking before I spoke.

'Well, I think I know who you fear it might be for, but rest assured it's not. It's for someone else not too far away.' He kissed my hair again and let me go, ducking his head to step into the kitchen. I stood in the yard a while, watching Izzy and Stanley walk away across the field arm in arm.

I didn't know what to think, but there were more interesting things to concern myself with, I decided.

In the kitchen, Dad was lighting a pipe from the fire. We had dinner late on a Sunday, and the smell of roast lamb filled the room and made me salivate. I felt in high spirits as I took off my coat and shoes and began to prepare the vegetables.

'I've been to see Miss Ashworth, Dad, and I was telling her all about our plans.' I was hoping to prompt him into telling me whether any progress had been made, but he merely answered, 'Oh aye?' and carried on sucking on his pipe in a concentrated manner.

I took the meat out of the oven to baste it, and as I straightened up from putting it back in, I caught his eye, which was twinkling.

'What?'

'Plans, eh? What plans are these?'

I was always easy to tease. They all took great delight in telling me things they knew would upset me. But this time, I was having none of it, and went over to poke him in the ribs with my basting spoon.

'Oh, you mean the housekeeper who starts a week tomorrow?' I gaped at him, and my face must have been a picture, because he laughed out loud, a great guffaw that rattled the pots on the dresser.

'Really? Who is it?' Suddenly I was assailed by doubts. Another woman in my kitchen, rummaging in my cupboards? I was no longer sure it was what I wanted.

'Oh, I think you'll like her. It's your Aunty Nellie.'

'Dad! That's wonderful! Are you sure it's what she wants?'

'She was delighted. She's got time on her hands now her girls are off and married, and you know how much she loves housework. She's made one condition, though.'

'Oh, what's that?'

'Electricity and running water by Christmas or she's off.'

My face fell. 'Oh, we can't afford that until we sell the land.'

'Well, don't get your hopes up love, but that might be quicker than you think. I'll say no more for now.' He went back to his pipe, but I wasn't having that, so I approached him again, brandishing the spoon in a threatening manner.

'No! No! Not the spoon!' he laughed again, and I felt my eyes filling with unexpected tears. 'This is between you, me and the gatepost. I mean it Esther. Don't even tell Stanley, and especially not Izzy.' He looked round and lowered his voice. 'I didn't tell you at the time, but Mr Farnworth came to see me in the summer. I knew he'd been to see Joseph Alker already, so I knew he was looking to buy land. I told him I'd think about it, but when he comes home this week, I'm going to see him.'

'Mr Farnworth! But what does he need land for? With an estate like that?'

'Thing is, and here's another secret. I don't know whether I should tell you this, but I will anyway. He's planning to marry.'

I was dismissive, 'Well, I know that, Izzy told us that was the rumour.'

'Well, this was from the horse's mouth. And his fiancée is a farmer.'

119

'A farmer! You mean, not a farmer's daughter or a farmer's wife?'

'No, an independent farmer. In fact, independent in more ways than that. It seems she's quite a character, Mrs Hertig. He met her in Manchester at the Corn Exchange. She was there to make some enquiries about buying a farm and moving back to the north. She's been married before, and moved down to Essex, but she was widowed young, and just carried on running the place by herself. It seems she has ideas about the future of agriculture, and it's a condition of marrying him that she can run a home farm.'

A condition of marrying him! This was indeed a brave new world.

'Well, that's marvellous, Dad. Let's just hope he hasn't changed his mind or found somewhere else.'

'Yes, here's hoping. We'll find out on Wednesday.'

I regretted changing the tone, but I was beginning to think I was the only one who'd remembered. 'You do know what else is on Wednesday, don't you Dad?'

'Yes, I do, love. I was hoping you'd not notice the anniversary. We'll not mark it. We'll mark his birthday instead, shall we? Every year. We'll have a special tea and mark his birthdays. One day he might be with us, you never know.'

Chapter Sixteen

The next day was Monday, and I was woken by Beth's front door slamming. Two teenage boys' voices passed under my window, laughing conspiratorially as I struggled to consciousness. I hadn't slept well: my mind was teeming, and I'd been disturbed to find the unwelcome presence of 'Mad Max' in my unconscious. I must find out his real name: I couldn't carry on calling him that.

After breakfast, I drove to the big supermarket outside Chorley and bought secateurs and gardening gloves as well as a coffee-maker and the other things on my list. As I turned into Park Road, a black Range Rover was just pulling out, and although I hadn't seen the driver, I had a strong hunch it was him, so I dumped my shopping and quickly changed into old jeans and walking boots before packing my rucksack and setting off towards the Common at a trot. I was anxious to get past the farm before he came back or I was going to look like a stalker.

If I hadn't seen an aerial view, I wouldn't have believed there was a path beyond the gate: I stepped from the impacted mud of his tyre-tracks into knee-high grass and followed the line in my mental image, going gently downhill until I reached the trees. The air was warm and humid, and surveying the apparently impenetrable wall of vegetation, it struck me for the first time that no-one knew where I was.

Directly in front of me, I could see that the route of the track was blocked by self-seeded ash and sycamore, although I identified a large oak to my left, and once I'd stepped into the darkness and my eyes grew accustomed, I saw there was another to my right. Their lower boughs were denuded of leaves, presumably because they could receive no light, being entirely hemmed in by these upstarts.

Stifling the thought that I was being foolhardy, I plunged in to the darkness, lifting my feet high over the dense undergrowth of ferns and shielding my face with my arm. The air was densely green and aquatic with humidity trapped by vegetation. A tortuous tangle of brambles and nettles snagged my jeans and jacket, and my secateurs struggled to hack through stems as thick as my thumb. I struggled on for half an hour or so, getting increasingly weary, and then got myself in a real fix and nearly fell. Stooping to hack away at the ensnaring octopus of brambles, I had just lifted my head when something whipped across my cheek with a sting and drew blood. Enough.

Defeated, I turned to retrace my steps, deluding myself that I'd cleared a path, but found myself surrounded by a massed army of dark trunks: my sense of direction had deserted me. I fought on, feeling the first fluttering of panic rising in my chest. Until I finally perceived daylight through the trunks, I'd honestly thought I had lost my way completely. By the time I stumbled out into the field, I felt exhausted, overheated and entirely defeated, and slumped onto the damp grass, shrugging off my rucksack and lying full-length on my back to get my breath. No sooner had I begun to appreciate the clearer air and the fresh warmth of the midday sun on my face than a shadow blocked it. I lay still, waiting for the cloud to pass and that welcome sunlight to return.

The air was still and I was so relieved that I think I could have fallen asleep, so you can imagine how I jumped when a man's voice came from directly above me.

'What on earth were you trying to do?'

I jumped up like a startled rabbit and staggered backwards, off-balance, until a huge hand clamped around my upper arm. I stifled a scream. It was him.

'How..? How did you know I was here? You can let go now, thanks.' I tried to gather some scraps of dignity and keep my voice from shaking.

'Your tracks. I thought perhaps a herd of wildebeest had come down here.'

'Well, why did you follow them? It's common land. You really made me jump. I could have had a heart attack!'

'No-one comes down here. I make sure of it.'

'Why? It's a free country.'

'Hmm, you think so?'

I didn't know whether to make a run for it or try to engage him in conversation while I casually walked away backwards, but I was seriously startled and my heartbeat felt too loud and erratic. He reached out a hand towards my face and by a real effort of will I stood still while he brushed a thumb across my cheek which came away smeared with blood.

122

'Come on, let's get you cleaned up.'

I was nervous and simply couldn't hide it. My voice shook slightly when I said, 'No, no, it's ok. I'll be home soon,' and started walking hastily away up the hill, my breath coming in pants.

Suddenly he was walking beside me in easy loping strides, 'You forgot your rucksack.'

Ridiculously, I said, 'It's ok, I'll get it later.'

Without breaking his stride, he swung it out in front of him. 'No need, I've got it.'

By the time we reached the gate, I had managed to calm myself by sheer force of will, reasoning that if he was going to attack me, he'd have done it down near the woods. Then a new worry struck me. 'Where's the dog?'

'I've just dropped him off at the vet's. He's being neutered.' 'Could they take away his fangs and his voice-box while they're at it?' Even as I said it, I didn't know whether I was attempting to lighten the mood or whether the residue of fear was anger.

He smiled down at me, 'Then he wouldn't be able to do his job properly.'

'His job? Terrifying innocent ramblers?'

'That's a curious route to go rambling. As far as I'm aware, there's no path.'

'Ah, but there is, you see. I looked on Google Earth.'

'Well don't go opening it up, because Seamus will have to put in some overtime.'

'Seamus?'

'The dog.'

'I'm not with you.'

'Clearly,' he said patiently. 'He's a guard dog.'

'Well, that's all very well when he's on his own property, but he has no business guarding land that's not his. Like the wood. Or the field with the horse-chestnut tree.' I squinted up at him, cast in darkness by the sun at his back, and jutted my chin. My confidence was back, and I was annoyed by the barely-concealed threat. 'Does he?'

He didn't answer and his shadowed smile was inscrutable.

We stood for a few moments just looking at each other, him thinking I knew not what, and me thinking several things: I was trying to read him, trying to decide whether I trusted him enough to accept an invitation into the farmhouse, realizing that he really was rather handsome and underneath it all was the slow realization that I could smell alcohol on his breath. The recognition of this arrested my thoughts and I had just decided that there was no way I'd go into the house with him when he startled me by stepping back and extending a hand for a formal introduction.

'Richard.'

I looked stupidly at his hand and slowly extended mine. "You already know my name.'

'Yes, it wasn't the most auspicious of meetings, but in my own defence I have to say that I hadn't invited you to climb over my gate.''

His hand had not moved, and mine was hovering parallel a few inches away. I looked at them both, extended in mid-air like two halves of a rope-bridge. I knew with a sudden startling clarity that this would be my only chance. If I walked away now, if I rejected this hand, which was offered at who knows what cost, I would be walking away from any chance of seeing inside the farmhouse, perhaps even of getting to the remains of the manor. And ... and...?

I moved slightly and his hand folded over mine, surprisingly gently but with an undeniable firmness. A slight lift and then it was released, but aftershock prickled the hairs on my neck and I could still feel the warmth of his palm pressed against mine. Unsettled, I took a step back and reached for my rucksack, still dangling from his other hand. 'Well, nice to meet you. I'll be off now.'

'Don't be frightened. I intend you no harm. If you still want to see inside the farmhouse, you'd be welcome. If you'd feel happier, I'll stay out here.'

The blush that had risen to my neck spread rapidly up my cheeks and I had no answer. He had turned to open the gate and now he stood holding it ajar to allow me to pass through, indicating the way with a slight tilt of his head like an imposing butler.

I stepped through with a tight smile, and he closed the gate behind us. He reached into his pocket. 'Here, you'll need the key.

Help yourself. The light switch is behind the door. The windows are small and it's quite dark inside.'

It felt wrong: he was clearly such a gentleman. 'It's not necessary for you to stay outside. I'd appreciate it if you'd show me round.'

He smiled more naturally than before, and his shoulders visibly relaxed as he led the way. I didn't attempt to keep pace, and by the time I reached the door, he was holding it open and the lights were on inside. Instantly, all my fears forgotten, I was entranced. It was exactly as I'd imagined it. The ceilings were low and the casement windows leaded. The curtains were faded chintz and the wooden floor was knotted and worn by decades of footfall: my own ancestors had lived here. Where once there had presumably been a range, there was a gleaming green Aga. Delicate porcelain teacups painted with spring flowers dangled from hooks on a dark oak dresser, and an enormous aged kitchen table of the same wood was spread with newspapers, books and magazines.

The air, though, was stale and slightly rancid: the unmistakable smell of gin caught my nostrils. 'Do you mind if I open a window? I feel a bit hot.'

'I'll do it, they stick. I'll leave the door open for the draught. And for your peace of mind.'

Inside the room, he looked like an Action Man in a doll's house, and I saw him dip his head as he passed under the beams.

'Would you like to sit down? I'll get you a glass of water.' His tone was formal, even sombre, and I realized my fears had vanished.

Chapter Seventeen

When Wednesday dawned, it was raining, which seemed fitting. If it had been a golden day like the last 27th September, the memories would have been even more immediate and I'd have been too raw. As I wiped the condensation from my casement window, I saw that the sky was leaden and the rain bounced off the eaves and gushed down the gutters: puddles in the yard were joining into lakes. I saw a figure walking quickly towards the gate with a tarpaulin draped around his head and shoulders: Stanley on his way to work. I must be late, or he was early. Instead of going into the smithy, he opened the door of the workshop and stepped inside, leaning out to shake his cloak fruitlessly before closing the door behind him. I was suddenly overwhelmed with an urge to go to him. What would happen if I simply appeared and closed the door behind me? The air in the workshop would be moist with the smell of resin and damp clothes. Perhaps he would have to take off his waistcoat and shirt. I lost myself then, and dare not tell you any more of my reverie.

Dad was in a thoughtful mood when he got up. He squeezed my shoulder once, but we went about our business in silence. By lunchtime, the rain had stopped. I had prepared a rabbit pie and vegetables, and the three of us ate with relish: there's something about a meat pie on a sad, cold day. I had made a plum crumble and as I watched Dad pour on the custard, I hoped that next year's plums might be from my own trees.

Nothing had been mentioned of any visit to Mr Farnworth, so I asked, as I often did, what they were working on that afternoon.

'I've an appointment this afternoon, and Stanley's just got a few things to finish off. Don't forget Laurie Topping's wheel, will you lad? It's stood there that long I'd forgotten it wasn't mine.'

'No, I've got it on my list, Tom. That crumble was delicious, Esther, thank-you.' He got up from the table and took his leave without another word. Dad left soon after, and I cleared away the pots, washed up and then sat down with my plans. I had measured up the area and drawn a diagram to scale. I was working out what area I would ideally be devoting to which crop, and how to arrange the beds to maximise yield. I was absorbed in my work, so I didn't hear the kitchen door open. I suddenly became aware of being watched, and jumped out of my skin, but it was Stanley. 'Good grief! I'll have to ask you to wipe the oil off that hinge. At least when the door squeaked I couldn't be scared half to death!'

'Sorry, I didn't mean to frighten you. I just came in for some tea, but you looked so absorbed I didn't like to disturb you. What are you doing?'

'I'm making a plan for a market garden.'

'Where's it to be?'

'Here. I'm going to have more time when Aunty Nellie comes to be our housekeeper.'

'That's champion: you won't know yourself. You've had a hard time of it, managing.'

'Yes, I have. It's been a terrible year.' I almost told him it was the anniversary, but decided against it: forwards, not backwards. 'But things are going to get better. Here, I'll put the kettle on. Sorry, it's past time: you must be parched. I lost track.'

He put a gentle hand on my shoulder and pressed me back into my seat. 'No, no, I'll do it. You go on with your work. That's a clever idea, how you've cut out templates for the different areas. I bet they're to scale as well.'

I looked up with a flash of temper. 'Of course they're to scale! Don't patronise me!'

He gave me a slow smile and turned to the kettle, muttering.

I couldn't stand it any more. I needed to know how he felt. 'What? What are you saying?'

'I said, you are such a red-head.'

'What do you mean?'

He turned to look at me. 'I love how you flash with temper then subside, all serene.'

I felt the blush rising from my neck, but simultaneously felt a build-up of suspicion and resentment.

'What are you playing at?'

'How do you mean?'

'You're walking out with Izzy. I don't think she'd like you making eyes at me.'

'I'm not walking out with Izzy,' his tone was reasonable, not surprised or indignant.

128

'Well it certainly looks that way.'

'Izzy's a great girl, full of fun. She's done a lot for me, brought me out of myself. For a long time, you know, I couldn't smile or laugh. Thought I never would again, but coming here, being with you, all of you I mean. It's saved me. I didn't care whether I lived or died. I felt nothing until I came here. She knows I don't feel that way about her: we've talked about it. She feels the same: we're great pals. She has aspirations, that one.'

It was the longest speech I'd ever heard him say, and I was profoundly touched. I thought hard before I replied, aware that I could have responded in several different ways. Finally, I said, 'Have you got time to take a break and sit and have a chat?'

'If you're sure I'm not disturbing you, I'd like that.'

The hour we spent together at the kitchen table is etched on my memory, not as words, but as emotions and pictures. I can still see his face, so serious and watchful at first, caught in the light from the window like a sepia photograph. At one point, I got up and lit the oil-lamp, and its glow cast his face in amber light, his features so fine and regular that he could have been a painting by Rembrandt. And all the time, his eyes were on me: even when I looked up from explaining something about my plans, I was aware he was looking at me and not the paper. We spoke of families and of what made us happy, of the wider world and the changes wrought by the cataclysm that we had lived through, the war to end all wars. At one point, I remember he astonished me by quoting Tennyson: 'The old order changeth, yielding place to new, and God fulfils himself in many ways.' My face must have been a picture, for he said, 'Who's being patronising now? You forget I was taught by Miss Ashworth too.' He did not speak of his own experiences beyond what he had already said about how he felt when he came to us. I loved every minute of it, and felt alive in every fibre of my being. By the end of that hour, my world had shifted on its axis. I told him this some time later, and he replied that that was exactly how he had felt when he first saw me after the war.

The spell was broken by the sound of iron on cobbles: Dad had ridden Dolly, the grey Shire, to Farnworth Manor, and when we heard the sound of hooves, an unspoken question and answer passed between us: we remained where we were. By the time Dad had stabled the horse and looked in on the cold forge, I think he knew what to expect when he opened the door. He stood silhouetted in the light from the doorway and beamed into the room, looking from one to the other. He behaved himself though, and there was no teasing: the beam subsided into a satisfied smile and he stepped inside to take off his coat and warm his hands at the range. 'Brr, there's a real chill tonight. I'll make a fresh pot of tea: I can see no-one's leaping up to put the kettle on!'

I wanted to know how his discussions had gone, but felt unwilling to let go of the feeling of liquid euphoria in my veins. When neither of us spoke, he sat down at the end of the table and looked at us both, and I could see that he was bursting to tell and I would not need to ask.

Finally, he could hold it in no longer. 'Well, I have news. Wonderful news. Though I must admit to a twinge of guilt - breaking up our inheritance and all that. Mr Farnworth has agreed to pay a generous price: he will buy any land that I decide to sell. I have agreed to re-draw the boundaries, and go back tomorrow with the deeds. We will then agree the price, formalise it with the land registry and sign the deeds with the lawyer. What do you say to that?' He directed his question at me, but his looks included Stanley.

Stanley, however, was embarrassed now. He stood up, and was about to take his leave, evidently seeing this as private family business. Dad stopped him, and I froze inside, praying that he would not make any assumptions, or trample on the tender shoots of our feelings for each other.

I need not have worried: 'No lad, I'd value your opinion if you've a mind to stick in your four penn'orth. I know you're no farmer, but if you're to stay on and finish your apprenticeship, you've an interest in the family business. I've a map here, look.' He took a crushed roll of paper from his back pocket and spread it on the table. As Stanley bent his head to look at the rough diagram, Dad winked at me with a broad smile.

And so, dear reader, you will wonder when we kissed, and whether the course of our love ran smooth. I don't know you, but you know me by now. I am a creature of discretion and shall draw a veil over our first kiss. Suffice it to say that it happened the very next day in the workshop, just as I had dreamed, although Stanley

130

wore a dry shirt and a soft corduroy waistcoat for the occasion, and I my prettiest dress. I will tell you that when I entered the workshop, my hair was pinned up, and when I came out, it was down. And tousled. I will tell you that I entered as a pale young maiden, untouched by human hand, and I left with a blush that extended from my face to my toes and all parts in-between. I had also learnt to generate my own electricity, and if you had touched me as I floated across the yard, your hair would have stood on end.

Chapter Eighteen

I sat at the table, running my fingers over the watermarks, knots and cracks with a sense of wonder. 'I'm amazed at this place. It looks just as I imagined it would. Was all this furniture, the dresser and pots and things, was it all here when you came?'

'Yes.'

'I wonder how much of it is original?'

'I'm afraid I know nothing of its history.'

'Why did you choose to live in a house like this if you have no feeling for history?'

'I didn't say I had no feeling for history. On the contrary.'

'Sorry, I mean, given that you must hit your head on those beams fairly often, it seems a strange choice.'

'It was the only choice. At the time.'

He had remained standing, his back to the sink, but now he came to sit down at the other end of the table, where he remained, unnaturally still and looking at his hands clasped on the table in front of him. I saw that the knuckles were clenched white.

There was a ticking silence while I considered how to proceed. I genuinely wanted to know, maybe even to help, but I felt as though I was circling a minefield.

'When did you move in?'

'Last year.'

'Alone?' That was stupid, but I couldn't help it.

He glanced up at me, and I saw that his eyes were the grey-blue of the sea under cloud.

'Yes, alone.'

'Except for Seamus.'

'No, I got Seamus a few weeks later. The natives were too friendly.'

'I guess you're not into coffee mornings?'

'No.'

'You wear a wedding ring.'

'Yes.' He hadn't looked up.

I tried a change of tack, but it came out clumsily: the answer was so patently clear. 'So, are you happy here?'

133

He looked up at me then, and his eyes were darker than before. Abashed, I blinked and looked away. When I looked back, he was studying his hands again.

The clock ticked on.

'So, what do you do with your time?'

I fully expected to be rebuffed, maybe even asked to leave.

Instead, he sighed deeply and involuntarily and turned his eyes to the empty grate. 'I read, I watch films, I keep abreast of current affairs.'

When I spoke, the ice trembled under my foot. I knew it was too soon. 'And drink.'

He looked up at me sharply, defensively. 'Yes, I drink.' For a few moments, I really thought he would open up, but I saw him reach a decision and rise to his feet slowly. When he spoke, his voice was tired. 'Now, if you've seen enough, I'd like you to leave.'

I stayed where I was, my face impassive rather than defiant. 'I'm sorry. That was crass of me. Can we just pretend I never said it?'

I held my breath while he stood still: he seemed to be considering forgiveness as a new concept. Finally, he placed his chair back under the table neatly. 'I find I can forgive your intrusive question, but I am still asking you to leave.'

I stood up and watched as he went to the door, standing back to let me pass. The oblong of bright sunshine seemed dazzling and I felt my pupils contract. I stopped at the doorway and extended my hand. His formality had touched me, and I was anxious to leave on the best terms I could salvage.

It was his turn to pause, but only briefly: I felt again the warm frisson of his hand closing over mine. This time the blush seemed to start at my wrist.

I walked home slowly, my rucksack slung over my shoulder, and it was only when a little girl pointed at my face as she passed that I remembered what I must look like. I speeded up and was thankful to get to the house without seeing anyone from next door. I needed to digest what had happened before I thought about telling Beth.

When I emptied my rucksack, I saw that I'd missed a call from Rosie: it must have come as I was crashing through the undergrowth. She'd never normally ring me in the working day, so I guessed she'd heard about the job with Booths and I was right. She was ecstatic, chattering on and on about what they'd said, her new contract, how she was going to break it to her boss. She was so excited that I forgave her completely for forgetting to ask how I was, besides which, I'd hardly have known how to answer.

I stayed in the shower for a long time, musing about things and trying to get my thoughts in order. I was going to be phoning Paul that night and it helped me to focus. I'd only been here three days, but a lot had happened and I was quite certain I was going to stay, for lots of reasons. I genuinely did want to renovate the house, and I wanted to pursue the family research. I decided that these were both valid reasons, ones he could blandly tell other people: it seems uncharitable, but I knew that was what mattered to him most.

The bathroom mirror cast my face in a flattering light, and as I dabbed antiseptic on the cut across my cheek, I studied my reflection. The skin was clear and pale, with lines in the right places, recording the smiles not the frowns. My freckles had faded since I was a child, but a touch of sunshine brought them out again, and my nose and cheeks were speckled like an egg. Without mascara, my lashes were practically invisible, giving my eyes a striking alien look which reminded me of Tilda Swinton. I'd been in the habit of putting on the same make-up first thing every day, barely pausing to look at myself objectively, just anxious to put the best gloss on reality: I was haunted by that Sylvia Plath poem where a woman sees her future self rising towards her in the mirror like a terrible fish. But now, when I took a step back and really looked, I liked what I saw, even the wild curls, and I gave my naked face a tentative smile. It felt like a re-acquaintance with an old friend.

I made myself a sandwich and went out into the yard to sit on an upturned crate and eat it. Surveying the yard, I was thinking about starting some home improvements when a male voice I didn't recognize said, 'Are you going to get rid of that shed?'

A tall dark figure in a grey hoodie emerged from the shadows at Beth's back door. This must be Jason. Behind him was a replicant who neither moved nor spoke.

135

I decided to play it his way. 'No, why?'

'It's crap. It's falling down.'

'I like it though. It was my granddad's.'

'It takes sun off our yard.'

'For what, about an hour a day in a strip two metres wide? You'll be ok for vitamin D, don't worry.'

With a dismissive snort, he melted back into the shadows.

There's something about September sunshine: it's so precious because we know what's coming, and the days are getting shorter. I definitely needed some garden furniture: in fact we still had that green plastic set that I'd kept for Rosie, only for her to turn her nose up at it. I decided to go and get my trusty A4 pad and sit out there whilst I thought through my plan of attack: priorities and decorating. Come to think of it, there were several things we had at home that I could use here without them being missed, and I started making a separate list and thinking about hiring a van. I was quite engrossed, and I knew I'd heard Beth's front door slam, so I was surprised a while later when Jason's voice came out of the shadows again.

'What you doing?'

This was progress. 'Writing a list. What are you doing?'

'Just hanging, y'know.'

'I'm Annie, by the way.'

'Yeah, mum said.'

'And you are …?'

'Jace.'

'Good to meet you Jace. Shall I call you Jace?'

'Nah, sounds stupid. Jason.'

I'd thought about jumping up to shake hands, but was pretty confident I'd be rejected as he hadn't moved from the back door, so I stayed where I was and I went back to my list.

Maybe he expected to be bombarded with questions and my apparent indifference intrigued him, who knows, but after a few minutes I became aware that he'd left the doorstep and was watching me from the shadows.

'What's the list?'

I considered teasing him about his curiosity, but decided against it. Softly softly catchee monkey.

136

'Stuff I want to do to the house.'

'And the yard.'

'Yes, and the yard.'

'If you're getting rid of that shed, I'll have it.'

This stopped me in my tracks and I gave him a quizzical look. 'What, for revenge? So you can take my sun?'

He looked a bit abashed as came out into the light. I saw that he was tall and lean and stooped, with a dark raven-wing of hair that fell across his eyes. 'No, just somewhere to ... hang out.'

It sounded so plaintive that I nearly offered to buy him one, but instead said, 'No, I'm really attached to it.'

There was no response, but he was still there, so after a few moments, without lifting my head, I asked him where he and his friends "hung out".

'Nowhere.'

'Well, as the great philosopher Eccles once said, everybody has to be somewhere.'

'Eh?'

'Never mind.'

'That the Goon Show, is it?'

Astonished, I looked up at him and there was actually a little smile at one corner of his mouth.

'Yes, yes it is. Have you heard them?'

'Yeah, my granddad used to play them. Most of it was crap, but his laugh made me laugh.'

'Ah, that's nice.'

The scowl was back. 'Yeah, anyway.' He turned to go, but I felt we were getting somewhere, so on impulse I said, 'Have you got a job?'

He practically spat the words, 'Yeah, right.'

'Would you like to help me?'

Suspicious now, he looked back at me over his shoulder. 'Like what?'

'Well, that depends on you. What are you good at?'

'Nowt.'

'No, really, are you good with your hands?' What a thing to say to a teenage boy, but there was no other way of putting it.

137

Predictably, he smirked as he turned away again, suddenly bashful. 'Dunno.'

'Well, did you do anything practical at school? Woodwork? Metalwork?' Even as I asked the question, I knew the answer. The National Curriculum had made sure such subjects were squeezed out.

'Nah.' But he wasn't walking away.

'Have you done any practical stuff for your mum or anyone? Decorating? Made anything?'

'Nah. Made a cake once.'

'Would you like to try?'

'What? Making a cake? Nah.'

I waited. One, two, three. 'No, not making a cake. I'll need help with quite a lot of things I plan to do to the house. If you know anyone who might like to help, who's got some aptitude,' I looked at him and saw that he knew what it meant, 'tell them to call round and we'll talk about it.'

He didn't answer at first, and I thought he'd gone, but then: 'I made a rabbit hutch.'

I was delighted, but kept my voice neutral. 'Did you? Can I see it?'

'Nah, gave it away.'

'Why?'

'Rabbit died.'

'Why?'

'It didn't like being in a cage.'

'Why?'

He regarded me with an amused smile: he was a good-looking lad when he smiled.

'It was a wild rabbit.'

'Oh dear. How old were you?'

'Bout twelve.'

'How old are you now?'

'Nineteen.'

'A-levels?'

'Yep.' It was like squeezing blood out of a stone. I gathered up my things.

'Look, Jason. I'm offering work, cash in hand, to the right person. Boy or girl, but I need someone reliable, physically able to help me lift things, climb ladders, decorate, maybe a bit of woodwork, things like that. I'm willing to pay above minimum wage. The hours will be unpredictable and they won't earn enough to interfere with jobseekers. If you or any of your friends might be interested, come and see me. Okay?'

'Okay.'

'Okay. Good. Nice to meet you, anyway.' And with that, I went inside and shut the door.

When six o'clock came round, I rang the house. Paul picked up after the third ring, something I'd seen him do before, even if he was right next to the phone. He didn't speak.

'Hello Paul.'

'Hello Annie.'

'Did you have a nice weekend?'

'Let's dispense with the idle chit-chat. When are you coming home?'

'I'm staying here, Paul.'

There was silence. Then, in a quieter voice, 'How long for?'

'I'm not sure, just for the time being. I'm going to renovate the house and I'm going to research my family tree.' I'd felt confident about saying this, but it sounded a bit lame now.

No reply. After a few moments, despite myself, I said gently, 'Is that ok with you?'

A deep sigh whistled down the line. 'It'll have to be.' But he didn't sound too heart-broken.

Heartened, I carried on, cheerfully, 'Are you away this week?'

'Yes, London three nights.'

'Back on Friday?'

'Yes.'

'Ok if I bring a van and collect a few things I'll need?'

He was on the alert now: the air between us hummed with suspicion. Finally he said, 'Have you got someone else?'

'No, have you?' The silence was loaded.

Finally, I broke it. 'Quite. Let's not go there, hey?' It was the first time I'd spoken to him with anything like sarcasm and I could feel him taking it in. When I spoke again, my voice had a new confidence. 'I'm just coming to get things like the wallpaper table, the tile-cutter, spare bedding and that old garden furniture. It's pointless me buying stuff when there are things I could use just sitting around in an empty house. I'll come while you're away so there won't be any embarrassing scenes.'

'What have you told people?'

I knew what he really wanted to know was whether I'd told them about his mistress. 'Nothing, don't worry. Just tell people whatever you like.'

'Right, ' his voice was hard. 'I will.' And he put the phone down.

I sat for a few moments with the phone humming in my hand, and I took the temperature of how I was feeling. One word summed it up: liberated.

Chapter Nineteen

I was free. My father's plans were agreed: money came to Chestnut Tree Farm. And soon after, mains water and drainage and electricity. Our lives were transformed. That spring was such an optimistic one for all of us, full of new life and hope and ideas and experiences, made all the more vivid because of what had gone before. It's a strange thing about grief. You think you will never get over it, that it will always be raw, always accompanied by physical pain, but over time the pain becomes muted and eventually it is absorbed into your body and your psyche: it simply becomes part of who you are.

The new mistress of Farnworth Manor burst upon our lives like a firework display. One beautiful May morning, I was planting my new plum trees when a gleaming chestnut mare clattered into the yard. I saw that the rider wore trousers and sat astride the horse, so I took it to be a man come to see the blacksmith, and turned back to my work. A few moments later, I was on my knees in the soil with my posterior lifted to the sun when an unfamiliar female voice with a pronounced accent bade me good morning and laughed aloud. Indignant, I sat back on my haunches and swept my hair back off my face as I turned and squinted up at the figure silhouetted against a single pristine cloud. In what must have been a rather hostile tone, I returned the greeting and bent to carry on with my work. I resented being approached by a stranger unannounced whilst I was in such an undignified position, and assumed she was waiting for someone. To my alarm, she came round the front of me, grasped both my soily hands and pulled me to my feet, still laughing. 'I vould rather address this end of you, if you don't mind!'

I stumbled to my feet, treading on my skirt hem, and felt my temper rising dangerously.

'Vhy do you wear skirts for zis job? I haf trousers. Life is so much better!'

Straightening up, I looked into such a clear, candid smiling face that I was instantly disarmed. She would then have been almost fifty, but her suntanned face and athletic build made her look much younger, and her auburn hair was touched with natural blonde highlights. I said, 'I'm sorry, who are you?'

She held out her hand and shook mine firmly. 'Freya Hertig, pleased to meet you. We will be neighbours.'

The penny dropped. 'Are you ... soon to be Mrs Farnworth?'

'In a manner of speaking, yes. I am soon to marry Mr Farnworth, yes, but I shall not be taking his name. It is, how do you say, a bone of contention. Ha!'

Astonished that such a thing was even possible, I was instantly intrigued by this woman, and instinctively grasped her hand again, 'I'm so pleased to meet you. Would you like a drink? Please come into the house.'

We walked together through the yard, where her horse was slurping thirstily from the trough, and looked in at the forge, where I introduced her to Dad and Stanley. Both went to wipe their hands, but Freya stepped in and grasped first Dad's then Stan's in her firm grip. She then turned back to me, saying, 'Esther and I have much to discuss. I will look forward to speaking to you later', and putting her arm through mine, she turned me back towards the kitchen. This was so unexpected and such a novelty that I found myself quite shy.

Whilst I made two jugs of lemon barley water and cut four slices of Aunty Nellie's lemon cake, Freya asked me questions: in five minutes she had extracted from me a concise history of my family. By the time I had handed a tray to Stanley (and snatched a kiss) and she'd carried the other to the picnic table he'd made, she had told me a concise history of hers: born in a village near Offenburg in southern Germany, she had moved to Manchester with her parents at eighteen, studied botany at Manchester University, married a fellow student and moved to Essex where they'd taken over his parents' farm. He'd died suddenly eight years later and she'd carried on alone. Now her parents were elderly, she'd decided to come back north, met Hugo, fallen in love and here she was!

Leaning backwards precariously, she surveyed my plot, which at the time was in its infancy. 'So, Esther, tell me about your plans.'

I told her everything: how I had left my vegetable garden unchanged for another season whilst I concentrated on planting a greater variety of flowers and fruits, both of which would bring in good money at market. As I went on outlining all my ideas for the coming years and gathering a head of steam, I became aware she was watching me with a wide smile. I faltered and came to a stop, taking a great swig of lemon barley water: I suddenly realised I was parched. Well, we were talking as equals, so I said with a smile, 'So, Freya, tell me about your plans.'

'Well, Esther, there is much to tell. I have many ideas. Have you heard of Rudolf Steiner?'

'Vaguely. I think Miss Ashworth must have mentioned him. She was our teacher.'

'Yes, I was introduced to her through a mutual acquaintance, Edith Rigby.'

'Oh yes! Miss Ashworth, Maud, has told me about her. She runs a school for mill girls in Preston, doesn't she?'

'Yes, I have known Edith for ten years: in fact, we met in Germany at a seminar given by Dr Steiner. He is an amazing man: a scientist, a philosopher and a social reformer amongst other things. Some of his more spiritual ideas give him a bad name in certain circles, but I don't let that put me off. Edith is keen on those ideas.'

'But what does Dr Steiner have to do with your plans for the farm?'

'Well, as Dr Steiner would say, your soil is pure. Your livestock are fed on plants grown on the farm, and your animals' manure is the only fertiliser you have used. Many farmers have trusted new science and bought industrial fertiliser. Do you know what this is made of?'

'No.'

'From crushed bones, from basic slag from steel-works, from chemicals such as postash, nitrates, superphosphates.'

'That sounds horrible.'

'It is horrible. In Essex, the farmers make a lot of money supplying London with milk. But London is greedy, so the farmers get greedy. They demand more and more of their land. The climate there is dry and the soil is clay. They plough more to grow more corn to feed the cattle. The soil is exhausted so they buy more chemicals and seed-mix. The soil gets sick, the crops do not thrive: the animals eat the corn made from sick soil and industrial chemicals. You see?'

143

'Yes.' I was horrified. She smiled gently and took a sip of lemon barley water.

'This is understandable, Esther. People have to live. They trust scientists to help them. It is the same in Europe. Dr Steiner is a famous man, a thinker. People ask him for his thoughts, and in Germany he is the focus of worried farmers who wonder why their land is sick. He is developing ideas: how to make our compost more dynamic, how to control pests and weeds without chemicals. These ideas I follow.'

She lifted her slice of lemon cake to her nose and inhaled deeply. 'Mmm, delicious! To sit in the spring sunshine in a lovely garden and eat delicious lemon cake! Truly we are blessed!' We ate our cake in silence: she in blissful contemplation of her blessings, and I in horrified contemplation of the farms she had described: I had never heard of such vast farms being worked so intensively, and I was fascinated to know more.

'How big are their dairy herds?'

'Some have thousands of cattle.'

My incredulity rose. 'But the milking! It must take hours and hours!'

'You have heard of milking machines? Well now there are huge industrial ones.'

I fell silent, thinking of the warm intimacy of the cowshed.

'You have no machines on this farm, Esther? None at all?'

I felt indignant now: 'We have a horse-rake! And a reaper!' I felt a huge hand settle on my head, and the bench creaked as Dad sat down beside me.

'Mrs Hertig means powered machinery, Esther. No, Miss, the rake and reaper are powered by Dolly and Prince, bless 'em, and I wouldn't have it any other way. George Roper gets a steam-engine in for threshing and baling, and the Toppings are buying a tractor that runs on petrol. Can't stand the smell meself. And another thing, what about the fellers?'

'Fellers?' It was clearly a word she hadn't come across.

'Well it was alright while the fellers were away in the war, but they're back now, and they need jobs. Tying the sheaves, building the stacks. Come harvest or ploughing, you get a contractor in with a bloody big binder, and what's the fellers going to do?

144

Stand and watch it? That doesn't put bread on the table! I've heard there's even a machine for muck-spreading! I'll have to go and see one of them in action, flinging manure hither and yon! Stand back Mr Contractor, or you'll get a bloody big lump of dung in yer smug gob!'

I think Freya only caught half of what Dad was saying, but she was so entertained by the sight of him laughing uproariously that she joined in. As we all subsided, Dad became serious again. 'But you know, I mean it. I don't know where all this is headed, but my gut tells me it's not going to be good for us.'

'No, I believe you are right, Mr Grenfell.' Freya's voice was grave and low, but when she stood up, she had a smile on her face. 'We can only do what we can do. We can look after our own. Our land, our animals, our families, our village. I want to be part of this village, and I hope my plans will help us all.' Turning to me, she held my hands across the table and I got to my feet. 'I feel we will work well together, Esther. I would like you to come to see me soon at the Manor. Will you come?'

'Yes, of course. When?'

'One week from today. Would that be fine for you? Any time after 2pm. We shall have afternoon tea together. What do you say?'

'That would be lovely, thank-you. I'll be there.'

When she'd gone, I leant on the fence for a while watching her ride away: not back towards the Manor, but off down the track towards the river, presumably exploring, or perhaps just letting the beautiful horse enjoy the day. I closed my eyes and let the spring sun warm my eyelids. A gentle tickle below my ear became warm breath, and Stanley's voice murmured, 'Mmm, the smell of sun on your skin,' as his lips caressed my neck. Trembling, I turned into his arms, whispering, 'Mmm, the smell of woodsmoke on yours.' Catching something distinctly less appealing, I pushed myself away from his chest: 'And the smell of an oily rag in your pocket!' With a rueful grin, he pulled a length of filthy cotton out of his leather waistcoat and tucked it into the back pocket of his trousers, then put an arm around my shoulders and guided me around the side of the barn, where we could be alone.

145

When we eventually emerged back into the sunlight and strolled back towards the forge, he asked me about Freya's visit.

'You should have come to meet her: she's lovely. Why didn't you come across with Dad?'

'I'm shy.'

'No, why didn't you?'

He faltered and looked away. 'It was her accent, to be honest. It'll take me a bit to get used to hearing that accent around here.'

I stopped and looked at him, unsure how to respond, and faintly irritated that he'd even thought of her nationality. Finally, I said, 'Well, she and I are going to be great friends, so you'd better get used to it.' And with that, I walked away. Looking back, I recognise that moment for what it was.

Chapter Twenty

The following morning, there was an old rabbit-hutch on my side of the wall. I smiled when I saw it and wondered whether Beth had had a hand in its appearance. No matter: I had a quick look over it and saw that despite the bottom being rotten and buckled, the hinges were level and the door still swung open freely. The groove in the screw-heads had been lined up in a way that indicated attention to detail. The piece of wood used as a swivel-fastener was smoothly honed and the screw was neatly central. It was good enough for me. Now there was just the matter of his personality, and of course I'd need to talk to Beth. I reached over and put the hutch back in their yard and went inside to sort out the van-rental.

An hour later, there was a knock at the front door. It was Jason. He was still wearing the hoodie, but he was standing up straight and he looked me in the eye when he spoke. 'Hi.'

'Hi Jason, come on in.' I can still see him that first morning and remember how sullenly nervous he looked, how he attempted to cover his evident interest with monosyllabic answers. I spoke to Beth that evening, and although she was keen to come and 'have a neb', she agreed that Jason and I should go alone to Knutsford to collect the stuff. It would be his first-ever paid job, and he wouldn't want his mum with him.

In the van, he relaxed entirely and was even quite chatty as we circled Manchester and slipped into the leafy southern suburbs. He told me the kind of music he was into, and was patient with my complete lack of awareness of whole genres; he told me some funny things to look for on YouTube, and a bit about how he and his friends spent their time, how dead Adlington was, how they all wanted out but didn't know where they wanted to go or what they wanted to do. He told me that nobody had any money, and although they'd all done a bit of shop-lifting in their time, only one of his mates had been in real trouble with the police: 'He's a dickhead.'

When we got to the house, he went silent and I saw him taking it all in. It seemed so big to me now, and so profoundly quiet. I had my list, and I went round briskly collecting things in boxes while Jason carried the garden furniture out to the van. We both went into the garage, where gleaming tools were arrayed on the shelves, all top-of-the range, of course, and barely used.

'Right, I'll read you what's on my list and you put them in these two plastic boxes. Hammer drill, tile-cutter, set of screwdrivers …'

'Woah, slow down, these are heavy.' He bent to put the boxed drill into the box. 'Is your husband not going to mind us taking this stuff? It's all new. The tile-cutter's still in its box.'

'No, he won't miss it, don't worry. He used to do a bit of D.I.Y. when we were first married, but these tools are just for show. We pay other people nowadays.'

'Cool. Doing your bit for the economy, eh?'

'Yes, you could put it like that. Look, can I leave you to do this while I go and pack some clothes and stuff from upstairs? If you're hungry, get something to put you on. I want to get this over with. Then I want to go to Booths, and I'll treat you to lunch at their tea rooms. I'll be ready to go in about an hour. Ok?'

'Cool.'

It didn't take me long to pack my full-sized suitcase, and I resisted taking any pictures or anything Paul would miss. I got mum's old photograph albums and a box of her things that I'd kept, packed a couple of crates of books, a few other oddments and I was done. We loaded the van and drove away singing.

We did a lot of singing that autumn, Jason and I, often in different rooms to different tracks, loudly, competitively, cacophonously: him often accompanied by one of his mates. Beth never complained, in fact she and Adam sometimes competed, but the neighbours on the other side had occasion to object. I didn't blame them, and we moderated our volume after that.

Friends of Jason's often appeared, sometimes volunteering to help, but more often just sitting on the wall at the front and 'hanging out.' They didn't bother me, in fact I enjoyed their company and was quite touched at how well-behaved they were, politely asking to use the toilet or offering to hold a ladder. I sometimes used to see neighbours cross over to avoid walking past them, and wanted to knock on the window and shout, 'They won't bite!'

Leonard, though, was an exception. I saw him one day standing talking to a group of four lads and two girls who'd been there for a couple of hours, and I paused to watch. They were all attentive and apparently respectful to him, chuckling at whatever he was saying. He looked up at the window, caught my eye and waved, then reached down to pick up his shopping bag. One of the girls was bending down to stroke the dog, and when she stood up, she'd picked up his bag and was clearly going to carry it home for him. That was sweet enough, but when one of the lads leapt off the wall and took it off her, I initially thought there was going to be some inappropriate horseplay. I was just about to bang on the window when I saw that the pair of them walking away with Leonard: the girl had taken his arm and the boy was carrying the bag. I watched for a few minutes and when I saw the young couple come back arm-in-arm, I wished the whole little playlet had been witnessed by some of my more sceptical neighbours.

The noisy, sociable and productive days left me physically tired and ready for a night of quiet solitude, and I often used to get straight into the bath and spend the evening in my dressing-gown. I stopped doing that the first time I had an unexpected visitor.

It was a cold, windy, wet October night, and I had lain in the bath wishing I'd put the central heating on. When I got out, instead of going straight to pyjamas and fluffy dressing gown, I put on a warm grey wool maxi-dress, a cardigan and some thick socks and padded down the bare boards of the staircase. I'd made a Lancashire hotpot in the pressure cooker, and I was just eating it from a tray on my knee while I watched something I'd recorded when there was a knock on the front door.

When I saw the outline of a man's head in the semi-circle of frosted glass at the top of the door, I fleetingly thought of Paul, but not only did I know he was in Germany, but also this figure was too tall. Still, I opened the door with confidence and was astonished to find it was the man from the farm. Richard. He stood immobile, looking down, seemingly unaware that his face and hair were drenched and his Barbour was slick with rain. I didn't know whether to slam the door and ring for help or commiserate and invite him in. I know I made a surprised noise, and he slowly raised his eyes.

What I saw there gave me an involuntary chill, and my misgivings dissolved into pity. In the end, he spoke first.

'Hello Annie.'

'Hello Richard.'

He gestured towards my car: 'I saw you driving the MX5 last week, so I guessed this must be your house.'

'Yes.'

'I'm sorry to turn up unannounced, but I ... I wanted to tell you that I've found something you might be interested in.'

Now I was genuinely intrigued and decided to defy my remaining reservations. I stepped back. 'I'm sorry, do come in.' Knowing there would barely be room for both of us in the hallway, I took a few paces backwards and watched as he loomed onto the front step.

'Thank-you. '

'Come through, but mind yourself on the skirting board: the gloss is wet.'

As he emerged from the hall, I saw him notice the tray on the sofa. 'I'm sorry, I'm disturbing your meal.'

'No, no, it's fine, I'd pretty much finished.' I'd switched off the television and picked up the tray to take it into the kitchen. From there, I saw him standing still in the doorway, looking into the small room, his face reflecting the warm glow from the wood-burning stove. It was only the second time I'd lit it, and I'd been fully expecting to spend the evening barely able to concentrate on my book, constantly being lured to stare into the flames, rapt. Although I didn't yet have carpets down, a creamy new sheepskin rug was spread invitingly across the bare boards where I could wriggle my toes in it while I read or watched television. The reading lamp was lit, and a couple of tea-lights on the book-case. I had never loved a room as much as I did this one.

When I came out, wiping my hands, he was still standing in the doorway staring into the fire.

I smiled, 'It draws your eyes, doesn't it?'

He turned and looked at me with a dazed smile and I tried to ignore the effect on my insides. 'Yes, it really does. This is a lovely room.'

Delighted, I cast a glance around proudly, 'I know, I love it. Do come in, you're letting all the heat out.' I was only teasing, but I saw a flicker of something, and hastily tried to make amends. 'Are you hungry, by any chance? There's some stew: I make big quantities, more habit than good planning. The freezer's not big enough to store all the stuff I've made. You'd be very welcome.'

He stayed where he was. 'No, really. I don't want to intrude. I just came to tell you what I'd found.'

It surely struck us both that this was a strange time to turn up. I couldn't imagine that he'd just found it and dashed out into the rain to tell me, nor could I believe that he was just passing: I'd seen him drive past a couple of times, but as far as I knew he never walked anywhere away from the farm.

I hadn't answered, too preoccupied with my thoughts, and acutely aware of his very masculine presence in my ivory sanctuary.

'Annie?'

'Yes, sorry, I was just thinking …'

'Pardon me, but I probably know what you were thinking. I found it soon after your visit, and I've kept an eye out for you since, but haven't seen you around.' I had in fact been back to the Common twice since then, but had deliberately avoided going anywhere near the farm. 'I didn't want to draw attention by coming here in daylight, and I walked because there's rarely anywhere to park along here.'

Despite myself, I said, 'I understand,' although it still left the question of why come out in the rain, why tonight of all nights. And it struck me that he was wetter than I'd have expected for a ten-minute walk in intermittent light rain, especially at his pace.

I said, 'What have you found?' but I was thinking, 'Why are you here?'

'It's a small leather suitcase. I found it in a space at the back of the attic. It contains papers and photographs. Old ones. When I saw what was in it, I didn't go any further. I thought you'd like to be the first.'

My face must have expressed my excitement, as he went on, 'I knew you'd be pleased. I hadn't looked in the attic until then, and when I climbed up, at first I thought I was empty. I thought while I was up there, I might as well check it for leaks and so on. Anyway,

151

that's when I found it. Whenever you'd like to come and see it, just let me know.'

'When would be good for you?'

'Any time, really. Afternoons are best. My sleep patterns are somewhat erratic, but I'm always awake in the afternoons.'

'Would tomorrow be ok? I could come at about 3 o'clock?'

'Yes, three o'clock would be fine. I should say that I wouldn't be able to let you take it away without the owner's say-so.'

'Oh! You're renting?'

'Yes. Three o'clock then.' And then he was gone.

When I turned on the news at ten o'clock, I saw that four young soldiers of the 2nd Battalion The Royal Lancashire Regiment had been killed that day in Helmand province.

Chapter Twenty-one

I had the following morning to myself, and I roughly sketched out what I knew of the family tree to stretch my memory: the idea of seeing photographs was inordinately exciting to me. At that point, I hadn't done any work on it as we'd been so busy with the house. I saw myself spending cosy winter days reading and researching. Perhaps I could make a framed tree with photographs for any future grandchildren who might materialise.

My mum's single album of old photographs had nothing earlier than her wedding to Dad in 1956, although there was a large formal portrait of her, taken on her twenty-first birthday, which must have been during the war.

I was working on the small folding table I'd got from Ikea, and deliberately hadn't opened the laptop in order to make myself concentrate and assemble whatever memories and snatches of information my synapses could produce. I must confess that my mind kept wandering: Richard's handsome, haunted face had become a kind of mental screensaver since his reappearance last night. Giving myself the excuse of reading about Granddad's regiment, the Lancashire Fusiliers, I reached for my laptop and put the papers to one side.

He'd died when I was only eleven, so I could hardly blame myself for not appreciating that he was one of the Tommies we'd been told about in school. The First World War had been an unthinkable miasma of horror to me since I'd seen a black and white photograph in a school textbook that showed a dead horse lying in a lake of mud, tangled barbed wire and tortured tree-stumps. It was only when we studied First World War poetry at fourteen that I really got it, in fact became quite obsessed with the nobility and innocence of their sacrifice, the foolishness of the officers, the challenge to belief, the poignancy of their love for one another: the poetry in the pity. But somehow I'd never made the link to my own granddad, or at least never had the courage to askanyone about it.

Reading the history of the regiment, my mind was elsewhere. What I was really interested in was how the survivors could begin to cope with normal life. All I could remember of Granddad was his sweet nature, his gentle quietness, the way he could show me something on a walk and I'd learn, seemingly by osmosis. In my memories, he barely spoke. There were times, of course, when what he said stayed with me: the Pennines were 'the backbone of England', the first one to see Blackpool Tower would 'get a shiny penny', a nice cup of tea was 'nectar of the gods', and his recitation of Albert and the Lion transformed him, but generally my pictures of him were silent vignettes: making a tiny splint out of a matchstick and tenderly fixing it to the broken leg of a female blackbird; reaching for the highest blackberries and passing them down to me instead of putting them in his own bag; bending his powerful back to awkwardly swing me to and fro in an upturned stool. I still had that stool with its woven rush seat, and I marveled to think I could ever have sat between its legs. I remembered my grief when I arrived one summer and could no longer twine my long limbs through the holes and the burning of my all-consuming jealousy as I watched him swing my baby brother. As soon as they'd gone, though, he took me on his knee and promised to build me my very own swing in the doorway of the privy.

The only time his wartime experience came to my attention was when they got their first television and we watched Blue Peter together. Someone had brought in a tortoise that her grandfather had picked up on the beach at Gallipoli in 1917. The place meant nothing to me: I was simply astonished that the animal had lived so long and was busily conceiving the desire for a tortoise of my own when Granddad whispered, more to himself than to me, 'I was at Gallipoli.'

And so, what of Richard? He was roughly my age, so could conceivably have been in which wars? What a dreadful thought: Granddad's was meant to have been "the war to end all wars." I scrolled through all the conflicts where he could have seen active service. If we were the same age, whilst I was at university he could have been in Northern Ireland; when I was getting married and setting up home, he could have been in the Falklands, then there was the first Iraq War, Bosnia, Afghanistan, possibly the current Iraq War. Even in my limited understanding of warfare, they were all very different. What horrors might he have experienced? Mines, grenades, snipers, internment camps, trenches full of massacred

154

civilians, possible capture, even torture. Perhaps he'd been involved in questioning enemy forces: who knew what that did to a man? My mind baulked from empathy, and I realised that any attempt was an insult as I had so little ability to picture even a fraction of the reality. Even when filtered images reach our screens, my eyes and my mind turn away. What can I do?

And what can the wives do, and husbands, for that matter? How must it be to wave your soldier away, shiny-booted, not knowing what he's going to? How must it be to hold your kids, answer their questions, instil pride when all you can feel is cold fear? How must it be to receive letters, phone calls and emails and know that he's not telling you the half of it? And when he comes home, what then?

Richard wore a ring. Whatever happened between us, if he felt he could communicate with me, I owed it to the woman it represented to do what I could to help him. I knew I had to keep that in the forefront of my mind.

Yet, when I went to get changed in the middle of the afternoon, I asked myself what I was doing. When I put some mascara on and a bit of bronzer, I avoided looking into my reflected eyes. When I applied a light, natural-looking lipstick and puckered up out of habit, I froze and asked the woman in the mirror what she was playing at, then wiped it off with the back of my hand.

I folded the scribbled family tree into my back pocket and, as an afterthought, slipped the small box containing Granddad's medals and ribbons into my bag, slung it across my body, and strode out into the autumn sunshine. I'd been so absorbed that I hadn't realized what a beautiful day it was, and I was too early, so I nipped back for my camera. I had a thing about that tree, and the leaves would be gold by now. Maybe I'd get into photography and make my own cards. It was Rosie's birthday the following week and we were going to meet for lunch in Manchester; I'd make her a special card. It could be my first craft project. I occupied myself with light thoughts while I walked, and when the chestnut tree came in sight, it was resplendent: well worth several photographs.

The conkers would be on the ground by now: I'd take some close-ups too: I had time. So I climbed over the fence and walked across, pausing occasionally to take another shot. It really was such a splendid specimen, its outline huge and symmetrical, its colours richly metallic: golds, coppers, bronzes, flashing and glinting in the sun, its trunk and boughs powerful, sinuous, enduring. There must be a national register of such trees, I thought: I'll Google it, maybe the Woodland Trust will know of it and be able to estimate its age. I had a powerful sense that Esther loved this tree too, who wouldn't, and us with hair the colours of its autumn leaves? I hugged a flare of sisterly affinity for her, and hardly dared hope I'd soon see a picture of her face.

Richard was standing at the open door when I reached the gate, and his smile as I approached was relaxed and genuine. We shook hands, and he showed me to the table, where a small, dusty brown leather suitcase lay neatly central on an outspread newspaper.

I put my bag on a chair and looked up at him, excited. The air in the room smelt much fresher, and I noticed all the windows were open. He stood still by the open door, in his habitual military stance, legs and heels together, feet slightly splayed. He was wearing a crisply-textured blue cotton shirt buttoned high and his arms were folded, shoulders raised and squared. I was touched to see that his hair was freshly washed and neatly combed. When he spoke, his breath smelt of mints. He smiled and nodded towards the case. 'Go on then.'

I sat down, straightened my chair and slid the newspaper towards me. The leather was old and stiff, with stains of damp and oil. The catches were rusty but I knew he'd had them open, so I flicked them with my thumbs and lifted the lid. The smell of the damp back room of a second-hand bookshop crept up my nostrils and I inhaled the taste of discovery, feeling the flicker of anticipation in my chest. I turned my face to him, eyes alight, and he smiled warmly, his face reflecting my excitement. On the top was a framed photograph or picture, about A4 size, lying face down, its mildewed back slightly bowed and stained. I hooked a finger into the rusty ring attached to the card and lifted it.

I took a breath and stared into my own face. Esther drew my eye immediately, though she was standing at the edge of a group of six people, one of whom had a baby on her knee. In the same way as you hear your own name spoken in a crowd, the connection was instant. Her eyes were my eyes, her expression was a quizzical,

156

slightly ironic one that I'd glimpsed on my own face. Her hair, though rendered in monotone, caught the light of the flashbulb in a singular way that I noticed to a lesser extent in the tendrils of her mother's disorderly bun and perhaps of the little boy on her knee. My eyes locked back on Esther and I must have sat there with my mouth open for several moments. The spell was finally broken by Richard saying softly, 'That's why I knew it should be you.'

I couldn't tear my eyes away from the picture: 'I can't believe it. She must be, what, eighteen or nineteen here? So this must be my great-grandparents, and this dark-haired girl must be my grandma Izabel, and the twins – oh, adorable! – Lily and Rosie. And a baby! It looks like a boy: I didn't know there was a boy.'

The proud father towered over his family, the width of his shoulders throwing the composition slightly out of kilter: Esther and Izabel, through clearly tall and well-grown, were dwarfed by his height. The hand which rested on his wife's shoulder entirely obliterated her dress from the top of her puffed sleeve to the lace of her high neckline, and his fingers were unselfconsciously spread downwards towards her breast. His eyes were large and thickly lashed with an habitual crinkle at their outer edges: his luxuriant moustache couldn't cover the breadth of his smile.

There was so much to absorb, and although it had clearly been taken in a studio, with a painted backdrop of a mountain and a lake, their faces had a familiarity which broke through the formality, the sepia, the sea of the years. I saw echoes of mine and my brother's faces, I saw my mum in her own mother Izabel, a likeness I'd never noticed when they were alive; and at first I told myself that the twins, standing coyly on each side of their seated mother, had a look of my Rosie, with their curly dark hair.

The baby was a sturdy little fellow, irrepressibly stretching forward from his mother's knee to wave his chunky little fists towards the camera. As I looked from his gummy smile to the expressions of his family, I caught a kind of ruefulness in their expressions which enlivened what might otherwise have been a static portrait: there had perhaps been several previous attempts which had resulted in him being rendered a featureless blur. As I studied his cherubic grin, I felt a lump in my throat. Hello little man, what happened to you, then?

I had barely been aware of Richard sitting down beside me: warmth and the clean smell of coal tar soap crept up my arm and shoulder to raise the hairs on the side of my neck. I didn't dare turn to look at him: unless my senses deceived me, he was extremely close. Instead I spoke to the picture with a nervous laugh in my voice.

'Richard, I'm sorry, I want this picture with every fibre of my being. Have you told anyone about it?'

He didn't answer immediately, so I had to look round or my tension would have been obvious. I hoped he was looking at the photograph, but I could sense he was looking at the side of my face, in fact he could well have been looking for several minutes, I'd been so absorbed.

When my eyes met his, he held my gaze for a few moments longer than could be ignored, before he abruptly stood up and moved away. He finally answered me from behind my back, thankfully a couple of yards away, so I guessed he was by the Aga.

'No, no I haven't. I thought I'd wait to see what you said.'

'Well, obviously I'd like to take the whole case away and explore it at my leisure, but I can understand you feel that wouldn't be right. Who have you dealt with, renting the house?'

'Just the agents.'

'So you don't know who owns it?'

'No.'

'Well, I don't know what to say. I suppose a lot depends on what else is in here. If it's all purely family mementoes, then I can't imagine anyone objecting to me taking it.'

'Unless it's the owner's family too.'

'I don't see how it could be. My mum was Izabel's only child, Esther had none, neither did Lily, and I'm in touch with Great-Aunt Rosie's son in Australia.'

'What about the boy?'

'I don't know, really, he was never mentioned. Perhaps he died in infancy.' I looked back at the robust little chap and wondered.

'I think you should look through the contents and then we can decide whether to write a formal letter for the agent to pass on to the owners.'

I laughed ruefully, 'Curses upon your conscience! Seriously, though, I don't like to impose on you.'

He didn't answer straight away, and then he said quietly, 'It isn't an imposition. Stay as long as you like.'

Embarrassed, I laughed again, 'You might be sorry you said that when you're pushing me out the door at midnight!' Instantly I was sorry I'd said it, but he chuckled and lifted the kettle from the Aga.

'Would you like a cup of tea?'

'That would be lovely. Thank-you. Incidentally, I brought my granddad's medals and ribbons: would you mind having a look at them? I don't really know where to start finding out what they tell me.'

'Yes, of course, I'd be honoured.'

I was touched by that, and decided to take a risk. 'Honour means a lot to you, doesn't it? It's a sadly outdated concept, I think. I miss it.'

'Yes, yes I suppose it does. I think … I think it's pretty central to my character.'

'For naught I did in hate, but all in honour.'

'What?' his tone was sharp, defensive and I was reminded that I should tread carefully.

'Othello. Do you know Othello? I used to teach, and it was my favourite Shakespeare play.'

'What was that quote?' Far from sounding reassured, his voice was still sharp, suspicious. The air had changed in an instant and I didn't understand why.

'It's when Othello has killed Desdemona, his wife, whom he loved. He was tricked into it by the man he trusted most in the world, his lieutenant. He's justifying himself, or at least trying to explain why he did it: "An honourable murderer, if you will, for naught I did in hate, but all in honour." The whole action of the play hinges on a soldier's sense of honour. It's the key to Othello's psychology.'

He was listening intently, the kettle almost comically still in his hand. I saw that what I'd said had clearly hit home. He seemed to be still absorbing it, and I got the distinct impression he was sifting it for its relevance. I cursed myself for not thinking before I

159

spoke. I'd better not say any more until I saw which way the wind blew.

Without speaking, he slowly turned and put the kettle down, then stood for a few moments, evidently deep in thought, with his hands on the Aga's rail and his head slightly bowed.

I turned back to the suitcase, but sat unseeing, alert to any sound or movement from behind me.

Finally, after what seemed an age, he said, 'I find that interesting. I don't know Othello. I've never seen any Shakespeare, and at school we read only Julius Caesar. Badly.'

I could have done a one-hour monologue about why I love the play, but I thought I'd said enough on the matter, so I just said, 'That's a pity.'

He came and sat across from me, his hands clasped on the table. He seemed to have relaxed again, so I was surprised when he said, 'Tell me more about Othello.'

'Are you sure? I was a teacher, you know: we never know when to stop.'

Abruptly, he got up and walked away, muttering, 'You're right. I'll find out for myself.'

I still didn't know how this was going, and I was beginning to feel stirrings of resentment that he was frightening me again, but I really didn't want to blow my chance to look through the suitcase. Then he was back, carrying a sleek silver laptop, and he sat back down opposite me to open it up. 'You get on with looking through the case: I'll find out about Othello.'

I didn't like this brusque tone and thought I'd risk a tease. Again, it was out of my mouth before I'd thought it through. 'You've lived alone too long.'

He looked up sharply, 'What do you mean?'

I raised a quizzical eyebrow. 'Well, I might be being over-sensitive, but you know, you're an intimidating man. I think you forget.'

He looked at me for a few seconds, clearly deciding which way to take it; when his face broke into a big smile, relief flooded me. It felt like a real step forward.

'You're right. I'm used to giving orders and I've been on my own too long. Sorry.'

'You might want to avoid just putting Othello into Google.'

'Why? What do you mean?'

'Well, you want a synopsis, so put that, or plot. Or if you just want to know about the theme of honour, put that. The internet is full of essays on Othello.'

'Really? How come?'

'Well, it depends. Some people put them there because they're proud of them, I suppose. Some might see it as altruism, but others might deplore the opportunities for plagiarism, in fact, the outright invitations to plagiarise. In fact, academic plagiarism is a business.'

'Seriously? This is a whole new world to me.'

'Yes, seriously. See? No honour.'

His face turned from wonder to bleak seriousness, 'Yes, I despair of the young.'

'Oh no, I don't feel that at all. I despair for them, but not of them.'

'What do you mean? It's a fine distinction.'

'I know they've been demonised, and they live in a very different world from the one we grew up in, but you know, they're still as caring and funny and inventive as they ever were. As we were. They just need opportunities.'

'I don't agree. Everywhere I look, I see decay: standards, behaviour, manners. I don't understand this country any more.' He said it with such utter conviction, such profound bleakness, that I was silenced.

Finally, I said, 'Do you have any children?'

Without looking up from the screen, he said, 'Two boys, eight and ten. Second marriage.'

I was genuinely surprised, 'Oh! Lovely! Where are they?'

'With my wife.' He still hadn't raised his eyes.

'Oh? Where's that?'

Now he did look up. 'Why do you want to know?'

'Just interested. Just being friendly. It's what people do when they're getting to know each other – ask questions. And then, you know, you get asked questions back. In an ideal world. It's called conversation.' I looked down into the case to avoid seeing his reaction, but finally, he did reply, and his voice sounded toneless.

'They're in the marital home. They're fine. I keep in touch by email.'

I thought before I asked it, but I had to know. I spoke gently: 'Does your wife know where you are?'

'No she doesn't.'

'She must be worried.'

'Oh, I doubt it.'

'Does she have someone else?'

'You ask too many questions, Annie. I know you mean well, but that's intrusive.' He was getting up. 'Have you finished?'

'What? With the questions?'

'No, with the suitcase.'

Indignant now, I stood up too, my voice raised in indignation. 'No, you know I haven't. I've been too busy treading on eggshells! How can I possibly concentrate on this when I'm thinking - any minute now he's going to throw me out?'

We glared at each other across the table for a minute, and then his face melted into a smile. 'I will confess something Annie. And it costs me a lot to tell you this, not being a man much given to trust. Not any more, anyway.' He looked away, and then back to me. There was a long silence. 'At the moment I am struggling not to come round there and take you in my arms.'

'Oh.' My annoyance instantly deflated. Never had I felt so conflicted in my life. My instinct was to say what's stopping you? but I had promised myself and we had just been talking about honour. The image of a wife and two little boys rose to the surface of my mind and I clung onto it like a lifebuoy.

Entirely uncharacteristically, I started slowly. 'I … I don't know what to say. I can't deny that I am attracted to you, but I hardly know you, and … it's complicated, and we're both married… and it's too soon.'

'I know.' He shook his head as if to shake free an image of his own. 'Forgive me, it was presumptuous.'

'And actually, I have to say, how do you know I haven't got a six-foot docker for a husband?'

'I'm sorry. It was an impulse. I haven't given in to an impulse for a very long time.' We looked at each other with sad smiles, and finally he said, 'What do you want to do?'

162

'Well,' I said briskly, 'we're both civilized human beings. I'd like us to get to know each other. How about that for a start?'

'I'd like that, Annie, I'd like that very much. I love your fearlessness, your quick temper. You're not afraid of me.'

'Oh, I think you'll find I am, or I was.'

'I have ... I have struggled ... with all sorts of relationships, for some time now. I don't need to tell you all about it, let's just say I'm fully aware I am... irrevocably changed. I left home,' he took a deep breath, 'before I did any more damage to anyone I loved.'

It felt like the moment when you close a glass over a bee on the window.

'I can only imagine.'

He looked at me with surprise. 'That's exactly the right thing to say. Only another soldier can come anywhere near, and even then you feel that their experience is not your experience. It becomes ... impossible to function amongst ordinary people, civilians I mean.'

'How long have you considered yourself ... damaged?'

'Look, I'll make that cup of tea. Unless ... you'd like something stronger?'

'No, tea's fine thanks.' Make no digs, Annie, no teasing. The ice is thin.

Behind me, he carried on talking, perhaps finding it easier not to look into my eyes while he spoke. 'Different jobs, different effects. Innocents. Corrupt politicians. Disguised intentions. The first Gulf: burning oil, not seeing the sky for days. Lads killed and maimed. The cowardice of car-bombs. Civilian massacres. Children. Northern Ireland: tension, duplicity, snipers, organized crime, horrors done in the name of religion. The Balkans, I cannot begin to tell you. The effects are cumulative I suppose. When did I begin to question? I don't know, but once I started I couldn't stop. Questioning orders, politicians' motives, arms sales, waste of life, cannon fodder. It's a slippery slope. I drank, we all did, but soon no amount can stop the flashbacks, let you sleep, escape the pictures in your head, the sense of it all having been for nothing.'

'But you know it was not all for nothing.' Now it was my turn to struggle: I was resisting the urge to walk up behind him, slip

163

my arms around his waist and rest my head against his back. Just to offer some comfort, I told myself, and nearly succumbed, but my conscience hissed Not your job, Annie.

He turned round in the nick of time, stood up straight and gave a sort of shrug. 'You're right. It's just the way it is.'

'Have you had any help?'

'Help? You mean counseling? Yes. But you know, it goes against all your training, everything you are.'

'So what happened at home?'

'Milk?' He turned from the fridge, his face impassive.

'Yes please.'

Bringing the two mugs to the table, I saw him consider sitting next to me, but to my mixed relief, he sat opposite.

'It became impossible. She tried, God knows. I'm not sure I did. The kids were just bewildered at all the shouting. They'd been so excited when I came home, it broke my heart to see the way they looked at me after the first row. And Cath did her best, she really did. I know how hard it must be for them, too, the wives: they've had all the worry and the jobs mount up and they want to tell you about what school said and the boiler and how they had to cope alone. And none of it means anything. It's like looking up from a deep mine where you're sitting in the mud and deafening pitch darkness and seeing people chattering about in the sunshine on the surface and not being able to hear what they're saying but knowing that they can't see you down there.'

'God, I don't know what to say.'

'So you drink because at least then you can dull the pain a bit, hit the mute button, but it doesn't stop the flashbacks or drown the memories and you can't sleep so you need distraction: people talking on the radio or tv or anything just to distract you from what's going on in your head. So then because you can't sleep you stay downstairs and she gets resentful and bewildered and you row and row, and she gets scared and goes for help and you feel betrayed and you get … out of control.' His voice had dropped to a whisper.

He looked up at me and his eyes were dry but red-rimmed. 'So I left before I really hurt somebody.'

I could only look, and my face must have reflected what he didn't want to see.

164

'Don't start pitying me, Annie.'

'How can I not?'

He stood up again and seemed to step away.

'I'll tell you what, let's lighten the mood and I'll tell you some good stories from my army days. It wasn't all sturm und drang, you know.'

'No, but it wasn't all beer and skittles either, was it? Not like the adverts. Join the army, see the world and all that.' I was off now, feeling angry about the waste of our youngsters, but he talked me down with a long anecdote about an elaborate trick a group of them had played on one of their number. As he talked, properly animated for the first time, and doing different voices, I saw him in an entirely different light, as one of the lads, and glimpsed what he used to be.

When he finished and subsided into chuckles, I felt real warmth towards him and he saw it in my eyes. He stopped laughing abruptly and his face became entirely serious and disarmingly intense. Slowly, he spread both his hands out on the table and reached across to mine. I didn't have to think about it this time: I lay both of mine in both of his and felt them strongly enclosed, but kept my eyes down.

'Thank-you, Annie. I haven't laughed for a long time.'

I looked up now, but made to pull my hands away, instinctively not wanting the physical contact at the same time as eye-contact. 'I didn't do anything, that was just a really funny story. It's strange to think of lads being so completely daft in such dreadful circumstances.' My hands were still in his, and to extricate them would have seemed rude. I found I could cope with both, because his smile was a kind one, and not at all intense.

'It's what keeps you going, the camaraderie. Gallows humour, I suppose. No, it's just good to talk to you. I really don't want to embarrass you, but you refresh me. Take me out of myself. Your attractiveness is beside the point, but I have to say it's a bonus.'

'It's a relief to hear you say that.'

'Why?'

'Well, I think in the circumstances it's important to make distinctions.'

165

'How do you mean?' Though I could tell by his eyes that he knew exactly what I meant.

'I think you take my meaning. I think it's hard for a man and a woman to be friends if they're attracted to each other.'

'Go on.'

'Well, obviously I can only talk from a woman's point of view, and no offence, but you learn quite early on that boys will misinterpret your friendliness if they get a chance. I think it's one of the reasons why many young women settle into marriage: it's protection. You're marked as taken.'

He looked genuinely interested in what I was saying, so I warmed to my theme, and as I talked, I gently slipped my hands away. 'I think girls are somehow conditioned or programmed to care, to please, to make sure everyone's ok, to keep people happy. Some of them get themselves into quite nasty situations because of it, get taken advantage of. And they're vulnerable: there's no male equivalent of 'slag' or 'tart' or 'slapper' or 'whore'. That's why I think all this social networking is so harmful to youngsters, girls in particular. All the cruelty, the baiting, the name-calling – it's all happening under the radar, with no civilizing controls from alert adults or concerned peers.' I took a breath, and almost continued my rant, but I caught a look in his eyes, a disengagement, and stopped myself. 'Sorry, it's the one thing that really gets me going.'

He smiled gently, 'No, don't worry, it's interesting, just not what we were talking about.'

'No, sorry, you're right. It's relevant, but not to the job in hand.'

'The job in hand?'

'Establishing a footing for our relationship.'

I must have looked over-serious, because he laughed aloud. 'Well, this is all new to me, do carry on.'

I didn't return his smile: 'I'm serious though.' I felt myself on unfamiliar territory and the soil was boggy. I was anxious for myself as much as for him. 'I ... look, when you said you wanted to take me in your arms, I nearly let you. And then I would have been lost.'

'Lost?'

'Yes. Probably. Carried away. Heat of the moment and all that. But that would have been no way to start a friendship. Not for me. And it's unfair. I was feeling .. um…receptive because of …the current circumstances.'

'I think you're over-intellectualising.'

But my blood was up now. 'No, I'm not. I'm looking after myself. And you, actually. I can't stop thinking about your wife and children. How they must feel to not know where you are.' I registered a hardening in his eyes, but carried on regardless. 'I want us to be friends, but ... It's too soon – we hardly know each other and once you've crossed that line, well for me anyway, once you've physically ... you know ... even if it's only a kiss or a cuddle. Look, I've spent years and years looking after people, thinking of others, often doing things I didn't really want to do because someone else needed me to do them. I don't want to live like that any more. I've … well, I've kind of broken free, or I think I have. It's early days for me. And I've got to find my way. I can't go falling in love or anything. So, anyway, the point is …'

'I get your point.'

'No, listen,' again, a line from Othello had popped into my head. I took a breath and got my thoughts in order. 'When Othello is explaining to the Venetian council how he made Desdemona fall in love with him, because they think he did it by witchcraft, he tells them that it was when she listened to his stories of his life in the military: "She loved me for the dangers I had passed, And I loved her that she did pity them." That's how it worked for them. You can see that that's how it would work. And I felt like that too, momentarily. But once you've crossed that threshold, of physical contact, it's difficult to get back on an even footing, if you regret it, you see.'

'Yes, I see.' I must have been looking anxious, because he said, 'Really, I do see, and thank-you for your honesty and openness, and actually, for your sense of honour. And for your insights into psychology.' His smile was teasing now, and I felt myself relax. 'Now, you've hardly had a chance to look at the suitcase, and that's what you came for. I'll let you get on.' He re-awoke his laptop with a click. 'Just let me know if there's anything you need, a drink or a pen or anything. Ok?'

167

I was so thankful, and as I turned unseeing eyes to the suitcase, my mind replayed the conversation with a kind of fascinated horror. How could I have got in so deep so quickly? Still, I reassured myself, if I hadn't had that presence of mind, I'd have been in an awful lot deeper, I had no doubt whatsoever.

I gradually brought my eyes to focus on the contents of the case, a drift of yellowed paper and card, with small objects gathered in the corners, which seemed mostly to be wizened conkers, some on strings. In the centre of it all lay an old envelope with the words "For Bertie And No Other" written in faded brown ink in a large copperplate script. The envelope was sealed with wax which must once have been red, but had now faded to the colour of dried blood. Putting it carefully to one side, I worked my way through the rest of the contents, carefully laying them around the suitcase so that I could put them back in the order in which I'd found them. I had a strong sense that no-one else had ever moved these papers: there were slight traces of indentation from one layer to the next.

The surface layers contained home-made birthday cards, the children who made them seemingly getting younger as I moved down through the strata. The first ones I came across were made of collages: pictures of flowers and trees, mostly, but some more evidently made for a boy, with trains and cars carefully cut from magazines and newspapers. Some had 'For Our Brother' written in neat copperplate on the covers. I counted seven signed by Rosie and Lily, sometimes Lily and Rosie, and smiled to think of them bickering over the order of their names. The one that really arrested me had evidently been made when they were very young: it was the largest and the only one done as a drawing, on faded thick paper which must once have been bright white. It showed the horse-chestnut tree in full flower, with huge pinky-white candles like piles of candy-floss, illuminated by a strip of impossibly bright blue sky. Beneath the tree, the dark silhouette of a small child was shown swinging from an upturned stool which was suspended from the lower branches.

I stared at this picture for an age: it moved me utterly. Whatever had happened to this little boy, his sisters wanted to preserve him at his happiest. Perhaps an adult had helped with the drawing: I had no recollection of the exact configuration of the

168

branches, but there was an attention to detail that I imagined would be beyond small children. A knot-hole was drawn in particularly carefully, with whorls like a child's ear, and attention had been paid to the formation of the line of earth around the base of the trunk. I would take a picture of this card and go to the tree with it, to see how accurate the drawing was.

There were no other figures save the solitary child in the swing, his chunky little legs sticking straight out in front and his fists flailing the air for joy, a mop of red crayon curls spiraling away from his head like a clown's wig. I became aware that my eyes were burning with tears.

Before I put it aside, I noticed that there were traces of dust in a neat line round all four edges: this card had been framed soon after it was made.

Dabbing my eyes on the sleeve of my shirt, I put the cards carefully to one side and lifted a layer of tissue paper to find a pair of faded blue knitted bootees and matching mittens with whitened blue ribbons threaded round the wrists and ankles. A tiny bonnet had slipped out of the tissue paper and was crumpled against the conkers beneath.

I saw that the next layer was composed of cottons and linens, with some small object wrapped in one and what looked like a folded handkerchief in another envelope. A little tin mug with Bertie painted on the side in wobbly blue paint clanked against the conkers as I lifted a piece of fabric free. At the bottom of the case I could see a large pane of glass edged in passé-partout.

The cottons and linens all had an ornate A embroidered in blue cotton, which puzzled me for a moment, until I realized that Bertie's given name was probably Albert. In one handkerchief, a small gold heart-shaped locket with no chain nestled in tissue paper. I carefully prised it open and found a whorl of soft red hair the exact colour of my own. I softly closed it again, tears brimming my eyes. Another handkerchief was folded into an envelope, and when I carefully opened it, I found a long strand of wavy hair which must once have been red, but had now faded and was threaded with silver.

The sheet of glass I now saw was doubled, and between them was carefully pressed one of the cones of blossom from the chestnut tree.

169

I had been so transported by the contents of the suitcase, which had entered my soul in a way that felt utterly transformative, that it was a surprise when I looked up and saw that it was dark outside: Richard must have got up and put the side-lights on, unless they were on timers. He wasn't sitting opposite me, and I looked around, somewhat bewildered and disorientated. Everything I had been looking at had had a previous existence in this room. I had a sudden, precipitous sense of the vortex of time which had swallowed these people and would one day swallow me. I was filled with a curiously wistful feeling of melancholy mixed with a strong sense of being alive: life is here and now, this place, this moment, always.

Richard was sitting in an armchair which faced the empty grate, reading under a lamp which cast a rich gold light over his book and caught his shoulder, illuminating the right side of his face. His long legs were stretched out straight, crossed at the ankle, and I saw for the first time the glossy shine on his boots. As I watched, he lifted a hand from the book to rest his head against it, his elbow on the arm of the chair and his fingers pushed through his hair, deep in concentration. My heart turned over. A woman could fall in love with this man if she wasn't careful. What would happen if I just went over to him and touched his hand, or stroked his hair? Would he take hold of my hand tightly, pull me onto his lap? I would inhale the clean fresh smell of him, the coal tar and Vosene smell, bury my face in his neck, allow myself to be lifted … I brought myself to a stop by a supreme effort of will, drowning in a mixture of arousal and fearful expectation. I had not felt these stirrings for so long, and had thought I never would again, but now I realized that my body had simply been asleep. It filled me with a sense of hope and excitement that I forced myself to see was wider than this moment, this place, this man. This man was not mine.

I had to know whether it was really all over between him and his wife. I had to conjure his family into existence: I needed to know what they looked like, and the suitcase could provide me with a way of getting him to talk about his children.

I stirred in my seat, making the legs of the chair scrape on the wooden floor, and he looked round, smiling indulgently. 'Well,' he said, 'happy?'

'I can't begin to tell you what I'm feeling.' I paused and stared into space. 'The baby in the picture is called Bertie. I had never heard his name before, so I thought he must have died in infancy. But there's a letter here, sealed, that says "For Bertie and no other" which must mean he went missing, unless whoever wrote it was deluding themselves. Perhaps his mother, though it looks like a man's hand to me. There's a strand of what must be her hair, wrapped in a handkerchief someone embroidered for him. And there's a lock of his hair, which is exactly the same as mine. I really can't describe how moved I feel, how connected. I feel as though I've been transported. And it's so strange to think that all these things were new once, in this very room.' I lifted a child's card, a collage cut from other cards and decorated with large, wobbly, copperplate script in faded blue ink. 'Look at this: Rosie and Lily made this for their brother's birthday. Look, they put the year on it – 1921. They would have been about thirteen, I think. It was probably made here in this room, perhaps at this very table.'

He was still smiling, but there was something in his expression that told me he wasn't thinking only of these long-lost children. Would it be wrong to bring the subject up? Was I over-empathising, or had he simply cauterized his feelings towards his boys? Was it better that way? I felt a sudden plummeting in my confidence and decided to go no further down that route. For now.

I got up and put my hands on the back of my waist to stretch my back: I'd been so immersed that I'd stiffened up. He was watching me attentively as I straightened my back, and I instantly dismissed the idea of doing a yoga stretch with my arms above my head, something I would ordinarily have done without thinking.

He still hadn't spoken or moved from the chair, and I realised he was waiting for me to take the lead. Everything about the man, the light, the room, the moment was so tempting. The only sound was the ticking of an old-fashioned mantle clock over the hearth. I had a strong sensation of time being suspended somehow. It brought to mind the strange feeling I'd had under the horse-chestnut tree. A pivotal moment, and it was in my hands. I could step towards him and the die would be cast. My body yearned for it, all senses directed towards his magnetic presence like iron filings, tingling.

171

I felt that he knew exactly what was going through my mind, and his smile took on another quality, of pleasure and expectation. It broke the spell. He didn't know me well enough: that had the opposite effect on me from the one he'd have liked. Always contrary, I bridled and looked away.

'Well, I'd better be going. I hadn't realised how late it was.' I started carefully putting things back into the suitcase. 'So would you mind contacting the agent to see how to proceed? I'd happily write a letter to persuade them to let me take this.'

He had got up and come over to the table, and my shoulders tensed: if he'd taken me in his arms, I knew I would have had no real resistance. I couldn't bring myself to look at him and didn't even know what I wanted to see there – disappointment or lust?

When he spoke, his voice was kind. 'Yes, I'll do that tomorrow and let you know what they say. Actually, there's something else.' In his hand was an old brown envelope. 'It's in here. It's something for you to read. You can take it away. Just promise to bring it back tomorrow and I'll put it back where it belongs. I'm sorry, I took it out of the suitcase: it was on top of the picture.'

'What is it?'

'You'll see. I'm sorry, Annie. That I read it first. It just drew me in.'

I took the envelope and felt the shape of the slim notebook inside. My heart fluttered and I looked at him in an unguarded moment of open warmth.

'Would you like to stay for tea? I have some fresh pasta and a nice bottle of wine.'

I was surprised and touched. He had planned this, and he would never know how nearly it had worked. I held his eyes, smiled warmly and lied smoothly, 'That would have been lovely, thanks, but I'm having Beth round tonight for a curry and a girlie film. Beth's my neighbour. But thanks, another time maybe?'

As he opened the door, it felt like the final hurdle, and I held out my hand for the customary shake. He took it in both of his and held it. 'Thank-you for coming, Annie. I've enjoyed your company.'

'Thank-you for asking me, I really appreciate it.' Nervously, I went on in a pathetic comedy-pirate voice, 'There's treasure in that thar suitcase!'

I saw that he knew it was nerves: he smiled kindly, and I felt again the spreading warmth of being understood. In answer, he lifted my hand in both of his, kissed it tenderly, lowered it and released it, saying softly, 'Until tomorrow.' I stepped out into the cold night feeling transformed in my essence: I made my wobbly way across the cobbles generating my own light and heat.

When I got home, thankfully unnoticed, I ran myself a bath straight away, and re-discovered the pleasures I could give myself entirely without complications. As I lay there in the glowing aftermath, I felt a calm confidence that seemed to feed a regenerative strength into every bit of me. I was learning to love myself in more ways than one.

I wrapped myself in my warmest dressing gown and went downstairs to put another log on the fire and make myself a bowl of pasta. It was only when I'd eaten and washed up that I finally curled up on the sofa and let myself open the envelope.

Inside was an old grey school exercise book with a brittle yellow label: 'St Paul's Church of England School, Adlington.' And beneath, in faded brown ink, the name Esther Mary Grenfell. The hairs on my neck prickled, and I inhaled deeply as I opened it. A tissue-thin piece of pale blue notepaper fluttered onto my lap, covered in neat writing with generous loops.

I write this in hope that the next eyes to see it will be those of my lost brother Bertie. If you are not he, please close this copybook and return it to the case in its place of safety, for we have gathered its contents for my brother, and him alone.

The Cottage
Farnworth Manor
8th March 1938

Bertie, my darling boy, as I write this note, I try to think of you as the young man you are now, for wherever you are, you are almost twenty-one, and I am a middle-aged woman of thirty-eight. (Imagine that!) Much has changed while you've been gone, Bertie, and here I have written things down for you so you might know some of what has happened to your family. There is so much to tell. Izabel has a daughter, Maggie, your niece. She is full-grown and lives in Manchester now. She writes that she often studies faces on the busy streets, wondering if she'd know you if you passed by.

The contents of this case we assembled on your tenth birthday. We always marked your birthday, all of us together, and in here you will find treasures of your childhood and cards that we made for you each year.

Dad wrote you a letter, Bertie. You will find it beneath this copy-book. If you are reading this, you will know that he is dead. I can say no more of this for my heart breaks.

For fear that I will never see you again, I have written down the story of what happened after you were taken from us. There are things that I could not tell while Dad was alive, but now he is no longer here to feel pain, and for that I am, in a way, thankful. Izabel and I are estranged and it can never be mended.

I wrote this mainly for you, Bertie, but also for the child who never was. But mostly, if I am honest, I wrote it for myself. I have set down the truth, my truth, and in writing our story I can, in a way, bring us all together again.

Writing this note to you directly, I find I cannot think of what more to say. I only hope that by the time you read it, I will have held you in my arms once more.

Your loving sister
Esther

My eyes brimmed and a devastating sense of grief overwhelmed me: Bertie had clearly never come home, and now all of these people, my people, were gone. Fragments might still remain in the farmhouse, a coil of hair beneath a floorboard, a footprint in the dust of the attic, but I could never know them.

What I wasn't prepared for, even by reading her note, was that Esther would speak to me so directly. Her words and feelings can be heard clearly down the long corridor of the years. You have read some of her story here, alongside mine, and the connections between us often feel uncanny.

By the time she wrote it, shortly after the death of her father, she was living in a cottage in the grounds of Farnworth Manor. As I started to read the final section, my most fervent hope was to find out what had happened between Esther, Izabel and Stanley.

Chapter Twenty-two

When I arrived at Farnworth Manor for that first meeting, dressed in my Sunday best, I found the estate a hive of activity. It had always seemed such a serene place, like something that had arisen from the earth, made of local sandstone and surrounded by native woodland. But now, banging and hammering rang out on all sides like an army of crazed woodpeckers. As I walked up the drive, the noise rebounded from side to side, bouncing off the trees and echoing round the valley: I found it hard to determine where it was all coming from, but as I approached the lake, I could identify at least one source: two carpenters were constructing a wooden jetty and a ladder, presumably so that bathers wouldn't need to plodge through the muddy reeds.

A long, low motor car was parked in front of the house, and as I emerged from the wooded drive, a young man got out of the driver's seat and strolled up the front steps, turning for one last look at the car before heeling the front door closed. The windows of the house were all open, and sheets flapped in a light breeze. There was music coming from somewhere, and on the lawn two sleek silver dogs bounded around playfully. More banging and hammering seemed to be coming from the back of the house, so I walked around the side and looked in at the kitchen, hoping to see Izzy or Mrs Cobham. A smartly-dressed middle-aged man was sitting at the big kitchen table reading a newspaper. When I told him who I was, he introduced himself as Francis, Mr Farnworth's valet: the staff were all busy preparing the rooms for the wedding party, but Mr Farnworth's fiancée was apparently in one of the outbuildings beyond the stables.

Thanking him and leaving a message for Izzy, I set off round the back of the house. The stables were built of the same yellow sandstone and surrounded a cobbled courtyard on three sides. I'd seen a few of the horses before, including Freya's chestnut mare, but the two huge grey Shires were new, and I went over to let them snuffle their velvet noses in my cupped hands.

177

A voice behind me said, 'There's two more o'them to come. Big buggers, aren't they?'

I turned to see who'd spoken, and recognised him the moment he said, 'You're Tom Grenfell's girl, aren't you?' Before I could confirm it, he shook his head and muttered, 'Bad business, that.'

I extended my hand, 'Yes. Esther. Pleased to meet you. I've seen you at the smithy.'

He took off his cap, his hair springing up like a magpie, and shook my hand, 'Alfred Poxon, groom to the gentry, at your service.'

'Busy stables. All to the good, hey? More work for my Dad and Stan.'

'More work for all of us,' he said gloomily as he flattened down impertinent hair before replacing his cap. His eyes rolled in a long, lugubrious face. Bending towards me, he whispered, 'Too much goin' on around here for my liking. I just hope her nibs knows what she's doin'.' He gave me a long look. 'And as for that sister of yours, she's no better than she should be.' And with that, he loped away.

I turned back to the Shires and considered what he meant. Deciding not to let thoughts of Bertie or worries about Izzy overwhelm me, I set my face towards the open side of the courtyard, held my head high, and strode towards the outbuildings.

I hadn't realised quite how many there were, or how far the estate extended behind the house. More hammering was coming from a vast barn, so that's where I was heading when I saw Freya emerge from another building, accompanied by a man with a clipboard. She saw me and raised an arm in greeting but didn't beckon me over, so I waited while they finished their conversation, shook hands and went their separate ways. Freya came directly to me and kissed me on each cheek, a greeting which left me somewhat bewildered and blushing, but which I came to depend on.

'Welcome, welcome, Esther! These are exciting times and my head it spins with ideas! There is so much to think about, and I'm hoping you will agree to become my right-hand man! Come, let me show you around, then we'll sit and have tea in the arbour and talk about our plans.'

178

I wasn't required to respond, for she took my arm and set off at a brisk pace, talking all the while of building renovations, greenhouses, pineapple pits, walled gardens and crop varieties.

Emboldened by her familiar manner and her friendly demeanour, at one point I stood stock still and pulling on her arm, I cried, 'Woah there! I can't keep up! Can we start at the beginning?'

She laughed gaily and apologised: 'I'm sorry, Esther, I'm so excited! I really should be thinking about the wedding, but that's all in hand, and my mind is full of possibilities!'

'Look,' I said, 'do you have anything written down? Any plans I can see? I'm finding it difficult to take in. I don't know how I can help, but I'd like to in any way I can.'

'Yes, we can go to my study. I'll have the tea brought there.'

'No tea, thank-you: if I could just get a glass of water, we'll go to your study and I can look at the plans and then I can ask questions, and we'll take it from there.'

Grasping both my hands and looking into my eyes, she said, 'You are exactly what I need, Esther. Come.'

The room Freya had adopted as her study was a beautiful library at the back of the house. French windows opened onto a walled garden, where an ornate wrought-iron greenhouse was being erected against one wall. Spread out on a large mahogany table were diagrams and floor-plans, scribbled notes and letters, gardening books and notebooks. It was chaos.

That afternoon, a vision opened up for me, and I like to think it became clearer for Freya. Despite the gap in our ages, she made me feel like an equal from the start. It transpired that she had brought with her a farm manager from Essex, and several trusted workers. Her focus now was on the possibilities of the estate.

'The gardeners here, they are, how do you say, unimaginative.'

'You're not going to sack them?'

'No, on the contrary, we will be hiring many more, but they will need leadership, inspired leadership. Could you be you inspired, Esther?'

'I'm ... I'm unsure what you mean. Please explain to me your vision.'

Just then, the door opened and the Squire came in. His warm open face lit up to see Freya, and he bent to kiss her cheek. 'Hello, my love, are you hatching your plans to wreak havoc on my garden?' He came forward to shake my hand, 'Miss Grenfell, how lovely to see you here. I trust you are well?'

'Yes, thank-you sir.'

'Please, call me Hugo. So, how is the summit meeting progressing? Has my wife enticed you to join her endeavours?'

'I was just beginning to tell Esther my plans, darling. Would you like to stay?'

In answer, he smiled and nodded and sat down at the table beside me. 'Yes, I would, in fact if you don't mind, I'd like to contribute and talk to Esther about what our project will mean for the village. Is that acceptable to you, my love? I won't intrude for long.'

He turned to me. 'As you know, Esther, I have barely lived here since ... since you were a child, but now the house and gardens are going to burst into life! We have great plans, Freya and I.' He slipped an arm round her waist and she bent her head to kiss his brow. It seemed the most natural thing in the world, and it touched me deeply.

'We have a very large estate here, Esther, and most of it is unused, either for pleasure or productivity, but that is going to change.'

I was alarmed, and my face must have shown it, for his voice became reassuring. 'Don't worry, we will not be changing its essence. We both love the land. Let me explain.'

'First, the vista. This garden was conceived as a spectacle to be viewed from the windows, but to my mind, it looks somewhat lifeless. I am working with a garden designer to re-imagine it into areas, as a succession of outdoor rooms. Rock and water gardens are already under construction. There will be rose-clad pergolas and arbours. Woodland glades are being cleared and semi-wild areas will be encouraged. Romantic trysts will abound.' Embarrassed, I looked away as they exchanged warm glances.

Mr Farnworth seemed to recollect himself, and he stood up briskly. Smiling down at me, he said, 'The front of the house, I fondly imagine, is my domain. My fiancée, however, has designs on all the rest!' He grew serious as he said, 'The people of this village will be included in these plans, Esther. There will be work for very many of them, and a portion of the land is to be designated as allotments for the mill-workers. You may tell your friends and acquaintances that we would be pleased to receive expressions of interest. Now I will leave my fiancée to tell you more.' He reached for my hand: 'I will take my leave. I look forward to welcoming you on board our great enterprise.' And then he was gone.

Freya sat down in the seat he had vacated, somewhat calmer now. I must have looked preoccupied, for she reached for my hand and said gently, 'What are you thinking?'

'I was thinking about what this will mean for the village. Apart from farm-work, there's only the mills.' I hardly dared mention my sisters, but hope was ignited in me that their future might not lie amongst deafening machinery. The germ of an idea was forming. 'Please would you show me how you intend to divide up the land?'

She jumped up and unrolled a large sheet of paper across the top of everything on the table. When I got up to look, I grasped for the first time the extent of the estate, now that Chestnut Tree Farm was included. Between our farmhouse and the first row of mill cottages, the Common remained thankfully un-marked, apart from the area adjoining the chestnut tree field, which was clearly designated 'Allotments'. Over all the rest, lightly pencilled notes allocated areas of pasture, three fields of crop rotation, orchards and woodland. Around the Manor, the stables were clearly marked, but a dense tangle of scribbles and question marks obliterated the outlines of all the outbuildings and walled gardens. Freya gestured to this area, 'I don't know where to start. There are so many possibilities. I know only farming, and it has been such hard work. I can hardly believe that now I have a farm manager. I'm free at last to grow more interesting produce, to meet new people and help the community, and my mind is ...'

'Overwhelmed?'

'Yes, most definitely overwhelmed. Will you help me?'

'I'd love to.' It was too soon to expose my idea, exciting though it was. For now, I must confine myself to Freya's immediate concerns, so I said, 'I've just been doing exactly the same thing on a much smaller scale at home. Shall we start by making a larger-scale plan of the area around the house?'

She jumped up again, 'I have one here! It's just been made by the surveyor, but I did not want to write on it until my mind was clear.'

'Well let's make a rough copy of it that we can scribble on. I'll tell you what, let me do that so that I can get to know the lie of the land. Meanwhile, you make a list of the crops you're interested in growing. Are you looking to simply supply the house?'

'At first, yes, but eventually I'd like to think we can sell our produce.'

'At the market?'

'Yes, I suppose so. What do you think?'

'I think it depends on what you want to grow. There's not a lot of money about at the market. Apples and pears will always sell, but if you're looking at growing more unusual fruits like pineapples and strawberries, you might be better investigating outlets in the bigger towns.'

'I had the most beautiful strawberry cream tea at Booths in Preston. Have you ever been?'

I gave her a long look. 'No, I haven't.'

Blithely unaware, she chattered on. 'The Tea Rooms are delightful! Ornate willow pattern blue and white china, and exquisite confectionery! The orchestra is superb! I took tea with Edith Rigby when she introduced me to your friend Miss Ashworth. The shop is wonderful! They import foreign fruits: lemons, oranges, limes, even olives! I had not thought to find such things in the north. In Essex, I had them sent from Fortnum and Mason! We must go to Booths, you and I!'

I demurred and quietly got on with my sketch, reflecting on the contrast in our lives and feeling the stirring of something I couldn't name at the time. I felt no resentment towards Freya for her lack of understanding of how my life had been thus far, but something was solidifying in my mind, and it was only later that I recognised it as ambition. The thought of Edith Rigby and Miss Ashworth gave rise to quiet aspirations in me: this was a new world, and I was going to be a part of it. I had heard of Booths grocery shops, and the fine things they sold. Known as 'Men of Taste' they had a reputation for the quality of their produce and the fair treatment of their employees. I had looked in at the window of the branch in Chorley, where carriages lined up outside and the assistants came out to greet their well-off customers. If we knew what kinds of things those customers would like to try, we could focus our growing to a specific market.

I would keep my powder dry. I did not yet know what terms Freya could offer me. If they were not to my liking, I would keep my ideas to myself and plough my own furrow.

She had gone quiet, and I glanced over at her list, which was growing apace. Finally, she looked up, triumphant. 'Thinking of those cream teas gave me an idea. I would like to develop creams and cheeses, perhaps introduce some German varieties to the British palate. A hop garden! German beers, too! What do you think?'

My mind went straight to Stanley's misgivings about Freya's accent, and I said softly, 'Perhaps after a few years have passed. I doubt the British public would take kindly...'

Slightly abashed, she looked away quickly, but then recovered her bravado and flourished her list. 'Bees, though! I would love to make honey! And perhaps even wine! There is already a wonderful fully-established vine in one of the glasshouses! Would you like to see my ideas?'

As I looked into her glowing face, as open and enthusiastic as a child's, I felt immeasurably older than Freya, though the difference in our age was over twenty years. She could be a bold and innovative free-thinker, and I might be about to hitch my star to a comet. But my sister had taught me that a person could, in Lady Macbeth's words, "Look like the innocent flower, but be the serpent under it." Whilst I could suspect no evil intent, the uncharitable thought came to me that Freya could be an over-indulged fantasist who never followed anything through. I might give her all my best ideas and see them squandered.

Then again, if I could harness her power and resources for the real and lasting benefit of the village, I would do so.

It was a realisation that changed the course of my life and perhaps the future of Adlington. Hitherto, I'd allowed myself to be carried along on the waves of her energies, but if I was to make something of myself, I must learn to value my worth. It was time to put my cards on the table.

I laid down my pencil whilst I thought how to phrase my question.

'Freya, I must ask you this. How do you see my part in your plans?'

I watched her eyes closely, and she seemed nonplussed by the question. She didn't answer immediately, but seemed to take a deep breath. She started slowly. 'I know I might seem flighty to you now, but I'm just so happy and excited about the future. Please believe me when I say that I am serious about this enterprise. We are both hard workers, Esther, and my life so far has been more difficult than you might perhaps think. There are parallels in our lives: we are each at a turning point, and it seems to me that fate has brought us together. I have never truly belonged anywhere, and now at last I feel I can put down roots.' She smiled with a kind of rueful sadness. " I know my ...'

Emboldened, I said the first word that came into my head: 'Limitations?'

She laughed, 'Exactly. Limitations. You, I think, complement me. We would work well together, I believe. I have imagination and resources. You have practical and local knowledge. I would like to appoint you to be my right-hand man.'

It was my turn to laugh, and as I did so, relief and excitement flooded through me. 'We'll have to think of a different title, I think!'

She held my hands and squeezed. 'Yes, yes. Head of Produce? Market Specialist? Business Manager? Assistant Lady of the Manor?'

'Fruit Queen? Plum Fairy?'

We dissolved into giggles and the tears in my eyes were only partly from mirth. Bertie, I tell you I could just as easily have wept, such was the tumult of my heart. I felt... how can I tell you? How can I put into words the swirl of ideas and emotions? Excitement, of course, ambitious ideas, heart-warming visions of all the things I might be empowered to do, the liberation of being given the power to

184

do good, relief that I could keep Rosie and Lily from the grind of the mills, that I could perhaps help those girls already trapped into drudgery to lift themselves out, to improve their lot: a great swell of realisation that the clouds had suddenly swept apart and a great golden glow of heaven-sent opportunities lay before me.

But beneath it all, Bertie, there was always you. Beneath everything I thought and felt, there was always the dull ache of not knowing. There still is.

What I did then is what I have done for years: I conjure you into existence as you are now. You are tall and big-boned like our father. Your hair is copper-coloured, like mine, and you have a fine sprinkling of freckles on your tanned face: you do not like them, but they suit you. The girls love you. Your eyes are green like mine, but your lashes are darker, and the corners crinkle, like Dad's. You are fit and well, Bertie, in my imaginings. You are strong and fine and you are good with your hands, like Dad. I think you work with wood though, like Stanley. You are well-cared for and always have been. You were taken by people who had no child of their own: a couple who, in their sadness, could think only of how well they would love you, the good life they could give you. They saw the little barefoot boy by the river, his red hair lit by the sun, and they took him while Izabel slept. I cannot countenance the alternative. Such was their yearning, they could not think of the pain they would cause. In my best moments, I imagine them wealthy. In their minds, they were lifting you into comfort. I think of their fine house: you are Oliver and your adopted father is kindly and good-hearted like Mr Brownlow. Perhaps, like Mr Brownlow, a realisation will come, a moment of recognition. He will recognise what he has done, and he will tell you the truth. Perhaps soon, perhaps when you are twenty-one. Perhaps your Mr Brownlow will tell you on his deathbed.

You will come home, Bertie. I know it.

And so, you almost have reached the end of my story. If I am still alive when you read this, you will hear the rest from my own mouth. If I am dead, know that I found happiness and fulfilment in my work for Farnworth Manor, for Booths, and for the mill-girls. There is much, much more to tell, but this is not the place, nor does it seem necessary to burden you with my personal life. If you meet your sister Izabel, I trust you to be discreet about what you know.

I do not believe in a God, but for lack of any other blessing to leave you with: God Bless you, Bertie.

Your loving sister
Esther Grenfell.

Chapter Twenty-three

I couldn't sleep that night, as you can imagine. Esther had entered my soul: I felt as though I'd gained a sister, only to lose her in the same moment. I felt, in a way, possessed. Thinking about her led me to all kinds of deep and depressing thoughts about existence and death and family and legacy. She'd achieved a sort of immortality just by writing that account, but only because it had reached me, and I would pass it on. How much flotsam and jetsam in junk shops and salerooms was other people's attempts to be heard by the future? Postcards, letters and photo-albums, paintings and stories, all coherent when they're clustered around a living person, but once that person's dead, the glue between them dissolves and their meanings and significance evaporates.

What's life all about, hey? That old chestnut. If only Douglas Adams was right, and the answer was just forty-two. My mind kept coming back to An Arundel Tomb, the last line: "What will survive of us is love." You know how your brain pings around when you can't sleep, synapses firing away uncontrollably? In the end I had to go online to find the whole poem because it was driving me mad. I was no further forward in knowing what had happened to Bertie or to my granddad's love for Esther: she could have been my grandmother, in fact she should have been! Perhaps she was! And then I felt ashamed, as I had when I was a teenager, loathing my mother and believing I must have been adopted. But I had to know, and alone in the darkness of my bed, I stared at the glowing screen as if into an oracle or a crystal ball. It's weirdly difficult, in this time of information overload, to simply accept that you can't find something out. I couldn't accept it and I wouldn't. There had to be a way.

I gave Jason the next day off: it was cold and wet, and I felt like staying indoors by myself to let my thoughts settle. I had to know what happened. I was going find out, and there was someone who might even have the full story. Whether he'd tell me was an entirely different matter.

When I knocked on Leonard's door, I thought at first there was no-one in, but presently I heard shuffling footsteps, then the door opened and he peered out like a dormouse. When he saw it was me, his habitual smile broadened, but I saw a distinctly wary look flicker across his eyes. 'Hello love, what can I do for you?'

Thinking about it now, I can see I gave the wrong reply: 'I think you know.'

Instantly, he was on guard, and I saw his mouth settle into a determined line. 'Know? Sorry love, I've only just woken up. Bit slow on the uptake nowadays.'

'Can I come in?'

'Oo, no, I don't think so if you don't mind. As I say, I've just got up. See you later. Bye.' He was actually going to close the door, so I blurted it out with my customary diplomacy, 'What happened between Esther and my grandparents?'

I couldn't see his face as the door was almost closed. For a moment, there was only the sound of raindrops splatting onto my umbrella and the swoosh of car tyres sloshing through the waterlogged road behind me, then the door opened slowly, but only enough for him to peer round it. For a few moments, his glittery little sapphire eyes looked into mine with what felt like pity, then he blinked twice. 'Ee love, I'd leave it alone if I were you. They're all gone now anyway. Least said, soonest mended.' And with that, his head withdrew and the door softly closed.

Well, I ask you. What would you have done? I turned on my heel and practically marched back to my desk to start the research proper. There would be other old people in the area: I'd find them and ask them, even if it meant grilling every resident of the care home. I'd become a volunteer, get them talking about their reminiscences, and find out whether they knew anything about the manor, and if not, move onto the next! When I calmed down, I realized how heartless that was as a plan, though there might actually be some mileage in trying...

I'd had an email back from the Local History Library which I'd simply filed in a folder in my inbox: having seen that it included plenty of information, I had replied expressing my thanks but saved the detailed reading of it for just such a day as this. I set about planning my approach: everything I wanted to know centred around Esther, whose life could have disappeared without trace but hadn't. The farm had yielded clues, but the Farnworths and the manor could yield more. I decided to concentrate on that: rather than work from the past, I would focus on the present: I needed to know whether the family still existed and whether the manor was really still standing. If it was, I wanted to see it and thereby make connection with the family.

When I opened the email, I saw that I'd got a far better answer than I deserved for my garbled question: their reply was astonishingly thorough. It gave details of who was living in the Manor and its outbuildings in the 1891 Census, then further information from 1901, 1911 and 1921.

During the Second World War, the main house had indeed been used by the Ministry of Food, and after that, there was no further information. If, as Leonard had said, Freya had been threatened with internment, I could see why they would have moved to Switzerland. If they had never returned, and Mr Farnworth's only son was dead, who could possibly own it now?

I set about making a list of the people who might be able to tell me more: the Land Registry, the Public Records Office, the National Trust, English Heritage. Then I wrote a carefully-worded specific enquiry about the house and grounds after 1945, tailored the email to each recipient and sent it off in four directions.

Thinking of the grounds, I had the idea of sending off similar enquiries to the Forestry Commission and the Woodland Trust to see whether they had any information on their databases. I found a world of enthusiasm and altruism on their websites, including an Ancient Tree Register compiled by volunteers, some of whom rather touchingly measure the circumference of candidates by 'hugs'. I resolved to go and hug the chestnut tree and get it on the register. Who knew what other huggable trees were hidden in that neglected wood?

After this burst of fishing activity, I made myself a sandwich, and as I looked out at the leaden skies through rain trammeling runnels down the windows, I hugged myself for pleasure. The day was dark, the house was cosy, my feet were toasty in soft bed-socks. All the people I cared about were fine, to the best of my knowledge, and I had everything I needed: nothing was being asked of me. The only thought that intruded was the expectation that at any minute, Richard might knock at the door, but I felt more confident on my own territory, safe and able to deal with anything that might arise.

But he didn't come that day, and it was late the next evening when his distinctive one-two knock came at my door. At first, I thought it was on the soundtrack of the film Beth and I were watching. We'd eaten our curry, and the plates lay discarded on the bare floorboards at either side of the sofa. Our bottle of red wine was almost empty, and I'd just been about to put the film on pause for 'pees and pints' as Beth called a comfort break. I looked at my watch – 10.20pm. I touched the remote and listened. There it was again. Beth looked at me, one eyebrow raised, and I rolled my eyes theatrically, disloyally. When I opened the sitting-room door, I was aware of her craning over the back of the settee for a look.

He had his hands in his pockets and his shoulders hunched, and when he raised his face, I saw huge pupils reflected in the hall light. His red-rimmed eyes with yellowish whites brought Van Gogh's self-portraits to mind. The pupils didn't contract, and I could smell the gin on his breath. I thought about asking him in: Beth was there, so I'd be safe, but somehow I didn't want her to see him like this. When he spoke, his voice was only slightly slurred. 'Mmm, curry. I love curry.'

Brightly, loudly, I said, 'Yes, Beth's here and unfortunately we've eaten all of it or I'd have offered you some.' I saw this register, and his expression changed instantly into an approximation of businesslike seriousness.

'I just came to tell you that the agents say I've to keep the case. They'll get back to me.'

I couldn't hide my disappointment. 'Oh. Right. Okay, thanks for telling me.'

He leaned in close and in a stage whisper, said, 'But you can come any time you like. To look at it.' And he winked. That and the breath that closed my throat helped my future willpower enormously.

'Thank-you. I will. I'll be in touch. 'Bye Richard.' And I shut the door, stifling the concern for his welfare that immediately rose to the forefront of my mind, shattering my mental peace. I resolved to go and check on him first thing in the morning.

Beth was all agog, wide-eyed and giggling, 'He was well pissed! Good job I was here, missis, or you'd have been in trouble! Actually, you should have invited him in and we could have kept him as a sex slave!' She subsided onto the cushions, thoroughly entertained by the idea, and I tried to join in, though my heart wasn't in it.

In the morning, I reasoned that it would be a really bad idea to go to the farm alone, but I didn't want to embarrass him by taking Beth or Jason. There had to be a landline number. I went to the internet, googled the name of the farm and soon found the number of the agent's central offices in Manchester. I thought of a plausible story and then rang their local branch.

The woman who answered was warm and friendly, and as I explained that I had a delivery for the farm and needed to check whether there was anyone in before I made the trip, an unrelated thought was developing in the back of my mind.

'Sorry, love, I can't give out the number, but I can ring it for you if you like. I'll ask him to give you a call to arrange a time for your delivery.'

'That would be lovely. Could you tell him it's Esther's Flowers, please?' I gave her my mobile number, and as an afterthought said, 'Would you be kind enough to ring me back if there's no answer?'

'Course I will love, no problem. I haven't heard of Esther's Flowers, new business is it?'

'Yes, I'm just starting up. Actually, where is the farm? I don't know Adlington.'

'As you drive from Chorley, turn right into Park Road, drive up there for about a mile until the houses stop, and it's out on what they call the Common. Turn in as soon as you see a lane on your left.' I waited, one, two, three: she was a chatterbox, and I knew if I kept quiet, she'd be likely to go on. Sure enough: 'It's lovely up there, all peaceful. You wouldn't know it was there. I went once when we were changing tenants. Wish I could afford to live somewhere like that.'

'Is it expensive to rent, then?'

'Oo, yes, that's one of our most expensive properties. It's been on our books for donkey's years. Old Mr Winterson wanted to buy it himself, but it's not for sale.'

'Who owns it?'

'I don't know, we deal with solicitors. The rent goes to them.'

I thought quickly. 'Oh, I need a solicitor, what's their name?'

'Grace and Powell, on the High Street. Been here ages. I think they must have built their offices round that big desk of Mr Powell's! Oh, someone's just come in. Been nice talking to you, love', and she rang off.

I waited for half an hour, increasingly worried about Richard: there'd been something about his demeanour last night, a different kind of darkness that I hadn't noticed before. I was just about to give in and put my boots on when I heard a text come in. It was from a blocked number, but it said, 'Thanks for msg. Am ok. Apologies. See you later?'

Relieved but wary, I texted back, 'Come for coffee this afternoon? Am out from 6.' Which was another lie, but I reasoned it was a white one: I had to keep control in this relationship.

To distract myself, I got a roll of wallpaper, cut a metre off and spread it on my desk, face down, weighting the corners with cups. Then I sketched out a family tree, starting with Rosie and Mark in the centre at the bottom, and working upwards and outwards, Paul's family first. As I worked, I reflected that I probably knew his family tree better than he did. I imagined that his relatives were beginning to wonder why they hadn't had any birthday cards or phone calls lately, and of course there was the looming presence of Christmas on the horizon. Time enough to think about that.

At three o'clock on the dot, two smart raps startled me out of my absorption. I had been playing lovely soothing arias to calm my nerves, and considered turning the iPod off, but dismissed the idea: let him see I was busy and not waiting for him.

This time, he was standing up straight and his eyes were focused. He'd taken care over his appearance and his breath smelt strongly of mints. He looked directly at me and said in a gruff voice, 'Sorry about last night. No excuses. I shouldn't have come.'

192

'No problems. It was my fault: I should have brought the envelope back. You were perfectly civilized. In fact, you could have come in to meet Beth.'

'No, I wasn't fit for human company. Even Seamus backs away from me when I'm like that.'

'Forget it, really, it's fine. Come on in and I'll put some coffee on. Cold samosa to go with it?'

I heard him chuckle behind me as I led the way to the kitchen.

'No, thanks. I'll resist.'

'Only joking, there are none left. I do however have some rather delicious lemon drizzle cake made with my own fair hand. Can I tempt you?' It wasn't meant to be coquettish, but when I turned to him, I saw that he'd taken it that way. His answer, though, was rueful rather than flirtatious: 'Oh, I think you know you could tempt me.'

'Sorry, I should learn to think before I speak.' Then, briskly, 'So cake, yes?'

'Yes please.'

'Do take your coat off: this is a proper, pre-arranged visit. Civilised, with etiquette. There may well be doilies.'

'No! Not doilies! It'll be fairy cakes and napkins next!' As I busied myself with my filter machine, he said, 'Mind if I look outside?'

'No, go on, help yourself. I haven't done anything with the yard yet: I'm saving that till spring. And don't for goodness' sake ask me if I'm going to knock down Granddad's woodshed. I'm not.'

When he came back in, he said, 'I see what you mean. It looks ready to fall down.'

'Yes, I think it's only held up by its contents. I prised the door open and it's stuffed to the gunnels with old deckchairs, tarpaulins, buckets, brooms, motorbike parts. I can't even see whether Granddad's workbench is still in there, let alone any of his tools. Jason and his friends keep wanting to empty it, but I'm kind of possessive about it. I want to unpack it in my own time, unobserved, kind of like the suitcase, and certainly Esther's story.' I glanced round at him, hoping to transmit how much I wanted to keep the notebook, but he wasn't looking at me. 'I'll leave it till the spring or summer, when I can spread everything out and explore at my leisure.'

'You might like to explore the outbuildings at the farm: I haven't opened any of them, just the barn I use as a garage. There's a huge bunch of rusty keys in the larder.'

'Oo, I'd love that! Who knows what I might find! So what did the agents say?'

'I think I told you last night. They're getting in touch with the owners.'

'Is that what they said? The owners?'

'Yes. Why?'

Just as I was wondering whether he had really rung them, or whether this was a cunning ruse to get me to come back, he said, 'Well, actually, maybe it was me that mentioned owners. Yes, come to think of it, I did the talking and the woman just said, "Right-o, will do. I'll ring you back when I hear anything." '

'Only I rang the agents this morning, as you know, to get your number, and she mentioned a firm of solicitors who deal with the farm. I made a note of the name because I'm trying to find out about the manor house.'

'What are you trying to find out?' his tone had changed: from pleasant chitchat I got the distinct sense we'd moved onto dangerous ground. I turned from the plates and cake-forks to glance at him, I hoped surreptitiously, but he was glaring at me, and looked away when I caught his eye.

'Well you know I'd like to get in there and see it.'

'You can't get in there. You've tried.' He was still sounding a touch aggressive, out of proportion to the topic, surely. I was a little unnerved, but I composed my face and turned to face him properly.

'What's wrong? Why don't you want me to find the house?'

He seemed to back down straight away, looking slightly abashed and ostentatiously going over to look at my bookshelves. I didn't catch his answer at first.

'Pardon?'

'I just think you should leave well alone.'

194

I was intrigued now, and went through to the sitting room, cake knife in hand. "I'm not with you. Tell me what you really mean.'

'Or what? You'll stab me with the cake knife? I'm terrified.'

I smiled, but I was on a mission now, and not ready for play-fighting. 'Why don't you want me to find the house?'

He looked at me for a long moment, then shook his head and looked away again. "It'll be dangerous in there. It's impenetrable.'

'Don't worry, I've got ideas about that,' I was relieved it wasn't something more sinister, and went back to pour the coffee.

When I came in with the tray, he was sitting on the sofa, which suddenly looked dwarfed. Only last night, Beth and I had lolled on here and it had felt as big as a double bed. Now there seemed no way of sitting next to him that didn't seem unduly intimate. I dreaded the feel of his thigh along mine: I had to keep my senses in order.

He was staring into the empty stove: I had deliberately not lit it: no cosy romantic glowing logs wanted here, thank-you very much. Maybe another time.

'Could you just open out that folding table please?' It was done in an instant and I set the tray down, settling into the other end of the sofa, as far away as possible from those lean muscular thighs.

As I poured the coffee, he started to talk: 'I read Othello after you left, and I have to say it ... not wanting to sound self-pitying or anything, but probably failing abysmally: it rather upset my equilibrium.' I looked up, surprised, but didn't interrupt his flow. Something about his manner told me that he had prepared what he wanted to say. 'It really got to me. As you said, there's a lot about the psychology of a soldier. How being in the military affects your views, of yourself, of duty and honour and ... and your relationships. I began to see myself in him, and when Iago causes him to doubt...' He straightened up and leant forward towards the empty grate to lean his elbows on his thighs. 'Doubt is alien to a soldier. We can't tolerate doubt. There isn't time. Doubt's a luxury.'

'Negative capability.'

'What?'

195

'Sorry, nothing. Go on, please.'

"'To be once in doubt is once to be resolved. I'll see before I doubt; when I doubt, prove: And on the proof, there is no more but this: Away at once with love or jealousy!'"

'Yes, quite.'

'When I read those words, I froze. I knew of course what he was going to do. He loved her so much, but he was an innocent. He'd found someone he believed in ... with all his heart. You don't use your heart very much when you're in combat. You can't. So it atrophies. And when Iago, his trusted comrade. made him doubt her, he couldn't deal with it. It was all or nothing.'

"I had rather be a toad and live upon the vapour of a dungeon than keep a corner in the thing I love for others' uses."

He looked round at me then, and his eyes were full of pain. 'Yes, that's it. That's it exactly. And I thought, that's what I did, to Kath. She went for help, turned to others, and I felt betrayed. And I thought, that's it. It's over.'

Gently, I reached across and touched his arm. 'But now you know. And you regret it.'

'No, no, nothing as clean-cut as that. But I woke up. I've not wanted to hear from her. I've forbidden her from contacting me. I delete her emails. She tried tricks. She gave one the title 'Luke ill' just to make me open it. He wasn't, but I was so angry that she'd tricked me. But it's understandable, isn't it?'

I kept my tone neutral, no reproach. 'Of course it is. She loves you and wants you back.'

'No offence, Annie, but you don't know the first thing about it. Don't reach for platitudes. The point is, I was forced to reassess my own conduct, admit doubt into my mind.' He paused. 'And I haven't slept since.'

'I'm sorry.'

'No, don't blame yourself. Maybe it's what I needed. Since I've been here, I've found some peace. But at the cost of cutting everyone out of my life.' He looked at me. 'I have an elderly mother, and a sister, too. I haven't wanted anyone. I had to be on my own. To control my environment, kind of insulate myself. I haven't felt lonely, not once.'

'Oh, I know about that. The only time I've experienced real loneliness, I wasn't alone.'

'Your husband?'

'Do you know what, I think that's the first time you've asked me anything about my life.'

'I know.'

'Why is that, do you think?'

'I'll be honest with you. I was attracted to you from the first moment I saw you. I've always had a thing for red hair, and you were so feisty, standing in that field confronting a scary man and his scary dog with your chin up and flashing green lightening from those eyes. I suppose I just didn't want to admit the existence of a husband, or children. I suppose you have children?'

'Yes, I do. They're grown-up and married. That's why I'm here, really, tasting freedom and independence for the first time since, well ever really.'

'You're still wearing a wedding ring, though.'

'Yes, I don't know about the future. It's early days. Paul's not pushing me for a decision. There's a kind of status quo at the moment. Maybe he's happier too. I don't know.'

'You haven't talked?'

'No, we haven't really. Just practicalities. I'll possibly see him next week: it's our daughter's birthday and I'm meeting her for lunch in Manchester. She'd like him to come too, and I've no objection. The more civilized we can keep it, the better.'

'I can't imagine a man letting you go.'

'That's a lovely thing to say, thank-you. You're good for my confidence, you are. Drink your coffee.'

We both sat back, and for the first time, I felt relaxed in his company. We were on an even keel. But then I had to spoil it all by saying something stupid.

'So what's your objection to me at least trying to get to the house?'

The face he turned to me was mutinous. 'I thought I'd made it clear to you that I don't want that path opened up. It took me a long time to find this place. Nobody bothers me, I'm not overlooked, no hikers or ramblers, and the locals know to stay away.' He regarded me for a long moment, his face serious and

197

frankly intimidating. 'I can see you're still not convinced. I imagine you harbour ideas of getting me back with my wife. Don't be tempted to meddle, Annie. You know not what you do.' He continued staring at me and I felt myself being assessed. Eventually, he took a deep breath. 'Look, this is serious. I will tell you this because I trust you.' He paused and moved his face fractionally closer to mine, speaking these words in a curious monotone: 'I have real reasons for not wanting to be found, and they are nothing to do with my wife.'

I had indeed been entertaining myself with an emotional reunion, ever since he'd spoken about her emails. This was an unexpected development, and I didn't know how to react, so I just said, 'Oh.' I was momentarily deflated, but even as I made the right noises, I knew nothing was going to stop me finding that house.

In fact, he hadn't been gone long before I was on the internet looking for ideas. I'd had a nice response from someone called Jack Garvey at the Woodland Trust, so I thought I'd start with him. His contact details were at the bottom of the email: it was just before five, so I decided to give him a ring. The phone rang for a long time, and I was just about to hang up when a friendly male voice answered. It's funny, I suppose I'm a creature of intuitions, and I have to resist making snap judgments about people, but there was something about Jack straight away. I suppose you could say we just clicked.

'Oh, hello, my name's Annie Keaton. You answered my email about Farnworth Manor.'

'Hi, Annie, you just caught me. I'm just going to pick my daughter up. Can I ring you back tomorrow?'

'Yes, no problem.'

'Or, I'll tell you what, I wouldn't mind coming to have a look and I'm out that way tomorrow afternoon. Are you around?'

'I can be, that's great. You go, and I'll send you an email right now with my contact details.'

'Great. See you tomorrow then.'

I must admit I felt some trepidation that something was happening straight away, but at least that gave me no time to fret about what Richard would say. As it turned out, I was in luck: Jack was due at 2pm, and at 1.30pm, I saw Richard drive past on his way out of the village. With a bit of luck, we could do what Jack had called 'a recce' and get out of the way before Richard got back.

At two on the dot, an old Land Rover pulled up outside, billowing smoke from a noisy exhaust: all I could see of the driver was a large green arm and a tweed cap. He appeared to be clearing the passenger seat, so I wrapped myself in a jacket and scarf, locked up and went round to open the passenger door.

'Jack? Hello, it's ok, we can walk from here.' What I really didn't want was a strange vehicle to be parked anywhere near the farm, and I was so preoccupied by that concern that I might have sounded a little neurotic. He stopped what he was doing, which was shoveling papers and files and binoculars and plastic bags into the passenger footwell, and looked up at me.

Afterwards, I tried telling myself that it was just in an overreaction. Maybe I was just hyper-sensitive because of all the sexual tension with Richard, but at that moment, I honestly felt as though an electric current flashed between us: I looked away, abashed, and started wittering about where we were going. I was conscious of the Land Rover rocking as he climbed out: I was still holding the open passenger door and standing in the middle of the road.

The driver's door slammed, so I shut mine and went to the pavement, still talking and waving my arm in the direction of the farm. We set off walking, and I eventually subsided into silence. I was really regretting this. I'd betrayed Richard's trust, just at the point when I might have cemented it: I'd acted rashly, and now, on top of all that, I was entirely discombobulated by a pair of the bluest, kindest, smiliest eyes I'd ever had the misfortune to be captivated by.

'Lovely day for a walk.'

'Yes, ' I turned to him gratefully, 'yes it is.' And indeed I hadn't noticed until then the clarity of the air, the mellow sunlight or the floating of copper clouds.

'I had a look on our records and there was nothing about this area, no notable trees recorded, but then I went to some older documents and I had an hour this morning to find out what I could about Farnworth Manor. There are some contemporary reports in newspapers from the twenties and thirties about the new landscaping and the farming methods of a Mrs Hertig. By all accounts, the estate

199

had some notable established indigenous trees as well as some more exotic plantings. The Farnworths were well-travelled, it seems, and the eighteenth century ones imported specimens from Europe. Could be really interesting, this. Thanks for contacting us.'

'Oh, you're welcome. I'm really pleased you responded. I .. it's just.' I stopped, partly because we needed to cross the road, but also because I was feeling so very highly-strung.

'What is it? Are you okay? If you don't mind me saying, you seem a bit, um, wound up?'

Now I really was grateful, and I looked up at him, got that spark again and looked away. When I think back, I must have seemed like a complete bag of nerves.

'I am, yes. Thing is, we have to walk past a farmhouse, and the man who lives there doesn't want me to. Doesn't want anyone to.'

'Pah!' he strode across the road, and to my great surprise, took me with him by the arm. 'Bloody Nimbies! Bane of my life.'

'No, it's not that. He's just very … private. I've only just got to know him, and we were getting on well. He's a bit of a recluse.'

He strode on, and I had to pick up speed to keep up with him. 'Don't you worry about that. We're just doing a recce. I won't let on what we're thinking of doing.'

'Oh, I think he'll know as soon as he sees us.'

'Oh well, I'll go and talk to him, shall I?'

'Well, it might not be necessary. He's just gone out. I think we'll have an hour at least.'

We'd just turned into the lane, and he stopped abruptly, 'Well! There's one for starters! That's the finest horse-chestnut I've ever seen in my life! That must be three hundred years old! Let's go and have a look.' Before I could stop him, he'd vaulted the fence and was off across the field.

'Jack!'

He stopped and turned to look at me: I saw him recollect we had time pressure, and immediately came striding back towards me, putting away a large notebook he'd produced from a voluminous pocket in his jacket. Before I knew it, he was back beside me in the

200

lane. He gave my elbow a squeeze, said, 'Next time, eh?' and set off down the lane.

When we reached the farm gate, he was about to plough into the grass, but I tugged his sleeve, feeling as though I was trying to stop a tractor rolling down the hill. "Jack, please could we kind of hide our tracks? If we just stride over the long grass here, he might not notice.' As I said it, I noticed that the grass was already dying back for winter, and we'd be unlikely to leave such a clear path of bent grasses as I'd done in September.

'Oh, ok.' And he took a giant pantomime stride, then reached back for my hands. Laughing, I jumped from a standing start, and he somehow spun me in midair, so that I landed as far behind him as I'd been in front. By then, I was helpless with laughter.

'Right, now you do that to me.' The prospect of me whirling sixteen stone of solid beef through the air had me in fits, but it didn't stop him going through the same procedure, with me helplessly hanging on.

By the time we got to the bottom of the meadow, I was bent double, completely unable to stop laughing or stand up straight. I'd wrenched my shoulder, but it didn't seem to matter. Nothing did. It was a great, cathartic release of all the tension and I felt so much better for it. I sat back on my haunches to get my breath back. Jack had disappeared and was crashing about in the undergrowth. By the time he reappeared, I was back in possession of my senses.

When he emerged, he was trailing ivy and brambles and there were leaves and twigs in his hair. It set me off again, 'Haa! You look like something from Where The Wild Things Are!'

'I think there might well be wild things in there in the crepuscular gloom. Nature run riot. It's anarchy in there! But there are two splendid oaks and a massively overgrown laurel hedge that must have lined the drive. I am Intrigued of Inglewhite!'

'Inglewhite?'

'It's where I'm from. Where are you from?'

'Salford, Nottingham, Knutsford, here.'

'Here?'

He sat down on the grass beside me, and I gave him a potted history of my life. 'So my great-aunt was the Estate Manager there, but I know nothing about her, and I'm intrigued to find out.' I looked at him and decided to come out with what I'd been thinking. To be honest, I'm wondering whether she's my real grandmother. She had a brother, too, a little boy who went missing, and I want to try to find out what happened to him, whether he ever came home. I'd love to get to the house, if it's still standing, which I think it is, because I could see chimneys from space.'

'That sounds like a good title for a poem. I Could See Chimneys From Space: the sad lament of Major Tom, floating in his tin can.'

I lay back, laughing and singing, 'Faaaar above the earth.'

He lay back too, and joined in, 'Planet Earth is blue, and there's nothing I can do.'

We both lay looking at a clearing of crystalline sky, quiet for a moment. I turned my head to look at him, a metre away in the long grass, 'Have you seen Gregory's Girl?'

'That's spooky. I was thinking exactly the same thing. That scene where they're lying in the park doing horizontal dancing and trying not to fall off the earth.'

I could have lain there all day, but suddenly became conscious that we should make ourselves scarce before Richard came back. As soon as I got to my feet, Jack stood up too, surprisingly swiftly for such a big man.

'Come on then, let's get back. We can talk as we walk. We have that capability. Are you ready for the reverse manoeuvre?' He was indicating the grassy slope with one eyebrow raised.

'Ha! I had enough trouble coming downhill! No, I shall get there under my own steam, taking giant strides.'

When we reached the gate, suddenly professional again, Jack said, 'Well, I think this is a job for the volunteers. I'll contact the BTCV.' Seeing my blank look, he said, 'British Trust for Conservation Volunteers. Let me think. It's November now, so no point in starting until after Christmas. By then, the vegetation will have died back a bit, and we always get lots of new recruits after Christmas. And then there's the Youth Offenders Team. Other voluntary organisations. We'll not be short of manpower. I've got a mate who'll be really interested in this, and he's well-placed to round up the troops.'

'What will be your approach?'

'Well, I'll put together a case study and make a bid for some money so we can get in some machinery if it comes to that, but first off we just want to clear a path along the drive so we can get to the house and see what's what.'

This was so much what I wanted to hear that I was beside myself with excitement. 'Oh, that's brilliant! I can't believe it's all happened so quickly!'

'Well, not really. As I say, I can't promise anything before Christmas, but you can be sure a volunteer workforce will be hacking through the undergrowth on Boxing Day.'

'You're joking.'

'Only partly. We do get a lot of enquiries and offers over the Christmas period. New resolutions and all that. Doing their bit. Putting back. Thing is, unlike a lot of new resolutions, people tend to stick at countryside volunteering. We get a lot of newly-retired types, still fit, released from their desks at last, rediscovering muscles they didn't know they had. All good stuff.'

'Any youngsters?'

'Not so much, no. It's a shame that. You get the odd one, budding Chris Packhams, people like that. The Youth Offenders who get roped in nearly always end up loving it. It's one of the best bits about the job, that. Seeing them open up and start to put their backs into it. The dignity of honest labour. It changes them. One of our officers started out as a young offender. He's great. Really knows how to talk to them.'

'I suppose a lot of them lack male role models?'

'Yeah, I suppose they do, but that goes for girls too, you know. It works both ways.'

We'd reached my house, so I asked him in for a coffee.

'Sadly I'll have to decline. Got to pick my daughter up from school. Another time, though, hey? I'll be in touch.' And with that, he climbed back into his Land Rover and vanished in a puff of smoke.

My phone was ringing as I turned the key, and when I saw that it was Paul, I ignored it.

203

Chapter Twenty-four

The next three weeks were a blur of activity and deliveries, and before I knew it, it was mid-December and the carpets were due straight after New Year. This had always been my mental marker: the carpets would go down last: they were all wheat-coloured, which might have been a mistake, as it meant I would have to impose a new shoes-off regime, on myself as well as others. I'd promised Jason and his friends some kind of celebration, so I bought a used gazebo from Ebay and was struggling to erect it by myself as a surprise for Jason when I heard the front doorbell. It was Jack.

'Hello, I was just passing and I thought I'd call in for that coffee. Is it a bad time?' I must have looked harrassed as I'd just dropped a pole on my head: it had left a slight bump that I could feel through my hair.

'No, in fact it couldn't be better. Will you just come and hold some poles up? I know what I'm doing, I'm just struggling to do it by myself. I've got the roof on, I just need to raise the legs and get the last poles to lock in.'

When I explained what the gazebo was for, Jack laughed appreciatively. 'That's great, that is. You could keep it up permanently as a youth club.'

'No fear. I'm already thinking I might have been a bit too friendly to the local young people. I can't get rid of them! This is to kind of draw a line under things. Yesterday, open house: tomorrow, private dwelling. The shame is they've nowhere else to go.'

'Is there nothing for them in Adlington?'

'Nope, nothing at all. There's a church hall but that's just used by the WI and the scouts. The rest of the time it's £30 an hour. Their secondary school's in Chorley, and there's a youth centre there, but the kids who've been helping me are all over nineteen. A couple even have degrees! It's appalling. No chance of a job because no experience. No chance of experience because they can't get a job.'

'Oh well, you've done what you can. And may I say what a nice job they've made of it? These doors are new, aren't they? Nicely fitted. And the surrounds, who did them?'

'Yes,' I said proudly, 'Jason next door did them. He's got a real aptitude for woodwork. His granddad came along and gave him some tips, but generally he just watches how to do things on videos on YouTube. It's really bolstered his confidence.'

'But you'll have had to get a plumber in, and an electrician?'

'Yes, the plumber wasn't as amenable as I'd thought when I took him on, but the electrician was great. Jason has a friend who wanted to watch what he did, and the guy let him feed cables, pass him tools, take readings, that kind of thing. The plasterer was a nice guy too. Bit gruff with them, but he let one of the girls have a go in that alcove, behind the bookcase, and she did really well.'

He was smiling hugely. "That's great to hear. You chose the workmen like that on purpose, didn't you?'

'Yes, I did. Once a teacher, always a teacher I guess.'

'It's just that I was reading about an initiative in Scotland, just community-based, that matches school-leavers with local workmen. You've been doing something similar off your own bat. That's really good.'

'Tiny acorns and all that. There!' The last pole slotted into place and we stood underneath; it was just starting to drizzle. "It's good, isn't it? I've got some fairy lights too.'

'I'll help you put them up if you like: I've got an hour. If I eventually get that coffee.'

'Ok, I'll go and put it on. The lights are in a bag in the hall. If you could just untangle them, that'd be great.'

We sat under the gazebo with our coffee, and I found he wanted to talk more about the nation's youth. It was clearly a subject he felt strongly about: 'I think about it a lot, the way kids are today. Claire's only young, but you know, I worry about her future if there's no jobs. You see them all just hanging around, and you think, just do something! Something productive. It's all staring at tiny screens. As cousin Guy says, Build A Rocket, Boys! There's so much they could be doing that costs no money. We can always use volunteers: I go into schools sometimes and you always get a few who respond, and then when they get involved, they love it. Practical stuff, connecting with nature, making a difference.'

'Yes, tiny acorns again. I blame the National Curriculum for that: it stopped teachers having the freedom to teach what was right for their kids, right for their community: it left no space for initiative. In the classroom anyway: there's always after school. But then there are so many pressures on the staff – results, league tables – and for extra-curricular stuff there's all the paperwork, insurance, risk assessments; and besides, there are so many other distractions for the kids. I couldn't do the job now, I couldn't cope.'

'When did you leave?'

'When the kids were small: it just got too much, and Paul was getting promoted, working longer hours, entertaining and all that. He started to want a different kind of wife, and of course I wanted to be there for Rosie and Mark. We could afford it, so I left.'

'Do you think about getting involved again?'

'I do, yes. I've always liked working with teenagers. I thought maybe I'd see whether there was anything I could get involved with here, but the village seems to … lack a heart. Don't get me wrong, the people are lovely, but there's no centre, no library, nowhere you can go to find things out and get involved.'

'Yes, it's lost a lot, and it's a funny-shaped place isn't it? Not like it's all been built round a village green. It's cut in half by the main road, and I suppose when the houses were built it was for the cotton mills, just long lines of terraces down one hill and up the other.'

'The local shops provided a bit of a hub, but they've all closed. The paper shop does well as a tiny convenience store, but that's not what I mean. It's actually in the back of my mind that if the manor's still there, maybe we could do something with it. I know it's a long shot, but you can dream.'

'That's right, because after all…' I somehow knew what he was going to do, and we laughed and sang together, 'If you don't have a dream, how you gonna make a dream come true?'

When I waved him off I reflected that I'd never before felt so comfortable with a man so quickly, and if I could avoid looking into those eyes, I had made a good friend and a wonderful ally.

On impulse, I'd invited him to the party, 'and you can bring your family if you like: the more the merrier. It's Indian food mostly, but there'll be a big pot of stew for anyone who doesn't like it spicy. I've said five o'clock onwards, but I'm hoping they'll all have gone by ten!'

He'd said, 'Thanks, that's lovely. I'll bring my daughter if that's ok. She's only twelve, so we won't stay long.' So I was none the wiser about any partner.

I thought about asking Richard to the party, although I knew he wouldn't come. He had been incredulous about the young people hanging round my house, but I'd defended my approach with verve. 'The thing is, Richard, there's this quotation by Goethe that used to hang in the entrance hall of the first school I worked in: "Treat people as though they were the best they could be, and they will become the best they could be." It can backfire, and of course you get bad eggs who try to take advantage of what they take to be your naiveté, but I've always stood by it as a way of dealing with young people. I find it works.'

I hadn't yet mentioned the volunteers to him. I simply didn't have the courage. He seemed to think the subject was closed and that the prospect of exploring the outbuildings would satisfy my curiosity.

Suddenly I heard Beth's voice emanating from the letterbox, 'Who's a stud-magnet, then?'

When I opened the door, she was standing with both hands on her hips and a quizzical expression on her face. 'Well? Who's the hunk?'

I laughed, 'Come in. I know, turns out men are like buses – none for ages and then two come along at once.'

'He's lovely. He even waved at me and he doesn't know me from Adam. He looks like Thor's dad in a Barbour! My kinda man. Who is he then?'

'He's called Jack. Married though. At least, he's got a daughter so I presume he's got a partner. He's from the Woodland Trust: I emailed them about the Farnworth woods, and he came to have a look. Want a drink?'

'No thanks, I want a shower: just been cleaning an old biddy's house and it was filthy. Hey! What's that in the yard?'

'It's for the party. Come and have a look.'

We both went outside to admire the gazebo. 'I'll put the fairy lights on, just a minute.'

'Oh Annie, that looks lovely! I'm quite excited now. It'll be great to have a party right next door and just fall over the wall at bedtime! I hope you've invited the neighbours.'

'I have, yes. They've put up with a lot. They were really nice: they didn't think they'd be coming, but thanked me for asking them. I assured them I wasn't turning the place into a youth club. Leonard's coming, though, bless him. He's really enjoyed having the kids around.'

'How many are you expecting?'

'Well, there could be twenty actually. Anil's daughter's doing the food, and I said she could bring a friend.'

'Priya's the same age as Ellie. I haven't seen her for ages, didn't know she was back.'

'Yes, she's been working in Leeds but got made redundant so she's home. When's Ellie home for Christmas?'

'She could be back this weekend, actually. It'd be great if she could come too. Have you invited your hunks?'

I laughed, 'They're not my hunks, but I have to admit I seem to be overdosing on testosterone at the moment. You bringing a beau?'

'Hmm, I've been seeing a bit of Adam's dad again. I might invite him if there's no other spare talent.'

' 'Fraid not. It's for the kids, this. If I had more room, I'd have invited all their mums and dads, but then it wouldn't be their party.'

'No, you're right. Tell you what, though, if we're getting our glad-rags on, why don't we get a taxi to town after they've gone? The girls sometimes go clubbing on a Friday night. Fancy it?'

'I'm not a clubber, Beth, but if we've still got the energy and the night is young when they've all gone, we could go for a drink and you could show me the bright lights of Chorley.'

'You're on. What are you wearing?'

'I'm not sure yet, I'll have to have a trying-on session. I've lost a bit of weight with all this hard work.'

'Show-off.'

In the event, it was a no-brainer: my cherished green lace dress with long sleeves fitted a treat, and as I slipped into high heels for the first time in months, I surveyed myself in the mirror with

209

confidence. I'd left my hair loose and wore my emerald earrings. It might have looked a bit formal for a back-yard gazebo party, but I felt good in it, and I wanted the kids to see I'd made an effort.

When Beth arrived, resplendent in red, I surveyed the tightness of her skirt and said, 'You look fantastic, but I can't see you climbing over any walls in that!' She really did look gorgeous, with her hair up and dangly tinsel earrings.

'Do you think these are a bit Bet Lynch?'

'Yes, but they suit you.'

Indignant, she slapped my arm with her clutch bag. 'What are you saying, posh totty? Mine's a Bacardi.'

I'd given Priya and her friend Rachel free rein with the front room, and they'd been in there an hour setting up the decorating table and bringing in the buffet. I'd left it all to them, so I was a bit nervous about how it would look, but finally they opened the door with a proud, 'Ta daaa!'

Quietly tinkling sitar music issued from an iPod on the shelf, and they'd lit the room with tea-lights in sparkly little red and green glasses. Big floor-cushions covered in twinkling multi-coloured sari fabric were propped up against the walls. Beth and I gasped when we saw the table: they'd covered it in a beautiful red sari, and laid out the finger food on green paper plates, lit by more tea-lights.

'Girls! That's beautiful! I can't believe the transformation! Can I keep those floor-cushions?'

Priya laughed, delighted, 'No, but I can make you one if you like.'

'I'd love one, Priya: I'll pay you, of course!'

'I thought we could put the cushions out when people have got their food, and we've got a couple of playlists ready for later, for like a chill-out room.'

Rachel was smiling, and I saw her whisper to Priya, who turned back to us and laughed. 'Did you two plan your outfits to go with our décor?'

The doorbell rang at that moment, and the two girls panicked instantly: 'We've not started heating the curries yet!'

I opened the door, and our first guest was Jack. I saw his astonishment at my transformation, and he didn't hide his admiration, saying loudly, 'By gum, lass, you scrub up well!"

I laughed and stood back to let him in, only then seeing his daughter, who'd been entirely hidden by his bulk. She was clearly shy, a young-looking twelve-year old in a sparkly pink top, so I made a point of introducing myself and taking her through to meet Priya and Rachel, who immediately took her under their wings. After that, they were inseparable, and I saw her later, serving with them and helping them collect up plates and glasses.

Others arrived in quick succession, and soon I stopped answering the door and just left it open. I briefly entertained the idea of texting Richard and asking him to stay on the door like a bouncer, but I'd been assured by Jason that he'd put the word out that no-one should consider crashing the party. He was also touchingly protective of my new wallpaper: I actually saw him point it out to a girl who was leaning against the wall. When I saw two couples entwined on my cream sofa, their drinks balanced on the arms, I was glad I'd thought to cover it with a layer of bin-liners covered by throws.

I saw Priya's parents arrive and go straight into the front room, from which they emerged beaming with pride. I hadn't thought of having music outside, but when I was asked for an iPod dock, I was relieved to hear music playing at an acceptable level: the neighbours had promised to ring my landline if the noise became too much.

The bar was in the kitchen, and Jason's friend Alex was keeping an eye on it: they'd promised that he and Adam would make sure no-one over-indulged. The older ones were going into town later, and Adam knew which of the younger ones was most likely to take advantage. There were plenty of soft drinks to keep them happy, and for the over-eighteens I'd stocked up on alcopops: even though I disapproved of them, I reasoned it was better to let them have them than help themselves to the spirits.

Jack was immersed in conversation with someone different every time I looked, his head bent down to hear; he was at least a foot taller than anyone else, including Anil, the only other adult male there, apart from Leonard. Once, as I stood on the back step and looked at all the people eating and drinking under the gazebo, he caught my eye and beamed across the assembled heads with fairy lights reflecting off his long wheat-coloured hair: maybe it was

211

alcohol, maybe the magical night, but he looked to me like a character from Lord of the Rings.

At ten o'clock, people started to leave, and when a minibus pulled up at 10.30 to take a big group into town, Priya and Rachel cleared up the last of the glasses and packed them into Anil's car. I closed the door and leant against it with a feeling of complete euphoria. It had been a wonderful night, everyone had been thoroughly appreciative, and there was no damage. What I would like now most in the world would be to sit out under the gazebo and look at the crystalline stars, wrapped in my angora shawl with a whiskey. And Jack.

I had barely spoken to him all night, and I knew he was sitting on a floor cushion behind this very wall next to Beth. His daughter had just emerged from the bathroom and was coming downstairs. I stood up straight and smiled up at her, 'Did you enjoy that, Claire?'

Instantly shy, she blushed and mumbled, 'Yes thank-you.' Standing in the doorway of the front room, she said, 'Dad? Are we going?' in the slightly whiny voice of a tired child.

I heard Jack answer, 'Yep, just coming petal.' And the floor creaked as he got to his feet. He appeared in the hall, and put his arm round Claire's shoulders. 'It's been a lovely evening, Annie. Thanks very much for inviting us. What a great bunch of kids. Are you going into Chorley with Beth?'

Beth had appeared at his side, her face a pantomime whose meaning I couldn't initially catch, but then it belatedly dawned on me that she was seriously smitten with Jack and trying to indicate as much to me.

'Yeah, Annie, get your bag. I've texted the girls and they're in Sasha's. Jack's giving us a lift.' Unseen by Jack, she gave a slight shake to her head, which clearly signaled that she meant the opposite to what she'd just said.

I took the hint thankfully. 'No, I'm whacked Beth. I'm just going to get a nightcap and go to bed. It's been a long day.' I was right. Her eyes lit up and she winked.

Her curtains were still closed when I left the house after lunch the next day: I would have to wait to find out what happened. I'd expected at least a text, but there had been nothing, and I must have been sound asleep when she came home. If she came home.

Richard was at the gate to meet me, and he had a huge bunch of rusty black keys in his hand. 'So, how did the party go?' Something in his tone told me he was hoping to hear tales of damage, drunken adolescents and misplaced trust, but I gave him my best breezy smile and told him all about it as we walked across the cobbles to the huge double doors of what must have been the forge.

'Have you really not been in here?'

'No, no need, and I've not been in the mood for exploring. I've brought some WD40 in case the locks stick.'

'Well thought, thanks for that. Allow me?' I reached for the keys. 'Which one do you think it is?'

'Well, it's the biggest door, so I'd go for the biggest key.'

I bent down to look inside the lock, but it appeared to be blocked. 'Have you got anything I could poke into the lock to clear it?'

He reached into his pocket and brought out a penknife, chose an attachment and I stepped aside to let him gouge out whatever was blocking the hole. It turned out to be just general debris, wood shavings, a rolled up strip of cardboard from a cigarette packet and a couple of dead spiders. Then he squirted a jet of WD40 into the lock, and gestured to me to try again. The key turned first time, and the great door creaked open on rusty hinges.

Straight away, as the wan winter light bathed the empty walls in a grey wash, it was clear that the place had been cleared and swept clean. The walls were blackened and the hearth looked like the unused backdoor to hell, but there wasn't one single item left in the forge. Disappointed, I stepped inside onto the worn flags, and tried to work out by the markings where the anvil would have stood, where my great-grandfather had forged horseshoes, plain useful objects and ornate wrought-iron decorative work to support that beautiful family.

I stood there for a long time in silence, trying to conjure noise and people by sheer effort of imagination, but nothing caught light, and I turned from the effort to close the door sadly and turn to the next door. The waft of sawdust that drifted out onto the chill winter air told us that this was a carpenter's workshop before we let the light in. Somehow, the same daylight cast a warmer glow of pale gold on the worn workbench and faintly illuminated a cabinet of many drawers that ran its full length. There were no tools hanging from the many hooks and nails, but their ghostly outlines spoke of recent use, and when I saw that there was a beautiful carved oak chair in the back corner, I felt a rush of warmth. This was more like it. I stepped through the brittle sawdust on the dusty floor, and went to look at it more closely. Only then did I see the cradle and, beside it on the floor, a stool with a rush seat exactly like mine.

My eyes burned with tears and I found myself completely unable to speak. When I turned, Richard was standing close behind me, and I lifted my watery eyes to him with a rueful smile. His eyes softened when he saw my tears, but then immediately took on an intensity and before I knew it, he had my face cupped in both of his hands. I was completely taken by surprise: I had thought we were past this, and an alarmed fluttering started in my chest. He was holding me quite tightly and his face was too close, too alarmingly intense. I could smell the mints on his breath but beneath that the sour note of alcohol. He must have seen the flicker of fear in my eyes before I looked away, anxious to evade his eyes. I didn't want him to think he saw any encouragement, nor did I want him to sense my fear. I started to try to move my head out of his grip and put my hands on his wrists in what I hoped wasn't too panicky a way. I didn't want to anger him, but nor did I want to give any indication that I was submitting to this. Suddenly, abruptly, he let go, and turned and left the workshop. I stood a few moments to compose myself. If he had gone into the house, I would not follow to talk about what had just happened. Although my caring senses wanted to sooth his embarrassment, I knew from previous experience that would not be a wise move.

He was standing outside in the wan sunlight with his back to me, his hands in his coat pockets and looking down at the damp cobbles beneath his polished boots. This I could handle. Instead of touching him, I walked around to the front of him and handed him the keys. As he took them, his hand briefly closed over my fingers, and he said, 'I'm sorry.'

I didn't answer immediately. I wanted him to know he'd frightened me, and I wanted him to be absolutely clear that it wasn't just that the circumstances weren't conducive. In this clear, bright, cold day, my thoughts were crystalline. I knew what I was about to tell him would be make or break for our friendship.

'You did frighten me, I have to say.'

He looked up at me and his eyes were sad and ashamed. He looked down again. After a few moments, he looked up again and said, 'Can we just forget it happened?'

'Yes, let's.' Immediately his shoulders lifted and he stood up straight, pride restored. 'So, thank-you for letting me have a look in there. That stool must be the swing in the picture. The cradle is probably Bertie's. It's so sad. I don't suppose we'll ever know what happened to the little chap.'

'No.'

There was silence, and I found it hard to guess what he was thinking. His face had taken on that immobile, difficult to read expression that I'd seen before. Well, I thought, here goes.

'What will you do at Christmas?'

'In what way?' I sensed a stirring of interest. Did he think I was going to invite him?

'About your family. Will you see them?'

'No.' His tone forbade discussion, but I was going to try.

'Couldn't you just meet them somewhere, for lunch? Your boys will be missing you.'

'No.'

'You just don't want to think about them, do you?'

'No I don't.'

I was getting annoyed at this obtuse refusal to admit the existence of two little boys, no matter what the relationship between their parents. 'Well, you know what, I don't think that's right. I can see how you'd go from day to day, blocking them out, but it's Christmas. Families should be together at Christmas. Whatever is going on between you and Cath, they deserve to see their dad. Don't you want to see them?'

'Of course I want to see them, Annie. I miss them, but I'm no good for them. They're better off without me.'

'How can you say that? How can you know? Just let them in, just try it. You have nothing to lose. You have no peace of mind anyway. Just see them. If you don't want to go to the house, then

215

meet them on neutral territory. You can plan it so that you keep control. Just think of their faces, Richard.' I saw a flicker of distaste cross his face. 'Not how you last saw them. Don't think of that. That's the past. Think how they'd look when you walked in on Christmas Day. I can imagine that whatever the circumstances of you leaving, the boys' faces are not images you'd want to remember. Think of how they look when they're happy and joyful. How they looked when you came home the last time. How proud they are of you.' His head was bowed, and I knew I was hitting home. I softened my tone. 'Just think, for just a little effort on your part, just arranging a visit or a lunch, you will make them so happy. And even if you find it painful, it's worth it for them. You might see them and find that you and Cath have moved on, that you can get back some semblance of what you had before. But if that's not to be, at least you will have tried. At least they will know that you are still in their lives, that you care.'

There was silence in the courtyard when I stopped speaking, and Richard stood with his head bowed. I saw again the dignity in his posture and thought bitterly of the cost of combat to him and thousands like him. And their families.

When he raised his eyes to me, they were red-rimmed but dry, and there was a fierceness that disarmed me for a moment. He said, 'Enough, Annie. You've made your point. I'll think about it.'

'Promise?'

'I've said I will think about it.'

'Ok, good. Thank-you.' Well, I thought, in for a pound. 'I'm going to my daughter's for Christmas, staying a few days, and then down to my son's in London for New Year. My husband might well be joining us for Christmas lunch, we'll see.'

There was no response. Ok, I thought, here goes.

'Um, there's something else I need to tell you.'

He looked at me and his eyes were hard and cold and distant. I swallowed and then came straight out with it. 'You're not going to like this, Richard. But I'm asking you, for my sake, and maybe even for your own, to accept it.'

He was interested, I could tell, and his look was suspicious, wary. It was only later that it occurred to me he might have thought

I had traced his family and was going to produce them with a flourish from behind the barn.

'In the New Year some time,' I tried to keep my tone light and casual, but I was genuinely afraid that there would be an explosion of temper and all contact between us would be severed. I think there might have been a slight wobble in my voice when I raised my chin and said, 'there will be a group of volunteers coming to clear a path through the woods to tend to the trees and ... to see whether we can find the house.'

You know that bit in Lord of the Rings where Galadriel turns from white to black? Richard seemed to expand before my eyes and his eyes sparked fire. He gave me what I strongly felt was one last look, a look which should have left me a smoking pile of ashes on the cobbles, turned on his heel, marched across the yard and slammed the old door with a force that must have split its timbers. The sound echoed around the buildings like a gunshot and Seamus exploded into barks, flinging himself against the bars of his cage. I stood still, dumbfounded, possibly even frozen with fear like a greyhound looking down the barrel of a rifle, and the thought crossed my mind again that he could very well come back out with a gun. In the ensuing silence, I found that I was trembling. I turned and made my way unsteadily to the gate.

Chapter Twenty-five

Christmas passed peacefully, although Paul almost wrecked it for all of us. He was due to arrive at Rosie's at midday, for Christmas lunch at 2pm, and when the phone rang at twelve o'clock on the dot, I knew it would be him, but I was unprepared for what he would say.

Rosie answered the phone in the hall, and I saw her shoulders droop when she heard his voice. She turned her back on me, and hung her head, listening. When she turned round to look at me, still listening to his lies, her yes were narrowed and brimming with tears. I stood in the doorway, making no secret of the fact that I was waiting. When she started to twist her finger in her hair, something she'd always done when she was upset, I went over and gently took the phone from her. I heard him say, '...so I just can't face it.'

He'll have been startled to hear my firm voice, 'I'll ring you back Paul.' And I put the phone down.

Rosie was sitting on the bottom stair, sobbing quietly into a Santa tea-towel. I sat down beside her and put my arm around her shoulder. 'What did he say, sweetheart?'

'He loves you so much. He says he can't go on without you. He's been trying to be strong and let you have your freedom, hoping you'll come home, but it's gone on so long Mum!' her voice had raised and she turned a tearful, accusing face to me, pushing my arm away from her shoulder. 'You should go home! It's where you belong. I can't bear to think of him all alone. It's Christmas! Ring him back and tell him to come, tell him you'll go home to him.'

I stayed silent, torn between anger at him and pity for my daughter, caught in the middle like this. Being used, though she didn't know it. My confidence wavered only once, but the more I thought about how he had planned this, how calculating and manipulative this was, how coldly he had planned to ruin Rosie's first Christmas in her married home, all for his own ends, the thought crystalized that I actively loathed him: it gave me strength.

Firmly, I put my arm back around Rosie's shaking shoulders and turned her face up to mine. 'Listen, Rosie. I'm going to ring your dad back now and talk to him. Don't worry, we'll work things out. I'm not promising I can persuade him to come for Christmas dinner, but…'

'Oh do, mum! You've got to! You owe it to him, and to us! He doesn't deserve this! I know he's been unfaithful, but that's all over now, and he's so sorry! You've been gone four months now, that's enough! You've made your point, he won't do it again. He loves you, mum. ' She subsided into sobs again, but she was calming down now she'd had her outburst.

Now wasn't the time to tell her. From somewhere, I summoned tears of my own. I held her face to mine and made her a promise: 'I'll do my best, sweetheart. Don't let this ruin your day. Come on, the house looks lovely, you look lovely, you've got a wonderful husband, a great job, so much to look forward to. Don't let a tiff between two oldies upset you.' She gave me a watery smile. 'Oh dear, you look like a panda. Go and see to your face, then look after your guests. I'll go outside and ring him on my mobile.'

I got my coat, put my phone in the pocket and stepped out into the frosty air. For a few minutes, I walked around their garden, following the billows of my breath. The sky was high and clear, crystal blue like my thoughts. When I was ready, I called him.

Just before it went to answerphone, he picked up but didn't speak. He would wait, pick up my tone, adapt his tactics accordingly and lead the conversation from there. He thought.

He'll have been surprised by the jolly, 'Happy Christmas!' He wasn't used to me being confident enough to be sarcastic. I wanted to reach down the phone and throttle him for making our daughter cry, but I was going to control this conversation. 'Any plans for the day?'

'What?'

'Any plans? Where are you going to spend Christmas, now you're not coming here?'

He faltered. I had honestly never heard him falter. Ever.

'Well, I … at home, of course.'

'Which home?'

'What? What do you mean, which home?' He was trying to gather himself. I knew the pattern: indignation first, then anger, but he was rattled. I could hear that too.

220

'I just thought you might have someone you'd rather spend it with. That you'd thought better of it, driving over here, not able to have a drink. Understandable really.'

'What are you talking about? You think I'd do that to my own daughter?'

'Yes, actually. I do.'

'You're fucking crazy! What do you take me for?'

'Do you really want me to answer that?'

'What? What?' he was incandescent.

'Calm down, Paul. You and I know the truth of what's going on here. Why did you say those things to Rosie? What are you trying to achieve?' Although I knew the answer.

A great sweeping sigh that I could almost feel as hot breath on my ear. He was gathering himself for a final assault on the Annie that he used to know. Deliberately lowering his voice, he sounded like a hammy actor from a black-and-white film: 'Come home, Annie. I miss you.'

I waited before I answered.

'Really? There's no other reason you want me to come home?'

'Of course not, what other reason would there be?'

It was time. 'Well, there are three that I can think of. There's a woman in her thirties, a little boy of about four and a toddler. She looked about two.'

The silence was deafening. It stretched so long that I thought he'd rung off. Finally, I was the one who spoke.

'Here's what I think, Paul. You want me to come home so that you can carry on your comfortable life. You want me back as an excuse. I imagine you say, "Poor old Annie, I can't leave her. She'll fall apart. Things are fine as they are, aren't they? We can be together whenever we like. I look after you and the children, don't I? I pay for the au pair." Because you do, don't you Paul? I can imagine you'd do anything to avoid living with two little children and a demanding young wife. If I come home, you can carry on having the best of both worlds.'

Another long silence, then finally, subdued and strangely sulky: 'How long have you known?'

221

'That doesn't matter. What matters is that I won't be coming home, Paul, not ever. I'll be filing for divorce in the New Year.'

Silence while he absorbed that. Finally, 'Have you told the kids?'

'I thought about it when you stopped my allowance, but no. No, I'm leaving that to you.' We were both quiet while we imagined how that would go. 'Just be sensitive, Paul. They know you're unfaithful, they've known that for several years, just not … the extent.'

He didn't speak, so finally, briskly, I ended the conversation. 'Right, now we're both clear, I'm going back into our daughter's house and I'm going to tell her that we're going to meet next week. Which we are. To talk about the divorce, but she doesn't need to know that just yet. Today, the main thing is that we have a lovely Christmas. So whatever it is you've planned to do, Happy Christmas, Paul. I'll be in touch.'

By the time she came out of the kitchen bearing the turkey on a large china platter, Rosie was all smiles. Danny's mum and dad were good company, and we ate in fine spirits: it was a lovely feeling to be hosted in the young couple's first home.

The dinner was a triumph: as a person whose profession revolves around quality food, Rosie had bought everything from Booths and ensured that everything possible was locally-produced: we finished with a delicious selection of artisan cheeses washed down with a fine port. As I crawled into bed that night, replete with fine food and good company, I felt an enormous sense of satisfaction. This was the first Christmas dinner I'd had in my adult life that was made by someone else. No stress, no sense of responsibility and a capacious well-stacked dishwasher hummed away downstairs. I fell asleep feeling more independent and optimistic about the future than I had for years.

When I got off the train from London on the 3rd of January to change trains at Manchester Piccadilly, it felt so good to be back, and as we rolled north, I watched the lines rise and dip and the familiar scenery roll by with a real sense of homecoming.

I'd only seen Beth briefly before I'd set off on my Christmas break: she hadn't surfaced the day after the party, and when I'd nipped round with the Christmas presents the following morning, it had been Jason who answered the door, so I was none the wiser about what had happened in Chorley. She'd sent me a rude Happy Christmas text with a trouserless Santa picture, and we'd exchanged texts again when the new year was only a few minutes old, but beyond that I knew nothing. I might well return to find that she and Jack were in a fully-fledged relationship, but then again, maybe not. If I put my mind to it, I could convince myself in either direction.

I'd just stood up to put my coat and scarf on when I heard a text come in. I wouldn't say Jack was the last person I expected it to be from, but when I saw his name, I felt a blush rise up my neck. 'What time do u arrive Chorley? Want a lift? Ps happy new year. Jack.'

I didn't have to think twice. 'Happy New Year 2u2! Arrive 1.34, & yes please!'

He was there in the slushy car-park when I walked out of the station, his Land Rover parked at the bottom of the ramp with the passenger side perfectly positioned so that I wouldn't have to step down into the grubby melting snow: I imagined other emerging passengers giving me resentful looks as they negotiated around it, but I cared not a jot. My one concern was whether Beth had sent him to pick me up, or whether he had really remembered for himself that it was today I got back.

He was turned round with his arm along the back of the passenger seat when I opened the back door and greeted me with a warm, 'Hello you! Can you manage that?'

'Yes, it's deceptive: I took a big case of heavy presents and all mine are little and light thankfully.'

I climbed in beside him, and the steamed-up cab was warm and smelt of sweets and damp wool. 'This is really kind of you, thanks. I don't know why, but I always get taxi drivers who have something they want to get off their chests. How was your Christmas?'

'Oh, quiet, you know. Granny and Granddad's as usual. Claire got spoilt as usual. I got socks, as usual. What about yours? Tell me all about it.'

As we drove to Adlington, I gave him an account of my travels, the joys of being hosted by my own children. 'They couldn't be more different: Rosie working for Booths, all the food's top quality. Mark lives on takeaways, but they seem to agree with him.'

'And Paul?' I didn't even know Jack knew my husband's name, but however he'd come to know it, I took it as a promising sign that he'd remembered.

'Oh, he didn't come in the end. Not really a surprise to any of us, but Rosie couldn't help being disappointed. It didn't spoil anything though.'

'And you? How did you feel about it?'

I was so struck by the novelty of being asked about my feelings by a man, that I didn't answer for a moment.

'I … well, I was relieved, I suppose. We're having our Big Serious Talk next week, but Christmas at Rosie's would have been a powder keg if we'd both been there. I'm not in any rush. I think now I've laid all my cards on the table we'll be able to keep it amicable. Besides, I'm not exactly independently wealthy, but we were so far apart when my mum died in the spring that he never even asked me about my inheritance. I put it away, so even if he does start cutting up rough, which I doubt, I'll be ok.'

'I wasn't really asking about money, it was more how you were feeling about your marriage. Not that it's any business of mine, sorry, just interested. I'm often told I ask too many questions. Mostly by Claire.'

'She keeps you in hand, does she?' I smiled. 'Can I ask you a question? It seems nosy, but while we're on the subject of families…'

'Where's her mum?'

'Yes, sorry, it's just you haven't mentioned her.'

'She died when Claire was four. Breast cancer.'

'Oh God, I'm so sorry. How awful.'

'Yes, well, we do fine, me and Claire. Christmas is a … a bit of a trial, but generally we're ok. She's got plenty of aunties and cousins. We're ok. Anyway, what about that party, eh? It was great. Claire proper enjoyed it. She's kept in touch with Priya and Rachel. They're a couple, you know! Who knew? Claire just took that in her stride. I don't let her do Facebook, but they text, and Priya's told her she can help next time she gets a catering job.'

'Oh, that's great. It was a lovely night, wasn't it? Seems ages ago now.'

'Yes, I really enjoyed it, we both did. Thanks again for inviting us.'

We were both quiet for a minute then and I cursed myself for not moving smoothly in to asking about Beth. In the event, I didn't need to, because as we turned into Park Road, he said, 'Did Beth have a good night, then? They were a right lot, those girlfriends of hers. There were three of them outside the club having a ciggie and waiting for Beth. I barely got away with my life.'

I laughed, flooded with relief. 'I don't know, she never surfaced the next day, and she wasn't up when I went for my train the day after that.' I felt happy enough to burst. 'If she's got me some milk in, I can offer you a cup of tea.'

'That'd be great, thanks.'

The house was cold, so I nipped upstairs to switch the heating on while Jack filled the kettle, and we stood drinking our tea in the kitchen in our coats. I was touched to find Beth had bought me some bread, eggs and bacon too. I asked whether he was hungry and was surprised when he suggested going for a walk. 'I though maybe, with sitting on trains all day, you'd like to stretch your legs?'

'Yes, I'd like that. Where shall we go?'

'Well I thought maybe just along the Common.'

'Ok, I'll just change my boots.'

When we stepped outside, the clouds were low and heavy with a yellowy-grey tinge and the air had taken on that pregnant hush that often predicts snow. It was slushy underfoot, but warm enough to keep the slush liquid. We chatted inconsequentially, and I increasingly got the sense that his mind was not on what he was saying. When we reached the lane, I was all for carrying straight on, but Jack stopped. 'Let's go this way.'

'Why? I don't want to go past the farm.'

'Oh, I think we should.'

'Why? Let's just carry straight on along the road.' I set off again, arms swinging to keep me warm, enjoying the bracing air in

225

my lungs, but stopped again when I realised Jack hadn't followed. 'Jack?'

'Come this way, Annie,' he said, smiling, and as he disappeared behind the skeletal hedge, I heard him mutter, ' just do as you're told.'

Bemused, I retraced my steps and called after him, 'I heard that!' I still felt unwilling to go anywhere near the farm, but Jack was trudging along the lane unstoppably. I saw that there were no tyre tracks at all, and I judged that the snow had been on the ground for almost a week, so I reasoned the odds were that Richard was either hibernating or he'd gone away. Concern for his well-being rose in me, but I pushed it down and followed Jack, my eyes on the ground.

He was waiting for me beyond the gate, and offered me his hand, looking away from me and downhill towards the woods. I took it gratefully, and we crunched down the field on the thin layer of brittle snow, through which a few feeble grass stalks bristled. I didn't look up until we reached level ground at the edge of the woods, so I didn't see until I was standing in front of it that an opening had been cut into the undergrowth. I looked at him in surprise, 'Oh! You've made a start?'

He was beaming. 'Kind of. Come with me,' and he turned, ducked his head and stepped in amongst the trees. I followed, intrigued now and not a little excited. It wasn't so difficult to adjust my eyes as it had been last time I'd ventured in here. This was partly to do with the yellowy light outside and partly to do with the leafless branches above, but it was mainly due to the fact that I saw immediately that a clear pathway had been cut into the vegetation. Jack was already a good ten metres away, and I saw him look round, beam again, and disappear behind a dark trunk the width of a barn door. By the time I got there, he was a further ten metres away, this time standing by a huge dark evergreen whose glossy leaves bore a fine frosting of snow: the heat of the sun couldn't possibly penetrate down here, and the flakes which had trickled down through the treetops had stayed where they landed. I heard the shuffling of a small band of birds clustered in the lattice of branches like dark fruit.

I laughed to see the excited pride in his face as he waited for me by the hugely overgrown laurel hedge. 'We noticed an iron archway amongst this laurel, look! Some of this stuff's fifty foot high. It'll have to be cut to the stump to encourage re-growth. Anyway, we cut through and found the route of the actual driveway. It must have been gravel: you can still see it in places, and it's lined with beautiful ancient elms! Next day, we came back with an axe to take out some of the self-seeded ash and sycamore saplings. Come and look!'

'When did you do all this? Who helped you?'

He smiled over his shoulder as he carried on striding away in front of me. 'Phil, that mate I told you about. He's really into this, what I call the slash and burn, Genghis Khan school of gardening. We used machetes at first, then axes. It was great. Trouble is, Phil's a lot smaller than me, little wiry fella, fell runner. He missed a lot of the higher up brambles, so watch your head.'

'This is brilliant! How far did you get?'

'Just you wait and see.'

When he said that, I knew, and I felt tingles of real excitement. The rest of the way, I kept silent, barely able to breathe in the cold air and the anticipation of what they had found. I hardly noticed the afternoon darkening ominously. Once, I felt a bramble snag my sleeve, and when I looked up from disentangling myself, a snowflake touched my cheek.

We must have been walking for about half an hour when I saw that Jack was waiting for me up ahead, and his smile of anticipation lit up the monochrome wood. I grinned back and carried on walking, still scanning the path for roots and branches and tangles of brambles, so it was a surprise when I reached the elm against which he'd been standing to find that he was still there, waiting. I sensed his heat before I saw him.

'Right. Give me your hands and close your eyes.' I didn't hesitate for a moment, and felt my right hand firmly enclosed in his. The skin was rough, as I'd expected, but my fingertips lay on his broad wrist, and I felt there the strong pulse beneath the softest skin. My foot caught on something: when he felt me stumble slightly, his great arm came round my shoulders and he held me firmly by the waist, still holding my hand, which was now across his body. His

227

coat was open, so the action brought me in against his chest, and I felt the heat he was generating under the soft wool of his jumper and shirt.

He spoke not a word until we had taken another ten paces, then he let go of my hand to hold both my shoulders, positioned them slightly to the right and touched my chin lightly to lift my head. Then he spoke softly. 'Ok, you can open your eyes.'

We were standing at the bottom of a flight of sandstone steps, and at the top of the steps was a large doorway. Panels of wood had been nailed across it, but above them an ornate glass panel was intact. My mouth must have dropped open as I raised my head to look at the floor above, because I felt snowflake dissolve on my lower lip. The sandstone wall was almost obliterated by ivy, but the distinct shape of a boarded-up window high above the door could be discerned. It took me a moment to realize that the whole of my peripheral vision was filled by the front wall of a great Georgian house. Rampant tentacles of what looked like Virginia Creeper and tenacious ivy had spread across walls and windows with complete indifference. Winter bones of Valerian and sycamore saplings had sprouted from gaps in the mortar and frozen brown fern fronds decorated the gutters. Outstretched tips of branches grazed the walls and more sycamore saplings sprouted from the gravel, but the front of the house, made of huge yellow sandstone blocks, was entire.

I turned an astonished face to Jack and he was beaming at me with undisguised glee, then he stepped back and surveyed the house with his hands on his hips, feet apart, like a builder surveying a particular challenging job. 'Well, what do you think of that, then? Amazing, isn't it? It was boarded up at the end of the war when the Food Ministry vacated. Me and Phil went all the way round, and they've done a really thorough job of it. It looks like all the windows and doors are intact, amazingly! There's been no vandalism as far as I can see. Too far out of the way. It's just kind of gone to sleep, the whole place.'

I still hadn't spoken, torn between astonishment, excitement and a sudden overwhelming wish to walk into this man's arms. If he had given me one iota of encouragement, I'd have done it, but he was all practicalities, so I took my cue from him. He didn't seem to have noticed I hadn't said anything: evidently my expression had been enough. 'Anyway, come on, we'd better be getting back. I was just keen for you to see it straight away. It's getting dark now and this snow's making its mind up. Shall I lead?' and with that, he plunged back into the darkness of the tunnel.

As I followed him back through the hushed maze of vegetation, I thought about the house. Jack's mind was entirely on the trees, and he kept making remarks as he went along, more to himself than to me: 'That needs to come down. Never seen one of them in this country. Corsican Pine, that! Beautiful cones, pale and rounded. Squirrels will have got them or I'd show you. It'll thrive when we've cleared round it, you'll see.'

We came out into the open just as the last of the daylight was fading, and soft snowflakes floated in the air before our faces. He reached behind him and took my hand to stop me slipping, and we climbed the field together. When we got to the farm gate, I glanced towards the buildings, but there were no lights on.

'Did you see anything of the tenant when you and Phil came?'

'No, no sign.' He gave me a quick look that I couldn't interpret, and we made our way along the lane, imprinting our boots through the fresh layer of snow to the slush beneath. I saw him look over to the chestnut tree silhouetted against the metallic glare of the clouds. 'I still haven't registered that. I need to measure its girth.'

'In hugs?'

He smiled down at me briefly, but without a trace of flirtatiousness. 'I'll bring a tape-measure.'

When we got back to the house, he took his leave without coming in. 'So we'll wait for this snow to clear then make a start. Those new volunteers are raring to go! It's quite a project, this. Biggest challenge I've ever been involved in. We'll need to record it all. Lots to do. Anyway, I'll be in touch, Annie. Bye.'

Beth must have heard my front door, because I'd only just stamped the snow of my boots and shaken my coat out to hang it up in the hall when the letterbox opened and a spectral voice came through, 'Ooooo, I am the ghooost of Christmas past. Let me in, my bum's cold!'

Laughing, I opened the door and we had a big hug. 'Ghosts don't have bums and they don't feel the cold! You're an imposter!' It was great to see her.

'So where've you been with hunky boy? I saw you, madam, nothing gets past me!'

'Well, you won't believe it. Come on in and I'll put the kettle on.'

'Sod the kettle, hot toddies and hot gossip is what we need! I've got some mulled wine, come round to mine. You can have some turkey risotto, turkey burger, turkey lasagna, I've got the lot!'

'Oo, yum, go on then! Just give me half an hour to get changed. It's been a long day and I've got loads to tell you.'

Beth's house was like Santa's grotto: I could barely get through the hall without garrotting myself on paper chains or impaling myself on the outsize tree, which was actually in the corner of the front room but encroaching substantially on the passageway. When I finally made it to the kitchen, she was sitting at the table, two bottles of red wine and a steaming lasagna on the table before her.

'Oo, you're a gem! And thanks for getting the milk and stuff. It was great to be able to have a cup of tea as soon as I got back.'

'So, yes, I watched out for your taxi, and lo and behold, it wasn't a taxi but a Land Rover! Come on, spill!'

'Nothing to spill on that front, sadly. Purely business. He just texted out of the blue while I was on the train and offered to pick me up. He must have got my mobile number from my email. Actually, my first thought was that you and he were an item and you'd asked him to pick me up. Not, then?'

'Nope, no dice. I did my best, I thought we were getting on really well, but he just dropped me off, fought off my harpy friends, and drove off into the night. Must be sweet on you, though, to have remembered when you were coming back.'

'No, nothing doing. Like I say, purely business: I think he only has eyes for trees. This mulled wine is certainly warming my cockles! Yum.'

'So?'

'So what? Oh, so yes, the walk. So we get back, and he suggests going for a walk, to stretch my legs. Only he's got something to show me.'

'If only.'

'Yes, quite, if only. Thing is, he and a friend have gone into the woods with machetes and axes and hacked their way in, and found the manor house! We've just been there! It's all overgrown and boarded up, but it's still standing, in fact it looks undamaged! They even think there's still glass in the windows and doors!'

'You're joking! That's amazing. I thought it was knocked down years ago. How did he find it? What happens now?'

'Well, Jack's all about the woodland, but I'm interested in the house. I want to know who owns it. Just think! If it's watertight and intact, and it's been sealed up for over sixty years! It'll be fascinating. And, I was thinking, if nobody claims it, why not open it up? We could make it into something, for the community. Maybe for the kids.'

'Hold your horses, missis, don't get carried away. It's not going to be as simple as that. Anyway, so Jack. Are you seeing him again?'

'Well, yes, he said he'd be in touch, and the Woodland Trust are getting volunteers in to clear the woodland and record the trees and things. Maybe at the very least we could make it into a park. Anyway, I'm going to find out what I can about Farnworth Manor.'

Chapter Twenty-six

I drew a blank with the Land Registry, who eventually referred me to the same solicitors that the agent had mentioned, but when I rang, the receptionist was singularly unhelpful. Eventually, when she refused again to put me through to a solicitor, I asked her what she suggested I should do.

'In what regard, madam?'

I took a deep breath. 'In regard to the ownership of Farnworth Manor. As I said, I am trying to find out whether it can be opened up, or whether we'd be trespassing.'

'Hold the line please.' After being forced to listen to Greensleeves for what seemed like hours, she came back and said, 'Mr Powell suggests you write a letter to the trustees.'

'The trustees? Who are they? Can you give me an address? Please.'

'Just write to them care of these offices. Good day, madam.' And the line went dead.

So I wrote the required letter and waited almost two months before I got a reply. By that time, the work on clearing the driveway into the woodland was well underway, and two or three times a week, I would see Jack's Land Rover passing the house, followed by a Woodland Trust minibus and sometimes one from Lancashire Rangers. I went along to help a few times, but it was backbreaking work. I was constantly astonished at the cheerful stamina of the volunteers: even the surly young offenders put their backs into it. I often used to see the smoke from the fires on the field where they burnt the rotten wood. Good wood was stock-piled, and a lorry came one day to take the logs away.

I never saw Richard in the whole of January, and no-one else mentioned him. Every time I passed, the place was in darkness and there was no sign of the dog. By February, I'd reached the conclusion that he'd moved out. I didn't know how to feel: I supposed I would never know what had happened, but decided for my own sanity that he had gone home to his wife and children.

When a reply finally came from the solicitors, I opened it with trembling hands. By then, I was full of ideas about how the manor could be used, though I'd shared them with no-one. Jack happened to be there when I opened the letter: he occasionally called in for a coffee, always by prior arrangement and often with Phil or one of the other supervisors.

'Well? What does it say?'

I re-read it to make sure there was absolutely not one iota of hope. 'Nothing. A stone wall. "Held in trust ... trustees have conferred ... no entitlement ... blah ... held in perpetuity ... terms of the trust...Any attempt to enter the property shall be deemed trespass." Just legal guff saying hands off, leave it alone.'

I was so disappointed I actually felt tearful. 'That's such a shame! I had such plans!'

'What plans?'

'Well, I haven't done anything about it, and I haven't tried the council, but I thought we could use it as a kind of skills-sharing place, something for the young people.'

Jack was clearly surprised: 'A youth club?'

'No, not a youth club, something for the older ones, what I think of as the lost generation. Eighteen to twenty-four, say. Maybe involving older people, too. All the people with knowledge and skills who've found themselves on the scrapheap. Maybe business start-ups, but more creativity. Art. Music. Carpentry. Skills that are dying out. Even just sewing! There are teenage girls who I'm sure would love the chance to learn. All the ones who are into vintage clothes who just don't have sewing machines or the skills to do alterations. Lads who never got a chance to do woodwork or metalwork because of the bloody national curriculum. Look at Jason! What he's done here, that he never knew he could! Some of these kids have only ever sat at desks, they've never made anything. They don't know the pleasure of it. Even if there's no jobs or apprenticeships, they could do stuff, learn stuff, get experience, get pleasure out of making things. They just need a place and people to get them started.'

I was so carried away with expressing my vision for the first time that it took me a minute to come back to earth, and when I did, I found Jack was looking at me in away that I found disconcerting. I was so resigned to the idea that he regarded me as a colleague, with brotherly affection at best, that I was entirely taken aback to find those blue eyes focused on me with an unmistakably different expression. But then it was gone. He shook his head, as though dislodging a thought, and abruptly got up. 'Well, I'd better be off.' But he stopped at the front door and came back into the room, where I was still sitting disconsolately clutching the letter. 'Tell you what, though. If you fancy doing a spot of trespassing, I'm your man. Unless…'

'Why not? Yes, let's, before anyone else has the idea. When?'

'What about Sunday morning? Claire's on a sleepover. Will you be here at say 11 o'clock?'

It crossed my mind to wonder where else he thought I'd be, but I dismissed the thought and just said yes.

'Right, I'll bring a few tools in my rucksack, a crowbar and some screwdrivers. If I can't get the paneling off without breaking anything, I've got a good idea of how to get in, but it'll be dirty. Be prepared! See you at eleven then.'

I was ready on the doorstep when he arrived. It was a beautiful early spring day, and I was raring to go, excited my the idea of doing something illicit, let alone the thought of what we might find. I doubted there would be anything left from Esther's time, but it wasn't beyond the bounds of possibility that I'd find something. Just the idea was thrilling to me.

We left the car at my house and walked the rest of the way, and today of all days, Richard was just pulling out as the lane as we reached the turning. Through the darkened glass, I saw him register it was me, scan Jack, then look back at me. He turned his head and drove away, accelerating hard.

Jack looked puzzled when I glanced at his profile as we walked, and finally he said, with what struck me as studied nonchalance: 'Problems?'

Now it was my turn to be puzzled. "Sorry? How do you mean?'

'With … um … Richard, is it?'

'Oh, yes, you could say that. He objected to me instigating any of this. I'm just relieved he hasn't come out with a gun.'

We'd reached the gate now, and I saw that the path down the field was well-worn with tyre tracks, and an area was completely

235

bald where people had been parking and storing wood. There was a big circle of burnt earth half way down the field.

We walked a way in silence, then Jack said, 'Got over it now, has he? The invasion, I mean.'

'I don't think so, no. That oak tree's beautiful, so kind of potent and melancholy! How old would you say it was?'

'Not sure, we had a tree surgeon out to that one, and he thought maybe three hundred years. It looks fine, now, doesn't it? There's a much older one deeper in, but we haven't cleared around that yet. We've been concentrating on the road itself and the laurel hedges on the right side. We're nearly at the house, which is why I suggested this expedition. Once the road reaches it, and vehicles can, we might have problems.'

'Has there been much interest locally?'

'We haven't seen much, just a couple of curious dog-walkers. When the weather improves, it'll be a different matter I expect.'

'I can't wait to bring Leonard. He was briefly a pot-boy here, you know. He's really keen to come and see as soon as it's accessible for an old chap with a dodgy hip.'

As we walked along the cleared drive, Jack pointed out features to me, 'We think there's a small lake or a big pond over there. There are really dense bulrushes and the land's very boggy. When we get to the right point, we'll get some of the big guns out from English Heritage and the National Trust to see where we go with it.'

'Oh, it would be such a shame if it got fossilized and people had to pay to come in. I wonder if they'd consider making it into a working museum, or something, like Beamish. Then at least there would be local jobs.'

'Well, it's funny you should mention Beamish: I was round the back the other day, and I found a barn and stables. There's quite a lot of old farm machinery, and I wondered whether to contact the agricultural college. I think the thing is to get the measure of what we've got here, then decide what we want to do with it, then bring in the experts and find out what we actually can do with it.'

It was wonderful to walk the route and be able to occasionally see the sky, and Jack set such a pace that soon we were both slipping off our coats and filling our lungs with fresh spring air. We soon reached the limit of the cleared path, and our progress slowed. I'd tied my jacket round my waist and Jack carried his. At one point, he stopped to hold a branch back for me, and his shirt was open at the top: he seemed unaware that he'd lost a button. His chest hair was golden and the skin smooth and unblemished: I averted my eyes hastily and passed under his arm with my head down.

Once we reached the front steps, we had to decide how to go about this, but Jack had clearly thought it through. 'We'll go round to the kitchen extension: there's a window there we might be able to open, and if all else fails, there's access into the cellar through the coal chute.'

He lead the way to where one of the panels on a back window had split and was hanging off, and suggested that he could lift me to see whether the sash window could be opened. Before I could come up with an alternative plan, he stood behind me and I felt his two huge hands encircle my waist. He lifted me easily, but the window wouldn't budge. 'Plan B, then,' he said. With a crowbar, he broke the lock on a small pair of doors set into the base of a wall, and then lowered himself down, though he had to squirm to the diagonal to get his shoulders through the opening. He suspended himself from a railing, then swung for a moment, looking down to adjust his eyes to the darkness below. Then he dropped out of sight and I heard him land with a thump and a clatter. A moment later, I was relieved to hear his voice: 'Don't worry, it was a bucket. It's actually ok down here. It's been swept clean since the last coal delivery, thank goodness. Come on.'

I felt a bit self-conscious about lowering myself into his arms, but needn't have worried: he clasped me firmly round the shins as soon as my legs came within his reach, and then held my legs with one arm while he took me round the waist with the other. When my feet touched the floor, my face brushed the warmth of his shoulder, and the musky masculine smell of him made my knees go weak. He held me briefly against his chest as he straightened up, and became suddenly aware of the firmness of his stomach. He looked a big man but it was clearly all muscle. When he released me, I felt a little unsteady with sudden awareness of my body's responses. I kept my head down, feeling entirely confused. If he'd seen my eyes in the light from above, I was sure the dilated pupils would have given me away.

The beam of his torch found a doorway in one corner and beside it a brush and shovel leant against the wall, for all the world as if they'd just been left there. With the briefest resistance, the door opened easily and we followed a narrow corridor and a short flight of stone steps up to a small room which contained only a grimy Belfast sink with brass taps shrouded in a dark mesh of cobwebs.

Beyond the next door was a whitewashed kitchen dominated by a large oak table very similar to the one in the farmhouse. Jack was all for going straight through, but I paused here to look around me. Such a human room, a kitchen, bearing the resonance of human needs and edible pleasures: the engine room of the house. All the pots and pans and implements lined up in the places they'd earned through frequency of use, all ready for service if anyone wanted them.

The stone sink in here was much larger and relatively cleaner, with a sloped and ridged wooden draining board on which stood a solitary white tin mug, evidently rinsed and left to drain almost seventy years ago, long before we were born. This poignant object drew my eye: perhaps the person who swept up and left this room for the last time didn't know they'd be the last, that no-one would ever side that mug away. Others like it hung from the shelf nearest the stove, and when I saw there was an empty hook, I couldn't resist. I lifted the mug from its sleep and tenderly wiped it on my coat. Its rim and handle were dark blue, lightened in places where thumbs and lips had touched. The upper part of the inside of the handle was scraped bare of paint by the metal hook on which it had hung, and to which I now returned it. Neither of us had spoken, and when I turned from the shelf, I saw that Jack was watching me with a gentle smile; he opened the door and gestured for me to go first. As I passed the sink, I noticed the pale circle of wood where the mug had stood looking vulnerable, exposed to the light for the first time.

The rooms beyond were hushed and haunted, wistful and waiting. Light seeped under boarded-up windows to show us the eerie outlines of shrouded objects and drift in the dusty air like pale wraiths. Startling shafts of coloured light refracted through glass to illuminate a patch of rug, a wafer of floorboard, a wallpaper rose, the rise of a stair, lending significance to randomness. And everywhere, just beyond the periphery of my vision and the scope of my hearing, spirits wafted and whispered.

As if by agreement, we didn't speak a word in that churchlike atmosphere, communicating on an instinctive level by the touch of an arm, an indicative nod, a glance of confirmation. The place entered us both by osmosis, and when we took our leave the way we had come, we reached the sunlight quite changed. For me, there was the quiet formation of a kernel of determination that the house would be woken from its long and lonely sleep. For Jack, less prone to anthropomorphism of inanimate objects, there was a new interest in the future of the building as well as the woods. And beneath this quiet conversational fugue was a subtext: I began to wonder whether only I could hear it.

By the time we reached the lane, I had decided it was make or break. I felt sure the attraction was mutual, but something was holding us back. For me, it had been uncertainty about how he felt: I wasn't sure about what his reservations were, but I found I had to know, and something had just occurred to me. We had been walking in pensive silence, but as we emerged from the woods into the sunlight, I said, 'I'm wondering whether to try and patch it up with Richard while you're with me. He can be a bit scary.'

He was ahead of me, so I didn't see his face, and there was no reply until we reached the gate. He'd stopped and was looking at me curiously. 'How do you mean? Scary how?' There was an ominous note in his voice that I hadn't heard before.

'Well, he suffers from post-traumatic stress disorder: he's ex-military, you know.'

'No, I didn't know.' He'd turned and walked on, but then he stopped and looked back at me standing by the gate, and he was glowering. 'So are you saying he mistreats you? You're scared of him?'

'No, he doesn't mistreat me because he doesn't see me. Not that I think he would mistreat anyone anyway. We haven't spoken since before Christmas when I told him about the woods.'

239

He was quiet, clearly struggling to grasp something essential. 'So, let me get this right. You broke up over this, over opening up the woods, but you want me to come with you to see if he's willing to give it another go?'

'To be friends again, yes.' He turned and walked away again, so this time I followed him, but I wasn't going to spell it out. Let him get there by himself.

He'd stopped again, and was looking at the chestnut tree. 'Tell you what, let's go and measure that tree. I keep meaning to do it but never get round to it.' Without waiting for an answer, he vaulted the fence from a standing start and left me to climb over and follow him across the field, quite bewildered by this turn of events.

By the time I caught up with him, he was standing holding the budding branches apart and his face was serious. I passed through the gap he'd made and again experienced that frisson, that sense of space out of time. I know I had a passing thought that when I got home, I must read Four Quartets again: there was resonance here that evoked Eliot's lines and images. All was still and quiet, expectant.

I brought myself back to the present and said, 'Have you got a tape-measure?'

When his voice came from close behind me, it sounded different, slightly lower. I felt a tingle down my neck when he said, 'No, I thought we could measure it in hugs.' I turned round slowly, and faced him with a quiet smile on my face.

'That sounds like a nice idea.' His smile was tentative, suddenly shy. He needed just a touch more reassurance, so I said, 'It was Beth, wasn't it?'

'Yes, she said you were heavily involved, "in deep" or something like that. I just thought you were out of bounds.'

'But I'm not, in fact, if I may be somewhat forward, just the opposite.' He paused only for a moment and then I was in his arms, enclosed by a ring of iron with the side of my face pressed against the soft golden hair on his chest. I slipped my arms around his waist and he lifted my face, tenderly, looking into my eyes with wonder. I lifted my mouth to his and kissed his lips softly, light butterfly kisses. I felt his hand slip into the hair at the back of my head while he kissed me, softly at first, and then more firmly when he felt my

240

response. I found myself pressed against the bark of the tree, feeling its roughness through my shirt until other his hand came up and protectively spread across my back while we kissed and kissed. I felt that if he hadn't held me in such a firm embrace, I would have swooned to the ground with the pleasure of it. In fact, if I hadn't swum to consciousness of where we were, if we'd been hidden from sight by the fullness of the summer canopy, I fully believe we would both have let our bodies take control of the moment.

When we surfaced, I stayed inside his coat, my arms wrapped around him, inhaling the masculine smell of him through the soft cotton of his shirt while he rested his head above mine, gently kissing my hair. At length, I murmured, 'You know something?'

'Mm, what?' I felt the words vibrate in his chest and his voice was husky.

'I've never made love outdoors.'

After a moment, he said, 'Then I would like to make you a promise, if it's not too presumptuous.'

'Oh, it's not presumptuous, not presumptuous at all.'

'I promise you that I will ensure that your first experience of making love outdoors is one you will never forget.'

I raised my head to smile at him and plant a lingering kiss on his warm lips: 'I shall look forward to that.' I snuggled back into the warmth of his coat. 'But for now, how do you fancy coming to see my new bed?'

The thought of sex with another man had held its fears, but Jack could not have been more loving, tender or appreciative of my body, and I have to say the feeling was entirely reciprocated.

Chapter Twenty-six

He fulfilled his promise in May, on the eve of my birthday. He'd made it known that I shouldn't make any plans for that night. We were going out for a meal with friends and family on the day itself, but we were apparently having a private celebration the night before. All I knew was that everything was taken care of, we were staying overnight, and I should dress comfortably and warmly: he would pick me up at six. I'd asked whether it was a posh hotel, a country-pub, an outdoor concert, or a camping trip, and he adamantly refused to give me even a hint, so I wore a comfortable maxi dress, some dressy jewelry and sandals I could walk in.

When he arrived in a jacket and tie, looking smarter than I'd ever seen him, I naturally expected to be getting into the car or a taxi. Instead, he took my overnight bag in one hand and my waist in the other, and guided me past the car, towards the Common. I knew then, but had one concern, 'Please tell me it's not a surprise party!' I had a horrific vision of all the volunteers gathered under a marquee erected on a patch of ground that had just been cleared near the manor.

'Well, it's a surprise, and it's a party, but don't worry, it's a very very private party.'

It was a beautiful evening, the air still and warm with the fresh moist promise of summer. In the hedgerows, the bright green peas of young buds were visible, and the first dandelions glowed in the shadows. The meadow grass had grown feathers which tickled my legs as we walked. The sky had been clear all day, and as we entered the woodland, I saw that many of the leaves had started to unfurl.

When we were getting close to the house, we turned off the main drive into a gap in the laurel hedge and followed a narrow path I hadn't taken before: it wound between the grey-blue trunks of old oaks. I hadn't realised how dark it had seemed until we came to a clearing in which a tree had been felled. A circle of pinkish-blue sky lit the treetops, and wraiths of woodsmoke lingered in the air.

On the other side of the clearing, a huge elm towered above its neighbours, and beneath this tree, Jack stopped and turned me to face him. He smiled and lifted my chin for a gentle kiss, then said, 'Right, we're nearly there. I'm going ahead, and I want you to wait here, ok? I'll be no more than ten minutes. Lean against this trunk and don't move. In fact,' he produced a silk scarf from his pocket, 'I'm going to ask you to put this on. Ok?'

I laughed, 'Oh no, you're not going to go all Fifty Shades of Grey on me, are you? Not my cup of tea, no siree.'

He smiled and gave me a kiss on the nose before tying the scarf round my head. I felt his fingers loosen my hair, then his hands on my shoulders and his whisper in my ear gave me a tremor. 'Ten minutes.' And then I heard his footsteps cracking away to my right.

It was a strange feeling standing there all alone, unable to see. My smile faded as soon as Jack's footsteps receded, and I instinctively reached my hands back to spread them on the smooth trunk and steady myself. A jackdaw cawed in the trees above me, and something skittered through the twigs over to my left. The smell of woodsmoke was curiously comforting: I found myself quite relaxed, with a delicious tingle of anticipation.

Soon I heard him coming back, felt his hands around my waist and his lips on mine. It was curiously arousing that he hadn't spoken and that I was feeling so entirely in his power. I trusted him completely, and the abandonment of my own will produced an unfamiliar sensation that I felt deep in my core.

He took both my hands and led me, and I didn't stumble once. When we came to a standstill, he stood behind me and his arm came down around the back of my shoulder to encircle my waist and hold me against his body while he undid the scarf and lifted it from my eyes. I blinked in the semi-darkness and saw that we were on the edge of a hollow filled with wildflowers and lit by candles. All around us, ancient trees stood sentinel, and the floor was a dark sea of bluebells, encircled by tall church candles which illuminated the shores like lighthouses. It took me a moment to notice that there were tea-lights suspended from branches and others from long hazel twigs embedded in the earth.

An involuntary gasp escaped my lips. 'Oh, it's beautiful!' Behind me, his arms wrapped around the front of my body, Jack whispered into my hair, 'That's not all. Come with me.' And he took me by the hand and led me around the edge of the hollow and over a small rise, where a line of trodden grasses led to a crumbling door in a high wall made of warm red bricks. When we pressed ourselves sideways through the doorway, I saw that a small shed leant against the wall, the inside warmly lit by candles in jam-jars. On the floor was a duvet and pillows on what looked like a large inflatable mattress, and by the side of the makeshift bed was a bottle of champagne on ice. 'Only the ice melted. Sorry.'

'Jack,' I took his face in my hands and lifted on tiptoe to kiss his lips, 'this is utterly wonderful. I could cry.' In fact, my eyes were brimming, and when he saw that and kissed my eyelids each in turn, my heart brimmed over too.

'Champagne? The picnic's in the cool-box, and I've got a rug, and there's an old table over there,' he pointed across the darkening walled garden, 'but I thought you might like to choose where we ate ... and when.' He looked at me meaningfully then popped the cork of the champagne with a wicked grin.

As we drank our champagne, we wandered the garden, our arms round each other's waists as the sky darkened and tiny pipistrelle bats swung through the sweetness of the evening air. Champagne kisses in a dark garden, oh the bliss of it! Soon, our glasses were empty, and we didn't need to speak our agreement that it was time.

Lying on a rug among the bluebells, inhaling their musky scent, I watched him undress. My clothes lay at the edge of the hollow, where I'd felt the cool fingertips of night-time rise up my body as he raised my dress. He had lifted me into his arms, naked, and kissed me, almost shy, his face full of wonder, and I saw how my skin glowed in the moonlight, opalescent and ethereal. He carried me down in the hollow and lay me down tenderly, then stood and watched me stretch out, luxuriating in the liberation of body and sense: of night-scents and woodsmoke and celandine and soil and the rising sap of spring. An owl called in the distance and another echoed its response. The sky shimmered like mother-of-pearl, illuminating the treetops above me. When he stood naked, candlelight touched the outline of his powerful body with gold. He looked to me then like a god and came to me, silent and elemental, a being of the earth, of the trees. I felt more open, more molten, more at one with the universe than I had ever imagined, and then everything was warmth and sensation and long rhythmic movements, and I was borne completely away on deep seas and tides pulled by the moon and the rotation of the earth beneath us and the unseen stars above us and the surging and the swell and the tension impossible to sustain and then the constellations burst into brightness and the release and then the suffusion of warmth within warmth and the sigh and the slowing and the slowing and then stillness and softness and peace.

Later, wrapped in the blanket and sitting together on the bedding in the hut, our food spread about us, heedless of crumbs or spills or cold or nakedness, I had never felt so alive, so free or so safe. We had hardly spoken: the night seemed almost sacrosanct, words banal and unnecessary.

We slept a little, woke a little, made love again, heard owls and skitterings in the undergrowth, slept again, woke again, and saw that pinkish light was creeping up the skies. Even then, there was no haste, no need for words, just a quiet agreement, a rounding up and a wander homeward in the half-light of dawn, to creep unseen along the cold streets and slip into bed for a cuddle and a warm snooze.

When I woke before him, I lay looking at his peaceful face and kissed the curve of his sleeping smile before slipping out of bed to shower and bring a tray of tea and toast. We had a whole day to ourselves, and I knew exactly what I wanted to do. It might have seemed a strange choice, but there was one big present I could no longer wait to unwrap. When I told him, far from being surprised, he acquiesced with a sleepy smile. 'I had a great dream.'

'Me too. Wonder if it was the same one.' I still felt utterly euphoric.

After breakfast, there were cards and visitors and phone calls and a bouquet of flowers was delivered mid-morning. For one moment, I wondered whether they could be from Paul, but I needn't have worried: Mark had enclosed a card and a promise to ring later. There was nothing from Paul, but in a way I was glad: it simply made things easier, more final.

It felt momentous when I finally turned the key in the lock: although I knew that my granddad hadn't been the last to close that door, I still felt an immediate connection to him. Jack helped me lift out all the detritus which blocked the doorway and sort it into three piles: Keep, Freecycle and Tip. Soon we were staring at Granddad's five-foot workbench, which ran the full length of the back of the shed. His tools were still hanging from the neat array of hooks and nails on the back wall, and three open-topped wooden drawers were lined up beneath, the words Plumbing, Electricity and Misc painted on in his neat copperplate. I felt my eyes fill. "That's the tin where he stood his Mint Imperials in an open paper bag. That's his flask. There's the butty box he used to strap to the back of his bike.' It seemed a miracle to me that all this had been left untouched: I'd imagined my grandma would have thrown everything out, no sentimentalist she, but instead it appeared that she'd simply locked the shed and left everything as it was.

'Well?' said Jack, his arms round my shoulders. 'What would you like to do? Some of those tools would still be useful, with a bit of sharpening, a bit of oiling, some tlc. Some are outdated now, but it's up to you.'

'I need to think about that, but for now, I wouldn't mind a bit of time on my own in here, just to poke about.'

'No problem,' he kissed my hair. 'I'll walk along for a paper and sit and have a read. It takes it out of a chap, giving a woman the night of her life, you know.'

I turned and hugged him tight. 'It was like a wonderful dream, Jack. Thank-you so much. How can I repay you?'

He bent to kiss me, smiling, and raised an eyebrow like James Bond. 'We'll think of something.'

When he'd gone, I stood for a while and breathed in the woody air, surveying the bench, the tools, the vice, all the things my beloved granddad had loved so much. He once told me he used to shut himself in here, his bolt-hole, and showed me the wooden peg that he used to turn to stop anyone opening the door while he was in there. By anyone, I knew he meant his wife. I'd thought nothing of it then, and I thought nothing of it now, passing over the memory with a wry smile.

But when I found the journal, I understood.

It was in a box hidden under the workbench, wrapped in a cloth at the back. When I pulled it out, I thought it was just a box of tools, but it was too light. I lifted it out onto the bench and when I unwrapped it, I saw that it was a hand-made wooden chest with the initials E and S carved on the lid in ornate lettering like vine leaves. Esther and Stanley.

It was locked, but in the instant I tried to open it, I knew where the key was. I had once picked up the old tobacco tin in which he stood his packet of Mint Imperials, and seen a tiny paper pocket taped to the bottom. I hadn't investigated at the time, and I'd never given it a thought since, but now the memory flashed on me from nowhere. I reached across the bench for the tin, and the pocket was still there, fixed forever by black electrician's tape. With my thumb, I felt the shape of a small key and pulled it out, conscious that my hands were shaking slightly. It was almost as though I had a premonition.

Chapter Twenty-seven

The Cottage
Farnworth Manor
May 1939

Dear Bertie

If you are reading this, then I am dead. It occurs to me that soldiers in The Great War must have started their last letters in this way. (Perhaps you wrote one too, my love: I am ashamed that I have never asked you, but I know you cannot bear to speak of that time. I can think of no other words with which to begin. Forgive me.)

It seems I must write a conclusion to my story. Perhaps we all have a yearning to believe our voice will still be heard when we are gone. I want to feel some control, although I have none: my fate is sealed. This account will at least bear witness. I will not hold back in what I write: it is strange how inhibition melts away when we know we will die. All any of us really wants is to be known and understood, and I count myself blessed that you know my soul and understand everything about me, my Gabriel Oak, my love, my Stanley. I will tell the rest of my story for Bertie, though some of it would shock him. I have to accept now that I will never see him again, but for some miracle. I will leave it in your care, my darling.

I know I leave a fine legacy here at Farnworth Manor: I am so proud of all we have achieved in the past seventeen years: all the lives we have touched and, I hope, improved. But this is the story of my heart.

As I walked home from that first meeting with Freya, my mind was ablaze with possibilities. The following day, I went to see Miss Ashworth, and she arranged for us to visit Edith Rigby that weekend. On Sunday morning, we walked to the station in bright sunshine and caught the train to Preston, and all the while we talked. Not of the weather and the scenery, but serious talk of working conditions and wages and food prices. By the time we stepped off the train, I felt bigger and stronger, animated by a new energy. Things had fallen into place: the lives of fictional characters, of Oliver Twist and Mary Barton, the poetry of Blake: the writers were real

249

people who wanted to expose the reality of working class lives to their readers, the people with the money and education: the power to help. Well now I would have power to help, and I was going to find out how to go about it.

When the pony and trap appeared in the lane outside the station, I took the driver to be a man, for I saw dark breeches and a farmer's smock. But when she called out, 'Woah there Bramble!' and the trap pulled up beside us, she raised her felt hat in greeting and I saw wheat-gold hair cropped short, like a man's.

'Maud! Beautiful morning, is it not?' she jumped down from the trap and held out her hand, leaning in towards me as I took it, and regarding me intently with eyes the colour of cornflowers. 'And this must be Esther. Welcome Esther, it's a delight to meet you. Maud has told me your exciting news. Climb aboard.'

I clambered into the back of the trap and sat on a box, whilst Miss Ashworth (I still couldn't bring myself to call her Maud) climbed into the front. As we turned a slow circle and then set off at a trot down the wooded lane, I was aware of the two of them talking and laughing, but could catch only the gist over the clopping of Bramble's hooves and the creaking of the cart. The cottage was near a hamlet called Howick, about a mile down a sandy lane which wound through woodland bright with buds and blossom. Once, as we passed by a beautiful apple tree, I heard Edith declaim, 'Behold the blossom! It is a butterfly fettered to the earth! Behold the butterfly! It is a blossom freed by the cosmos!' and I smiled to hear it.

When the rocking of the cart slowed and we turned into a gate, I turned to get my first glimpse of Edith's smallholding. Maud had told me all about the house at Winkley Square where Mrs Rigby had never felt at home: she had recently bought Marigold Cottage, having finally tired of Preston society. Ever since she took to the streets on the first bicycle Preston had ever seen, her exploits had been deemed eccentric and unladylike. As a teenage girl, she had been pelted with fruit as she rode by flashing her bloomers, and the disapproval had grown with each new exploit. I could imagine the derision accorded a youngster who left her leafy square on Christmas morning to distribute her presents to the children of the poor, now the doctor's wife who wore trousers and spent good money pointlessly teaching mill-girls poetry. And as for the radical feminist

250

and activist for the suffragette cause who brought shame on Preston and evaded the police by climbing out of windows dressed as a chimneysweep! It simply could not be countenanced!

In Marigold Cottage, she had finally found peace and happiness, and I could see why. It was a pastoral idyll, with glowing orange walls and donkey-brown thatch, surrounded by a blossom-filled orchard in which hens pecked contentedly and kittens gambolled. Transfixed, I was startled out of my reverie by an aggressive gander, which ran towards us hissing and flapping its wings, but Edith ran at it flapping her arms and shouting, 'Yahhh! You don't scare me!'

After a guided tour of the orchards where fresh blossom filled the fruit trees and bees beat a steady airborn path back to their hives, we were taken to admire the rows of vegetables. Then we had to see the sheds, where precarious pyramids of potatoes towered and full sacks leant against the walls, ready for market. By the time we were taken to see the compost heap, I was seething with frustration. I would have been more patient if it hadn't all been accompanied by a self-congratulatory narrative littered with bursts of what seemed to me ridiculously fanciful poetry: "A leaf of grass is no less than the journeywork of the stars…And the running blackberry would adorn the parlours of heaven."

This was not what I'd come for. The beauty of nature, the benefits of contact with the rhythms of life, the oneness of the universe: this seemed to me the romantic indulgence of townspeople for whom these ideas were new. (Lest you think ill of me, Bertie, remember I was young, newly-charged with fire and I had come here with an agenda.) By the time Mrs Rigby lead the way into the cottage, I was impatient to talk of something other than produce and poetry.

I excused myself and walked away simmering: I was convinced that she had lost her taste for battle against injustice. Miss Ashworth had brought me here on a fool's errand. But as I relieved myself in the earth privy, I reminded myself that both Maud and Freya had warned me that Edith's ideas were becoming increasingly drawn to the spiritual: she was clearly today in the mood for "Walking the sky". As I rearranged my clothing and stepped out into sunlight, I scolded myself for my impatience: none of this detracted from her achievements, and she more than any woman I had ever met, had surely earned her little slice of heaven.

They were seated at a small table in the window-nook and looked up as I came in. Edith's eyes gleamed with mischief, 'And how did you find our earth-closet, Esther?'

Embarrassed, I muttered, 'Fine, we had one the same until recently,' and sat down at the table, which was spread with heavy pottery of delphinium blue.

'Our strawberries last year were huge!' I looked up in time to catch her winking at Maud, and caught her meaning. I was surprised by what she implied: our horses and cows produced plenty of manure, and we'd never considered using human waste. But I would not show her my disgust: I was inspired to surprise her: "From where we have gathered in we must put back –life-in full measure."

She looked at me, clearly delighted. 'You are a student of Steiner?'

'No, it's something Freya said to me. We were talking about the plans for Farnworth Manor's produce.' I considered launching into what I really wanted to talk about, but at that moment the interior door opened, and in came a woman shaped like a cottage-loaf, bearing a tray.

'Ah, Miss Tucker, this is Esther, and you know Maud.' The woman peered at me over think pince-nez glasses, grunted an acknowledgement, placed the tray on the side-table, and withdrew.

Edith winked at me. 'Be not offended, Esther. Miss Tucker is my right-hand man and a gallant little body. She would normally have partaken of this repast with us, but is clearly not in the mood.'

Maud laughed. 'You'll get to know Edith: she sees charm where no others find it. She was famous in Preston for treating servants as equals. It got you into no end of hot water, did it not Edith?'

Edith chuckled ruefully as she poured the tea. When she looked at me again, her expression was quite transformed. 'So Esther, you have the opportunity to benefit the people of your community? Tell me about Adlington.'

At last, here it was, my opportunity to find out how it could be done, how to maximise the benefits of the Farnworths' plans. So

I told her about our town, Bertie, about the three mills which dominated it at that time. I told her that Freya had given me the opportunity to represent the needs of the community and that I wanted to do so in a considered, business-like way.

When I had finished, none of us spoke for a while. We drank our tea and the others took cake. I had no stomach for it at that time: I found myself agitated and nervous, full of the wish to do good but conscious of my ignorance of the world beyond the dry-stone walls of the farm. Even the life of the mill-girls was a mystery to me, I am ashamed to say.

When she broke the silence, Edith had regained some of her old fire. 'The mills are hell-holes where capitalist fortunes are made. The conditions are dismal. A child of eleven, plucked from school, earns sixpence per week as a weaver's apprentice. If at twelve she is promoted to the status of a full-timer, she may earn five shillings for working twelve hours a day and six hours on Saturday.' There was silence again whilst we contemplated what she had said.

When she looked at me again, her eyes had softened. 'I have done what I can, Esther.'

Maud spoke up: 'You have worked marvels, Edith.' Turning to me, she said, 'Edith has done so much, I cannot begin to tell you Esther, and her work continues.'

'Yes,' Edith brightened suddenly, straightened her spine, and began a long speech which I have often recollected. 'The working conditions of the people in your mills cannot be your priority Esther. Instead, think of this: Steiner speaks of the threefold being of man – body, soul and spirit. Do what you can for the souls of those workers. Provide allotments in which they can reconnect with nature and reap the benefits in mind and spirit. For the children, perhaps a school. Maud tells me of your enjoyment of education. Share your joy. If you do not wish to teach yourself, suggest that the Farnworths dedicate one of their outbuildings and employ a teacher. Maud and I have many connections who will be happy to help, and more will appear in your locality.

'Negotiate fair wages for the workers on the Farnworth estate, and employment terms which will feed their spirit. Perhaps a bonus scheme, or shares in the profits. Introduce the Farnworths to the Booths. After payment of dividends, Booths employees receive

253

one third of the company's profits: imagine the benefits not only for their pockets but also for their spirits, for the effect it has on their pride, their sense of the dignity of labour and their sense of ownership, of joint endeavour. John Booth has a fine house and grounds - we have taken our Brook Street girls there, haven't we Maud? – and he is not afraid to share its pleasures: on Bonus day, he holds a garden party for all his employees. The Farnworths are perhaps new to the idea of business, of providing employment beyond the necessary. The Booths, not the mill-owners, are the family we would wish them to emulate. We can provide introductions, Esther, we will help you.'

And it worked, Bertie. The Farnworths are such good people, and they were grateful – imagine that! – grateful for my initiative, for the ideas and the contacts. I planned it all out and then wrote it all up as a business plan. It took me two weeks of solid work and meetings. If it hadn't been for Aunty Nellie and the twins, we'd all have starved and the house would have gone to rack and ruin. I barely slept! But never was anything more worthwhile in the whole of my life or, I'll wager, in the history of this village. When you come home, Bertie, you will be so proud of all we have achieved.

And so to the story of my heart. The first year of my employment here was a blur. I was ablaze with ideas and used to crawl into bed long past midnight, only to wake a few hours later to scribble notes before falling back into exhausted sleep. There was so much to think about, so much research to do, so many meetings with suppliers and buyers, soil specialists and irrigation engineers, and I loved every single minute of it.

Stanley was patience itself. He and Dad were working long hours too: all the new horses and horse-driven machinery kept them so busy that soon they were able to take on two new lads, so Dad could ease off a bit. As he said, he wasn't getting any younger. I knew Aunty Nellie was taking good care of him though. Her husband had been invalided out of the Lancashire Fusiliers, and had died soon after she came to us, so she was often still there when I got home. Lily and Rosie were usually still up, too, heads bent together at the table, plotting their next venture in the flower gardens that were now their responsibility. They are fine women now, with families of their own, and I count it a blessing that they can still have the fulfilment of running their business: I know it is hard work, but they have strong support and they both know how lucky they are.

One June night in that first year, it was so light when I looked up from my books that I was astonished to find it was 8 o'clock. It had rained for most of the day, and I had been hunched over books all afternoon in the study, reading about the optimum growing conditions for exotic fruit. Now it was dry and warm, so I decided to walk instead of taking the pony and trap: I knew Stanley would wait for me under the chestnut tree. As I walked, I consciously stretched and breathed deeply, feeling an appreciation of the easy fluidity of my body and looking forward to being in his arms. The canopy was at its thickest at this time of the year, so I knew the ground would be dry, and the outer skirts of the tree hung down to the ground, affording us privacy.

By the time I stood on the stile, it was almost dark and the air felt oppressive. My shirt was sticking to my back and damp tendrils of hair coiled on my neck. The clouds had an ominous, leaden look, and suddenly lightening split the sky. I jumped down and ran as fast as I could across the field to the shelter of the tree, bursting in under its branches just as the first heavy raindrops hit my head. I was laughing breathlessly, my face alight and eager to see him. But all was still and quiet in the cool cave of leaves. 'Stanley?' I spoke softly, and a shape emerged silently from the shadow of massive trunk and enfolded me. Only later did I think about how quiet he was. I suppose I was so wrapped up in myself that I was taking him for granted, but it didn't seem to matter. I was to find out to my cost that love needs feeding like a tender plant, else it weakens.

I think of that night often. It was the last night we were together before it happened, and I felt so fulfilled in every way, so full of energy and optimism about everything. Stanley was always part of my future; I had no idea of his doubts. All was right with my world.

My demeanour must have been transformed during that year: the Manor's established workforce in the gardens and stables were frankly astonished to find themselves being governed by two women, but we soon won them over with a combination of skill and charm. I learnt a neat trick when I wanted something I knew they'd resist: I only had to begin a sentence, "I was talking to Mr Farnworth about ..." to find their expressions changed in an instant.

And what happened between me and Izabel, you ask? I take you back to the words with which I opened the story of what happened when you disappeared. You may have wondered what action of my sister's occasioned such condemnation. Well now I will tell you.

When Dad married Aunty Nellie and I moved into a cottage in the grounds of the Manor, I was twenty-one. Stanley and I were deeply in love. He still lived at home with his father, and we planned to marry when the time was right. Unavoidably, I became more and more absorbed into Freya's circle. Encourages by Edith Ripley, other members of the WSPU had come forward to help in the education and recreation centre we set up in the largest barn. Freya's ideas and her friends stimulated me, and I suppose I neglected Stanley a little. But only a little. My heart never waivered. He, however, became increasingly insecure, thanks in no small part to my sister.

We would often take lunch together in the gardens: I was so busy, and Dad happily gave him a long lunch break to enable him to walk the mile to Farnworth Manor and join me in the garden or the greenhouse for a picnic. Sometimes Izzy would join us, and it seemed to me she took every opportunity to tease Stanley. I put it down to her mischievous nature, and seriously misjudged her malign intent.

'That was a handsome chap I saw you with in the orchard, Esther. Another of your admirers?'

Stanley would turn his face towards me, serious and watchful, and I would blush despite myself.

'No, Izzy, he was a buyer from Booths: he came to look at my peaches.'

'Ha ha! I bet he did!' She would laugh uproariously, but Stanley could never join in, and I would have to spend time reassuring him again.

Izabel had been disappointed in love. Her devotion to young Edgar continued unabated, and she clung to the belief that he would marry her when he finished university. He returned home in some university holidays, but not all, and was frequently in the company of young men like himself: urbane, privileged, spoilt. Their arrival was invariably announced by the roaring of engines, for he was the proud owner of a Bugatti, which he had bought on reaching his majority and coming into an inheritance from a grandfather. His father greatly disapproved of this, and I often heard him express his concerns to Freya about Edgar's latest exploits.

Needless to say, all my cautionary talks with Izzy went unheeded. She professed to have 'an understanding' with Edgar, and their liaisons took place in secret. She assured me that they were careful that she should not become pregnant. She had never told him about the miscarriage, but she promised me it had taught her a lesson.

In the spring of 1922, Edgar's university education was drawing to a close, and shortly after he had been home for a month at Easter, Izzy confided in me that she was carrying his child. I was horrified by her complacency, and certain that she had engineered this with the intention of forcing his hand.

In May, he came home for a short period of revision, and she told him. I was not aware of any of what I am about to tell you. You must understand that these days were saturated with work and people. I was loving every minute of my life, and I was confident that just one more year would see everything established and that Stanley and I would be married. I had one deep concern: I still felt no stirring of maternal cravings. I had told him this honestly, and he had seemed unperturbed. I know now that he was confident I would change my mind when we were married.

At the time, there was a gentleman staying at the Manor, Alexander Campbell, an engineer who specialised in irrigation systems. I knew that he was smitten with me but I did nothing to encourage him. We spent a good deal of time about the place, looking at ways of maximising the natural water supply.

Unbeknownst to me, Izabel had been dripping her poison into Stanley's ear. He had been quiet, but no more so than usual, and I had been especially busy, but I assured myself that I would make it up to him at Whitsuntide, when we had agreed a period of holiday to coincide with the mill closures.

One evening at 9 o'clock, I had just got out of the bath when there was a knock at the door of my cottage. I was in the habit of bathing at 8.30 and being in bed for 9 o'clock. You may think this was early to retire on a May evening, but I always loved the mornings, and usually awoke at 5am to make the most of the long spring days.

My first thought was Izzy. Edgar had been home for two days, and knowing her impetuous nature, I doubted she would keep her news to herself any longer than she had to. I feared for her. An unmarried mother was a social pariah: the term 'bastard' applied to her child without compunction. Reader, you live in a much kinder world in so many ways.

I threw on my dressing gown and rushed to the door, ready to take my broken sister in my arms and comfort her. We would work out a plan. We would defy convention. I would look after her. The irony of it sends shivers down my spine.

The figure at the door was Alexander. I folded my arms across my dressing gown, which I hadn't even fastened. His eyes lit up, and travelled the length of my body in a most presumptuous way, and to my horror, he took me in his arms.

I pushed him away immediately and held him at arms' length, scandalised. 'What on earth are you doing?'

His response bewildered me entirely, 'Your note.'

'My note? I gave you no note.'

He understood his error straight away and his face fell.

'There was a note left on my clipboard when I came back from lunch.'

'What did it say?'

'Simply "My cottage, 9pm tonight."'

'Well, I'm sorry to disappoint you, Mr Campbell, but it wasn't from me!' I stepped back to slam the door, but he reached for me again and spoke earnestly into my face.

'I'm so sorry, Esther. I can't think what it meant or who must have left it. It is a mistake, clearly, meant for someone else. Please do forgive me. Don't let it spoil our friendship.'

I relented immediately. He was such a charming man, and we had indeed built up a close friendship over the past two weeks.

I stood still, waiting for him to let go of my arms. He was giving no sign of doing so, so I looked down pointedly, and he dropped his hands.

'Say you'll forgive me.'

I smiled, and relief covered his face. 'I forgive you. Some other person will be waiting for someone in vain tonight.'

He laughed, relieved, and then his face grew serious. 'I would like to get to know you better, though, Esther. Would you like to come for a drive tomorrow evening? Perhaps we could take a meal at the inn on Rivington Pike? They say the views are tremendous.'

'I'm sorry, Alexander, I'd love to, but I doubt my fiancé would approve. Unless he could come too, perhaps?'

'Your fiancé? I had no idea! Who is he?'

'He's my father's apprentice, the blacksmith in Adlington. You may have seen him with me and my sister.' But come to think of it, Stanley hadn't been to Farnworth Manor for well over a week. Nor were we actually engaged, but that seemed immaterial.

He took a step back and smiled ruefully. 'I really have made an ass of myself, haven't I?'

I smiled too, and leant forward to kiss him on the cheek, an impetuous gesture which I have since had cause to regret: my excuse is that I was genuinely fond of him and pitied him in his embarrassment.

'Well, no hard feelings then. I think my disappointment is clear, but I wish you every happiness with your blacksmith. When do you plan to marry?'

'In a year or so, I think. I want to get everything established here, and then we can think about it. It wouldn't be fair to marry before then. I've too much to do to be a good wife.'

'He's a very lucky man.' He reached for my hand, bent to kiss it, and then left.

The whole encounter was witnessed by Stanley. Izzy had chosen her spot well: she was with him, and she had ensured that they would hear none of the dialogue. Later he told me how he felt to see the woman he loved, but had only kissed and embraced fully-clothed, a woman he respected and revered as chaste, apparently naked under a loosely-draped dressing-gown, saying goodbye to her lover. Izabel had held his arm, which at the time he felt as a comfort, but when the truth came out, he realised she had meant to restrain him in case he went to confront us. She had prepared him well, with a constant drip of comments meant to weaken the foundations of his faith in me. When I think of it even now, my heard pounds with the evil that she did that day. I can see her simpering face as he turned away from me, his heart broken. She will have had the same sly smug smile she had slid towards me in the bedroom window that first day when she lured him away.

'I'm sorry, ' she said. 'I didn't know how to tell you. It's been going on for more than a week now, and I'm afraid he's not the first. This place has turned her head. She doesn't deserve you Stanley,' and here she sobbed, turned her face away. 'I can't bear to see you unhappy. I can't bear the way she takes you for granted, treats you like a lapdog. You deserve so much better. All she cares about is impressing Freya and the Squire, hobnobbing with all their fine friends. She'd never marry a blacksmith, Stanley. You know that in your heart of hearts. Oh!' and here she started to cry, something she always did easily when she wanted to get her own way, to manipulate Dad usually. She knew Stanley's soft heart. 'I can't bear it, Stanley!' and here he took her in his arms to comfort her, as she knew he would, and she cried and cried. She had only to think of her plight, of Edgar's rejection and the end of all her dreams, and she could cry her heart out, cry to her heart's content. And he fell for it, as she knew he would. 'I love you Stanley! I've always loved you, since we were children! We were meant to be together, can't you see? Think how happy we were when you first came to the farm, how I made you smile for the first time in years, you said.' Gulping, she was, gasping out her lies through her crocodile tears, wetting his shirt-front, accepting his handkerchief to wipe her eyes, then reaching up to kiss him, to kiss him and kiss him and seduce him and steal him. My Stanley. How could she do it? I cry even now to think of it. The betrayal, the cold selfish betrayal.

By the time I knew anything was amiss, the banns had been read for the first time. By the time I heard the full story, it was Whitsuntide and they were about to be married. She had played him perfectly. She had 'proved' that I had betrayed him; I was not interested in marriage; I was stringing him along and taking him for

260

granted. She, on the other hand, loved him dearly and always had; she had saved him from grief, neglect and deceit; she had made a mistake, and she regretted it; she needed him. He married her in full knowledge of her pregnancy: some misguided sense of honour told him it was the right thing to do. She married him in full knowledge that his heart, broken as it was, belonged to me.

But that's not the end of the story. Others may read this beside you, Bertie. I expect the disapproval of some: others will cheer for me.

They had been married just over a month when Stanley first came to me. It was early July, and the night had been a warm one. I had not slept well: the knowledge that I had lost him was still breaking over me afresh every morning like an icy wave. I admit there were times when I didn't want to wake up at all. Once I was dressed, I knew I could put on my cheery face and go about my business as normal: the curious looks of others were best fended off that way, and people had quickly accepted the unexpected turn of events. Only my father suspected the truth.

I always slept with my windows open: my bedroom window is at the back of the bungalow and faces east, so Stanley had made me a pair of slatted shutters which effectively block out the morning light but let the air in. I got out of bed now to open them and saw that it was still too early to get up, but I stood awhile to breathe in the sweet woodland air and listen to the birdsong. My window opens onto the woods, and a faint pinkish light could be discerned through the trees. I traced a cold curve of iron foliage with my finger and remembered him proudly fixing the shutters in place. I had planned to paint them blue, but when I saw the beauty of the wood and the delicacy of the decorative ironwork that he had made, I was moved beyond words and my eyes had involuntarily filled with tears. He is not a man to whom words of love came easily, but he expresses himself eloquently with his hands.

A twig snapped and a blackbird lobbed away through the trees, calling its alarm. Had I seen a movement from the corner of my eye, a shape melding into a tree trunk? What intuition made me speak his name I know not, and it seemed like a dream when he emerged from the trees ten yards away and stood still. I said his name again on a softly rising note, and held my breath until the word came like a dying echo: 'Esther.'

What happened next is a blur to me, I thought of nothing and was all instinct: I raised my arms and he came to me. Suddenly, he was in my room and I was enfolded in his arms, weeping into his chest as though my heart would break. He held me tight, stroking my hair and speaking not a word. I abandoned myself to my grief in a way that I had hitherto resisted, and I have no awareness of how long I cried. Eventually, I began to struggle to calm myself, letting go of the back of his waistcoat to wipe my eyes on my nightdress, and though he loosened his hold, he did not let me go. His arms felt like iron across my back, and his hands cupped my shoulders and held me close. Calmer now, I began to breathe more deeply and inhale the familiar smell of him, and felt a melting warmth suffuse my body. I slipped my hands under his waistcoat and felt the heat of him through his shirt. Running my hands over the powerful muscles of his back, I turned my head as he lifted my hair from the side of my neck and I felt his breath heating the skin beneath my ear. A gentle kiss sent tremors down my shoulders and I felt my nipples harden against him. Suddenly I was finding it hard to breathe deeply and I was conscious of a warm moistness between my legs. Something took over me then, took over us both. No words were spoken, but I found myself slowly pulling the back of his shirt free of his belt so that I could touch his skin, and at the same time, he took my face in both his hands and turned it upward to receive his kiss. For the briefest moment, we looked into each other's eyes and mutually acquiesced, then his lips brushed mine and we were lost.

We had kissed before, of course, and caressed, but this was so different. Our minds were silenced, custom and convention forgotten. We were all instinct and need. My mouth opened to receive his in a way that was new to us, and every probing thrust of his tongue caused a melting and an opening in me that reduced me to warm liquid. When he raised my nightdress and lay me down on the bed, his eyes drank me in and his fingers trembled to undo his shirt. He was so beautiful, carved like Michaelangelo's David, with soft light brown hair on his chest and in a line down his stomach. I reached for his belt and undid the buckle, softly brushing my fingers over the place where his manhood pushed against the fabric of his

262

trousers. He caught his breath, and holding my hand, he gently but firmly placed it beside me on the bed, then bent to kiss my hip. I groaned softly and folded myself round him: suddenly his mouth was on my breast and I gasped as an electric current ran down my body. He softly kissed my other breast and I could wait no longer. My fingers twined in his hair, and my hips lifted of their own accord. Then he was above me, and I felt the leather of his belt hard against my leg. We could not wait. He twisted to release himself from his trousers, and I reached to push them down over his buttocks, surprised to find a fine covering of soft hair over the hard muscles. Now he lay fully between my legs and his eyes held a question, but I smiled up at him and gently drew him into me. Never had I felt more certain of anything in my life.

We did not discuss our betrayal of his vows to Izabel. He had promised to take care of her, and take care of her he does: he is a good husband in every other way. Maggie was born in December, and everyone agreed how lucky they were that a premature baby should be so fine and healthy. The Farnworths do not know, for Edgar left suddenly the day after Izzy's revelation, and never came back. Straight after his final examinations, he and a friend set off for Europe in his Bugatti, and came off the road in the Alps. Maggie will probably never know that she is a Farnworth: that is for Stanley to decide.

Izabel has known about our relationship for all these years. I do not doubt that he has endured difficult times: I choose to believe we have an unspoken agreement, the three of us.

Two years after they married, Izzy became pregnant again, and Dad bought them a house in a terrace not far from the farm. They have a beautiful boy now, the image of his grandfather: both Maggie and Aiden have Dad's curly dark hair. He adored them, and part of the reason he retired was to spend more time with them. His last years were contented ones, though he never ceased from watching the road and lifting his eyes quickly whenever he heard the gate-latch. He tended his garden and pottered in the wood-workshop he shared with Stanley: he was happy and seemed healthy. He died in his sleep, Bertie. I hope I shall go the same way, but I fear not.

They agreed to close the smithy: there was not enough work nowadays for it to support a family. Stanley got a well-paid job as an engineer in the dye-works, and he does carpentry in his spare time.

War is coming again, but I will not live to see it. I am not yet forty, but it seems I have had my allotted time. We thought at first that I was pregnant: there's a savage irony there. The thing that is growing in my womb does not bring life but death. Stanley is devastated, but I am at peace. I have loved and been loved. I have had a wonderful life, touched by tragedy as it was. If I have one wish, it is of course that I'll see before I die. It seems impossible now, but miracles do happen. Whoever took you, your Mr Brownwell, must have links to our town. I have made no secret of my illness: perhaps news will spread to wherever you are, and one day the latch will lift and there you'll be.

If that is not to be (but the hope sustains me) I nurture a hope that whoever took you will one day tell you where you belong, and you will come home again. And then, although you will not find your favourite sister here to hold you, you will read my words and know me, Bertie, know who I became.

I hope you will meet Stanley, the love of my life. He will tell you all about me: his deep abiding love will bring me back to you both.

The box in which you no doubt found this journal was made by Stanley: you will have seen his initials entwined with mine on the lid. He made it in secret that first autumn, before he had even spoken to me of his love. It is carved from a fallen branch of the horse-chestnut.

Chapter Twenty-eight

Esther's journal changed everything. It's no exaggeration to say it changed my life: in fact, it changed very many lives. Through Esther's account I learnt the truth. My mother had not been the biological daughter of the man she called Dad. She adored him, and I was glad she had never known: it would have been a terrible shock to her. At the distance of a generation, my adoration of him was unaffected: it flickered but then the flame came back stronger than before.

The realization that my mother was a Farnworth was entirely secondary, and it took a long time to dawn on me quite what the repercussions could be: my mind did a kind of slow-motion double-take.

Things moved quickly after that. I wrote a new letter to the solicitors, outlining my claim to the estate and was astonished when I received an answer only a week later. It said very little, but requested sight of my birth certificate and if possible, that of my mother. More in hope than expectation, I took both along to the offices, where the receptionist photocopied them, looking at me with a curiosity that she didn't dare voice.

I heard nothing then for a fortnight, and was just about to ring the offices again when a letter arrived asking me to make an appointment with Mr Powell. I saw him that afternoon.

When I was shown into his office, the solicitor was standing next to an enormous oak roll-top desk which filled one wall of the room. He was a tall, ascetic-looking individual with silver hair, and he came forward to lay a cool hand in mine before motioning me toward a group of chairs over by the fireplace. I hadn't noticed the elderly gentleman who was sitting there staring at me fixedly. As I turned to him he attempted to rise from his seat unaided to extend a shaking hand towards me. Mr Powell held his other arm to support him and introduced us: 'Mrs Keaton, this is my father, Ernest Powell.' Once the manoeuvre was accomplished, the old man subsided into his chair gratefully, and I took my seat opposite the two of them.

Mr Powell Senior spoke first, and his voice was surprisingly strong for one whose body was so evidently weak. 'I'm very glad to meet you, Mrs Keaton. I am long retired, but curiosity has propelled me out of my incarceration.' He bestowed a meaningful look on his son, who seemed unaware of it as he continued looking at me with a grave smile on his face. 'I have to say, it was well worth the effort. You are the very image of your great-aunt, as no doubt you are aware.' I was about to respond, but he went on: 'However, your mother's maternal line is not at issue: as you know, we are here to discuss your putative claim to the Farnworth Estate.' He paused to ask for a glass of water, and his son rose to pour one from a decanter on the desk. I noticed I wasn't being offered any refreshment, and began to feel a little uncomfortable. I needn't have worried: it seemed that the circumstances were so unusual that custom was suspended. As the younger Mr Powell sat down again, offering his father a folded handkerchief, it crossed my mind that he was the most solicitous solicitor I'd ever met, and the thought caused a bubble of hysteria to rise in me which I stifled with a cough.

'I was well acquainted with Mr Farnworth, God rest his soul. As you may be aware, Mrs Keaton, his only son was killed in his twenty-first year, and of course it was thought that there could be no heir. Mr Farnworth was a widower who remarried in his forties: his second wife was of a similar age.' He took a sip of water, while I waited, all intuitions twitching: I still could not tell which way the wind blew.

'After his son's funeral, however, Mrs Farnworth, or Hertig as she liked to be known, was contacted by one of the boy's university friends who had attended. This young man told her that Master Edgar Farnworth had boasted, in his cups no doubt, that he had impregnated two young women, one in England and another in Paris.' He looked at me over his glasses, blinking meaningfully. 'I need hardly tell you that this revelation produced a hope in Hugo Farnworth that an heir would yet appear. He had an agency make enquiries in Oxford and Paris to no avail. I think, ' and here he paused and blinked at me again, 'that Mr Farnworth was too much the gentleman to enquire in Adlington. This is to be regretted: if he had divined that the boy had, as it were, fouled his own nest, things might have turned out quite differently.' I bridled at his terminology, and was just deciding that he was a sanctimonious old fossil, when he carried on. 'I need hardly point out, Mrs Keaton, that the trust will need to verify your claim by scientific means, a procedure that my son has investigated for me.' Here the younger Mr Powell flashed an apologetic half-smile my way, possibly having detected that my feminist sensibilities were prickling.

The elder gentleman took another sip of water, and when he spoke again, his voice was creaking. I briefly reflected how it must feel to him, this final taste of his old life. He must have read my mind. 'I know not whether you are acquainted with Tennyson, Mrs Keaton: Morte d'Arthur comes to mind frequently these days: "The old order changeth, yielding place to new," here he flashed an openly resentful look at his son, "and God fulfills himself in many ways." What is at stake here, my dear, is the inheritance of a fine old family, their name and their legacy. Under the terms of the trust, it is just possible that Farnworth Manor might be placed into your hands "to be used for the benefit of the people of Adlington." Moreover, there is an extremely substantial quantity of money, currently held in Switzerland, which, if your claim is verified, would be made available to you for the same specified purpose, to whit "for the benefit of the people of Adlington."'

When I came home, Beth was sitting on the front step waiting for me. She took one look at my face and leapt up, clapping and squealing, 'Wow! I can't believe it! Do I have to bow?'

'It's not a done deal quite yet: I have to assemble a proper bid, which will have to be put before the board of trustees. I'll need professional help with that. The big thing is, Beth: if we succeed, there's a massive pot of money that will be put at our disposal. It's so exciting!'

We got down to work straight away and assembled a steering committee made up of me, Jack, Beth, Jason, Anil and Priya. Our first brainstorming session was enormously productive, and Rachel could hardly keep up with taking the minutes. She and Priya were full of ideas about food production, having just been to Hebden Bridge to stay with friends.

'It's fantastic! There's stuff growing everywhere, even outside the police station and on the roundabouts! Every patch of land grows edible stuff, tended by volunteers, and you can just help yourself. And it's all free!'

Priya joined in: 'Yes, and we were saying on the way back that there used to be allotments on the Common, but nobody uses them anymore apart from a couple of old men, and why is that, and could we get it all going again?'

'But then we thought we wouldn't know where to start, everyone's so apathetic. Let's just move to Hebden Bridge. They have loads of small local shops and businesses: we could set ourselves up, but then we thought we haven't got any money and where would we live and how do we get known? It's starting from scratch.'

'And we were kind of a bit defeated and depressed, so we couldn't believe it when Dad told us about this and said you wanted to talk to us.'

Anil turned and smiled at me and said quietly, 'Yes, sometimes it needs someone with vision and charisma to make things happen.'

'That's right, Dad. In Hebden Bridge it was two grannies from Todmorden apparently, and now it's a whole movement called Incredible Edible. They don't have any money, and like the watering cans are ones the police gave them that had been confiscated from a cannabis farm!'

Rachel laughed. 'They pulled in support from all over, there's something called the Plunkett Foundation that supports community initiatives. In fact, I'll tell you what, they had a conference there last year, Ambitious Communities or something. I'll get in touch with our friends and find out who to contact. Maybe we can get someone up here to talk to us.'

Jack said, 'That'd be brilliant, Rachel. There's no point in re-inventing the wheel. If you can get someone here who knows about all the agencies we can tap into, we'd have a head start. While we're on growing things, I'm seeing someone from Myerscough College tomorrow.'

'Where's that?'

'It used to be Lancashire Agricultural College. They're interested in a joint venture, using the farmland. I also thought we might want to consider contacting people who work with special needs and horticulture, or Care Farming. People with mental health issues often benefit enormously from working in agriculture.'

It was time for me to take charge of proceedings. 'I'm not sure about that, at least not initially. I think it's important to have a clear idea of what we're aiming to do, and as I said at the start, it's the 18-24 year-olds I want us to concentrate on, the ones with no jobs.'

Priya looked disappointed. 'But I thought you were interested in small business start-ups?'

'Yes, you're right, Priya, I am. There's so much swirling around in my head at the moment that I can't think straight! I think we need to clarify the order in which we tackle this.' I took a deep breath and tried to get my thoughts in order. 'Priority number one is the bid. If we succeed with the bid and my understanding is right, we're not going to have money problems, at least at the start. The bid specifies the people of this town. So we need to decide what they need, what would benefit them.' I saw that Beth was about to speak, so I said, 'Let me just outline my vision: we provide a place and resources where young people who are out of work can do productive things. Some of those things may lead to jobs and small businesses, but that's not the initial intention. My idea is that we harness all the skills and knowledge that are already here, in this village, in unemployed people and retired people.'

No-one spoke at first, and then the dam broke and they all spoke at once. Everyone knew someone who would want to get involved, and we kept coming back to food. No-one liked shopping in huge supermarkets, and when it came down to it, the idea of food grown locally appealed to all of us. I told them about a documentary I'd seen called A Farm for the Future, where Rebecca Hosking deconstructed a supermarket sandwich in terms of what it showed about our dependence on oil: everything from the transport of the out-of-season ingredients to the plastic packaging involved oil products, and the oil is running out. The range of references that we produced between us was impressive: the community supported agriculture movement in America in the sixties, Cuba, solidarity gardens in Italy, the Slow Food Movement.

Shy Rachel was moved to speak: 'And like, the Olympic Opening Ceremony last year, how England moved from agriculture to industry, people being swallowed up, losing their connection with the land.' We were all diverted for a time by our own memories of the highlights of Danny Boyle's extravaganza, but Rachel brought us back to her point: 'The thing is, it's all gone now, the industry, and what are we left with? We've lost our feeling for the land.'

'Yes,' said Priya. 'That ceremony kind of explained the nation to itself. It was the first time me and Rachel understood, anyway. And we've got to build a new future. And not depend on oil. Because the other thing is, there's wars being fought for oil. It's all failed us: capitalism, consumerism, whatever you want to call it. We've got to kind of…'

'Take possession of your future?' I offered.

'Yes!' she turned to me with shining eyes. 'Yes, that's exactly what we've got to do. We've got to help ourselves. All of us, because it's not just the young that have been failed, it's the old too. It's all of us.'

By the time the meeting ended, we all had jobs to do, contacts and agencies to investigate, and each one of us had come up with one other person that they would approach about being on the steering committee.

I already knew I wanted Rosie, at least as a consultant. Her role with Booths would provide us with a focus for our food-production. She'd already identified some gaps for us to investigate: we wouldn't be ready for livestock for some time, but meanwhile we could certainly get started on jams and chutneys: the orchards were well-established and the trees were already being prepared for the growing season. One of the retired women who'd been involved with the clearing of the driveway was a keen flower-grower, and was already developing plans to resuscitate the beds and look at breeding hydrangeas and camellias for the cut-flower market.

There was one other person I wanted to approach, more out of politeness and curiosity than any expectation I could really get his co-operation. It had become clear that Richard was still living at the farm, although I'd noticed his absences were getting longer. I hadn't seen him drive past at all during April, and fervently hoped that he was spending the school holidays with his family.

There was also the matter of the farmhouse: it would only be right for me to give him the 'heads-up' that it might be withdrawn

270

from the rental market if our bid was successful: I'd specifically asked about it, and Mr Powell junior had confirmed that it was part of the Farnworth Estate. I had an idea brewing about its future.

When I stopped at the five-barred gate, I realized that I'd been walking straight past for six months now. Apart from that one time when he saw me with Jack, we hadn't made eye contact at all. The Range Rover was parked in the yard: I'd seen him drive past an hour ago, so I knew he was in. There was no sound from the kennel, in fact there hadn't been a peep out of Seamus for months now, so either he'd become used to the vehicles and fires, or he was no longer there. I took a deep breath and opened the gate.

I walked very slowly across the yard, partly in fear of Seamus leaping out at me, and partly to have a better look round: every previous visit had been stressful in some way. In one corner of the cobbled courtyard I noticed what looked like an old chicken coop, a well-stocked wood-store and beyond it, another five-barred gate that let onto the chestnut tree field. When I knocked on the door, there was silence apart from two collared doves billing and cooing on the roof.

After a few minutes, I knocked again, more insistently, and deliberately banging so hard that I bruised my knuckles. The doves stopped cooing and a blackbird's alarm call made me jump. Nothing. I wasn't having this: I wouldn't be ignored. One more knock on the door then I'd try the windows.

I'd just raised my other hand to inflict similar bruising when the door opened, and I froze, my fist raised on a level with Richard's corduroy-clad groin.

'I wouldn't do that if I were you.' I slowly raised my eyes, my fist still comically frozen in position. 'People have died for less.'

Relief flooded me and I gave him what I hoped was a mischievous smile. 'I have other methods of extracting conversation, fear not. But for now,' I lifted my right hand and withdrew my left, 'shake? But gently,' I added ruefully, 'my knuckles are somewhat bruised.'

He left it a few moments before he responded, but then he briefly and lightly shook my hand, without moving from the doorway.

271

'What can I do for you?'

'Well, are you going to keep me on the doorstep?'

'Yes.'

'Oh. Right. Is it a bad time?'

'No, it's not a bad time, I just don't want to invite you in.'

'D'you mind me asking why not?'

'Because I presume this is not a friendly visit.'

'Why not? We are friends, aren't we? Well, we were. I know things went badly wrong but I hope by now you've got used to all the coming and going. Seamus certainly must have: there's not been a peep out of him.' I was nervous now, feeling on the back foot.

'Seamus has moved on.'

'Moved on? As in, to a better place?'

He gave a tight smile. 'A better place for Seamus, yes. He's got a new job as a professional guard dog.'

I made a bid for humour. 'Uniform, pension, that kind of thing?' Silence.

'So, I repeat, what can I do for you?'

'Well, how've you been? I've often wondered.'

'Fine, thanks. What do you want?'

Exasperated now, my temper rose quickly, as it does. 'Look Richard, we were getting on really well, and you know I care about you, and you know I would have liked to carry on being friends, but you had such a fit when I said about the woods. You did that, not me. So in my book it was up to you to make amends. I mean, I could make allowances up to a point, because I know you've got your problems, but it's been six months now and that's beyond a joke, and life's too short, you know. And I'm sorry about the disruption, obviously I am, but it's not just about you, all this. All the people that have got involved are so lovely, and it's been so worthwhile: we found the manor, you know, and the woods are going to be tremendous, a real resource, and as for the house and the Home Farm and the gardens ... there's lots going on and there's a great deal of excitement. Things are happening that I came to tell you about, and I would have come before now if you'd made just one single move to say I was forgiven, but you didn't, you just zoom past with your blacked-out windows, not giving a fig for anybody.' I

272

ran out of steam, and in the same instant surprised myself by feeling suddenly tearful. 'I really did care, you know. I do. How are you? I want to know.'

When I looked up, I saw that his face had softened. He thought for a moment, then came out, shut the door behind him and sat down on the worn sandstone step, patting the space beside him. 'Come on, sit here beside me in the sun.'

I didn't have to think twice, and we sat in companionable silence for a few minutes, our faces raised to the early summer sunshine.

'I've missed you, Annie. The reason I don't want to ask you in is that I don't want to upset my equilibrium. Or yours, for that matter.' He gave me a gentle nudge with his elbow. 'I've seen you with that big chap. You look very happy together. Are you?'

'Yes, yes I am.'

'We can't always choose when we fall in love, can we?'

'What do you mean?'

'Well, you memorably told me that you "couldn't go falling in love or anything." But now you clearly have.' His sideways smile was a warm one.

Quietly, I said, 'And you?'

He looked straight ahead, and spoke slowly, reflectively. 'Well, I think you were probably aware that I was falling in love with you. Which I welcomed at first. It was a new feeling that broke in on me when I thought I'd just about managed to kill off all emotion. It was a novelty for a time, and a distraction. I knew it could go nowhere, and that it should go nowhere, so in a way, it was a relief when I stopped seeing you. Perhaps I deliberately sabotaged it, I don't know.'

"She's gone, I am abused, and my relief must be to loathe her."

'Yes, exactly. Like Othello, all black and white, no shades of grey. You got the brunt of that, as Cath did.'

'How it is it with Cath?' I held my breath, and he didn't answer at first.

'It's getting better all the time, thanks.'

'Tell me.'

273

He turned to me and looked steadily into my eyes. 'Can I ask you something? I'll always wonder what it would have been like to kiss you. May I kiss you? Just briefly?'

It was the gentlest kiss. His lips were warm and soft, and they lingered on mine just a fraction too long, but then he withdrew and looked ahead again, leaving me to recover my composure.

'Thank-you. That was lovely. It shall never be spoken of again, but I shall always remember it.' We sat in silence, both lost in our own thoughts.

It was me that eventually broke it. 'So Cath?'

'Yes, thanks to you, I did contact them at Christmas, and went home for Christmas Day. It was good. The boys were ecstatic. Cath and I were careful with each other. I didn't drink, not at the house anyway. I stayed at a hotel.'

'And then?'

'Then on Boxing Day I went to see my mother, and that was fine too. Everyone was a bit careful of me, understandably. What was it you said, treading on eggshells?'

'Yes. It must be hard to make them relax.'

'Yes, it was. So then Cath asked whether I'd like to go away for a couple of days, just the two of us, so I decided to give it a try. So we did, and it was fine.'

'Fine?'

'Yes, we were all talked out from all the rows, so we just agreed to forgive each other everything that had gone before. Try and start a new slate. I couldn't face just plunging straight back into family life, though. Call me a coward, but I'd become so used to my own company, so dependent on the peace.'

'No-one would ever accuse you of being a coward, Richard. Did Cath accept it?'

'Yes, she did. She does. We've spent stretches of time together, on our own and with the boys. It's working well. I know I've got somewhere else to go if I feel myself losing it.'

'Losing it?'

'Losing my temper. Little, unpredictable things can set me off. I'm much better than I was though.'

'And the drinking?'

'Not nearly so much now. I have an iron will you know.'

'I know.'

'I stopped with the spirits and went onto beer. I've put weight on, though.'

'It suits you.'

'Thank-you. In fact, thank-you for everything, Annie. You snapped me out of it.'

I held that thought, looked at it from all angles like a rosy apple. An idea was growing.

'So where do you go from here?'

'I'm not sure. For the first time, this morning, it seemed silly to be driving away from home to here.'

'You said home.'

'I did, didn't I?' He looked delighted.

'So you think you might leave here?'

'Yes, I think I might.'

'Can I ask you where home is?'

'Why?'

I laughed, but I was stung, 'I just wondered. I have an idea. It might come to nothing, but if you're interested, I'll run it by you.'

When I'd outlined my idea, he said, 'I'll give it some thought. Thank-you.'

'So will you come to the meeting?'

'Yes, yes I will. In fact, how many people are there? '

'Not sure just yet, but twelve to fifteen.'

'Do you think they'd all fit round this table?' He gestured over his shoulder.

'Yes, I'm sure they would.'

When we finally assembled the full steering committee, Richard looked as though he regretted offering as we all piled into his peaceful kitchen: we had someone from the WI, a representative of the Volunteer Council, a recently-retired headmaster, and a woman in her thirties who had run her own business until she'd had children. We soon had a network of contacts and a presentation with which to drum up publicity and support. We kept everything very local, involving the WI, the Soroptimists, the few local businesses, the bowling club and a book group. Our mission was to make sure the people of Adlington had ownership of the ideas.

It was clear from the start that a minibus had to be high on our shopping list if we did succeed: the manor was too far away from houses, particularly those on the other side of the main road, so we envisaged a service running continually on a route around the village, free to local residents.

I was concerned all along that the young people at whom this initiative was ostensibly aimed should be invited to contribute ideas, but didn't know how to go about it until Jason revealed that he'd set up a Facebook page with settings which apparently restricted access to people he trusted and approved. I was soon gratified to be approached by individuals and groups who wanted ideas and requests put before the committee. It grew like Topsy.

The Manor has been established for just over three years now, and is managed by Richard, whose imposing presence and natural authority have an instant impact on the young people we draw in, as well as some of the older ones. His understated insistence on mutual respect and old-fashioned courtesy imbues the Manor with an air of quiet industry and collaborative creativity. He travels every day from his home in Lancaster, and when he was first considering taking the job, he brought Cath and his sons for a look around. I was nervous about meeting her, but needn't have worried: when we were introduced, Cath held my hand slightly longer than convention dictates, and a look passed between us that said all that needed to be said.

Beth's daughter Ellie is the main administrator. Beth had the job to start with, but she found she preferred the flexibility of her previous life, with 'a bit of this and that.' It was a relief, actually, as she'll be the first to admit that she's not the best with paperwork!

Individuals and groups put in bids for the use of rooms in the main house or the outbuildings for an initial period of six months. After that, their lease can be renewed, depending on how it's going and what the waiting list is like. We currently have a good range of occupants: a thriving batik workshop; a film-maker and photographer who has recently done his second wedding and is recording the development of the whole place for a book and a film; the second-hand bookshop in the old library added to our coffers significantly by selling Mr Farnworth's collection on the internet to antiquarians and collectors around the world; two rooms are devoted to second-hand clothes and sewing; there's an independent book-keeper, and one of our great successes is a bespectacled young man who has an uncanny way with recalcitrant computers and confirmed Luddites. Metalwork is going on again in the forge, and carpentry in the workshop. Priya and Rachel operate their catering business from what we think was Esther's cottage.

There are many more projects based outdoors, notably the honey products, which will shortly be moving to a recently-renovated outbuilding near the walled-garden where the hives are set up. The orchards and espaliered fruit-trees are tended by Mrs Partington and her devoted team of helpers, and the increasingly-ambitious Allotment Co-operative is soon expecting its first crop of asparagus. I saw their head honchos gathered round the derelict pineapple houses yesterday, and there was a distinctly speculative tone to their conversation.

The farm is thriving, and our artisan produce is much in demand. Booths have been wonderful, providing sponsorship and publicity as well as expertise. We took out a lease on one of the boarded-up shops on the main road as soon as we had produce ready to sell, and there was a huge celebration when the quality of our honey, jams and chutneys was judged good enough to be sold in Booths stores. Now the challenge is keeping up with demand.

Jack is the Estate Manager, and he and Claire live in the farmhouse that comes with the job. I stay over sometimes, and sometimes Jack stays with me. Maybe one day I'll move there properly, but we like it like this, it suits us. We both have our private space and time spent together is always special.

I did re-read Four Quartets, and it turned out to have so much relevance to my story that my indulgence is to have framed extracts adorning the walls of the Manor. One of them kept running through my mind today, when we received a very special visitor.

"We shall not cease from exploration
And the end of all our exploring
Will be to arrive where we started
And know the place for the first time."

277

I was walking home yesterday when I saw a smartly-suited man in his early sixties standing in the open door of a dark blue Rover. I recognized him as a director from Booths who had come for his first visit: I'd seen him with Rosie earlier. His name is Patrick Robinson. He was looking at the horse-chestnut tree with a curious fixity. I called out hello, and strolled up to stand and admire it with him. It did look particularly glorious in the autumn sunshine, and we both stood with the sun on our faces, looking in the same direction. He was shading his eyes and hardly seemed to hear me or register my presence, until I said, 'It's beautiful, isn't it?' when he turned to me, his face serious.

'Does it have a swing, do you know? Under the branches?'

It's a strange thing. I don't often have premonitions, but when I do they're big ones. The certainty rose up in me instantly that this was something to do with Bertie. The image of that child's drawing had never faded from my mind's eye.

'Yes,' I said, 'there was. A long time ago. It's not there now, but you can see where it hung. And I know where it is, or at least I think I do. Why do you ask?'

He had been watching me closely as I talked, and I saw that his eyes were full of wonder. 'My father. All his life he kept an eye out for just such a tree, near a farm, standing alone in a field, with a swing underneath it. He didn't know whether it was just a dream or a real memory from his childhood.'

With a voice that slightly shook, I asked where his father had grown up.

'In a hill farm up beyond Rivington. We never came here, it's a bit out of the way.'

I couldn't help myself. 'Did he have a happy childhood?'

'I'm sorry, that's a curious question, but yes, yes he did. He was an only one. His parents had apparently given up hope of having any children when he came along.'

'Was he called Bertie?'

He looked at me in astonishment. 'Why, yes he was, when he was younger anyway. Robert.'

'I don't suppose by any chance he had red hair?'

He looked at me more closely now, and I saw him take in my own hair, which was tied back. He spoke slowly, 'He did indeed

278

have red hair, curly too, very much like your own. Do tell me what you're thinking.'

I took a deep breath. 'I don't know how you're going to take this.' His stare was intense, and I noticed for the first time that his eyes were green flecked with hazel. I looked at the tree and ordered my thoughts. 'In 1919, a two-year old boy, a relative of mine, disappeared from this farm.' I saw him swallow and his eyes widened. 'He was called Bertie, but his full name was Albert Thomas Grenfell.' His mouth had dropped open. I put a hand on his arm. 'I'm sorry if this comes as a shock. I'm guessing from your face that your father would have been the right age. If this has come right out of the blue, I'm sorry.'

His gaze slowly swept the tree, the farm, the woods and the tree again. When he looked back at me, his eyes were full of tears. 'I can't take it in. I can't believe it. We just dismissed it – oh there he goes again, wanting to stop and look at every big tree on its own in a field. I can't believe it.' Recovering himself, he dabbed at his eyes with an immaculate handkerchief. 'I never knew my grandparents: they died before I was born. They were quite elderly when they had him.' He looked at me again, the enormity of what he was saying dawning on him. 'It was remote, the farm. They used to take their pork products to the markets all over.'

I didn't need to say it, but I did. 'Bertie disappeared on market day.' He looked stricken, and I tried to imagine how this must feel for him. 'Look, would you like to come into the farmhouse and I'll tell you everything I know?'

'I won't come in just now. I need time to absorb this. But if you'd tell me the story, I'd be very grateful.'

'There's so much to show you. There's a photograph of him with his parents and sisters. There are cards his family made for him. They always believed he would somehow find his way home. There's actually a letter for Bertie written by his father. You could open it, when you feel ready.'

He didn't speak at first, and when he did, I felt the blood drain from my face in a rush that almost caused me to faint.

'I think my father would prefer to open it himself.'

And so today, a shiny black cab pulled into the cobbled yard, and a ninety-seven year old man in a wheelchair was lifted to the ground. I watched from inside the farmhouse with Rosie and Jack, the three of us leaning on the windowsill to look out through the net curtains. Richard had gone out to help with the wheelchair, and I deliberately stayed back to give Bertie time to take in his surroundings.

I could only see that he was tall: his legs were long and he was thin but clearly extremely broad-shouldered. He wore a dark suit and tie and though age had stooped him, he held his head erect. Patrick stood beside him and I saw him bend to speak into the old man's ear. When his son stood back and I saw his face for the first time, I thought of the cenotaph, of Harry Patch and Henry Allingham, the last of the Tommies: I had the same sensation of looking history in the face. He was staring at the house, and I saw him look up at the roof, where the bedroom windows peered out at him from under the eaves.

We'd agreed that I should be the one to open the door, though I was faintingly nervous of him seeing me for the first time. When Rosie whispered, 'Go on, Mum,' and gave me a gentle push, I reached for the handle, put my hand to my hair, took a deep breath and opened it. I saw him looking into the darkness of the doorway from the bright September sunshine, and I saw his expression change. His fingers gripped the arms of the chair and he bent forward, straining to see, so I moved out of the doorway into the light. He gasped and lifted a hand to his mouth and then spoke the name softly, disbelievingly, 'Esther?'

I was just starting forward when I saw that his son was holding his shoulder and speaking clearly into his ear. 'This is Annie, Dad. Your great-niece. Your sister Izabel was her grandmother.'

'Izabel?' He seemed to be trying the word for the first time, wonderingly.

I went forward and bent down so that we could see each other properly. We were both crying silently. I smiled and reached out to touch the backs of his hands, which were as soft as the finest cotton. The green of his eyes was clouded with age and with tears, but he saw me clearly and a warm acceptance spread across his familiar features. He nodded, just once, and turned his hands to hold mine. Behind me, Rosie had come out of the house, and I saw him look up and study her face, before nodding again, then shaking his head and dabbing at his eyes.

Richard spoke. 'Would you like to come inside the farmhouse, sir? We can lift you in the wheelchair.'

More forcefully now, he shook his head, still weeping quietly, and let go of my hand briefly to waft a damp handkerchief at his feet. I looked up at Richard and Patrick. 'He wants to walk.'

It was the most moving thing I've ever seen. With Richard on one side and his son on the other, he was steadied onto his feet and supported across the cobbles. He reached the sandstone step and paused, staring down at the worn hollow where so many feet had trodden since the last time he was here. And then he lifted his head, straightened his back, and lifted his foot onto the step. Bertie had come home.

Chestnut Tree Farm
Adlington
,17th May 1928

My boy

    I hope one day to give this letter into your own hand, for if you have come home you will find me quite unable to speak. You are my own darling boy and I will love you always. Your mother, God rest her soul, was quite unable to bear your absence, and she left us in the winter, just four months after we lost you. My only hope is, my boy, that wherever you have been, you have been loved and cared for and that one day those who took you will tell you where your true home is, and your people.

    I picture you now as a fine tall lad, nearly ten years old. You are going to be a big man, like me, for your fists were the size of a cat-hammer when I saw you last, and you were but a baby of two. I love to think of you working in the forge with me one day. As I write this, I reckon if I am spared I have a good ten years of hard work in me still, time to train you when you come home to your old dad. By then you will be as big as me, a fine fellow of twenty. I can see you now. You have your mother's copper curls which I so loved, and her eyes of green, like your sister Esther. I saved a lock of your mother's hair for you, Bertie. You will find it in this case, folded in a handkerchief she embroidered for you. A curl of your own baby hair you will find in her locket.

    Your sisters love you so, you were their pet, their dolly. You were their baby brother of whom they were so proud. We think of you always, though it is hard to speak of you. Each year on your birthday, we celebrate, and if it is fine, we have a picnic under the chestnut tree. I have taken down your swing, for we could not bear to see it. I have kept it though: it is in the woodshed with your cradle. One day you will have children of your own, and it is a comfort to believe these things will be brought out, dusted down and full of life again. In this suitcase you will find cards your sisters have made over the years and some little presents. The twins pressed a stem of chestnut flowers for you: they call the blossom Bertie's Candles, for they are always full and fine on your birthday.

    Welcome home, my own boy, my son, my Bertie.

A big THANK-YOU to:

Kachi Ozumba and Ann Coburn at Newcastle University for their help and encouragement.

David Almond for everything he's said to help me on my way.

Andreina Cordani of Good Housekeeping for running the Novel Competition which spurred me on, and Ajda Vucicevic of Luigi Bonomi Associates for all her subsequent support as the manuscript grew.

Edwin Booth for his time and help in my research.

Kathleen Hatch for letting me poke around the farm where my mum was born.

All the staff and volunteers who work so hard to make Gibside and Cherryburn (National Trust) such wonderful and inspiring places to visit.

Kev for his constant patience, pride and faith in me.

All the friends who read the manuscript and contributed in any way, but particularly Margaret Bone and her mum Sheila Nicholson.

And last but by no means least, Jane Nicholson for her friendship, for being an inspirational funny feisty redhead, and for saying, 'Jfdi.'

Val Boyle
Newcastle upon Tyne
6th January 2014